GUARDIAN FORCE

Galaxy Quest Books are published by:
Ocean Quest LLC
Cambria CA 93428

Printed in the United States of America

For information address:
Ocean Quest LLC
2100 Ogden Drive
Cambria, CA 93428

ISBN: 978-0-9839630-6-6

10 9 8 7 6 5 4 3 2 1

This book is dedicated to the memory of
Ollie Mayberry Van Sickle, my Mom
and Lorna Gusner, my daughter.

Inspiration from Gepeto, a gift of love from
Guide Dogs for the Blind, San Rafael, California.

Acknowledgments:

Kind patience and encouragement from
The Rough Writers Group of Cambria, California.

Cover design by Lorna Gusner

Moral support, layout, internal graphics,
and proofing: Brian Gusner

Cover Attribution:
Eskimo Nebula, Telescope Gallery, NASA.
Object Names: Eskimo Nebula, NGC 2392
Image Type: Astronomical
Credit: NASA, Andrew Fruchter and the ERO Team
[Sylvia Baggett (STScI), Richard Hook (ST-ECF),
Zoltan Levay (STScI)]

Book layout and production:
Nancy McKarney, Diversified Graphic Design

Guardian Force

D. Arthur Gusner

GalaxyQuestBooks.com
Ocean Quest LLC
Cambria 93428

Contents

Contents

"Since the mathematicians have invaded the theory of relativity, I do not understand it myself anymore."

Albert Einstein

"A circle is a round straight line with a hole in the middle."

Mark Twain

Author's Foreword

There are many branches on the paths we follow in life. Some lead to adventures and others lead to mysteries. When I was a small boy, I happened onto the path that led me to the County Library. There I found both adventure and mystery in abundance. Among the shelves of dusty books, I encountered James Churchward's works on Mu. That starting point led me to the broad field of speculative history and to wondrous tales of forgotten cities and lost civilizations.

When contemplating the massive stone figures of Easter Island, the towering pyramids of Egypt, and the mysterious structures of Stonehenge, I asked just how did they shape and move those massive stones? In Machu Picchu and other Incan ruins, very large stones with irregular surfaces were precisely fitted to match adjoining similar stones. They fit so precisely, a cigarette paper could not be placed between them. How was that done?

The spate of UFO sightings in 1947 prompted further youthful exploration. One book I located, *The Book of the Damned,* was from the early 1900s. This was the first published nonfiction work of the author Charles Fort. Within the pages of Charles Fort's work, I found remarkable descriptions of UFOs similar to Ezekiel's wheel within a wheel. Could these have been modern hoaxes? My conclusion then favored an unsolved mystery, and it still does.

The Guardian series is an imaginative story winding through the widely spaced pillars of incomplete human history. *Guardian Force, Earth Guardian, Guardian Probe, Guardian Strike, and Guardian Thunder* are pure science fiction brimming with high adventure and military strategy. The author's hope is that the books will provide science fiction enthusiasts an enjoyable and memorable read. So relax, lean back, and enjoy a modern imaginative fable set both in the past and in the year 2511 and beyond.

D. Arthur Gusner
Cambria, California
2011

Editor's Foreword

In any good story, telling it well is the critical piece, and in sci-fi writing, telling it well is what defines the masters. Anyone can tell a story, but telling a story that easily flows forward while building tension is either a gift or it has come at the price of working hard. Sometimes, it is both. *Guardian Force* tells a wonderful, fast-moving story of people in a time and place far away, yet the story and its vibrant characters easily connect to that part of us today that sees compassion and caring as an integral part of who we are as human beings.

Brandon Jones, editor
Affect Writing

Prologue

And it came to pass, when men began to multiply
on the face of the earth, and daughters were born
unto them, that the sons of God saw the daughters
of men that they were fair; and they took them
wives of all which they chose.

KJV Genesis 6

Chapter One:
Detection

Within the infinity of blistering cold space, like a fleeting apparition flowing among dark shadows, the small Scout ship was an anomaly, a lethal precision instrument supporting fragile human life. Well cloaked by advanced stealth technologies and searching for a potentially deadly enemy, survival demanded that no light gleamed or was reflected from the ship's flat black and energy absorbing hull. Being near the heliopause boundary, the vessel was far from its home world, Glas Dinnein, and even further from the life supporting warmth of the radiant solar primary, Tearman.

"If they're really out there, then they're well shielded," Zorn commented.

Roan's slate-gray eyes scanned his control display, studying the instrument readouts. "Agreed."

Within the subdued ambient lighting of the command compartment Roan and Zorn were sitting side by side; each wore restraining harnesses attached to their command chairs. Both men were dressed in the informal shipboard uniform of Guardian Force Scout ship personnel, forest green fabric of woven natural fibers loosely fitted for comfort and ease of movement, a long-sleeved tailored tunic top, and pants that hung in neat folds above soft low topped leather boots. Their collars bore military and rank tabs showing the subtle insignia of Guardian Force commanders and the elite badge of Scouts.

"One perimeter early alert isn't much to go on. It may be another false detection. How long are we going to remain on station?" Zorn said.

"As long as it takes. Something triggered that detector. There is an intruder, and unless you want a Dargon long-range reconnaissance fighter or a Kreel Scout to punch new holes in Shey's pristine hull, you'd better pay attention to your tactical screens."

"New holes are a bad idea. Confirming, I'm focused on my tactical screens. But, based on what I saw, what the detector indicated was likely a probe and not a Kreel or Dargon fighter. Besides, with Shey, you, and me on patrol, no Kreel or Dargon would dare send anything they valued into Glas Dinnein's solar system."

"Sorry Zorn, but there's a bug floating in your ointment. No one may have told the Kreel or Dargon that we're out here."

"Oops, in that case, we just may have a problem to resolve," Zorn cheerfully replied.

"What we're looking for may have serious firepower. And, I have no intention to provide anyone target services. Whatever it is, we need to identify it, and if appropriate, dispatch it," Roan said.

During the next few minutes, only the soft whisper of Shey's life support systems and the occasional tapping of keys punctuated the silence in the compartment. Then, a tone sounded. Turning, Zorn glanced at one of his screens.

"Contact. Roan, I've definitely got something. Check the higher band for a plasma emission."

"Got it. The signal is on Alpha-23, faint but steady. Azimuth 23 relative, elevation 47 degrees. I don't recognize a signature, can you see anything resembling modulation?" Roan said.

"No. The signal isn't a modulated linear or non-linear temporal gravitational field wave. There're no observable harmonics," Zorn reported, even as he switched the signal to the ship's analyzer for signature identification.

Shey's calm and rich feminine voice promptly announced, "No match found."

Roan activated his external view screen and maximized its optical magnification along the signal source vector. What he saw was the normal background of space, the plasma source was not apparent.

Roan turned toward Zorn. "The signal is barely distinguishable from white noise. I don't see anything I can identify. And, it's the things you can't see and don't know about that can bite you when you least expect it. Whatever the source of that signal is, we're going to assume it has big sharp teeth, until proven otherwise."

"Got it, sharp teeth. In that case, I recommend we diligently avoid all fair fights."

"Agreed. No fair fights," Roan replied.

Roan switched the incoming signal to Shey, and the computer began to digitize and compress the data. He then keyed in a description. *Unknown target detected, beginning Target Motion Analysis.*

Once compressed, the computer divided the message and signal data into packets, then encoded those packets into short bursts of modulated ultraviolet-laser pulses. The network would route the packets of data to their designated recipient. Roan observed the Message Ready indicator turn golden, and he pressed the send key, launching the message across the network to Guardian Command on Glas Dinnein.

"Shey, with you positioned at its center, display a relative motion polar plot," Roan said.

On the previously blank forward bulkhead, a maneuvering plot appeared. A small golden icon indicated Shey's position, and her course vector appeared as a thin golden line that originated at the center of the plot. A thin green line, representing the current target's true bearing, passed through the center, bisecting the plot. The green line was the initial reference for beginning the passive target motion analysis maneuver.

The bitter lessons learned during space warfare deeply etch the cautious wisdom on those who survive, and Roan and Zorn were survivors. In the stealth world of space warfare, any stray energy pattern could become a beacon for a homing missile or conversely be a baited lure to attract careless investigators to their destruction. Operating in full stealth, Shey would not be emitting any active energy probes while searching for the target, but strictly rely upon passive analysis.

"Zorn, set Condition 3, we're beginning our bearings-only analysis."

With a rising faint yet deepening resonant hum, Shey began accelerating across and normal to the signal vector.

Responding to Roan's Condition 3 command, Zorn initiated the Scout ship's defensive and offensive systems' test routines, confirming all systems were battle ready. Throughout Shey, compartment doors slid shut and sealed. All non-essential systems began shutting down. Both light and medium missiles began running internal diagnostics, preparing for possible deployment. Shey was inwardly flexing her muscles and preparing for a potentially hostile meeting with the unknown.

Glancing toward Zorn, Roan noted his colleague and friend focused and busy. They had for decades served together in Guardian Force, and they were widely recognized as a smooth and efficient team, bound tightly together by mutual respect and trust.

Zorn looked up, and catching Roan's eye, he smiled. His blue eyes held a hint of amusement.

"I'll wager a cold brew we'll have the target localized within a day."

Roan moved against his shoulder restraints, seeking a more comfortable position. Returning Zorn's smile, he indicated with a negative nod that the proffered wager was not accepted. Aware of the inherent risks, he issued the necessary commands to move Shey, Zorn, and himself directly into harm's way.

More than forty Astronomical Units distance from Shey, the Admiral commanding Guardian Fleet Operations, Dylan Cord, responded to an alert tone, "Computer, display the new contact data."

Scanning the report, Dylan first looked at the "from" and only then the "what" data blocks. *It's from Roan and Zorn. Now, what are those two rogues up to?* After studying the data, he then sat back in his chair, frowning.

"Computer, display the current positions of our patrolling Guardian cruisers within the Glas Dinnein system. Highlight the cruiser nearest to Scout ship Shey's location."

The computer displays changed, a list of ships and their coordinates appeared. Dylan examined the list and then keyed his communicator.

"Connect me with Captain Harlow on Lux."

A moment later a three-dimensional image of Captain Harlow, a young and promising captain, flashed upon Dylan's communicator screen.

"Good morning Admiral Cord. How might Lux be of service this fine morning?"

"Harlow, it's good to see you again. I've got a Scout ship out on its own and near the heliopause. It's Shey. Roan and Zorn were on some development work involving Fleet Intelligence when one of our outer detectors triggered. Shey, being the nearest

Guardian asset, was directed to check it out. My problem is from the available data, we don't have a clue what's coming into the system. Since Lux is the nearest cruiser to Shey, I want you to slip over and back her up, in case the target proves hostile."

"Yes Sir, Lux is on it. Please transmit Shey's coordinates along with any target data you may have. Lux will move out at once."

"Fair winds be at your back, Lux. Cord out."

Swiveling in his chair, Dylan instructed, "Computer, transmit a message to Cruiser Lux. Provide him with Shey's last reported coordinates and her communications ID. Include all current target data provided by Shey. Next, transmit a message to Shey. Fleet Operations is moving Cruiser Lux to support. Keep Lux in the loop. Good hunting."

Shey was moving through the solar wind, striking across the incoming signal vector, running a leg of the TMA. Shey was doing her job, and doing it well.

"Hey Roan, I've just received a message from Fleet Operations. They are vectoring Cruiser Lux to back us up."

"Sounds good, but let's hope we won't need the firepower of a cruiser to handle whatever is out there...."

Chapter Two:
Localization

While Roan and Zorn were analyzing collected on-ship dynamics and target bearing data, Shey was moving across the target true bearing line. Ending the first TMA leg, Roan brought the ship about and began their second analysis leg.

"Good news, the horizontal and vertical bearing rate components are smooth. Looks like the target is maintaining a constant course and speed," Zorn reported.

"Anything new on signature identification?"

"No, it's just hash. There is nothing recognizable. Shey's navigation is solid; we're getting crisp on-ship's dynamics and location data."

"Zorn, bring up a new tactical x-y plot. Make the initial axis the target true bearing line and the second axis parallel with the Galactic plane."

The polar plot on the forward bulkhead promptly transformed into a standard Cartesian x-y plot, showing Shey's track as a golden line extending across the initial green reference bearing line. A golden symbol marked Shey's location on the plot.

"Given its constant velocity, whatever that target is, the computer should soon have it localized," Zorn said.

Once again Roan brought the ship about, beginning the third TMA leg.

Soon thereafter, a bell-like alert sounded.

Shey's vibrant feminine voice announced, "Target localized."

The tactical display promptly updated and a red line appeared, projecting the computed horizontal target track. Where the red line intersected the updated green-bearing line, a red icon appeared, indicating the target location.

"Shey, reset the tactical plot axis. Set the first axis to the calculated target velocity vector, and set the second axis parallel with the galactic plane," Zorn ordered.

The plot immediately altered. Taking several minutes, Roan and Zorn studied the plot, noting the calculated relative motion vector and the target's closest point of approach. Zorn then

7

initiated a computer analysis of the target's trajectory in relationship with the solar system's major planetary bodies.

"Now, just where is that target headed?" Roan mused.

"It looks to be slowing. If there are no significant changes in its dynamics, the analysis indicates it's heading for a solar orbit near Glas Dinnein. The apparent intent seems intelligence gathering," Zorn reported.

"Agreed."

Keying in a brief report, Roan entered - *Determined trajectory inserts target into solar orbit near Glas Dinnein. Analysis data attached. Shey is commencing a visual fly-by.* With a flick of a key Roan sent the message, along with its bundled data block to the nearest communications node. The node then routed it on to Fleet Operations on Glas Dinnein and to Cruiser Lux.

"Zorn, set up for a slow visual inspection fly-by. I want every available scanner focused on the target."

"Making it so. Bringing all full spectrum detectors and optical monitors to active operation. I'm diligently preparing to grab the data, as we sneak past, preferably undetected and without shooting," Zorn responded.

"Shey, activate verbal command sequence functionality," Roan ordered.

"Sir, acknowledged. Voice command and response algorithms activated."

"Shey, on the plot, display a moving tactical sphere. The target is to be located at its center. Set the radius of the sphere to our medium missile effective range. Set our first defined Closest Point of Approach to be directly below the target. Our CPA is to be 80% of effective missile range. When approaching and entering the tactical sphere, our closing relative speed is to be 100 milli-lights. Report any ambiguities in your orders," Roan instructed.

" No ambiguities detected."

"Shey, bring us smartly about and proceed as ordered. Bring us to and through the designated CPA. When beyond CPA, you're to maintain your course and speed."

"Executing; as ordered, adjusting my velocity vector. Intercept the set target CPA in twelve minutes."

Rolling starboard, Shey briskly turned toward the target. Accelerating, her propulsion was softly humming with reserve vitality.

"Roan, I'm a bit curious. Since one-thousand lights equals the speed of light, isn't a relative closing velocity of 100 milli-lights akin to getting out and leisurely strolling past that target?"

Smiling, Roan glanced toward Zorn. "Are you in a hurry to be somewhere? Be hereby advised, I just might decide to strap you on a lifter disk and send you out with a hand-held camera to get really close-up images of that target."

"Hand held camera? Oops, I'm not that curious."

"Good. Now, set combat Condition 2. Set stealth to 85 percent. Bring two medium missiles on line, and obtain passive locks on that target."

Shey was small by design, but her armaments were formidable. As ordered, Zorn first brought Shey's defensive systems to full combat readiness, including laser and gun point-defense systems, electronic jamming, ballistic shells filled with metal foil, self-propelled and evasive drone decoys, laser energy deflectors and absorbers, and holographic generators. Then, with defensive systems activated, he proceeded with activating Shey's offensive systems. These included medium and light missiles; short range and high-rate-of-fire ballistic projectiles; and moderate power laser turrets. With experienced proficiency, he brought two medium missiles to ready-standby and established hard passive homing missile locks on the target's radiated signature.

"Confirming, Condition 2 set, battle ready. Stealth is 85 percent. Two medium missiles are ready-standby, each with solid passive homing lock."

Shey's intercept trajectory assured that at CPA the target would be at an optimal firing position. The target aspect angle of 90-degrees would provide a maximum target profile, taking full advantage of the opportunity to examine the target's construction and apparent function.

"Optical target lock," Zorn said.

On the screen, a small point of light appeared. The target's range was still too great for the photo-multipliers and their related discrimination circuits to provide a clear image, however, for the first time they had something visual to observe.

Roan initiated a video link and keyed the image to the nearest command node, setting the interval of subsequent automatic updates to a random sequence. His accompanying message was brief- *Optical target lock*.

"I'm not detecting any active laser scanning or EMF, phased or pulsed. Mark, five minutes to CPA," Zorn reported.

"Shey, update set missile homing. Lock one of the medium missiles to the target optical image," Roan ordered.

"Acknowledged and set."

"Shey, set evasion pattern to Tactical six and evasion acceleration to seventy percent."

"Set."

As the object drew closer, its expanding form and shape became evident on the forward bulkhead screen. Zorn gave a low whistle.

"What is it? Roan, have you ever seen anything like that before?" Zorn said.

"By Nodons' whiskers, never."

Chapter Three:
Stone Hammers and Flint Knives

As Shey approached the CPA with the target, its image on the bulkhead screen continued expanding. Its appearance was unanticipated.

"That thing must be more than 200 meters long. Just look at the clutter of stuff attached to its open framework, for sure it was never intended to enter an atmosphere," Roan said.

"I'm not reading any life-signs, not even in hyper-sleep. There's no crew; it's just a probe, but from where and sent by who?"

"Do you recognize anything that appears remotely like a weapon system?" Roan said.

"No. There's no detectable EMF or laser scanning, and I'm not seeing anything structural that indicates a weapon. I'm, however, detecting low level fission radiation. It's probably from the main power source being used for propulsion."

"Mark, CPA," Shey said.

"Fission powered propulsion? That's hard to believe. Whoever sent that thing must have built it using stone hammers and flint knives. That thing isn't capable of high acceleration, and isn't going anywhere in a hurry.

"Hold tight to our Condition 2, and be ready to go to Condition 1. I'm bringing Shey about to match the target trajectory. Shout if you see any indication the target detects us.

"Shey, we will be coming about. You are to roll out wide 45-degrees to port, then roll tight starboard, while climbing to the target's altitude. Close on the target. Keep it on our port side. At CPA, the target is to be abeam and at 80% of medium missile effective range. At CPA you're to match the target's velocity vector. Then hold on station. Execute,"

Roan ordered.

"Executing."

Shey's propulsion systems promptly produced a deep growl, as she began decelerating and rolling out to her left. Soon thereafter, while pitching upward, she reversed her roll, coming

11

sharply right. Continuing her deceleration, as Shey completed the maneuver, her propulsion system once again sounded as a faint purr. Leveling off, precisely at CPA, Shey matched the target's velocity vector.

"Mark. On station, at CPA."

If the target were a Kreel scout, Roan knew the intense burst of energy Shey had required to decelerate and alter her trajectory would have looked like an erupting nova on a Kreel sensor screen.

"See anything?" Roan said.

"Nothing, not even a flicker on any bandwidth."

As Shey paralleled the target, keeping station, both men carefully studied the image of the odd spacecraft. Someone had obviously gone to considerable trouble in sending the ungainly looking thing into the solar system. While it didn't appear to offer any threat, the questions of why and who built it, where did it come from, and its functionality remained a mystery.

"The primary signal source we've been tracking is being generated by a braking ion thruster. It's emitting a pronounced trail; however, the solar wind is beginning to disperse it."

"Can we use that ion trail to compute the target course?" Roan said.

"Yes. It's pronounced."

"Good. Now, get a standard laser scan of the target's surface. I want to know how long that machine has been in space. When finished, attach the analysis to our next transmission to Command and Lux."

Roan keyed in a brief message - *Target is an unmanned probe. No immediate threat detected. Strong ion trail. Shey is now breaking contact and backtracking target inbound path before ion trail dissipates.*

After Zorn attached the data block, Roan sent the message. The odd-looking probe was no longer Roan's problem. He knew that when the target came nearer to Glas Dinnein, those receiving the message would devise an appropriate intercept action.

"Our next job is to determine the probable origin of that probe, if possible. Do you have the ion trail mapped?" Roan said.

"Yes, there was no apparent evasion. That thing came in smooth and straight as an arrow."

"Sorry Zorn, but I've got some bad news. There'll be no cold brews at McBride's tonight. We need the longest baseline possible to get a boresight on where that thing came from, and we're going to back track that ion trail to get it.

"Shey, load Tactical's map of the ion trail into navigation. Set your new trajectory back along that trail. Then, bring us about smartly, and proceed along the trail. Accelerate at 70-percent, until you attain 220 lights. exccutc."

"Executing."

Rolling smoothly starboard, Shey's mild purring propulsion system became a deep rich and resonant thrum. With reserve energies, accelerating, Shey came about, setting her trajectory back along the ion trail and toward the heliopause boundary.

"Hey Roan, no cold brews at McBride's qualifies us for hardship pay. Might this humble sailor inquire, just how long do you anticipate we'll be following that ion trail?" Zorn said.

"Well, that sorta depends upon how many rations we have in our provisions locker."

"Ouch, emergency rations? Then, there'll be no cold brews for weeks upon weeks. It looks like not requesting a transfer to cooks and bakers' school was a huge mistake," Zorn said.

"Shey, initiate long-range active sensors. Search along the ion trail. If a target is detected, sound an alert," Roan ordered.

Active sensors came online and began seeking any potential threat lurking ahead. Sweeping a large volume of space, no threat was detected.

"Zorn, analyzing your preliminary result from the laser scan, that probe has been in space for more than a hundred years. It must have traveled across interstellar distances."

"Agreed, but from which star system?"

"Hopefully, by getting a solid boresight back along the ion trail, we can narrow down the possibilities."

"Shey, suspend active sensor search. Continue full spectrum passive scanning. Sound an alert if a target detection occurs.

"Zorn, retain our stealth factor at 60% or better. Reset our combat status to Condition 4."

"Acknowledged. resetting to Condition 4, standard alert status."

Passive tracking systems remained active, but weapon systems spun-down, resetting to an inactive state. Internal compartment doors slid open. Throughout the ship compartment lighting increased to normal levels and non-critical systems activated.

"Roan, the muses are at it again."

"What's troubling you this time?"

"Well, it's that odd probe. The muses are whispering It's more important than we can imagine. Rations aside, I'm getting an uncomfortable feeling we'll not be seeing Glas Dinnein or getting a cold brew for a long time, maybe even years."

"Years? Not likely. We're only backtracking a short distance to get a simple baseline measurement, not starting out on some interstellar junket. But, if the muses should prove correct again, then all bets are off. On the brighter side, just remember, when we do get back that first brew will taste really good."

"What do you think we'll discover out there?" Zorn said.

"Sorry, not a clue. But, when we find it, I'll let you know."

"After that bit of sage wisdom, I need a hot mug of neab. Do you want one?" Zorn asked.

"Sounds good, and let's get something to eat."

Moving aft toward the mess area and their living quarters, Roan and Zorn departed the control room. Shey was even then hurtling out along the ion trail at ever-increasing speed, busy working a fading trail into the void of space and the unknown.

If Roan or Zorn had been looking back toward the sun, they would have seen the image of Glas Dinnein steadily diminishing in size until it was only a pixel. Then the last pixel simply blinked out.

If it were possible for a Scout-ship AI to smile or feel emotions, then Shey would be considered happy and smiling. Alertly, she was surveying space all about her, even as Roan had instructed, looking for any threat. Until ordered otherwise or else prompted by some inner command protocol, she would continue doing so.

Except for the soft resonant thrum of Shey's temporal-gravimetric field generators, the control room was once more silent.

Shey held course and continued accelerating. Later, her sensors detected crossing the turbulent boundary between the inner solar system and outer interstellar space. Given her command protocols, Shey logged the event and sent a short text message to the nearest Guardian navigation beacon and to Roan

-- *Shey now exiting the solar-system, entering intergalactic space....*

Chapter Four:
A New Puzzle

Filled with the warm sunlight of a beautiful Autumn morning, the day outside Guardian Command HQ was bright and inviting. Inside, while holding a full mug of hot neab, Guardian Fleet Admiral Mer Shawn was entering a small conference room. Its functional working setting was enhanced by warm sand-tone colored walls, a dark tile floor, and leather-bound books, which complimented highly polished wood bookcases. The single picture on the walls was that of a sleek Guardian L-Class cruiser that was shown adorned with its brilliant white with gold trim parade colors. The cruiser was surrounded by the blackness of space, with a brilliantly glowing nebula framed in the background.

The obvious focus of the room was the polished wood conference table, where two men were sitting. Admirals Ron Cloud, Fleet Intelligence, and Dylan Cord, Fleet Operations, were already seated and waiting. Like Mer, they were wearing comfortable Guardian shipboard uniforms. Both men looked up as Mer entered.

In the relaxed manner of old friends, they smiled. Mer eased into his familiar chair at the head of the table, put his mug of neab down, and returned the smile of his friends.

"Good morning, gentlemen. It seems we have a new puzzle to evaluate. Please open your individual indexes to file K-172, then review its unrestricted portion," Mer said.

Picking up his mug, and turning away from the table toward the nearby window, Mer allowed his associates the time necessary to review the referenced file. The outside facing wall of the conference room was wall-to-wall glass, offering an elevated and stunning view of the harbor, a forested coastline, and the wondrously blue ocean.

Mer's thoughts turned towards the ongoing war, an interstellar war that was a desperate fight for humanity's survival, a war where no quarter was asked or given.

The Kreel were a merciless humanoid lifeform, whose imperative was absolute dominance and the expansion of empire. From their unanticipated first encounter, the Kreel had exhibited a savage hatred for humanity, and soon thereafter humanity had come to mirror that sentiment.

With the outset of war, in pursuit of their common defense, the elected representatives from the eleven dispersed human Planetary governments had convened a federated governing assembly. The Assembly was located on Glas Dinnein, the home world of humanity's new beginning.

More than eight centuries had elapsed since the Kreel launched a planetary scale invasion. They attacked Kintana, one of the eleven worlds that humanity had over the preceding thousands of years settled. During that devastating attack, before the Kreel were beaten back into deep space, Kintana and Guardian Force suffered horrific losses.

Since the battle of Kintana, improving stealth technologies had sharpened humanity's drawn sword to a keen edge. It was the stealth advantage that had enabled sharp increases in Kreel ship losses, thereby effectively blunting the Kreel aggression. Nevertheless, Kreel probes entering humanity's space, hit-and-run raids on human interplanetary shipping, and their brief bitter skirmishes with Guardian Force demanded constant vigilance and readiness.

Strategically, the Kreel remained a mystery. There was an obvious imbalance in military resources, and post-battle analysis concluded the Kreel Empire occupied a larger volume of space than did humanity. The question remained, just how much larger?

The lack of hard Intelligence had prevented humanity from turning the tide of battle to its favor. It was harsh necessity that committed Guardian Force to hold the line and wage a defensive campaign against the Kreel.

The Dargon were another savage species. Like the Kreel, they had no known allies. An insectoid lifeform, the Dargon were not humanoid. Whenever they appeared, it was as a swarm, ever bent upon short term pillaging. The Dargon made no attempt to remain on a planet, focusing rather on swift raids designed to rapidly pillage a selected sector of a planet. After they struck their prey, as swiftly as they had appeared, they disappeared back into the abyss of space. The last three Dargon attacks, which occurred centuries past, were detected and defeated long before they reached a planet. Since their last defeat, the Dargon had not returned.

Holding the now empty, but still pleasantly warm mug between his hands, Mer's thoughts shifted from the Kreel to the cabin that he hoped to someday build in the coastal foothills. While the burdens of his job dealt with battles in space, it was the oceans, rivers, windswept hills, and the forests of Glas Dinnein that were his real love.

Returning his attention to the men at the table, he observed both were just completing their review of the file.

Ron was the first to speak.

"Primitive."

"I disagree. The engineering is dated and basic, but there's nothing primitive about its design, or its simple functionality. The probe displays a balanced use of polymers, sophisticated digital processing, and sound engineering. In my opinion, there's a simple elegance to the entire design. It demonstrates careful planning, a scientific rather than a military or economic purpose, and social patience measured in centuries. None of those qualities are what I'd classify as being primitive," Dylan said.

"I've no disagreement with your engineering assessment. Still, whoever sent the probe had no concept of who or what might intercept the probe en route or at its intended destination. They might as well have sent up fireworks, or hung out a banner proclaiming easy pickings. The culture that sent that probe has fundamental engineering talent, I'll give you that much, but it's utterly naive as to what dangers might be in deep space. In my view, that ranks it as primitive," Ron said.

Mer smiled. If left alone, he knew the two men would most likely have continued their discussion for some time. Unfortunately, time was a commodity in short supply.

"Gentlemen," Mer interjected. "Now open and read the restricted section of the report, and evaluate the results of the forensic analysis. Please note, it is classified, and not to be discussed or mentioned outside of this room, without a confirmed need to know."

With interest, Mer studied the countenances of his old friends as they read the report.

Ron looked up first, letting out a deep sigh, his expression having become troubled. Dylan continued to read for several more minutes, then he looked toward Mer.

"Is the data here fully confirmed?" Dylan said.

"Yes. The forensic team found traces of blood and tissue in the probe. Apparently during the orbital phase of the construction, there was an accident. Although the blood and tissue specimens were small, they were sufficient for analysis. It's confirmed, the blood is human," Mer said.

"Then, the logical conclusion is humans built that probe," Ron said.

"Yes. The results of the analysis are documented and beyond doubt. The probe was designed and built by human beings," Mer said.

"If I fully understand what I've just read, forensic analysis shows the probe was manufactured on a planet, and then assembled in orbit. There is ample evidence that the builders ran a very clean operation, and the analysts believe this attention to detail suggests a genuine cultural concern for preventing the proliferation of disease vectors. Whoever they are, that awareness and attention to detail speaks well for them," Dylan said.

"Do we know where the probe originated?" Ron asked.

"Given our initial investigations, we've established a probable origin. Commanders Roan and Zorn ran back for some distance along the probe's braking ion trail. They have obtained a solid boresight pointing to the probe's probable origin. Given Shey's measurements, the launch solar system is about twenty-three parsecs distant. Shey's preliminary report also supports Ron's assessment. The probe made no detectable effort to conceal its flight path."

"It seems Commanders Roan and Zorn have, as is typical for those two rogues, shown exemplary initiative," Dylan said.

"Agreed, and on both counts," Ron said.

Troubled, with quiet intensity Dylan asked, "Mer, could the probe be from First Home?"

"Dylan, you know there is no evidence to support a First Home ever existed. Those ancient legends are based on nothing more than oral tradition and oft-told whispers," Mer retorted.

"Mer, on this I'm siding with Dylan. Although ancient, the legends of First Home have never faded. It may only be folklore, but there are no tangible records other than legend concerning our beginnings. And, our recorded history emerges from those oral traditions. Fables or otherwise, the stories all agree. There was a time of an immense solar-system scale disaster. That fragment of racial memory is clear. What remains vague is where it all happened, and how our forebearers survived to be flung out among the stars," Ron said.

"Given that probe, I'm somewhat inclined to give those old fables a little more credence. We know the probe was constructed and sent here by human beings, sent from somewhere we've never been. It's indeed a real puzzle. So, just what are we going to do about solving that puzzle?" Dylan said.

Chapter Five:
A Bold and Naive People

Mer's frown had increased as he listened to his colleagues. "Gentlemen, actual Dargon and Kreel forces are a real and present threat. We need to stay focused on known hard facts, not fables.

"Our galaxy is 100,000 light years across, and within a radius of twenty-three parsecs, there are approximately 2,600 solar systems. We don't have the luxury of over abundant resources, which might permit us to go scampering about searching for a mythical First Home.

It's because of the active rumor mill around here that the human DNA found on that probe is classified. And, on my watch, we're not going to begin feeding the hungry gossip dragon," Mer said.

"Well, if we exclude a first home theory, there're several possible, although admittedly implausible, explanations how human DNA might be found on that probe. Perhaps the human DNA came from a dominated world, where the Kreel or Dargon are exploiting human slave labor. Otherwise, it might be from a trophy or breeding pen world. Given our limited resources, sending a full-fledged exploratory mission in force to investigate is altogether out of the question. Still, I submit the two improbable possibilities that I've just mentioned do warrant our making a limited long-range reconnaissance. " Ron said.

"I doubt the Dargon would stand idly by and permit a captive human population to build a probe. That is doubly true where the Kreel are involved. We all know what the Kreel do with humans they capture. Besides, that probe is programmed to resume its voyage and return to its launch point, with whatever Intelligence it has collected. The Dargon and Kreel know more about us than that simple probe will observe in a hundred years. Still, I agree with Ron. The existence of the human factor demands that we send a long-range reconnaissance," Dylan said.

"Humph, I've just thought of another possibility. If our people truly were scattered out among the stars during some long-ago disaster, then perhaps that probe originated with another group of far-flung survivors. What we know for certain is somewhere out there, a human culture fashioned and sent a probe across interstellar space and parked it neatly on our doorstep. I'm impressed that so basic a machine could reach this solar system from such a distance, let alone expect to find a planet worth examining. Just how they managed to do that is of some interest to me. Frankly, I would like to meet such a bold and naive people. If nothing else, they must have a fascinating story to tell," Ron said.

"Gentlemen, then we've reached consensus. Accordingly, I'm authorizing sending a long-range reconnaissance mission. It will consist of a single cruiser. Henceforth, information concerning the mission will be tightly compartmentalized.

"Dylan, as Guardian Operations, you will take charge. All related information concerning the mission will be skillfully blended into our normal fleet operations reports. The risk level and the long-range nature of the mission is not to be overtly mentioned. And, that goes double for any summary reports or updates going to the Planetary Assembly."

"Mer, is your intention not to tell Admiral Secretary Eryan Kyrie of the mission?" Dylan said.

"No. Our esteemed Admiral Secretary will be informed, personally by me, verbally, unofficially, and discretely, and at a time of my choosing. That strictly means no mention of a long-range deployment is to be made or referenced in any report sent to the Assembly. I have no intention of pouring fuel upon our General Administrator's raging budget-cutting bonfire."

"Mer, while I understand your reasoning, we are talking about a high-risk mission. We'll be deploying a single cruiser twenty-three parsecs into unknown space, and standard operating doctrine specifies we should be sending at least three cruisers. The increased risks associated with sending one cruiser are significant. That cruiser and its crew may be going out on a one-way mission. Your decision not to tell the Assembly is fraught with political hazards. You know that. My earnest recommendation is that you bring Eryan into our conspiracy as soon as practicable," Ron said.

"Acknowledged," Mer said.

Turning, Mer spoke toward a small console located on the table. "Computer, show me the present location of Scout ship Shey."

The large picture on the wall was replaced by a graphics display showing a compressed representation of the solar system, as if looking down on the ecliptic plane. The planetary orbital paths were shown as concentric blue rings. Beyond the outermost blue ring was a thin red ring, defining the heliopause boundary. The display shifted, the set of rings diminishing in scale and moving toward the lower left corner of the display. Near the upper right corner, A blinking golden icon appeared. At the bottom of the display, a set of coordinates were shown.

Studying the coordinates, Dylan gave a low whistle. "For a Scout ship operating alone, Shey is far from home."

"Computer, display the list of cruisers that are currently ready to deploy," Mer said.

The image of the solar system was replaced by a short list of five names. The three men studied the list for several moments before anyone spoke.

"Gentlemen, what are your recommendations?"

"They're all fine ships, Mer. Given, however, the extreme nature of the mission, I recommend Cruiser Lan. Captain Kellon and his crew have the greatest amount of combat experience. Considering where they're going, that combat experience might prove to be critical," Dylan said.

"Agreed. Lan is also my choice. "Ron said.

"Good. Computer, display the previous plot," Mer said.

The graphics showing Shey's position were displayed. Mer studied the coordinates shown across the top and down the left side of the display. With a laser pointer, he chose a set of coordinates.

"Computer, you are to append the plot to the following orders. To: Scout ship Shey: alter current trajectory. You are to rendezvous with Cruiser Lan at the indicated coordinates.

"To Cruiser Lan send: you are herewith directed to make immediate preparation for an extended three-year deep space reconnaissance patrol. The mission is classified Black Hole, and your priority is AA. You are expected to maximize use of your AA priority in fitting out for the earliest possible deployment. Upon receipt of your deployment orders from Fleet Operations you are to rendezvous with Scout ship Shey at the marked coordinates. You will thereafter provide hangar space for Scout ship Shey. After rendezvous with Shey, you will proceed with stealth to the destination that will be provided by the crew of Scout ship Shey. When arriving at your destination, you will conduct a full, detailed, and covert surveillance of the specified solar system. Afterward, return to Glas Dinnein.

"Computer, send both orders and validate they are from Fleet Admiral Mer Shawn.

"Computer, reset display," Mer said.

The picture of the Guardian cruiser and nebula immediately replaced the graphics, and Mer looked toward his colleagues. His voice carried with it an unmistakable deep fatigue.

"How simple it seems to send men and women into the unknown and possibly to their deaths. We are directing Lan out alone and further than we have gone before. Only the muses know what they are likely to encounter. I know that both of you would like to be going along with Lan, so would I.

"Dylan, you're to scrutinize every iota of Lan's preparation and outfitting. They are to be thorough and overly complete. Deny Lan nothing. When you are completely satisfied with Lan's preparation, issue his deployment orders.

"Ron, you're to set up a contingency plan to support the mission, should it turn into a firefight. You're also to provide backup for Dylan and are in charge of Intelligence operations. Meanwhile, continue with the analysis of the probe. You're to continue taking necessary steps to keep the mission under wraps.

"The code name for the project is Door Step and like Lan, your priority is AA. Are there any questions?" Mer said.

"No Sir."

"Gentlemen, Lan is among our best. May fair winds be with Lan and all those going with him, and may they all return safely home."

Mer stood, turned and departed the conference room. Carrying his now empty cold mug, he walked with the assured step of a military officer, without any outward appearance of his inward fatigue. He tried not to ponder how many people might not return from the mission they had just put in motion, and tried to keep under tight mental check the memories of former ships, families, and old friends who went out and never came home.

Mer Clamped hard down on his anger. *Blast the Administrator and his budget cuts. Three cruisers, not one, should be going out on the mission.* Fending off his rising sense of anger, Mer began to visualize the floor plan of his imaginary cabin in the coastal foothills. That, he rationalized, was something that could at least be controlled.

Chapter Six:
Lan

Shey was inert, her self-noise near zero, and searching for revealing ripples of energy within enveloping interstellar space. The illumination within Shey's control room was subdued, and both Roan and Zorn sat alert and monitoring their passive detection displays. The men were tired, but in good spirits. In back-tracking the ion trail, they had pushed Shey's performance envelope to its limits and were pleased with her abilities. She was stealthy, nimble, and well-armed, but not designed for long interstellar-space excursions. Her pantry was also limited.

When they had received Fleet orders to rendezvous with Cruiser Lan, Roan and Zorn were both happy to comply. The remaining journey home would have required several more weeks, and both men were beginning to feel their tight quarters.

"Roan, when we get home, you'll owe me dinner at McBride's. If I have to see another ration bar I may turn into a raving madman."

"Be careful with what you say, some people that I know might just consider that transformation as being an improvement."

"Be kind. I'm not that bad. What I'm really looking forward to is a cold brew. Our hitching a ride with Lan means I'll get that brew sooner than later. Even better, being on board Lan means I can get a decent breakfast."

Arriving early at the defined rendezvous coordinates, they had followed tactical doctrine, first searching for a rendezvous beacon. When no beacon was located, they initiated a helix-search of surrounding space. Their search yielded no trace of another ship. If Lan had arrived first, he would have provided the security sweep of surrounding space, then deployed a rendezvous beacon. Having verified local space was clear, Shey returned to the rendezvous coordinates, deployed one of her low power beacons, and withdrew to a safe distance.

"Shey," confirm we're within the standard rendezvous tactical sphere," Roan ordered.

"Sir, in strict adherence to Guardian doctrine, we are positioned 75% of the tactical radius from our beacon."

"Hey Roan, do you remember what the muses whispered to me before we began this little junket?" Zorn said.

"Yes. Are the muses at it again?"

"No, but I've got another uncomfortable feeling. Consider, just how many times has the Guardian Fleet Admiral personally ordered us to rendezvous with anyone?"

"Well, never."

"Precisely, our orders always come from Operations or Intelligence. So, why not this time? What's really going on?"

"I don't have a clue. And, it really doesn't matter. When Lan arrives, we get a free ride home. And, like you said, breakfast on board Lan will be a real treat."

"I guess you're right. For certain, we'll soon enough learn what is really happening.

"Hey Roan, I'll wager that I'll detect Lan before he acknowledges the beacon."

"Wager how much?"

"How about one cold brew when we get back to Glas Dinnein?"

"You're already down five cold brews on this trip. Is your credit that good?"

Shey's soft voice cut short their idle banter, "Scout ship Sheba is acknowledging our beacon."

"Roan, the bet is off." Zorn inserted.

"Shey, acknowledge Sheba's signal. Move cautiously toward the beacon, until we can obtain a solid fix on her location," Roan said.

"Acknowledged."

Troubled, Roan mused, *Why is Lan deploying Sheba to make first contact? Did we miss some threat? If not, then why would Lan be operating under strict mission guidelines? By all of Zorn's muses, he is on target again. Lan is here for something more than just to offer us a quick trip home.*

"Hard data link established with Sheba," Shey reported.

Zorn broke out in a broad smile, "Hey Roan, we're being congratulated by Sheba and Lan's other Scouts for our effort."

"Shey, return our compliments to Sheba and her sisters. Request her for the rendezvous trajectory to Lan; then, terminate our rendezvous beacon."

"Rendezvous beacon terminated. Sheba has provided the requested trajectory. We are now moving directly toward Lan."

Perplexed, Zorn was concentrating on his monitors, seeking a clue as to where the cruiser was waiting. "By all the muses, we should have detected Lan by now."

Shey's passive detectors showed no trace of Lan. Clearly Lan was running in full stealth and dark, not showing any navigation running lights. With the passing minutes, the tension within Shey's control room steadily mounted.

"It sorta looks like Guardian Force got its money's worth from Lan's last shield upgrade," Roan mused.

"Contact. We've a faint propulsion trace on him at 357, E40. He's close and is extremely well shielded," Zorn reported.

"Shey, inform Lan we've detected his propulsion signature, and provide him with the detection range information," Roan instructed.

"Lan has acknowledged. Hard link with Lan is now established. Data, voice, and video are now available," Shey reported.

"Shey, coordinate with Lan. Request a controlled approach to hangar and docking," Roan ordered.

"Now exchanging maneuvering data with Lan."

"Shey, show all coordinates on a maneuvering plot, with Lan at its center. "Roan said. The tactical display altered. Lan's position appeared as a stationary golden icon in the center of the polar display. Shey's symbol and a third golden icon representing Sheba were also shown. As Roan and Zorn watched, the two offset golden icons drew nearer to one another and to the center. Lan was responsible for the coordination of both Scouts; each was moving in accordance with Lan's instructions. Since the Scouts were the smaller ships, with less inertia, their responsibility was to make the majority of the required maneuvers, while Lan made only subtle adjustments. After five minutes of maneuvering, the massive bulk of the cruiser became discernible against the background field of stars. Shey maneuvered alongside Lan, matching trajectories. The blackness blocking the view of stars parted first with a thin seam of dim light. Then a large and dimly illuminated open hangar volume became visible. A coupling field extended out from the hangar, and it gently enveloped Shey. As she was drawn in, padded docking clamps extended to cushion and secure her into a snug berth. With a firm and reassuring thump, the hangar door shut behind Shey. Elsewhere, Sheba was returning to her own hangar.

As both men began to secure the controls and power down Shey, the lights in the hangar brightened. The hangar volume was small and nearly filled by the bulk of the Scout ship. Frost began forming around Shey as the disparity in temperatures between the hangar and Shey's hull began seeking a compromise. A gangplank smoothly extended from a platform near Shey's control room and nudged Shey's entry hatch. As it touched Shey's hull, with a pleasant and masculine resonant tone, Lan spoke through the intercom.

"Welcome Shey, and honored crew."

"Lan, we send our compliments. Your warm hospitality is greatly appreciated," Shey replied, in the formal fleet tradition.

"Atmospheric pressure is restored. The hangar is now safe," Lan replied.

"Nicely done, Shey. Set internal ship's status to standby and self-diagnostics to full operation. Notify Lan of our needs for provisioning and any discerned maintenance requirements. Open the hatch, and maintain communications with both Zorn and me," Roan said.

"Acknowledged."

"Hey Roan, see if you can use your rank and clout to swing us a cold brew," Zorn whispered.

In response, nudging his shipmate in the ribs with his elbow, Roan quipped, "Sorry, but McBride's is a long way from here."

Even as Roan spoke, Shey's hatch retracted and an inward rush of frigid hangar air greeted them. Coming with its cold embrace was the familiar and unmistakable aromas of cleaning compounds, electronics, and light machine oil, all blending together with a multitude of other odors. Stepping out of Shey and into the hangar, they heard the soft background hum of the interior of a cruiser. They were safe aboard Lan, and just like coming home, it felt good. Now, all that remained was to learn just why they were aboard.

Chapter Seven:
A Good Question

The bitter cold of deep space clung frostily to Shey's flat black hull. In spite of the influx of warm air, the entire hangar compartment was freezing to the point of discomfort.

Roan was smiling as he walked across the gangplank and received the brisk salute of a young woman, who was waiting for them. He could not help but notice she was a very attractive blonde, her brilliant blue eyes glowing with youth and intelligence. Her smile was genuinely warm. Dressed in the stylish but comfortable shipboard attire, the insignia tabs on her lapel declared that she was a sub-lieutenant, with a specialty in science. Roan formally returned her salute.

"Sir, I'm Lieutenant Elayne Cloud. I'm here to extend the Captain's personal compliments to Commanders Roan and Zorn. Sirs, you're both requested to join the Captain in his briefing room."

"Lieutenant Cloud, please show us the way," Roan said.

When they departed the hangar, its hatch slid smoothly shut behind them. After being in the cold hangar, all three of them welcomed the comfortably warm temperature of the bright passageway. Entering an elevator, they were carried up two decks.

"Is this your first tour?" Roan asked.

"No. This is actually my fourth tour with Lan."

"After being more than five weeks cramped inside a Scout ship, it's good to be aboard," Zorn inserted.

Exiting the elevator, they turned left and proceeded along a narrower passageway. As they walked, the closed hatches ahead of them smoothly withdrew into the bulkheads. Once they had passed, the hatches slid quietly closed again. Finally, they reached and entered into a modest sized compartment. It was a sparsely furnished, but comfortable conference room. Its color scheme was warm, the walls being a pleasant tan hue and the deck appeared to be dark earthy tiles. Two men were sitting talking with each other at a long table. Both were wearing shipboard apparel, with the subtle collar insignia of senior command officers.

Elayne saluted, and then announced the visitors. "Sir, as requested, Commanders Roan and Zorn are here."

The older man stood and returned her salute. "Thank you, Elayne. You may return to your duty station."

"Welcome gentlemen, I'm Captain Kellon. It's my pleasure to welcome you aboard Cruiser Lan. I know you must be tired, so let's get straight to the problem at hand.

"Commander Roan, I understand that you know my Executive and Navigation Officer, Commander Roy Grey."

"Yes, Sir. Roy and I were shipmates on the Cruiser Kyrie."

"Gentlemen, please take a seat. There's hot neab, if you wish a cup."

As Roan and Zorn settled into two chairs about the table, Roan looked toward the Captain. "Sir, we are somewhat perplexed. We don't fully understand why we're aboard Lan."

"Roan, there are two reasons why you are aboard. The first reason is to provide Lan with the details of your observations about the ion trail, and your conclusions as to the launch point of the probe. As for the second reason, Fleet Admiral Mer Shawn has personally selected and assigned Shey and her crew to duty aboard Lan for the duration of our mission.

"In accordance with standard protocol, as the senior Scout Officer aboard, you are also designated the lead Scout Commander of Lan's four Scouts.

"Our mission is to proceed directly to the solar system that you have identified. We're to make a complete covert survey of that system and then return to Guardian Command with the intelligence report. In fulfilling our orders, Lan will be required to survey a new route through uncharted space, and this is going to slow our outbound progress."

"Sir, speaking for Shey, Commander Zorn, and myself, we welcome the opportunity to serve aboard Lan. Shey, transfer a complete log and the specified astrometry profile to Lan."

A soft acknowledging tone sounded from Roan's collar insignia.

"Computer, display the astrometry profile provided by Shey," Commander Grey instructed.

The unadorned bulkhead at the end of the table transformed into a display and the lights in the conference room subtly dimmed. The men turned to observe the display, studying the screen for a moment. The display was in a standard format, consisting of a star field similar to what a high-quality telescope might show, but with a few informative additions. Stars were color-coded by type, and their intensity was directly proportional to their magnitudes. All known dark bodies were also shown. Over the entire display, fine horizontal and vertical lines created a reference grid. Two boldly colored lines were shown on the screen; one was the red-colored ion trail of the probe and the second was the golden track of Shey.

"What are your deductions?" Kellon asked.

"Sir, I will defer to Zorn concerning our observations," Roan said.

"Sir, based on our observations of the probe, our conclusion is it was not launched from a ship, but rather originated from a planetary orbital launch.

"Given the data from our laser scan of the probe, it was in transit for about 175 years. The probe is clearly a sub-light vehicle. Because of the elapsed time of a round-trip, we surmise the purpose of those who sent the probe was scientific rather than military in nature.

"Computer, rotate the star field image by ninety degrees. Sir, Regarding the probable launch-point of the probe, as you can now observe on the rotated image, the ion trail does not show any deviation along its measurable length. We extrapolated the course vector and corrected for the indicated dispersion, this being a rather simple approximation.

The indicated solar system of origin is a BG type star, located 24.57 parsecs or 80 light years from Glas Dinnein. We found no information concerning this particular solar system in Shey's database. Sir, those are our observations and conclusion, " Zorn said.

"Captain, with all due respect, the defined mission doesn't seem to make any sense. That probe was out there for nearly two hundred years. Given the tactical priorities in the region, and the value of Lan's tactical capability, why is Guardian command diverting Lan 80 light years in such an urgent fashion?" Roan asked.

"That's a good question, and you're not the first person to ask it. It seems that the examining forensic teams found proof that your probe was built by human beings."

"Human beings on a world eighty light years distant? By all the muses, this will prove to be a very interesting tour of duty," Zorn said.

"Roy, we now have the needed confirmation of where we're going. So, it's time to set condition for making our first jump," Kellon said.

"Yes, Sir. First jump coming up," Roy Grey said.

"Lan, ask Elayne to come to my conference room," Kellon said.

Shortly thereafter, the woman who had greeted Roan and Zorn returned to the conference room." Sir, reporting as ordered."

"Gentlemen, I suggest you get some rest and freshen yourselves. I hope to see you in the Officer's Dining Room for the evening meal.

"Elayne, please show Commanders Roan and Zorn to their assigned quarters, and then continue with your normal duties," Kellon said.

Kellon watched as the trio departed and the hatch slid shut behind them. Musing, he thought, *Given your orders, and where you are sending us, thank you Mer Shawn for assigning those two Scout officers to Lan. They are definitely two of the best among a very select group.* He then returned his attention to studying the image on the display.

"Lan, review all available historical records pertaining to the indicated solar system and all actions that have occurred between Glas Dinnein and that system. Cross correlate the data by time and contacts with either Dargon or Kreel forces. Cross-index any missing ships or personnel, with appropriate links to documentation. Have the report ready for my review by dinner this evening."

"Processing."

Problematically, Lan was outbound on a long trek and without resupply or backup. Kellon's long years of no-quarters combat with the Kreel and Dargon had honed his survival instinct to a keen edge. What might be lurking out there ahead of them was completely unknown, and his instincts were shouting a strident battle alarm....

Chapter Eight:
Transit

There was a subtle and resonant vibration within the laminar mesh of time, a point in space flowed outward; emerging from his third long jump, Lan was set Condition 2 -- alert and at battle stations. Lan was but an incongruous anomaly suspended within the boundless void of space. Enveloping him were the points of light from nearby stars, randomly intermixed with similar points from uncountable distant stars, galaxies, and nebulas. Immediately, He began collecting the star sightings required to calculate the current standard time and his precise jump-exit location.

A soft knock sounded on the conference room door, and Kellon looked up. "Enter."

When the hatch slid open, Commanders Roy Grey and Lorn Shaw entered. "Gentlemen, help yourself to the neab. There is also sharp yellow cheese and a few pastries on the side table."

"Why, thank you, Sir. My dear mother taught me never to turn down a kind offer of neab and pastries," Roy said.

After filling their cups, Roy and Lorn took their seats about the conference table." Sir, as your Senior Navigator, I am reporting the successful completion of our third long jump. All stations have reported Condition Gold. We're on the edge of the Badlands. Beyond this point, none who ventured forth returned to tell their tale," Roy said.

"Thank you for that troublesome reminder," Kellon said, with lighthearted derision.

"Lorn, what's our Tactical situation?"

"Sir, all bandwidths are clear. There's no indication of any other ships operating in the local volume."

"Good. Lan, order a stand-down from Battle Stations. Reset ship's internal security status to Alert Condition 3."

"Sir, acknowledged."

"Roy, as our Senior Navigator, how are you planning to keep us from running aground on uncharted reefs or riding off a cliff in the middle of the night?"

"Well Sir, as to that, we sorta got lucky there were even three long jumps through charted space. As for keeping our safety margins high, I'll be using a tight cluster of background beacon stars. Their spectrums and distributed positions about our destination afford Lan first-rate infrared, gravity lensing, and light perturbation analysis. Still, because of the possibility of unknown dark bodies, the best we can hope for are short jumps of less than a parsec. And, most jumps will be a light year or less."

"How soon can we make our next jump?" Kellon said.

"So far, the muses are smiling. When exiting the last jump, we initiated an analysis of the star field ahead. We've detected no aberrations in the apparent star positions or in their light path stability, suggesting there're no dark bodies or temporal sumps immediately ahead. I estimate another ten hours of analysis before I can certify our first short jump."

"Take whatever time you need. Accurately charting the outbound route is more important than is the covert survey of our target solar system. Our safety and the safety of every ship that follows depends upon our thoroughness."

"It was our safety that I had in mind, when requisitioning twice the number of navigation beacons that the Quartermaster had allotted for our mission. My own view is navigation beacons don't have crews and cost less than a cruiser, so, more is always better than less. At first the Quartermaster didn't share my views, and there followed a brief, but energetic discussion. Sir, I am quite pleased to report that I got my extra beacons. We'll be deploying a beacon at each and every jump-exit point."

"You wangled twice the allocated beacons? Given their cost and scarcity, how?"

"Well, Sir, you didn't hear me say it was easy, not even with Admiral Cord's approval. Sir, I am sorry to report, at first, the Quartermaster seemed inexplicably confrontational about my views. But we finally reached a compromise; the beacons only cost me two cases of brews."

"Two cases? Roy, you're as incorrigible now as when a cadet at the Academy. Do I dare ask, what was the wager you made with the Quartermaster?"

"Sir, regarding my Academy days, the memories of those far distant centuries are somewhat vague. Being prudent, I'll defer to your keener recollections of those times. As for the brews, Sir, only an unkind person might call the gentlemen's agreement between the Quartermaster and me a wager. At the outset of our discussions, he personally guaranteed me that the allotted beacons were more than adequate, and furthermore insisted each was perfect. While striving to avoid any hint of rancor, I merely questioned his objectivity; Sir, I was only being prudent. As reported, we eventually reached a consensus, and our gentleman's agreement is that I'll deliver him two cases of brews, but only after we get home safe; and then, only if I am able to confirm each and every beacon was, as he assured, perfect and without defect. Upon his reflection, given how far we are jumping, he agreed doubling the initial allotment was only a reasonable contingency, should his initial viewpoint be proven overly optimistic."

"Humph, I'll stick with incorrigible. Still, I suppose even the Fleet Admiral would agree, it's definitely a gentlemen's agreement. Well done, Senior Navigator."

"Why, thank you Sir."

"Lorn, as Lan's senior Tactical Officer, I want you to keep a sharp eye on our baffles. Lan is not to leave a detectable trail. We're not going to be responsible for leading the Kreel to a planet full of humans."

"Sir, I'll double check we don't."

"And, keep in mind there might be other space-capable species that we know nothing about and are native to these regions. Finally, since we don't have a clue where the Dargon hives are located, it would prove awkward if we stumbled into the middle of a Dargon swarm. Stay on top of our stealth profile and communications disciplines."

"Yes, Sir."

"Gentlemen, our mission is a deep exploratory probe into hostile regions. We're far from our families on Glas Dinnein, and that distance increases daily. My intention is to accomplish our mission, and then return home safe and intact-- without serious injury or loss of life. We're going to check and then recheck every action to make it happen.

"Are there any questions?" Kellon asked.

There were none. After Roy and Lorn departed the conference room, returning to their duty stations, Kellon remained sitting in the conference room contemplating the mission risks, including the seldom mentioned 80 light years long return journey. He well understood when dickering with energy, mass, and time, executing a spacial-temporal jump came with discernible risks, and doing so was always dangerous. Although there were now far fewer ships lost than in centuries past, occasionally a ship was still inexplicably lost during a jump.

"Lan, transmit a Black Hole encrypted message to Guardian Operations, to Admiral Dylan Cord: Lan has completed the last of three long jumps. First jump into Badlands is in ten hours. Morale is high and Lan's condition is Gold.

"Lan, include our current coordinates and standard time. Send it over my signature."

"I am sending the message, as ordered. Sir, might I say, I am in full agreement with Commander Grey. The extra beacons are an excellent contingency and seem well worth two cases of brews."

There was nothing routine about the daily ship's operations, and in increments, Lan moved painstakingly across the twenty parsecs toward his objective. At each jump-exit point, a navigation beacon was calibrated and deployed. Each beacon operated in tandem with adjacent beacons, and together they searched for mass and temporal anomalies occurring in their local space. The lengthening chain of beacons served as the superluminal communications network from Lan back to Glas Dinnein, and they also served as passive Intelligence gathering monitors, continuously searching for transiting superluminal spaceships, dark bodies, and temporal sumps. Remaining on its designated station, each beacon relayed superluminal communications and reported its collected astronomical data.

As the weeks and months slowly passed, Lan's crew meticulously filled in the blank pages of their logs, recording volumes of astronomical data.

Slowly, a sense of excitement began to build within the crew about where they were going and even more so about why.

"Roan, how can there possibly be human beings on a world twenty-five parsecs from Glas Dinnein? The more I think about this mission, the more important the answer seems to be."

Zorn was carrying a thermos of neab and two cups over to the small table in Shey's mess area. He placed them in the center of the table, and then sat down before continuing his thought.

"Our own origins are a mystery, as big or larger than any question of how humans might be living on a world 80 light years from Glas Dinnein. Where did our own people come from? No one has the answer for that question. We've all heard the rumors about First Home. Are they true? The good news is, during this mission we may actually figure it all out."

Sitting forward, Roan poured himself a cup of neab. "Agreed. For sure, humanity didn't spring forth simultaneously from the ether in more than one place. There has to be some link that ties the loose ends of humanity together."

"Sir, when we arrive in the target solar system, will the Scouts go back to work? Just sitting in hangar space is not what Scouts were made for," Shey said.

"Not to worry, Shey. There will be hard work waiting for all of us, especially the Scouts. I expect Captain Kellon will stay distant from the inner planets and rely on sentinels and Intelligence gathering probes for his initial data collection. But there will be plenty to keep us all very busy," Roan said.

"Sir, I just told my sisters what you said. They are happy to learn we will be busy again. Sir, may I have permission to ask an unrelated question?"

"Permission granted."

"Sirs, over the past months I have listened to your conversations about humanity. Still, my sisters and I remain perplexed. We do not understand your confusion relating to the origin of humans upon Glas Dinnein. Lan and my sisters agree, each person was born of woman. In cross-referencing Lan and my medical databases, human reproduction techniques, methods, and sexual relationships are fully annotated and explained. Admittedly, I find matters pertaining to human biological and reproductive functionality and its related behavior inefficient, and very strange. Nevertheless, fertilization and embryo development within the womb is well documented. Surely that knowledge explains where humans come from."

"Well, Shey, it sorta does, and then again, it sorta doesn't. What you have mentioned is well documented, however, you need to ask where did the first women who *had* the children on Glas Dinnein come from? We know from the legends of our people that we did not originate on Glas Dinnein or any of the other known ten worlds of humanity. All we really know is that we somehow found our way first to Glas Dinnein, and thereafter over the millennia we spread out to the other ten worlds. The real question is where were we *before* we came to Glas Dinnein? Why don't our legends or records plainly identify that place, other than simply referring to it in rumors as 'First Home'?" Roan said.

"Sir, does it really matter?" Shey said, puzzled.

"In some ways it doesn't matter, at least not on a day-to-day basis. But we simply *want* to know."

"Hey Roan, putting aside rhetorical questions for the moment, like Shey, I'm curious about our upcoming workload. Do we even have a clue how Kellon is going to organize Intelligence gathering? We are nearly there, and I don't even know where Lan will penetrate the heliopause."

"Zorn, I know where Lan will enter the heliosphere. Lan told the girls we are heading for an entry point near the Ecliptic Plane. Captain Kellon is planning to use an outer asteroid belt as cover when establishing his initial surveillance position," Shey said.

Roan looked over to Zorn, with a quizzical expression." Shey, does Lan often talk to the girls about what Captain Kellon is planning to do?"

"No sir. He only talks with us when he is involving the girls in working on some problem, where our analytical or computational capabilities are being employed."

"Shey, do you know how long we have before entering the heliosphere?" Zorn said.

"Yes, Zorn. We have made the last jump and are even now approaching the heliopause boundary. This was why I asked about the Scouts working again."

"Shey, you and the girls are all to begin a total system diagnostic. Cross compare all of your results. Since we're about to go to work, I want you to confirm the girls are fully operational and without glitches."

"Sir, the girls and I will immediately begin systems diagnostics."

Standing, Zorn swept up the dirty cups and thermos and carried them back into the galley, where he deposited them in the cleanse receptacle.

"I don't know what you're about to do, but as for me, I'm staying aboard Shey and will be nosing around inside Lan's databases. If we are about to enter the heliosphere, then Lan must have assembled files of interesting information about the planets in that solar system. And, my curiosity itch badly needs scratching."

"Good call. While you're poking around Lan's innards, I'll go up to Tactical and learn what Lorn has already developed. For sure, it's about to get interesting...."

Chapter Nine:
The Stuff of Nightmares

The glimmering ray of light from the distant star pierced the darkness; its steady gleam had been their guiding beacon for months. Long before Lan entered the target solar system, probes were sent ahead, being directed well above the Ecliptic Plane. The long-range surveillance had identified eight planets, several minor planets, and a significant outer asteroid belt. Continuing observations identified several other minor belts of debris material. Compared to other known solar systems, the target system revealed a stark history of catastrophic structural change.

Lan crossed the heliopause boundary at a reduced speed and in full stealth. To avoid detection, Kellon directed Lan to a position close to a comet belt near the orbit of one of the multiple outer planets. This placed Lan about six-thousand-million kilometers from the primary.

Kellon's orders were strict; Lan was to remain undetected and conduct a full covert intelligence-gathering operation and return to Glas Dinnein. He held no illusions about their lack of hard knowledge regarding the technical level of those who occupied the system; his information regarding their technology was derived from a single dated example, which by reckoning was nearly two hundred years old.

Three busy days after Lan reached his designated observation position, Kellon assembled his senior staff for a general conference.

Lan's main conference room was one of the most enjoyed spaces within the ship. While its primary use was for large conferences, the room was also used for special events and crew social gatherings. The room was circular, about ten meters across, having a low perimeter wall which was crowned by a transparent optically perfect crystal-steel dome. The low circular wall was radiant, glowing with a soft diffused light, which had a spectrum near that of sunlight. Normally, the clear dome was externally protected by covering panels. Once Lan had attained his monitoring position, the protective petals had been retracted, and the stunning and brilliant stars were revealed.

During their time serving together, the crew had become good friends, and there was a sense of comradery. The general excitement in the conference room was nearly tangible, as the senior staff gathered and took their seats. With a soft rap of his knuckles upon the conference table, gaining everyone's attention, Kellon brought the meeting to order.

Turning to Commander Shaw, Kellon asked, "Lorn, please brief us on Tactical's assessment of Lan's risk of detection."

"Sir, Lan is operating in full stealth mode. The risk of detection is judged to be low to non-existent. No active alien monitoring has been detected. All our primary energy systems are minimized and shielded. Our external communications are restricted to line of sight and UV burst pulse encoding."

"What steps have you taken to prevent leakage of Guardian technology?"

"Sir, in accordance with your orders, no Scout, monitors, or probes have entered within the orbit of the fifth planet. In all deployed equipment, redundant self-destruction protocols are activated and set to their maximum, including proximity, apparent detection, equipment malfunction, and self-destruction triggered by our remote commands. All instrumentality employs convex Q_7 charges that will utterly obliterate all vestiges of Guardian technology."

Turning to Commander Grey, Kellon asked, "Roy, in that Roan is on assignment and not present, please brief us on what the Scouts are doing."

"Yes, Sir. Shey, Sheba, Misty, and Cindy are now actively deploying intelligence gathering monitors. Shey is deploying a network of detection and communications monitors from our position inward toward the system's primary. Shey is using a standard cylindrical distribution pattern and will terminate her deployment at the orbit of the fifth planet. When complete, her monitor network will provide Lan an enhanced communications capability with our future probes that will be sent deeper into the system. They also form a high-resolution detection grid along the most probable path from the inner planets toward Lan's position. Shey is scheduled to return to Lan in twelve days.

"We've defined a rudimentary early warning detection sphere for monitoring this solar system; the sphere is positioned between the orbits of the eighth and the minor planets. Scout Sheba is now accelerating above and normal to the Ecliptic Plane, moving along the circumference of the imaginary sphere. She is deploying a string of Class III sensors and will complete her circumnavigation and return to Lan in twenty-two days.

"Scouts Misty and Cindy are, like Sheba, working along different circumferences of the same detection sphere, each being separated in counter directions at the equator by 60-degrees from Sheba's baseline circumference. Like Sheba, they're deploying sensors normal to the Ecliptic Plane. Both Scouts are scheduled to return to Lan in twenty-eight days. When Scouts Misty and Cindy return, this solar system will be contained within a coarse-grid, Level III surveillance network. At that time, Lan will be fully able to detect a superluminal wake or major propulsion source entering or leaving this solar system, but not necessarily ships or probes operating in a stealth mode."

"Roy, do we currently have telemetry with our Scouts?"

"Affirmative. By using the monitor grid they're deploying, we're maintaining an open com-link with each Scout. We're using normal line-of-sight, pulsed ultraviolet DTHS."

"Well done. Now for the grand prize, what have we learned during the past several days about the people living within this solar system?"

"Well Sir, I believe even my dear mother would be surprised, for sure there seems to be a whopping large number of them. Although Lan is using every available visual and passive broadband sensor in its automatic and full scanning mapping mode, he's completely swamped by the quantity of communications sources.

"So far, all identified communications signals are subluminal in nature. They include pulse-coding, compressed burst, and frequency and amplitude modulation methods. Oddly enough, no transverse communications signals have been detected.

"What is really off the scales is the density of communications on the third planet. By all indications, that planet is the primary occupied planet within the system. Sir, the sheer quantity of signals emanating from the planet indicates an extreme population density, with a complex social interaction. Even

49

scanning at full bore, we have only begun building a relational database for tracking all identified signals by their characteristics.

"Elsewhere, we have detected a few communications signals originating in the outer solar system. Given their low power and signal characteristics, these signals are most likely data telemetry signals from scattered unmanned probes. Most are in close proximity to the large outer planets of this system, especially the fifth and sixth planets.

"Additional signals are being transmitted from a few probes, which are in odd high solar orbits. These orbits are almost perpendicular to the Ecliptic Plane and their low amplitude signals indicate probes of a scientific nature.

"Regarding the inner planets, we've detected human-communication traffic between several moons of the fifth and sixth planets, and also all around an asteroid belt that lies between the fourth and fifth planets. Similar communications traffic exists between the third and fourth planets. We have not yet detected communication signals near or on the two innermost planets."

Frowning, Kellon turned to Commander Shaw, "Lorn, what is Tactical's assessment of the observed technical level of interplanetary traffic?"

"Sir, "So far, we have detected 207 ships operating in various positions throughout the solar system. The power profiles and velocities of the ships suggest they are all of local origin and are using either a crude anti-gravity or else an ion propulsion. No superluminal wake or high velocity ship traffic has been detected. The only temporal-gravitational propulsion wakes being observed are the faint wakes of our own Scouts.

"The majority of observed ships are in the inner asteroid belt between the fourth and fifth planet or between the fourth and third planets. The patterns of movement strongly suggest some form of economic activity, rather than military operations.

Still, 68 of the ships have a power profile suggesting performance several magnitudes higher than those of the remaining ships. Three of the observed high-performance ships are beyond the orbit of the asteroid belt that lies between the fourth and fifth planets. These ships may represent the characteristics of the military profile in this system.

If our evaluation of the higher performance ships is correct, that they're military in nature, then they don't represent a threat to Lan, since, we have the option to engage or not to engage, as we choose. Sir, that's what I have at this time."

"Roy, are we on schedule with phase 2?"

"Yes, sir. There's, however, one critical analysis result that must be further discussed before discussing phase 2.

"Given the density of communications on or about the third planet, our conservative estimate of the population is that it's greater than ten-billion people -- that Sir, is billion with a big "b."

Kellon sat back, startled. "Roy, ten billion people is more than the total population of all our planets combined. What is the variance of your estimate?"

"Sir, I caution that the value of ten billion is on the low side of the estimate. Given our initial data, the final value could be in excess of fourteen-billion people."

Kellon heard the number, but coming to terms with it was difficult to comprehend. Judging by the expressions of the others gathered around the table, they also were having trouble processing the information.

Kellon turned toward Lieutenant Cloud, "Elayne, your specialty is sociology. Can you provide us with an insight into how fourteen-billion people might come to live on a single planet?"

"Sir, such an over-population is a staggering anomaly fraught with catastrophic overtones. Because we don't have the history or any knowledge of the customs of the people, all I can offer now is speculation. Even so, there are only a few long-term influences that might produce such an anomaly."

"What are some of those influences?" Kellon said.

"Sir, it could be over-compensation for an abnormal and short lifespan, or else a result of natural or inflicted cataclysmic death rates. It's highly probable there has been one or more global conflict, disasters, or plague in the recent history of these people."

"That makes sense; what other influences might be involved?"

"Sir, well-educated and prosperous people do not reproduce themselves out of prosperity. The social pressures associated with such a massive over-population are enormous, and the environmental impact of so many people living together is immense. There are probably wide variations in education and access to natural and manufactured resources. From the exhibited technology, we know there is a degree of technical education and therefore a potential for prosperity. But, large regions of poverty and ignorance must also co-exist.

"This, in turn, suggests the population may be subdivided into conflicting political groups or belief systems, and a disparity in education, resources, and manufactured goods can cause social conflicts. Therefore, with some certainty, we can assume that there's a long history of distrust, social conflict, and warfare among different groups of people living on that world.

"Sir, while my views are based on pure supposition, I strongly recommend extreme caution in any prospective contact with those people, at least until we have a much better understanding of their history, social, and political structures."

Troubled, Kellon sat a moment considering what Elayne had just said. "The task which is set before us is difficult. This system is like a pressure cooker. When and if these people achieve superluminal interstellar travel, their movement into the stars will likely become a major factor in our own future. Our actions here and now could define our relationship with these people for millenniums to come.

"Lorn, you are to go over and reexamine every detail of our activity in this system. There is to be no failure in our stealth operations. Above all, there is to be no technology seepage. We're to do whatever is required to assure this mission remains covert.

"Additionally, Lorn, you're to set trackers on the three ships near the sixth planet and additional trackers on any ships moving in that direction. I want continuous monitoring and records of all their activities, maneuvering, and communications. If those outbound ships are military craft, I want to know every aspect of their operational and tactical procedures. Finally, reexamine the deployment of our Scouts. Confirm they are operating in a full stealth mode, Paying special attention to wake suppression procedures. I don't want even faint wake trails being detected."

"Yes, Sir."

"Roy, you're to proceed with development of the relational database. The technological development and density of communications suggests there must be both verbal and visual commercial broadcasts among the signals being monitored. I suggest the most powerful and continuous signals are most probably commercial signals. Assign a team to focus on at least five of the most powerful signals. Where spoken-language traffic is identified, begin linguistic analysis. We need to get access to the history of these people as quickly as possible.

"Now, heads up everyone, I'm to be immediately advised of any significant problems. Are there any further input or questions?"

Glancing about the table, Kellon observed Roy still looked troubled. "Roy, is there another problem?"

"Sir, possibly. If you would authorize launch of a full-intel Tattle-Tell probe inside the orbit of the fourth planet, it would greatly improve our ability to carry out your orders. At this distance from the third planet, what we're monitoring is more like white noise than discrete and coherent signals. With a Tattle-Tell in place, we could eavesdrop and snoop with far better clarity. Also, when the third planet moves along its orbit to the other side of its primary, we'll lose some of the signals now being monitored."

"Roy, for now, proceed as ordered. Once our Scouts return, we'll better understand what further procedures are viable. I'll give you my decision as soon as possible. Are there any further comments or questions?"

There were none. Kellon stood and brought the meeting to a close.

Having returned to his own conference room, Kellon poured a cup of hot neab from the thermos on the side table and with a sigh, he sat down. "Lan, Fourteen-billion human beings crowded onto a single planet is incomprehensible. How could such a runaway population exist?"

"Sir, I suggest answering that and related questions is precisely why we have been ordered to perform a covert reconnaissance of this solar system."

"I suppose it could be worse -- At least there're no Kreel anywhere about--"

When a light knock sounded on the compartment door, Kellon looked up. "Enter."

When the door slid aside, Roy entered. "Sir, requesting permission to discuss personal observations about this solar system."

"Roy, as XO, permission granted. But first help yourself to some neab. Then, let me hear what's troubling you."

After pouring neab, Roy took a seat and faced Kellon. "Sir, what we have found here is downright terrifying. If the Kreel were to stumble across this solar system, the carnage that would immediately follow is unthinkable. It's the stuff of nightmares. Sir, I urgently recommend we take some calculated risks."

"Even as you knocked, I was thinking the same thing. The billions of people squeezed onto that planet is an irresistible lure for the Kreel. Only their isolation has so far saved them from that terror."

"Sir, I recommend we put a minimum of one Intelligence Tattle-Tell near the third planet, and doing so should be a high priority. We must get closer, if we are to fulfill our mission criteria."

Swirling the dregs in the bottom of his nearly empty cup, Kellon looked up and met Roy's intense blue eyes studying him." Roy, I will give you my answer tomorrow."

"Sir, thank you."

After Roy departed, deeply troubled, Kellon sat pondering the mission criteria. "Lan, The Standing Orders of Guardian Force are plain. Our principal mission is protection of human-occupied planets. During all of Guardian Force history, we've done precisely that for all our eleven worlds. The people within this solar-system don't know we exist, but now I know that *they* exist. And, there is no turning aside from our duty.

"Lan, take a Black Hole message for Guardian Command. Direct it to Admirals Mer Shawn, Cord, and Cloud.

"Lan has attained his initial point of observation. Morale is high and status is gold. Initial observations reveal a teeming solar system with one primary occupied planet. The observed technology is early inter-planetary level. Initial estimate is that more than ten-billion people live on one planet.

"Lan, send it over my name."

Chapter Ten:
Contact

The massive bulk of the ship slipped through the darkness toward the distant sun, in what seemed a most leisurely fashion. The ship was large, nearly 8,000 meters in length; it was a Capital ship with a large array of potent firepower. Significantly, the ship was not constructed within the solar system it was entering, it was pure alien.

The beings serving on board the impressive ship were relaxed, their confident attitude being the product of previous successful military campaigns commingled with a long-held sense of absolute species superiority. These two well established psychological factors had combined to produce a self-reinforcing complacent attitude, which far surpassed simple arrogance.

As the alien ship penetrated the heliopause, its crew did not consider it necessary to scan surrounding space for Guardian monitors. Even if they had, the probability of their detecting them was infinitesimally small. Therefore, Lan's observing monitors remained undetected and efficiently noted the massive ship and precisely marked its passage.

The days that followed the staff arrival conference were busy and flowed quickly past. The complex effort involved in gathering and analyzing the incoming streams of Intelligence data was demanding and the work hours long.

Shey had successfully completed her mission sunward and had returned to Lan. Misty, Sheba, and Cindy had almost completed their assigned missions and were nearing Lan. The unfolding Guardian plans for conducting a detailed reconnaissance of the solar system was on schedule and proceeding smoothly; That was, however, before Contact.

For hours following the detection of an inbound target, the alert messages moved unerringly through the linked chain of monitors, arcing nearly halfway around the detection sphere.

Flowing at the limiting speed of light, the contact alerts ultimately arrived aboard Lan and in the Combat Analysis Center, the CAC. When the contact alarm sounded, Kellon was in his private quarters, asleep. Shortly thereafter, the irritating sound of Kellon's bedside communicator sounded.

Waking and reflexively rolling over, Kellon keyed the communicator, "Kellon here."

"Captain, Tactical here. We have just received a contact report. We've got an unknown Capital ship entering the system. Sir, I recommend you come to CAC," Lorn said.

Acknowledging the message, Kellon swung his legs out of bed, as his mind was considering possible intruders; *Have we led the Kreel or Dargons to this system or is this a new threat?*

As Kellon entered CAC, a soft voice from the general announcing system spoke, "Captain in Combat Analysis Center."

Looking about, Kellon observed everyone was busy processing and evaluating the incoming data streams from the deployed monitors and from Lan's own sensors.

Standing by the central command chair, Kellon scanned the symbols being displayed in each quadrant of the solar system, which were shown on the tactical displays. He quickly identified a blinking red icon in quadrant three. It was directly opposite from Lan's own position, shown as a steady golden symbol in quadrant one.

As Kellon stood studying the data, Commander Grey entered the CAC, still brushing the sleep from his eyes. "Good morning Captain, I hear we have some unexpected company."

"Good morning Roy. It does appear we've an unanticipated visitor dropping by."

Looking toward Commander Shaw, Kellon asked, "Lorn, what's your current assessment?"

While holding a cup of neab, Lorn glanced at his notes, then up toward Kellon. "Sir, our monitoring grid detected the target about thirteen hours ago, as it approached the outer orbits of the minor planets. From its wake and power characteristics, we know it's large and running unshielded. Its trajectory and propulsion signature are odd. Combined, they display a total lack of precaution. Either they don't have stealth capability or else don't consider stealth is necessary.

"Sir, the incoming target is definitely not a product of the technology native to this system. And, given the preliminary data, our estimate is the target is at least seven times the mass of Lan. With their size and mass, they're capable of carrying fighters, although none has yet been detected."

"Lorn, did I hear you rightly? It's seven times the mass of Lan? Roy said.

"Yes, sir. Given our current data, it's a real brute."

"Lorn, what does the data tell us about its propulsion? Is it superluminal capable?" Kellon said.

"Sir, there's no match for the wake signature, however, it's very similar to some old Kreel linear propulsion patterns. If this holds true, then it's definitely not superluminal capable. I have asked the analysis team to upload our old Kreel propulsion archive, and they're looking for a match within the older data set."

"Is there any possibility the ship has followed our wake?" Kellon asked.

"No, Sir, none whatsoever. The monitors deployed along our inbound path do not indicate any activity.

Also, the target's generated power signature, propulsion wave, and mass, when taken together indicate it's designed for long-term subluminal interstellar travel. This limited interstellar capability would explain its size. Given all these factors, it would have been unable to followed in our wake. The target, however, still represents a significant unknown technology; therefore, caution is recommended."

"Roy, what's the current status of our Scouts?" Kellon said.

"Sir, Shey is on board and Sheba will be back in her hangar late tomorrow. Cindy and Misty will be aboard the following day."

"Good. Having our Scouts aboard while that ship is in this system is helpful.

You're to alert Sheba, Misty, and Cindy of the visitor, and verify their wake nullification procedures are being fully implemented."

"Yes, Sir."

"Lorn, have you any idea where the inbound target is coming from?" Roy asked.

"Sir, at this time, all we have is supposition."

"At the moment, supposition is quite acceptable. So, give us your best guess," Kellon said.

"Supposition, yes Sir. Although the inbound ship must know this solar system is inhabited, still they're showing no cautionary behavior, none whatsoever. If the total lack of tactical discretion is its standard operating procedure, then it's reasonable to assume they took no evasive maneuvers to conceal their point of origin. Therefore, given their entry vector and performance profiles, reasonable probability indicates the target is coming from a BG star system, about 3.65 parsecs distant. This would be in keeping with their limited speed profile. With modest continuous acceleration and deceleration capability, that star system would require about fifteen standard years of travel time. Tactically speaking, the travel time factor puts the target considerably farther from its home than we are from our own home."

Kellon glanced again at the screen, with its slowly blinking red icon. "Have you calculated its intended orbit?"

"Sir, at present, the target is decelerating and approaching the orbit of the eighth planet. Its trajectory parameters suggest it intends to swing around the primary. Our best guess is it's heading for a solar orbit somewhere ahead of the third planet."

"Roy, do you remember the Tattle-Tell sentinel that you wanted to insert inside the orbit of the fourth planet, but never got?" Kellon said.

"Well, yes Sir."

"Times change, and that inbound target alters everything. We need information, and we need it now. Your previous request is herewith approved.

"Roy, we have a positional advantage. The target is entering the system nearly opposite to our own position, and the third planet is on our side of the primary. That gives us a little time to prepare and get out ahead of their arrival. You're to promptly launch a full spectrum Tattle-Tell sentinel and insert it into the anticipated orbit of the target before it arrives. Use the current data to make your best approximation of that intended orbit. We will fine-tune the final Tattle-Tell orbit after we have better data.

"Gentlemen, the sentinel and its companion probes will be our first resource insertions within the orbit of the fifth planet. They represent the cutting-edge of our own technology;

58

therefore, maximum protocols for self-destruction are mandatory. As for their communications with Lan, Security is the primary consideration, elapsed time of signal transmission is secondary. That sentinel and its companions are not to be detected or intercepted. Take every precaution.

"Once that target achieves its orbit and shuts down its propulsion systems, its self-noise will drop near zero. Then, their internal sensors will be operating at optimal sensitivity and capability. Let's not give these strangers any tactical advantage that we can deny them.

"Roy, work with Lorn and set up the sentinel to accomplish your planetary Intelligence objectives. Then, assist in calculating the necessary trajectories for the supporting probes. Both of you are to take every possible action to assure we remain covert."

"Yes, Sir. However, as my dear mother would advise, since we are going to be passing near the third planet, why not slip a probe past as tight as prudently possible. It would sure enough help in meeting your mission criteria of isolating those commercial broadcast signals."

"So, since I'm in for a gram, now you want a whole kilogram. Alright, be advised your dear mother's recommendation is acknowledged and approved; but, there're not to be any detections. Is that perfectly clear?"

"Yes, sir, perfectly clear. Absolutely no detections permitted," Roy said.

"Lorn, the arrival of this unknown ship is troubling. You mentioned their propulsion signature wasn't Kreel, but it looks somewhat like older Kreel signatures. So, are we dealing with a Kreel ship here or not?" Kellon said.

"Sir, with very little data available, my best guess is, no; it's not Kreel. In the past thousand years, I can't remember ever encountering a large Kreel ship that didn't have superluminal capability. Frankly, I don't know who is driving that thing. Even more important, I don't know *why* they've bothered to travel such long years to reach this solar system. What I do know is they are not native to this system, and therefore they constitute a potential threat."

"In that assessment, we are in wholehearted agreement. We're a long way from Glas Dinnein, and we've no backup or

59

resupply. Whatever we do here, we need to remember how far we are from our own homes.

"Roy, Have I forgotten anything?"

"No, Sir. I believe you've about covered everything, except perhaps for getting some more sleep."

Kellon returned Roy's smile. "More sleep is definitely in order. Good night, gentlemen."

As the hatch closed behind Kellon, a soft voice on the general intercom announced, "Captain has departed Combat Analysis Center."

Chapter Eleven:
Good Herd Management

The energetic vibrations of deceleration were heard as a low resonant sound; it permeated the entire massive ship and was felt by all on board. The vibrations emphasized the Arkillian's current position in space, they were approaching their destination, the Earth.

The three representatives of Scion's Ruling Council then on board the Nest ship were gathered in a lavishly appointed meeting room. Although the outbound crossing from Scion had taken more than twenty turns, during which time their conversations were many, the three Arkillians still held differing opinions concerning their mission objectives.

The room in which the three Arkillians sat was richly equipped with heavy and ornate furnishings, polished wood paneling, and thick carpet. The illumination in the room was dim and the warm air was dry. Most humans would have considered the room's temperature uncomfortably warm, but its occupants were not human. By Arkillian standards the environmental conditions were considered perfect.

Bipeds with two upper appendages, The Arkillian's arms extended to hands having four fingers and two opposing thumbs. Although humanoid in form, they were not mammals, having emerged from a different branch of life. Their heads were slightly larger than that of a human of similar stature, while their torsos were of a slighter build. Naturally occurring patterns of various shades and colors adorned their facial features, these being unique to each individual. They had no hair or fur. The multiple facets of their eyes, which were slightly larger than those of humans, gave them a distinct non-human appearance. Each eye had three lids, one was upper and two were lower. The innermost lower lid served as a protective transparent light filter and protection from blowing sand, the second outermost lid, like the upper lid closed and blocked light from entering. They had a well-defined center facial ridge and distinct nostrils. By human standards their mouths would be considered somewhat small. They had no discernible ears; their two aural detectors appeared like small white domes, one affixed to each side of their heads. Some observers might consider the Arkillians a handsome species – the Arkillians most certainly did.

For many thousands of years, the elite within the Arkillian culture had rigidly maintained a strict feudal system. Those who were hatched to rank used genetic manipulation, combined with life-long conditioning to cultivate and dominate a servant class, which was kept under abject subordination. For those Arkillians who were hatched to privilege, the established social order worked extremely well, and in Arkillian society, the opinion of the elite was all that really mattered.

Each Council member was attended by his own servants, each of who were conditioned from their hatching to provide personal services. Unheeded, six servants stood nearby, motionless, silent, and attentive.

The representatives, Kur, Ca, and Rin were sitting around a deeply carved and ornate table, which was crafted from exceptionally fine grain hard wood, which had long before been harvested on Earth. They were engaged in general conversation.

Kur was the elder and senior representative. Ca was second in authority, and at the moment he was expressing his displeasure of recent developments on Earth. Rin was the youngest of the three, and the journey to Earth was his first deep-space commercial venture.

Facing Kur, Ca was again complaining. "Something must be done soon. We have continued far too long observing the humans in this system without taking corrective action. Humans may be sentient mammals, but they are also filthy, disgusting, and perverse. Now they are also becoming dangerous."

"Ca," Rin offered, "it's not their perversion that troubles me. For thousands of turns our psychological warfare has properly focused upon the obvious inferior traits of the mammalian human species. Still, those same psychological methods we have successfully used for millenniums to promulgate our own proven and superior cultural foundations, a stable feudal system, a regulated serfdom, and a logical system of social caste distinctions, are apparently no longer effective on Earth.

"In spite of our efforts, most humans have recently resisted our influences. Why? What has changed?"

Momentarily disregarding Rin, Ca was inwardly seething. he knew Kur had heard his earlier comment and was disrespectfully ignoring him. Irked, he turned toward Rin.

"Rin, not all of the methods we use to control humans depend upon shaping their cultural traits. Remember, after we rendered human cultures primitive, we continued our suppression of the population through use of biological and genetic warfare vectors. We need all of these combined processes working together to assure our precise control."

Kur was listening to Ca's comments, but without enthusiasm or interest. His was an often-repeated and superficial viewpoint. Still, Rin's questions warranted meaningful answers, and as the elder, it was his responsibility to provide the young Arkillian those answers.

"Rin, always remember and then heed the Council's wise and standing policy; direct overt actions are warranted only if required to nullify a potential threat. During our initial assault, our direct action required the eradication of several billion humans and the obliteration of their culture and technology. Afterward, thousands of turns passed before Earth began to recover from our overt military action. It was only then that the Earth began to yield acceptable profits, finally justifying our significant initial costs."

"Then, honored Kur, everything we do here is to optimize our profits?" Rin said.

"Fundamentally, that is true. At this juncture, unless there is a clear necessity, the Council will not risk lessening our profits."

"Honored Kur, you are the eldest. May I therefore ask why humans do not remember the destruction we rained down upon their heads? If they were made to remember, would not their fear of us force them to their knees?"

Kur's facial markings brightened, revealing his inner pleasure. He was indeed the eldest and senior among the three council members on board the Nest ship. It was therefore appropriate that Rin, being the youngest, should seek wisdom and knowledge from him.

"Rin, about twelve -thousand Earth turns ago, during our initial rendering process, we exterminated about 95% of the humans living on Earth and eradicated their fledgling colonies on the fourth planet. On Earth, all of their cities were reduced to bleak and dismal ruins. The human species might then have become extinct, if we had not taken the prudent steps required to preserve the species for our benefit and future profits."

"Then, honored Kur, our war planners understood humans would forget we rendered them primitive."

"That is correct. The planners correctly anticipated any surviving records of human history, including their destruction, would be fragmentary and fade with passing millenniums. Of course, the eradication of their history was assured and accelerated after we modified human DNA and severely shortened the species individual lifespan."

"Do any memories of the rendering persist among the humans?" Rin said.

"A few. In spite of the passing millenniums, some vestiges of racial memory and scraps of fragmented records of the times prior to the rendering remain. Those rare fragments, however, are deeply shrouded within legends and seldom told fables. There are some surviving stone artifacts that have fostered mostly muddled and discounted theories about early human civilizations, such as tales of the lost lands of Mu or Lemuria and Atlantis. Some remnants of racial memory are also contained within their mysticism and religions; but nothing remains that correctly elaborates the truth of their previous high civilization, or reveals what agency ended that civilization," Kur said.

"Then the humans do not comprehend they once had a high civilization," Rin said.

"That is correct. As was foreseen by the war planners, most humans are ignorant that once they were highly evolved. Of course, we have labored diligently to assure that outcome."

Rin sat momentarily quiet, pondering what Kur had explained before proceeding. "Honored Kur, you mentioned we took careful steps to preserve humans as a species. Again, how did we do that?"

Kur was pleased, Rin was continuing to show proper respect.

"your question is perceptive, but it lacks a simple answer. Remember, it is always wise policy to preserve some members of a suborned inferior indigenous species. The intention of our war planners was the survivors would be cultivated and conditioned to perform the labors needed to produce what we desire to be harvested from Earth. To achieve this goal, we created several preserves and there provided some humans with basic tools needed for their subsistence and a means for sustaining their lives. In its immediate aftermath, most humans who survived the rendering did so by finding our established preserves. By creating the preserves, we were able to conveniently shape the evolution of the surviving humans.

"Later, we gathered selected groups from each preserve for the purpose of adapting their genetic makeup. Naturally, our goal was to adapt the species to be better suited for our purposes.

Following good herd management protocols, we thinned and culled out the surviving human mammals. Some of those culled-out specimens were then used during our long-term laboratories research projects."

"Honored Kur, none of my studies mentioned research projects were involved. What was their purpose?"

Rin's question delighted Kur. The old research projects were commonly considered an esoteric subject, but it was one that he had long studied.

"From the outset, we have understood that all sentient beings possessed some degree of telepathic communication, even if this capability is not well developed or understood by a lower species.

"Long ago, we learned advanced techniques for detection, monitoring, processing and how from a distance to manipulate mental functions at the level of brain waves. As you know, mind control is one of our most highly developed military capabilities.

"Much of our knowledge about mind control was gained using human specimens. The specimens we collected from our preserves provided excellent subjects for exploring and mapping of cognitive processes.

"Later, we were able to apply what we learned about humans to other sub-species. Once we systematically map a species' cognitive processes, we are able to selectively attack their minds across the entire spectrum of emotional and mental functioning --"

"Honored Kur, I apologize for interrupting, but just how does what you are describing apply to our current problem on Earth?" Rin asked.

A momentary irritation about being interrupted flickered across Kur's facial markings. "Rin, what you do not understand is that following our initial attack on Earth, we experimented on tens of thousands of specimens. For thoroughness, those experiments were conducted on all ages and both genders. The scientists were skillful and with practice learned how to extend a human's life, even when extreme vivisection was involved. Naturally, such vivisections were necessary in order to fully document human pain thresholds and responses. Each of the inflicted pain thresholds were carefully defined after each experiment. Through our precise research we were able to amass copious knowledge concerning the human genome, physiology, and human brain functionality. This knowledge continues to have a direct application to all that we accomplish on Earth, then and now."

"Did the experiments hurt the mammals?" Rin said.

"Yes. The scientific records of the experiments indicate the specimens experienced both mental and physical anguish and acute suffering. That of course was all part of the experiments. It was all done carefully and precisely, where each step of the experiment and its results were entirely documented. By using such precise techniques, our scientists were able to achieve a truly profitable outcome.

"If you are interested, Rin, you might choose to study those old records. In terms of applied techniques, I personally found them to be interesting and informative. Even now, we continue to exploit the knowledge we then gained."

Rin's facial markings revealed his perplexity. "Honored One, I do not understand. How are we exploiting that knowledge?"

When Rin asked his question, Kur noticed Ca suddenly sat up straighter, eager to participate and to insert his own viewpoint before Kur could respond. It required Kur's practiced effort, and he momentarily suppressed his displeasure.

"If Kur will but allow, I will explain some of the ways we still exploit that knowledge," Ca said.

Chapter Twelve:
Maximum Profit

Although carefully subdued, the tensions between Kur and Ca had increased steadily over the preceding weeks. Social rules of honor and personal conduct regarding elders strictly forbade any possibility Ca would openly oppose Kur's authority. This was doubly true, since Kur was among the most respected and senior elders sitting on the Council. His ultimate authority aboard the Nest ship was indisputable. Nevertheless, being second in official rank aboard the ship, Ca was aware of his rising sense of indignation. From Ca's perspective, Kur seemed to be unnecessarily snubbing him, and doing it openly before Rin. Now, it appeared to Ca that Kur was doing this again.

In turn, Kur perceived Ca's attitude as being rudeness, and his own lengthening silence before responding to him was intended as a clear rebuke. Being an elder, correcting bad behavior of a younger Arkillian was well within his right., Finally, with a permissive nod, Kur gave Ca his permission to speak.

With effort, Ca suppressed his own sense of annoyance, and turned to Rin. "We have developed the technical ability to directly interfere with human mental functioning on a subliminal level. We accomplished this feat by injecting a series of complex low frequency signals directly into the planet's magnetosphere. Then, using direct interference methods, which we learned during the old experiments that Kur told you about, we can produce a wide range of mental effects. These include sleep deprivation and the jamming of cognitive beta analytical functions within a target species. Our advanced technical systems can also generate signals that stimulate specific emotional centers within the human brain."

"But, Ca, how do we use these capabilities?" Rin asked.

"By using these selective and programmed subliminal patterns, we can establish deep-seated conflicts within the consciousness of an individual or even an entire population. By utilizing elements of strong emotion, combined with sexuality, doubt, and evoking fear, at the deepest subconscious levels, we are able to turn the minds of humans inward against themselves or outward against each other. We can even cause conflict between the genders. By skillfully utilizing available mental levers of fear and anxiety, we are able to induce stress, illness, and even madness in a specimen."

In deepening contemplation, Rin's facial markings darkened. "Ca, then our concealed low frequency ribbon transmitters on Earth are able to affect the entire human population."

"Yes. They can, and we subtly do affect all humans. One of our primary tasks during this voyage is to review what changes in programming are indicated, and then to make the necessary adjustments to the existing subliminal programming before we depart."

Kur had listened attentively to Ca and considered his explanation to Rin inadequate. "Ca, you must not forget that our knowledge of mind control is not limited to human emotions and general commerce. Our advanced technology includes the ability to directly assault the mental functioning of humans and also of a number of other species. We can also do this with lethal results.

"While our mastery of advanced mental technology has provided us with powerful weapons, they have also proven profitable. Very selectively, we have exchanged some restricted military mental weapons technology with a trusted and carefully selected hatchling species, the Kreel. In exchange for some of our mental technologies, we have obtained considerable wealth from the Kreel, including ships, weapons, and similar advanced military hardware."

"Honored Kur, other than our mind control methods, what other procedures do we use to maintain control over humans and other species?" Rin said.

Turning to face Rin, Kur's demeanor became solemn. "Rin, never forget that the agenda of those who will rule others is plain. To rule, it is only necessary to promote confusion, division, and conflict within a subordinated culture. A society at war within itself, should it survive, requires little effort to be effectively manipulated and controlled.

"In all such matters, time always works to our advantage, because those who are subjected to prolonged mental inducements become conditioned and increasingly susceptible to mental manipulation. Suborned species are also prone to impulsive behavior, which we can and do exploit. After millenniums of conditioning, even problematic humans respond to our manipulations."

"Then, is this why the Council is opposed to taking overt military action on Earth?" Ca said.

Kur was pleased, he recognized Ca's question revealed his growing understanding of deeper and subtler policies within the Council. "Yes, Ca. remember Council policy is always established on sound reasoning. We now deem there is no further need for overt military force.

"From our vantage point, the dynamics of our operation on Earth are most favorable and profitable. The humans living on Earth have no complaints. And, except for a very few human investigators and pliable agents, none even believe we exist. This carefully conditioned global state of unawareness was the initial long-term goal set by our war planners."

"Honored Kur, there is much in what you have said that requires additional reflection," Ca said.

"Good. Wisdom is the desirable fruit of such considerations. While reflecting on what I have said, do not forget an underlying truth. In order to realize the maximum profit from warfare, it is best that those defeated remain ignorant of their defeat."

"Honored Kur, there is a problem that the Council is overlooking, the humans' increasing technology and development of advanced spacecraft. If we do not intercede soon, they will most certainly become a threat," Rin said.

"I believe your assessment overstates the risk," Kur said.

"Perhaps, yet I need not remind you that forty turns past, we detected and destroyed another space probe that humans sent into our home system. That probe is a loud warning that something must soon be done about Earth," Rin retorted.

The main hatch opened and an Arkillian dressed in the robes of a senior command officer entered the room. He approached the three seated Council members, then stood quietly, waiting to be noticed. Out of his earnest reverence and respect for the members of the august Council, the officer remained formally silent, erect, and at attention.

With a slight motion of his hand, Kur granted the officer permission to make his report....

"Honored Ones, we are now crossing the orbit of the eighth planet of this system. Within three cycles, we will enter a heliocentric orbit, positioning ourselves at one of the three inline libration points, one eighty-five planet diameters from Earth. I also report that we are monitoring a number of rudimentary spacecrafts operating within the orbit of the fifth planet and between the orbits of Earth and the fourth planet. None of these spacecrafts represent a present threat. We are proceeding on schedule, in accordance with your instructions."

"Captain, what is the tactical capability of the observed space crafts?" Kur said.

"Honored One, there are several classifications. Some are using simple solar sails. Others are using rudimentary anti-gravity drives or else primitive fission-powered ion thrust technologies. All the monitored vessels have low power and acceleration profiles. My evaluation is the observed spacecraft do not represent a direct threat to this ship."

"Captain, if any of the ships being monitored appear to detect us or else approach, you are directed to block all their communications and utterly destroy the ships. Do you understand?" Kur ordered.

"Honored elder, it will be so."

Kur nodded his approval. "You may depart."

Turning quickly, the officer left the room by the same hatch he had entered. The servants standing about made no motion, nor did they appear to have noticed the officer arrive or depart.

Kur turned toward Rin. "That tactical report should ease your concern about the potential threat posed by human space technologies."

Rin's inner eyelid closed halfway and he clucked softly. "Honored Kur, while you make little of their potential threat, I notice that we are going into a solar orbit eighty-five planetary diameters away from the planet itself. I would wager that you well remember a time when we openly thundered across the heavens above Earth, and with our passage we made the mountains shake with sounds of thunder."

Sitting back, Kur remained momentarily silent, studying the fine-grain burl structure of the polished table, respectfully considering Rin's unexpected comment before responding. "Rin, it is plainly true that today we know more about humans on Earth than we knew millenniums ago. Back then, our military intervention was swift, absolute, and complete. Our disciplined policy of suppressing humanity was simple. Suppression meant utter destruction of their technology, culture, and the majority of the species.

"Today, we continue to enjoy the full benefits of our past conquest, and we need not overly work ourselves in extracting the Earth treasures we so covet and enjoy. To again destroy the majority of the species, along with its achieved technology and culture, would also certainly destroy our profits for thousands of turns. Therefore, the debate in the Council continues unabated. In principle, however, I agree something needs to be done to stem some of the more egregious human aberrations."

Ca considered Kur's admission to Rin provided him with an opening, and he quickly inserted, "Kur, you and I understand the war planners' intent was to fracture human society and thereby create a beneficial system of human government, one which we can manipulate. For millennia our psychological programs have worked. Recently our programs are no longer working. That is the core of our problem. I submit, we have not upgraded our methods adequately to compensate for recent changes in human culture. I must ask, who is at fault?"

Rin's facial markings flushed, revealing that Ca's disrespectful tone toward Kur was upsetting, and moved promptly to gloss over Ca's rudeness. "Most honored Kur, as Ca and I have both asked, what has recently changed to make our methods less effective?"

Chapter Thirteen:
Render the Humans Primitive

The three Arkillians sitting around the table were wearing lavish robes adorned with numerous items of meritorious jewelry. By comparison, the six servants were wearing simple garments of rather neutral colors. The only ornamentation on the servant garments was the rich ornamental badge that declared to which nest they belonged. The clothing they wore was not the only difference between those who sat at the table and those who waited attentively. Those sitting at the table were at least a head taller and physically heavier. Even the color patterns on the faces of those sitting at the table were brighter and more distinct than the ones seen on the faces of the servants.

In all matters the Council representatives held the lower ranked crew and servant classes in nearly as much disdain as they held humans. In Arkillian culture, rank had its definite privileges.

Having listened to Ca's tones of disrespect and Rin's effort to minimize that insolence, Kur was moved to moderate his own emotions. "Rin, you have properly asked an insightful question, indeed what has recently changed? The answer is complex.

"Our ability to control human social development is similar to controlling a broad river; over time, by placing boulders at selected points on the riverbed, the flow and course of the river may be altered. Similarly, by exploiting religion within a culture, combined with themes of strong emotions, like fear, avarice, hate, jealousy, and especially sexual mores, we can alter the course of an entire culture.

"Kur, I have listened with patience and respect. And, I have just heard you admit that the filthy mammals continue to hold to their fables and vile superstitions. Because they do, our ability to control the population on Earth is increasingly difficult. Consequently, our previous work is steadily unraveling," Ca said.

"Ca, your own viewpoint is askew. Remember, it is the gullibility and superstitious nature we have long inculcated in humans that has given us the advantage in shaping their cultures. Even now we maintain a significant control over the mass of humans. Without even use of superstition, we are effectively using greed as our most powerful motivator. All the same, superstitions do have their advantages. You must admit there is something quite amusing when a subordinated culture brings rich bribes as offerings."

"Kur, I did not come here seeking amusement. Our common purpose for coming here is to assure that our Nests obtain their just and full profits. As the humans have increased their auditing and communications capability, our ability to conceal what we have been doing on Earth has become more difficult. As our exposure increases, profitability and the simplicity of operations decrease. Something needs to be done--"

Kur held up a hand, silencing Ca. "The Council fully understands that correcting the perceived social aberrations on Earth may require some action be taken. Still, none sitting on the Council has yet to present an acceptable plan of action," Kur said, dryly.

Ca's facial markings revealed he was becoming emotionally upset. "Kur, given our own obvious superiority, why has the Council permitted an inferior life form, such as humans, to become a troublesome perturbation? I say, the real problem is the Council; it has done nothing for hundreds of turns to reverse the deterioration of our control on Earth."

Rin had sat respectfully, only listening, but now he interjected his own simmering thoughts. "Most Honored Kur, when in millenniums past we reached this solar system, we deemed it prudent to take direct and forceful action. We destroyed the humans and their flourishing cultures. Since its environment is at best marginal and most disagreeable, we have no desire to inhabit the planet. So, I asked, just why did the council then decide to render human kind primitive? Clearly, what the Council then refused to tolerate was a potential threat to our own established culture by an expanding neighboring species, and especially not when that species was of filthy mammals.

"Honored Kur, I humbly ask, why is it any different today? Since I cannot see any difference between then and now, I must agree with Ca."

Kur remained momentarily silent, and raising his cup, he drank the remaining mead. In Kur's opinion, the cool honey brew was adequate justification in itself for maintaining their firm control of this solar system. He held the empty cup right-side up and to his right. Immediately one of Kur's servants approached and exchanged the proffered empty cup with another that was full.

Both cups were made of pure silver and heavily adorned with intricate patterns of gold filigree. Kur had personally acquired the cups on Earth from an Etruscan merchant several thousand turns earlier. He was especially fond of them. Musing, Kur inwardly admitted, *Many things have changed on Earth since those times, those better times.*

Kur turned to Ca, and expressed his musings, "Ca, I tend to agree with much of what you say. Something must soon be done because of the expanding populations of Earth. Admittedly, we of the Council have become too complacent for too long."

Kur's admission prompted Ca to cluck, with pleasure. "Good. In spite of the significant genetic stumbling stones we have imposed and our mental damping fields, the mammals seem to be resolving their internal social conflicts. They are even overcoming the gender, racial, and genetic barriers we have engineered. The real problem stems from their filthy political doctrines of equitable law and social equality. Those vile concepts are not only filthy, they are dangerous. If for no other reason, the planet should again be rendered primitive. Besides, dealing with the ancient Egyptians was more profitable and far simpler. That culture at least had a proper respect for hatchlings, and respectfully acted with deference."

Ca's sharp-edged retort hit a sensitive mark. Kur did remember better turns.

"Ca, concerning this matter, upon our return from this journey I will submit your views before the Grand Council."

"Good. It is long since time that someone listens to my advice. We should have reduced the miserable mammals back to their primitive state two-hundred turns ago," Ca said.

Noting Ca's continuing inflections of disrespect, Kur looked up abruptly. "Be careful, Ca. We have prospered much from the ingenuity of humans, which has helped in our own development. While their honey is exquisite and it raises our joy, some of their music and many of the additional products of this planet hold great value in other markets. There exist many reasons to be aggressive, and there are as many arguments for continued patience."

"Continued patience?" Ca chided.

"Yes, Ca, continued patience. Remember, the little bee that makes the honey is native to this world. No effort to alter its genetics to enable it to thrive elsewhere has been successful, although many have tried. The same is true for silk, alpaca wool, cinnamon, and a host of other very desirable commodities.

"Be assured, Ca, if necessary, we will render the humans primitive again. Such action, however, will not be taken until it is deemed absolutely necessary."

As Kur spoke, he extended his right arm slightly to his side, holding the now empty cup upside down. Promptly, one of his servants took the proffered cup.

Ca's increasing disrespect had surpassed that which Kur would tolerate. Turning, Kur issued a formal challenge. "Ca, I look forward to meeting you upon the exercise sand tomorrow, precisely at zenith."

Ca recognized the implication of Kur's challenge. As a senior Council member, Kur had every right to call him out for any perceived slight, even one of a minor nature. Ca was also confident that Kur did not appreciate the intention of his rudeness was to provoke Kur into issuing a challenge to a formal contest of martial skill, with staff. Being much younger, Ca smugly expected to exploit the coming contest to teach Kur it would be wiser to show him far more respect.

Looking directly at Kur, with a slight bow, Ca formally responded. "Respected Kur, I am honored by your notice."

Ca's blunt manner and smug tone produced an irritation within Kur. *Ca is a brash youth,* he thought. *It is past time he was given a few hard lumps and good cause to reconsider his disrespect toward his elders. I am going to greatly enjoy giving him that overdue lesson in better manners.*

Returning the subject back to the real business at hand, Kur addressed his companions. "Fellow hatchlings, it is time for us to retire to our own nests. We will gather here again at twilight the first cycle after we arrive in our defined orbit."

Without further comment, Kur stood and with his servants departed the room. Like Kur, Ca and Rin next departed the room, each with their own retinue of servants, and in strict order of rank. As the last Arkillian departed the room, the dim lights softened further and shadows merged. the unoccupied meeting room went dark, filled only with the deepening rumble of the drive fields, as the ship decelerated, moving closer to Earth.

Chapter Fourteen:
Olympus- A Clear and Present Danger

Being far removed from Glas Dinnein, on a world nearly 24-parsecs distant, the people living on Earth in the calendar year 2511 had never heard of Glas Dinnein, the Kreel, or the Dargon. That did not mean they did not have serious alien problems of their own. One of those problems was all the governments of Earth refused to publicly acknowledge such problems even existed.

Looking up, Charlie Wilcox frowned, then sighed. His boss had just entered the Olympus deep-space Analysis Center, and he was wearing his *Well, where is it?* expression.

"Charlie, do you have the data ready?" Darrell Fann asked.

"Well boss, not quite yet."

"And, why not?" Darrell said, sharply.

"Well, it sorta involves a small problem in temporal mechanics. Before I can print out the results, there must first be some results to print out. Of course, if you can figure out just how I might speed up the velocity of light, then perhaps I might get the analysis report sooner."

"Sorry Charlie, but I'm a little on edge. The problem is Sullivan; he is calling me every five minutes demanding the report."

"I fully understand, I've got a boss just like that. But Sullivan is definitely your problem, and he is a problem one tier level above my pay grade. I suggest you remind him that the clear and present danger Executive Order, which we are still being funded under, was declared in November of 1947, right after the Roswell crash. That was about five hundred years ago. You could also remind him that patience is the key to successful reverse engineering."

"Perhaps you would like to come along with me and tell Sullivan that for yourself," Darrell said.

"Thank you, I appreciate the kind offer, however, I'll pass. Pacifying the head honcho of the top-secret Olympus Project definitely falls within your pay grade, not mine."

"Just keep it up Charlie, and you'll soon find that Sullivan is two pay grades above your own," Darrell retorted.

"Hey boss, look. It seems your timing is perfect. See what is hot off the presses and just dropped out of the data slot, it's your report, four copies collated and bound."

Nodding his head in sympathy, and heaving a sigh, Charlie watched as Darrell hurriedly exited the Analysis Center, clutching his reports, the door closing solidly behind him. "Honest boss, best of luck."

X

Out of breath, and at a brisk pace, Darrell entered the outer office of the Director of Project Olympus. Using the underground executive tunnels, he had hurried across New Washington to the Department of Commerce building, and then used the Executive express elevator to the top floor. When opening the door to an office, he noticed the copies of the reports were still warm from the toner fusing process. Charles Sullivan's executive secretary, Lois, looked up from her work.

With a smile and a wink, Lois cautioned, "You'd better be ready with an excuse for being late Mr. Fann. They've been waiting in there for at least twenty minutes."

The inner office of Charles Sullivan, whose official title on the outer office door declared to be an Under Secretary of Commerce, looked over the parks of New Washington from a prestigious vantage point, and this factor was accentuated by a wall-to-wall and floor-to-ceiling blast proof window. The office contained a massive and ornate executive desk, bookcases, an array of displays, and a small circular oak conference table. When Darrell hurried in, three of the four chairs positioned around the table were occupied. Two men and a woman looked toward him, with obvious recognition and interest. Taking the empty seat, Darrell turned toward and addressed the older man.

"Charles, my apologies for being late. New data was just coming in with the most recent analysis from the last download from NASA."

Darrell knew the people sitting around the small table, they were the Olympus Project Director and two of his three branch managers. The Director held overall authority with responsibility for all executive, administrative, and Congressional relations. Carl Suthaford managed the government agency liaison, field operations, and security affairs. Janet Rodgers was responsible for counter-intelligence, overall data analysis, and historical research. For his part, Darrell managed the Deep Space Intelligence and Research Division.

"Well, don't just sit there like a pumpkin, tell us what you have," Janet said, with humor.

Smiling with her friendly chiding, Darrell passed around the packets of information. "What I have is only our preliminary data, but Monstro is definitely back and about to swing around the sun. It's heading our way. If this data checks out, they're decelerating and about ten days out."

"That means we have about a week to gear up for full monitoring. The advanced warning helps," Janet said.

"Advanced warning? After hundreds of years of monitoring that ship and others like it, Whatever Monstro represents is still an enigma. History proves that ship or some of its counterparts have been nosing around Earth for millennia. But why?" Carl said.

"Carl, we all know what we're involved with is a game of cat and mouse. That ship, or as you say its counterparts operated openly, and during past centuries they made no secret of their presence. The recorded sightings over Nuremberg in April of 1561 absolutely proved that fact. But, since we began tracking them, those ships have taken ever more steps to minimize our monitoring of their activities. That tactical change in behavior underscores both our increasing ability to monitor them and their desire to remain anonymous. Still, as long as any of these ships are within our solar system, we must conclude they represent a potentially hostile threat. Each of you are to proceed on that presumption," Charles said.

"Charles, granted, we can now spot them coming, but we still don't have a clue concerning their intentions or purpose. After hundreds of years, what do we really know? All we have is frustration and speculation," Carl said.

"I disagree, Carl. It's not all been frustration. We've actually learned considerably about that ship, including its probable point of origin, vital details about its propulsion, and about its overall general operations," Darrell inserted.

"True, but just for sake of arguments, perhaps we've gone about this with a wrong mindset. Rather than framing the Monstro problem as being military, if we used an economic model as our frame of reference, maybe we might gain a better understanding of what they are up to. Consider for a moment, someone somewhere is spending an enormous amount of their limited capital in sending those ships here. This being true, then an economic model might help in our identifying the bottom-line profit motive that warrants someone taking such obvious risk, while incurring huge associated costs," Carl said.

"What you're suggesting is Monstro is here and involved in some form of commerce on Earth. If your premise is correct, then following that line of reasoning, there must be a corresponding commercial enterprise on Earth involving a mutually beneficial trade. If this were true, then there must also be mutually acceptable trade goods or some type of exchange currency. It also implies a huge conspiracy, which has remained concealed for hundreds if not thousands of years. Such a secret kept so well for so long would require unbelievable discipline and organization. Personally, I find your premise of a commercial basis for Monstro's visits highly improbable," Janet said.

"Improbable? I disagree. While some of Monstro's strange activities, such as cattle mutilations and the capture of wild animals, appear to be outside normal channels of what we call commerce, yet some form of commerce remains possible," Carl said.

"Janet, given your list of objections, I have a suggestion. With available data, it would be possible for your staff to initiate a basic economic analysis looking for import and export items. Are there notable fluctuations or underlying surge patterns corresponding with the dates of Monstro's visits?" Darrell said.

"Yes, in fact, I do have a qualified team member who might pull together some preliminary data. But, given such vague boundaries definitions, I have serious doubts about our obtaining meaningful results," Janet said.

"Janet, Since Monstro has visited Earth for centuries, you might simplify and speed up the analysis by narrowing the analytical boundary to only those trade goods that are common today and also common a thousand years ago. If my hunch is correct, and commerce is involved, somewhere there must be one or more common products being traded through the centuries," Carl said.

Leaning forward in his chair, Charles looked at each member seated around the table. "Janet, I tend to agree with your assessment concerning a well-oiled conspiracy. It's unlikely. We, however, really are working with a lack of information about Monstro's motives. Carl's suggestion has merit. Even if remote, the possibility of commerce must be examined. You have my authorization to initiate a preliminary analysis, one looking at the fluctuations in trade over centuries."

"Yes, Sir. I'll have a preliminary report ready for you at next week's meeting," Janet said.

"Darrell, you have less than ten days to insert your new monitoring equipment into orbit, can you make that happen?" Charles said.

"Yes, sir. I believe we can pull it off. It will require NASA to delay a scheduled launch, but I believe that can be achieved."

"Good. If NASA tells you they can't shift their priorities, let me know and I will see they alter their schedules," Charles said.

"Yes, sir."

Charles Turned toward Carl. "You're to tighten up the inner-agency liaison protocols with NASA and support Darrell's efforts. I'll contact and acquire the Administration's formal authorization to back you up. Schedule the appropriate meetings with the agency directors and confirm that they're informed and in sync."

Carl made a few notes, while nodding his understanding. "Yes, Sir."

Once again Charles looked about at his senior managers. "For years, we've prepared for Monstro's eventual return. While that ship is in orbit, we're going to extract every data byte we can. Are there any questions?"

The three branch managers in turn acknowledged "No."

"If you weren't as capable as you are, then you would not be sitting in those chairs. If there's anything during Monstro's visit,

83

any anomaly whatsoever, it is to be immediately brought to my attention. I expect you to call me day or night. Now, get back to work."

Charles watched as his team gathered their papers and departed. He then stood up and made his way over to the large picture window. It was a beautiful day outside. The sky was incredibly blue, not a cloud could be seen. The distant monuments on the new Mall were bright in the sunlight, the remnants of past glory. Old Washington DC had long ago ceased being the nation's capital. Politically speaking, he was not certain that the Government's building the new Capitol at New Washington near Independence, Missouri, constituted much of an improvement. Politics was not his favorite study, but right or wrong, politics continued to alter the landscape. Thinking about his library study at home, he suddenly wished he were there.

With a deep sigh, he turned and walked to his desk. Sitting down, he reached out and pushed the red communication button that was located on his communications console, and sat back. Within seconds the communications screen cleared, and a familiar countenance appeared.

"Mr. President," he began, "Monstro is ten days out and coming to visit."

Chapter Fifteen:
Interstellar Trade

Standing on the balcony with her dog, Susie was listening to the nearby colony of seals barking on Seal Rock, while enjoying the cool sea breeze off the Pacific. The ocean below the balcony stretched westward, the whitecaps on an aquamarine sea merging on the horizon with the marine layer. It was April, the day was clear, and the combined scents of jasmine, pine, and the sea itself filled the morning air with heady fragrances.

Standing there, her blue eyes sparkling with intelligence and pleasure, she felt like hugging someone, a warm sense of being alive and very happy coursing throughout her body. Not only was it a beautiful morning, but she was also involved in new research for the Department of Commerce. New projects always came with a feeling of excitement.

With a sigh, she turned and entered into her library-workroom, her handsome yellow Labrador retriever, Gepeto, walking by her side. The wood floor of the generous size workroom was grained hickory and there were two broad oak work tables, upon which was ample evidence of several projects in progress. Large windows facing west looked out over dark green pine trees that stretched away to the coastline of the nearby ocean. Filled bookshelves occupied much of the wall space, and on the remaining wall area were various award plaques and framed watercolors that were rendered in vivid colors.

Enjoying the warm sunlight streaming in through the windows, Susie moved with an easy grace, a slender young woman in excellent health and physical condition. Strawberry blonde hair fell below her shoulders and was contained in a ponytail, which swung in harmony with her movements. She wore an embroidered teal peasant blouse above a soft full skirt of matching hues. On her feet were hand-stitched moccasins that she had made from supple leather. A handcrafted silver and turquoise belt ringed her waist; a matching turquoise pendent on a silver chain hung about her neck. Like all of her jewelry, these were of Susie's own design and handcraft.

"Good morning, William," Susie said.

"And good morning to you, Ma'am," responded the house computer.

The computer was her personal AI, and it responded using the vocal qualities and inflections of a calm and assured British butler of the era. Since William's nuance, voice and manner, were the product of hours of her own programming skill and labor, the computer's response pleased her.

When Susie sat down at her work table, Gepeto also settled on his mat with the air of a dog repeating a familiar routine. Opening an anachronistic and well-worn leather notebook, she unclipped her favorite pen, an equally anachronistic silver-barreled beauty from the late 20th century.

"William, we've got a new job. Given the hypothesis that interstellar travel exists and there is interstellar trade, then, what would likely be the most valuable interstellar trade commodities?"

Sounding unruffled by the vagueness of the question, the computer responded, "Given that the term 'interstellar trade' presumes sentience and a high degree of technology, combined with goodwill commerce, then the most valuable trade goods would be those that promote life and improve health or the quality of life, such as new technology or small items of exotic character and intrinsic beauty. Such items, materials, and substances would need to have a low mass to value ratio, be easily transported, and have a high value in one or more sentient cultures. Examples are DNA, including plant and animal genomes, pearls, exotic woods, and music."

Susie smiled and made a note – music. "William, why do you specify pearls and not include diamonds or other gems?"

"Ma'am, because diamonds are naturally occurring minerals and most probably occur in other solar systems, whereas a pearl is the biological product of a marine bivalve mollusk indigenous to the Earth, and is unlikely to be found elsewhere. Because of its unique qualities and beauty, a pearl is considered of value by cultures on Earth. Accordingly, there is a high probability that other sentient cultures would also find a pearl of beauty and value."

William paused momentarily, then continued, "However, of even greater value would be the mollusk genome itself.

86

Possessing this, other cultures might then be able to produce pearls of their own. Such production would also allow them to begin to compete in the pearl trade. To maintain the value of such trade, wisdom and prudence would suggest a strict ban on exporting any DNA, plant or animal genome, seeds, or living organisms. Other reasons to strictly prohibit importing or exporting live organisms include the high possibility of biological and ecological contamination."

Susie made a few more notes and then continued her line of reasoning. "William, given that interstellar commerce exists, what would be the most valuable *non-trade* item?"

"In the physical sense of a single item, that of greatest value would be a habitable world with an abundance of water. Most local, and presumably interstellar conflicts, happen because someone wants access to and control of inhabitable territories and their resources, especially water. Naturally, degrees of compatibility exist when considering such habitation, and depends upon the specific requirements of the population seeking to expand its habitation and base of political power."

Susie considered William's responses, and mused, *Someday I must do something about William's verbosity settings.* She leaned back into the soft leather covered chair and it tilted smoothly in response to the shift of her weight.

"William, in referencing your condition of goodwill commerce, why have you made this a specific condition?"

Before William could respond, the communicator emitted an announcement tone. "Ms. Susie, the incoming text message is marked urgent and is from your friend, Janet Rodgers. Shall I display the text?"

"Yes. And, please remember while she's my friend, she also manages historical research at the Department of Commerce. Meaning, she's also my boss."

As Susie read through the brief message, she frowned. "William, this is strange. Janet never pushes for a report, at least not until now; Something or someone must be pushing *her hard.* But, why?"

In response to her question, William was silent and Gepeto only yawned. Frowning, Susie sent Janet a short acknowledgment. Then, she mused, *Where was I? Oh, I remember. It's back to the old salt mine.*

Referring to her notes, Susie repeated her previous question. "William, referencing your condition of goodwill commerce, why do you make this a condition?"

"Ms. Susie, the answer is based on commodities being traded between two or more parties in a mutually beneficial and fair exchange. By contrast, in times of warfare, or in willfully fraudulent trade, many items, such as fine art and gold, often change hands without goodwill or fair compensation. When two cultures with diverse technologies and mores make contact, the culture having the lessor technology generally does not obtain balance or fairness in commerce.

"Moreover, the culture having the dominant technology will often impose its own political, cultural, and belief systems upon the culture with the less developed technology. Examples of such exploitation and subornation of cultures, under the guise of fair trade, can be found in the history of national colonization by European countries during the last six-hundred years of the twentieth century.

"While history on earth does not expressly establish a corollary with potential interstellar commerce, it strongly suggests caution is prudent. This is why I expressed the restrictive condition of goodwill in my response."

Susie had not considered the possibility of fraud or warfare in her inquiry and analysis. All the trade articles that she had read relating to future interstellar trade held out the alluring promise of an unlimited expanding volume of commerce, citing new mineral and chemical resources, like those now being realized in recent interplanetary exploration. Those articles spoke glowingly of the wealth-building possibilities of new unpopulated inhabitable worlds, just waiting to be settled. Reflecting on her prior research, she could not recall a single professional trade article that spoke about possible risks or threats associated with humans taking the bold step into the larger universe. Given William's clear warning, it now seemed important for her to look at just such possibilities.

With rising hope, Susie picked up her line of inquiry.

"William, I've got a new postulate for you to consider. Given that interstellar travel denotes intelligence and a very high level of technology, and given that achieving such technology demands a social structure capable of bringing together the needed resources, then, evaluate the following hypothesis: any such advanced culture would possess a high level of ethical and moral development."

The computer remained silent for only several moments before responding. "That a society possesses a technology capable of achieving interstellar travel does not by necessity denote that the required technology was developed by that society. Technology might be transferred through trade or perhaps recovery from an off-world culture's crash site. Technology is but one narrow aspect of an evolved social-political structure, and there are examples in Earth history where one society has made an infusion of technology into another society, one that has a lower level of technology.

"Pertaining to your second stated postulate, the ability of a society to organize raising capital and fostering development of the technology supporting interstellar travel, is flawed. The advanced technology may be the product of reversed engineering of foreign technology. Otherwise, a society may simply trade for the needed technology from another interstellar capable society. For example, one society having an obsolete interstellar capability may trades the old technology to another society that desires interstellar capability.

"Given that both of your foundational postulates are not self-supporting, there is no meaningful conclusion concerning a corollary between technology sufficient to achieve interstellar travel and a presumed level of ethics and morality."

William's response was not what Susie had anticipated. "William, I believe it's time for a break. There is much for me to consider in what you have provided."

Susie stood up, stretched, then moved across the room, down the hall, and into the kitchen. One of Susie's small indulgences was coffee. The pot was empty, so she turned the dial on the grinder to produce the proper amount for a fresh pot. As the sound of the grinder rumbled, she rinsed the pot and filled the measuring container with filtered water. After pouring in the water, she leaned against the tiled kitchen counter and thought about how William's responses had directed her inquiry in a new direction and away from her anticipated endpoint.

Her initial focus had been the effects of interstellar travel on business and commerce. Now, William indicated there might be problems of a far more dangerous nature than a market index transitioning from bull to bear. *Still*, she thought, *if there are real dangers that have nothing to do with fair trade, then that fact must be considered as part of the market reality....*

Chapter Sixteen:
An Adequate Clarification

The delectable smell of fresh Kona coffee filled the entire kitchen. Reaching into the cupboard, Susie selected a large handcrafted mug. In a practiced series of moves, she filled it and added honey and cream. With the warm mug held snugly in hand, she retraced her steps, returning to the workroom and her favorite chair.

As she sat, Gepeto placed his muzzle on her knee, and looked up with an inquiring gaze, as if to say, *Can we go for a walk?*

Smiling, Susie stroked his head. "If you're a good boy, I'll take you for a walk in a little while."

Having heard this promise made and broken many times before, Gepeto looked disappointed, but being ever hopeful, he quietly settled down on his mat again. Susie returned her concentration to the problem at hand, pondering the computer's earlier responses. Checking her notes, she leaned back in her chair and asked a new question dealing with commerce.

"William, referencing one of your responses, why did you indicate that some trade might involve exchange of obsolete technology?"

"Ma'am, that response is based upon a proven commercial and military axiom; Do not provide a potential adversary with technology capable of causing you future harm. Trading sensitive technologies would not only provide potential commercial competition at levels proving less profitable, it could also increase the risks in potential military conflict that might later arise over trade or other political issues. Therefore, a prudent culture exploring surrounding star systems, and finding a second culture, would not provide the second culture with any technology that might compete with it."

William's response made sense. Susie made an appropriate note and then continued.

"William, you have referred to many examples of high technology being infused into a less technologically developed society. Can you give me a specific example?"

There was no perceptible delay before William responded. "Yes, Ma'am. During the last half of the twentieth century, about 500 years ago, there were a number of bitter fought regional wars. Opposing major foreign powers became embroiled in some of those local conflicts. In one case, the war in Vietnam, the Soviet Union shipped billions of dollars of armaments and supplied military advisors to the Vietnamese in the northern part of Vietnam. During the same time, the United States government increased its own support for the Vietnamese in the southern portion of Vietnam, providing both troops and resources. These direct actions by two major opposing powers resulted in massive infusion of military hardware and technology into a small and underdeveloped region. The conflict produced harsh warfare that killed more than one-million people."

Susie was perplexed. *Why would any country alter an entire society in so drastic a manner,* she wondered?

"William, why did the Soviet Union and United States infuse modern armaments into such a primitive culture?"

"Ma'am, the underlying cause was not for an expansion of territory or similar economic purpose. The ostensible cause was utterly failed political strategies that pitted two opposing and badly flawed national ideologies against each other."

Curious, Susie asked, " William, you used the odd term 'ostensible.' If the bloody conflict in Vietnam was not the consequence of utterly failed political strategies, then what was its true cause?"

"Ma'am, Historians refer to that historical period of international tension and constrained warfare as World War III. At that time, a minor political basis for international conflict did exist between the Soviet Union and the United States, however, the true genesis for World War III was not political--"

Surprised, Susie interjected, "Constrained warfare? William, you said more than a million people were killed. If the cause of the war was not expansion or political, what possible rational justification was there for killing a million people?"

"Ma'am, WW III is euphemistically called the 'Cold War.' The sole purpose for the constrained warfare was warfare itself, along with its associated international tensions."

"William that makes absolutely no sense. There must have been some meaningful purpose."

" Yes, Ma'am. The obvious purpose is it was mutually beneficial for the Soviet Union and the United States. Otherwise it would not have been prosecuted. WW III was a mutual strategic stratagem of international tensions, which allowed the opposing nations to justify and conceal their enormous investments in funding high priority secret research projects. These clandestine projects were expansive, involving reverse engineering of several recovered alien spacecraft. The immense research efforts did yield breakthrough advances in multiple scientific fields, especially those in solid state electronics and field effects."

"Alien spaceships? William, I am unaware of any reliable reports of alien spaceships, crashed or otherwise."

"Ma'am, the historical record identifies a number of such crashes. one notable and closely guarded alien crash occurred July 3, 1947. The crash occurred only a few miles from the United States nuclear arsenal and flight ready bombers, which were then located at the Strategic Air Command base located at Roswell in New Mexico. Does this information provide an adequate clarification?"

"Yes, sorta," Susie said.

She shook her head in wonder. Science should be pure and used only to increase knowledge. When bad people co-opted and exploited science for killing other people and destroying established cultures, it was a dark stain on all of humanity. Remembering reading the stories about the time following WW III, when there were tens of thousands of nuclear bombs and inter-continental missiles, she shuddered. Thankfully, sanity had prevailed and such weapons were outlawed and destroyed hundreds of years earlier.

William's brief reply disturbed her. Although having a reasonable understanding of history, details of clandestine international operations and intrigue comprised no part of her knowledge base. That went double for any discourse regarding the crashes of alien spaceships, factual or mythical. Such topics were generally deemed nonsense, and William's reference to such matters as being factual was disconcerting. She would need to determine where William had obtained the data, and then assess whether it should be purged.

Throughout her life, the entire space program had always been postulated to be rooted in peaceful research. She knew the first manmade objects to depart Earth and leave the solar system were purely scientific exploration robots called Voyager One and Voyager Two. The United States launched these two-robot craft in August and September of 1977. Smiling, she remembered the initial stunning photographs Voyager One and Voyager Two sent back to Earth. They remained extraordinary achievements for so young a space technology.

When their internal power systems finally degraded below useful levels and shut down, the two spacecraft had continued their journey beyond the solar system's ability ever to recall them.

Susie knew the objectives of these early spacecraft were to explore the solar magnetic fields and outer planets of the solar system. They were also the first probes to measure and cross the boundary that exists between the outward flowing solar winds and the vast interstellar medium. Both spacecraft had continued to provide scientific data to scientists on Earth beyond 2020, even sending information back to Earth after they had crossed the heliopause boundary.

Ground controllers did not direct the two spacecraft to a specific destination. As far as anyone knew, they were still traveling at the leisure speed of approximately 3.3 Astronomical Units each year, following their own quiet ballistic trajectory into the unknown, moving toward a destination somewhere in eternity.

Since the Voyager missions, other more advanced and scientifically ambitious probes had been sent toward specific adjacent star systems. These new probes employed fission-powered ion propulsion, allowing them to travel farther and faster, but they were still high-risk long-term missions with a very low probability of success.

When the interstellar probes had been launched, everyone understood it would be a very long time before any information was received from those missions. Even though the timeframe of such farsighted scientific projects was measured in centuries, the excitement of such interstellar ventures had lifted the interest of everyone on Earth to learn more about the characteristics and nature of the beautiful galaxy surrounding everyone.

Closer to home, such scientific enthusiasm also meant paychecks for Susie arriving regularly from the Department of Commerce. She sat holding her warm coffee mug and considered what William had told her, and much of it was disturbing.

Why must the possibility of something bad be permitted to disturb what should be a purely scientific problem? Why must thoughts of potential danger be intermingled with the pleasure of the expanding knowledge of our universe?

We have been sending out interstellar probes for centuries, Susie thought. But suddenly she began to question the wisdom and logic behind such high-risk ventures. *Perhaps sending out radio beacons and interstellar probes was not such a good idea after all.* Even as she began to think along this line of reasoning, she held tightly to hope. *Perhaps William's responses were not as dire as they first seemed.* She then thought of one more question.

"William, why is goodwill not to be presumed as the normal condition for interstellar cultural contact and commerce?"

There was silence for several moments as William sifted through his extensive database and structured a response based on topic relevance and priority of probability. Susie smiled at the delay and wondered for the umpteenth time if she could ever ask a question that her AI would not be able to answer. After several quiet minutes, rather than an answer, William asked a question.

"Ms. Susie, what do you call someone who does not believe in monsters?"

The question surprised Susie. She knew from experience by repeating a question asked by the AI, it would often provide her the answer.

"William, what do *you* call someone who does not believe in monsters?"

The computer responded with a single resonant word that any British butler would have envied -- "Lunch."

Chapter Seventeen:
Shadow Dance

Outwardly, they appeared to be typical small asteroids, similar to millions of ragged and craggy stony objects found in space. Launched from Lan, the small cluster of objects moved toward the inner planets in a precise and purposeful formation. Each disguised by a cast composite shell, the sentinel and its six escorting companions looked like perfectly natural objects. Their synthetic outer shells were coated with a layer of ground asteroid debris, and a cursory laser scan would detect only a natural stony body.

The sentinel with its accompanying probes dropped leisurely sunward, moving at a fraction of their full speed capability. Passing the orbit of the fifth planet, the sentinel continued toward its defined goal near the third planet, while its escort broke out of formation and dispersed. Three of the probes moved above the Ecliptic Plane and the remaining three moved below. Spreading out, each probe independently proceeded to its predefined position, forming a broad monitoring network.

The six dispersed probes nearest to the sentinel provided it with optional discrete data nodes, each potentially being the first in a chain of telemetry links leading back to Lan. They were the distributed connectors to the monitors Shey had earlier deployed between the orbit of the fifth planet and Lan.

Approaching the third planet from its night side, the first visual data the sentinel transmitted was an image of the planet and its large moon. Coupled by mutual attraction, they appeared as two gleaming slender crescents suspended in darkness. The stark symmetry, contrast, and their beauty was appreciated by the people watching their displays on board Lan.

The approaching alien ship had necessitated Commander Roy Grey to make changes in overall planning. With Kellon's approval, he had directed the intelligence team to program the sentinel for a multiple-discipline mission. Dropping sunward, it would brush the third planet's magnetosphere, then move into its long-term monitoring position -- seventy diameters away from the planet. To monitor communications on the third planet, the sentinel trajectory was computed to provide a three-day window prior to the arrival of the alien ship.

The sentinel was within the orbit of the fourth planet before the communications team differentiated and translated communications signals from the third planet. They were audiovisual transmissions, and rather than answering questions, the video images provoked surprised wonder. Some of the images were of city street scenes. There was an overwhelming hodgepodge of oddly shaped boxes, bottles, and sundry items. Other images displayed people talking together.

It was the images of the people that caused the exclamations. There were men and women having extraordinary variation in their physical appearance, including astonishing differences in their skin color. People on the Assembled worlds did not have striking physical differences, and the concept of different races was foreign to everyone.

While ship's linguists began working with their computers to isolate the languages, many of Lan's crew came to the CAC and looked at the displays. They wanted to see if the rumors spreading throughout Lan were true. They came in ones and twos, stood looking in astonishment for a few moments, and then went back to their work. The same question was in each of their minds -- how could such a striking variation in humans have occurred?

Roy was standing at one of the plot tables assigned to monitoring the incoming sentinel data. Roan, Zorn, and Elayne were working directly with him. As the sentinel brushed the outer reaches of the planet's magnetosphere, the observers on Lan were studying the very low frequency bands.

Zorn abruptly stood, pointing toward the data display. "Computer, freeze that spectrum profile. By Nodons' whiskers, there are Kreel pop patterns within that data structure. Those signals look like compressed brain wave-suppression patterns."

Roan moved over to Zorn's side and studied the display for several moments. "Roy, I concur. Those do look like Kreel subliminal patterns, but they are at variance with similar patterns I have seen."

"Elayne, can you provide an analysis of that signal?" Roy asked.

"Yes, Sir. It should not take long. Computer, isolate the signal pattern in monitor grid C6 to F8 and correlate for possible matches with known Kreel pop-patterns."

After several minutes the computer reported, "There is an eighty-three percent match between the pattern in monitor grid C6 to F8 and Kreel pattern K27r3. The Kreel pattern encodes a signal causing depression of self-esteem in humans."

"Blast, that really tears it. First, we've got an inbound Capital ship using obsolete Kreel-style linear propulsion, and now we've an eighty-three percent match with a known Kreel pop pattern. That is not a product of random chance. Since those pop patterns have long-term harmful effects on humans, it's a safe wager the people living on that planet didn't put those pop patterns in their own magnetosphere. Kreel is Kreel, and it's probable whoever is manning that inbound ship is accountable," Zorn said.

"Well, that answers one question. If they inserted those pop patterns, it means they've made earlier visits; that means they have prior knowledge of this system. That explains their lack of stealth," Roy said, with a hard edge in his voice.

Roan was becoming noticeably angry. "Such mind-altering signals on a planetary scale causes untold misery, even suicides. They constitute blatant acts of war."

"Agreed. I'm reclassifying that ship hostile," Roy said.

"Elayne, if the archive data is available, pull up the data concerning the older known Kreel propulsion signatures," Zorn said.

"Requested specifications coming up."

Elayne keyed in a query on her console, and the display shifted from the pop pattern and displayed four Kreel ship classifications. Each was shown with mass and general characteristics.

"There is only one Kreel class in that group with a mass-to-power ratio anywhere near those of the hostile ship," Roy said.

He selected and downloaded the selected data. Then, everyone studied the complete specifications for the ship class.

"Sir, while there are many similarities, that class of Kreel ship is a real museum piece. None of those ships have been observed in operation for more than two-thousand years. How can we be sure the incoming ship is the same class?" Elayne asked.

"It may be an antique, but potentially it's a lethal one. If our identification is correct, the inbound ship is an old Kreel assault ship, having hangar capacity for up to one-hundred scouts and fighters. The real problem is there is no data about what weapon systems upgrades that ship might be carrying," Roan said.

"Elayne's observation is astute. On the surface, the data does correlate with the mass, propulsion signature, and its being subluminal. While it may be an obsolete Kreel vessel, we don't have a clue as to who is driving that thing," Roy said.

Zorn had continued studying the incoming sentinel data. "That magnetosphere is literally loaded with pop patterns. The effort required to structure so many patterns is huge and would require considerable time."

Zorn pushed his chair away from the console and stood. He was obviously angry.

"I don't know who is aboard that inbound target, but the density of pop patterns proves someone with murderous intent is assailing the population on that planet. Elayne, if you're still looking for an underlying cause to explain the short lifespans and conflicts in the history of these people, you need look no further.

"When a purposeful action is taken to demean and injure people, the purpose is either simple ignorance or else willful intent. If willful intent, then the clear purpose is to bind people in ignorance and fear. Those are the brutal tools of tyranny, not righteousness. Those pop patterns prove we are dealing with a tyrant. What we don't know is how long that tyrant has oppressed these people."

Having read both of their service records, Roy knew Zorn and Roan had fought on Kintana, back when the Kreel attempted to invade that planet. Both of them had suffered the brunt of the mental torment caused by Kreel pop-patterns. He recognized the memories of that violation of their minds was rekindling an old bitter rage. Elayne also heard the anger in Zorn and Roan's voices, and wondered about the cause of such anger.

"Roan, like other Guardian personnel, I have experienced Kreel pop patterns during training. But I've never experienced such patterns in an actual attack. Have either you or Zorn personally experienced such a Kreel assault?" she asked.

"Yes. It happened about eight-hundred years ago, during a Kreel attack on Kintana. Zorn and I were both there. Each of us had come separately during the Spring Festival to enjoy the parties. Captain Kellon was also there, but he was not yet a Captain. It was Festival time and everyone was in a party mood. The beverages, music, and general excitement had done their work. Everyone was relaxing and having fun--"

When Roan's voice broke, and he paused, Zorn picked up the story. "The Kreel had timed their attack to begin at the peak of the festival. The initial pop patterns created a sense of unrest and general anxiety. At first no one understood what was happening.

"The patterns started at a low level of intensity. During the first night of the attack, the Kreel incrementally increased their signal strength and during the following days they maintained a high signal level. The patterns induce both mental and physical torment.

"Desperately looking for a cause for our mass illness, we discovered the Kreel were using complex electromagnetic bursts of coded information injected into the magnetosphere, which affected the underlying human circadian rhythms of our minds. Those patterns incorporated an entrain technology that made mental functioning extremely difficult."

When Zorn paused, Roan again picked up the story. "On the second day, the mental anxiety had ramped up until some people were driven mad with fear. Others were mentally overwhelmed to such an extent that even though they were fully aware they could not function. The effects were on a subliminal level, swamping our rational capability. There were associated physical and mental side effects, including hearing voices and visual hallucinations, eruptions of color, geometric symbols, and bursts of intense sound. Old memories flashed before us in sharp clarity and flashes of bright colors directly intruded into our visual field. It felt like our heads were in a vice with someone slowly increasing the pressure to a crushing point.

"Those pop patterns violate a person's very essence, they're a mental rape of a person's mind. And, it took a terrible toll on the people all about us."

As Roan finished speaking, his countenance expressed both anger and sadness. Elayne was aware of the Kreel assault on Kintana, it was a part of Guardian Force history. But she had not knowingly met anyone who was there. Her personal experience with such mental weapons was in a training environment, and it lasted only one minute. Thinking back to that experience, she shuddered. Roan and Zorn's countenances gave her evidence of the lasting trauma induced by such a prolonged experience.

Zorn again picked up the story," It was on the second day of the attack that we began to understand what was happening. We had problems with the Kreel before, but they'd never exhibited any form of mind-control technology. The entire attack was something new to us. It wasn't until the Kreel actually launched their physical assault on Kintana that we understood what was going on. To say we weren't working at a full combat efficiency would be a gross understatement. We were seriously outnumbered and our battle losses were heavy. Eventually, our counterattack blunted and broke through the Kreel offense. At a terrible cost in ships and lives, we located and destroyed the primary pattern transmitters. Then, our reinforcements broke the Kreel attack."

Elayne knew more about the history of Kintana than Zorn or Roan had elaborated. She sat quietly, remembering the history every Guardian cadet learned. The battle at Kintana was fiercely fought, with raw courage against overwhelming odds. Only 23 percent of all Guardian personnel who engaged in the initial battle survived. Even though afflicted with heavy casualties, Guardian Force steadfastly held the line until reinforcements arrived. Together they had crushed the main Kreel fleet.

"Zorn, from the level of the pop patterns, would you declare this to be a Kreel assault?" Roy asked.

"No, Sir. There are patterns in profusion, but their intensity and level suggest a general oppression field, not a ramping assault sequence. My opinion is that the pop patterns have been in place for a long time. They appear to be a covert suppression of the population, not a prelude to overt military action."

"I agree with Zorn's assessment, but stress what we're seeing here is not typical Kreel behavior," Roan said.

Elayne watched as Roy returned his attention to the large tactical screen. She did not envy his responsibility, difficult decisions needed to be made, and soon.

Lan's sentinel slipped past the planet's magnetosphere and reached for the anonymity of its defined solar orbit. As it continued, new probes began moving up and out from the third planet. They moved with apparent precision into their assigned observation positions. Like dancing shadows, they passed quickly out of the light, seamlessly merging with the darkness of space.

Alert, the Guardian sentinel detected and efficiently began monitoring each new probe rising up from the planet. It recorded the data concerning the progress and positions of each new object, incorporating that data into its random telemetry stream. Farther out in space, the six monitors reacted to the new probes, making subtle adjustments to their own positions.

On the fringe of the solar system, analysts on Lan were carefully scrutinizing every incoming data byte, as their probes pierced the void. Down on Earth, Olympus analysts were not looking for fleeting Guardian probes, they had other problems. Even if they were looking, they would not have seen the Guardian sentinel's minuscule shadow, as it quickly flickered past, disappearing into the deeper darkness....

Chapter Eighteen:
Occasional Research

With a sense of rising excitement, Susie placed the phone back on its cradle; the unexpected call from Janet intrigued her. She and Janet had been friends for years, ever since they were graduate students together at the University of Washington. After graduation, Susie had remained affiliated with the University, but Janet had chosen to follow a government career with the Department of Commerce. Over the years they gradually lost contact. Then, after reading an article Susie had published in The Solar Commerce Journal, Janet had contacted her. She was still working for the Department of Commerce and wondered if Susie might be interested in doing occasional research for the government. That was almost six years ago. There was no raging demand for Susie's narrow specialty in finance and market analysis, and she had jumped at the prospect of occasional Government work. It had definitely helped her in keeping dog food in Gepeto's bowl.

Janet's new assignment was urgent, and Susie cleared the desk of on-going tasks. Then, she opened her notebook.

"Hey, William, wake up sleepy head. We've got some work."

William's calm and resonant voice immediately responded, in a slow confident drawl of a British butler. "Ma'am, I am fully awake and merely waiting for you to start pushing my buttons."

Susie considered William's droll response, and smiled. It was the result of her recently installed nuance upgrade for his random responses. How William's AI interface would utilize new expressions often surprised her.

"William, please open my recent Govmail folder and isolate a message from Janet Rodgers, dated today."

Without a perceptible pause, William responded, "That message is now available."

"William, display the message."

The graphic display altered, the multi-hued seascape transforming into a page of text. It was typical government boilerplate and of little interest.

"William, scan the document for the first reference to Task Description and display the associated text."

Again, the monitor display altered, and a new page appeared. It was more government jargon, and Susie scanned down the page to read; *Provide an in-depth and detailed review of global commodity import and export patterns.*

Reading the sentence, Susie's smile broadened. *Well given a few dozen years,* she mused, *that should not pose much of a problem, but doing it by Monday morning, not so likely.* Then, she continued to read; *Narrow the study to only those commodities commonly being traded today and one-thousand years ago.*

That specification was odd, and it brought her up short. Sitting back in her chair, she wondered-- *What in the world does the Department of Commerce need with one-thousand-year-old commercial trade data?*

She continued reading; *Identify and report all unusual periodic increases in demand for the identified trade items that occur immediately prior to the list of dates provided on the attached schedule, Appendix 1.*

"William, scan the document and display Appendix 1."

The display altered, and the requested appendix appeared. It was short. Susie carefully scanned the list of dates and noticed the first date was about five hundred years back, 1947. Being an avid reader of technical journals, particularly those publications dealing with space research, she knew 1947 was immediately following the dropping of the first atomic bombs and the end of WW II. That was about the same time the hot space race between the United States and Russia began in earnest. The last date on the list was the current date. She was born naturally curious, and It was her curiosity that shaped those analytical qualities that made her a good researcher and annalist. Occasionally her curiosity also got her into trouble.

Sitting and looking at the short list of dates, she wondered, *What do those dates have in common? What collection of events occurring around each of those dates, when taken together, constitute a data set that the Department of Commerce is interested in?*

"William, begin a Global-Net search. Using the dates specified in Appendix 1, initiate a search for a span of time from six months prior unto three months following each of the listed dates. Then, isolate and analyze the news headlines in each of the intervals. Identify the headlines describing similar events occurring in each interval. Discard any category of headlines that do not occur in each and every interval. Notify me when your search results are complete."

Janet's recent conversation did not identify a cause or purpose for her urgent study, and Susie knew better than to probe into such topics. Still, Janet was most emphatic, the required study results must be in her Govmail queue not later than Monday morning, 08:00 Central. Once more, Janet was pushing her hard, and the new deadline was tighter than most.

Susie was uncertain about the true nature of Janet's job description. Whatever it was, Janet's new assignment was peculiar, and it sparked Susie's curiosity.

"Gepeto," she called. Now, where is my dog?"

Gepeto heard her call and recognized it as an invitation for an outing, and he came quickly.

Susie bent over and hugged him. "You're a special pup. Let's go for that promised walk."

She returned thirty minutes later. Breathing deep, she was feeling relaxed.

William then announced, "Ma'am, the list of common topic headlines within each interval is now complete."

Wonderful, she thought. "William, thank you. Now, sorting the data by topic category, display the results."

The displayed list was short, consisting of only four common topic categories. Scanning the list, she read, *Politics, Sports, UFOs, and Weather.*

She stood looking at the list for several moments, with only one item igniting her analytical curiosity- *UFOs.*

Then, she remembered during their recent work William had mentioned 1947 and something odd about UFOs. Curious, sitting down she picked up and flipped open her notebook. Leafing quickly back through the earlier notes, she read, *Notable and closely guarded alien crash occurred July 3, 1947. The crash occurred only a few miles from the United States nuclear arsenal and flight ready bombers, which were then stationed at the Strategic Air Command base located at Roswell in New Mexico.*

Quietly musing, she closed her notebook and sat back in her chair, then sighed. Dear Janet, it seems we need to have a long talk.

Chapter Nineteen:
Of Dragons

The Captain's conference room had a comfortable feeling, but the matter before those gathered there was anything but comfortable. Lieutenant Oster, Lan's Communications Officer, looked toward Kellon and cleared his throat before speaking.

"Captain, as you ordered, at 06:00 our initial situation report was coded Black Hole and transmitted to Guardian Headquarters. Given our distance from Glas Dinnein, the earliest possible reply will be in four weeks."

"Thank you, Will," Kellon acknowledged.

Kellon looked about the table at each person and then spoke with firmness. "Gentlemen, we are now confronted by difficult choices. Our mission orders are definitive. We're ordered to conduct a detailed covert surveillance of this solar system. Here, I underscore the word 'covert.' Does anyone have any questions?"

"Yes, Sir. Our mission orders are clear, but there are also Standing Orders. Those orders form the bedrock of the Guardian Force," Roan said.

"You're correct, and those Standing Orders apply to Kreel and Dargon attacks against any human-inhabited planet. In all such events, standing orders require Guardian forces to take immediate decisive military action to intercede or terminate any such attack. Without reservation, this ship, and all of its crew and resources, is fully committed to fulfilling our Standing Orders."

Kellon paused a moment before continuing, looking toward Roan. "Our current tactical situation has a potential of erupting into combat. If this happens, my intention is the battle will be on our terms and in the place and at the time of our choosing. Before engaging in combat, we need to understand who our enemy is, understand his military capability, and determine what he is doing in this solar system. For the moment, our primary mission is not combat, it remains covert reconnaissance.

"In keeping with our mission criteria, do we have anything new from our sentinel?" Kellon asked.

Lorn glanced at his notes, then looked to Kellon. "Yes, Sir. The sentinel detected and identified what appears to be a group of satellites being launched from the third planet. They are now in surveillance orbits and operating in a stealth mode. If our sentinel had not been on station prior to their launch, it's likely we would not be aware of them. In short, we got lucky."

"Have you determined the purpose for these new satellites?" Kellon asked.

"Sir, we've reached some initial conclusions. the satellites terminated their initial telemetry upon obtaining their observation positions, suggesting they are passive intelligence gathering monitors. This would mean someone on the planet knows the Capital ship is inbound. Additionally, the ability to accurately pre-position the satellites indicates the people who launched them have precise information concerning the target's expected orbit."

"Lorn, that's an important insight. Knowing there are people on the planet who're aware of the inbound ship alters some of our initial assumptions," Kellon said.

"Yes sir, and their ability to insert the new satellites also explains some of our earlier data. It implies they have an early warning system in place. Knowing this enabled us to reexamine our earlier data. Our analysis indicates satellites located in solar orbits, whose orbits are normal to the Ecliptic Plane and intersect the orbit of the fifth planet, are effective early warning monitors.

"Sir, our new data reveals those on that planet are employing stealth technology when positioning their new satellites. This argues they believe the inbound ship is hostile. If this supposition is correct, the people on the planet recognize the technological gulf between the inbound ship and their own technology. They also understand they're under siege and recognizing their vulnerability, they are prudently gathering additional information."

"Well done, Lorn. For now, we will avoid conflict, if possible. Those on the third planet have chosen stealth and the gathering of Intelligence. We will do the same. However, we're now also operating on the principle of Roland and the Dragon saga. Given that all dragons are not peaceful, when observing a hungry dragon with open jaws bending over a child, we'll act first and ask questions later."

Looking around the table, Kellon observed expressions of resolve and determination. "Gentlemen, we're a long way from home. To fight any prolonged conflict over such distances is prohibitively costly and a logistical nightmare. We are at best four months from possible reinforcements. However, the inbound Capital ship, given its subluminal speed, may be twenty years or more from possible reinforcement. If we can prevent the ship from sounding an alarm, then we might stretch that time interval significantly before someone comes looking for a missing ship. When they come, it will most likely be as a reconnaissance mission in force. This estimate presumes that we continue to deal with a subluminal technology. If that presumption changes, the entire situation becomes problematic.

"We can estimate what military force might be made available by Guardian Force to protect this system, but we have no way to determine the level of reinforcements that might respond to an alarm coming from the target. Our primary advantage remains that the enemy doesn't know who we are or even that we exist. Let's strive to keep that advantage.

"If a fight develops, we have the speed advantage and the benefit of surprise, and we will exploit them. If battle comes, our priorities are first protection of the planet from direct assault, then jam all communications from the target, block deployment of their fighters, force or decoy the target away from the planet, and render the target non-operational. If determined possible, we'll board the target and recover all hard intelligence, then destroy the target. Finally, we'll sweep the battle area clean, removing all traces of Guardian technology. In keeping with our orders, we'll remain covert in all actions at all times.

"Gentlemen, be advised, we're one ship, but what we do next will have a direct impact upon everyone living in this solar system and eventually involve everyone on Glas Dinnein. Our ignorance of the enemy is our greatest danger. Gathering actionable intelligence about that enemy is therefore our highest priority. The second highest priority is determining the precise location of the pop transmitters. Consistent with our Standing Orders, before departing this solar system, we're going to search out and destroy every pop transmitter on that planet."

Given Kellon's brief outline of battle, the staff planning meeting began in earnest. They continued late into the evening, looking for every option and searching out contingencies. If they were going to fight the dragon, they were determined the dragon's tail was going to be sagging.

Chapter Twenty:
Exercise Sands

Nearly a thousand turns in the past, an intense rivalry between competing Nests devolved into open combat. Two Nest ships were in Earth's lower atmosphere harvesting trade goods, when a trade dispute concerning conflicting territorial claims erupted. While the fighters from the ships were escorting their cargo carriers to designated upload points, an open combat between the fighters erupted over a major Earth city. Several fighters were destroyed and their crews killed. The Nest ship commanders were able to restrain their fighters before the combat spread and engulfed the Nest ships.

Later, upon returning to Scion, the High Council waxed furious with all the involved ranking officials. Following that near disaster, all subsequent trade ventures to Earth were restricted to cooperative endeavors and under the strict control of the High Council and its designated trade arbiter. To assure this, the Council established severe punitive sanctions, and hence no Nest dared dispute the Council's trade arbiter or again contemplate open warfare over a subjugated planet.

Fully understanding disputes were inevitable, the Council mandated a straightforward method of resolving disputes between individuals or Nests. That method was by the use of traditional martial contests waged upon the exercise sands.

The exercise room was large and warm, and by human standards it was dimly illuminated. Its floor was evenly covered by a deep layer of warm and dark brown sand. The ceiling at its center was light tan, however, it gradually darkened until it smoothly interfaced with the upper walls. Similarly, from their top the unadorned walls also gradually darkened in color until they flawlessly merged with the color of the dark brown sand at the bottom. The effect in coloration manifested a subtle illusion of space.

It was precisely the zenith aboard the Arkillian Nest ship, and nine Arkillians had gathered in the exercise room. Kur was there with his second and two servants, as was his opponent, Ca. The ninth Arkillian present was the official trade arbiter, his sole task being to adjudicate the upcoming contest, and to assure the rules and tradition of the duel were strictly followed.

A non-lethal conflict, the duel involved martial skills with staffs, and its traditions were lost in Arkillian antiquity. The contest served the Arkillians as a means of resolving personal disputes, and it also provided those of senior status a method of addressing perceived affronts from someone of lesser status. It was a personal matter of perceived affront that had brought those in the exercise room together.

The duellists were barefoot and attired in loose two-piece garments. Each wore a long-sleeved full blouse and generous ankle length pants. In color, all the garments were deep burgundy. Both contestants also had a narrow white headband, and wore a similar white sash tied about their waists. A large embroidered emblem designating their respective Nests was sewn on the backs of their blouses.

The duellists' seconds removed long slender wooden staffs from their protective slipcovers. Like all facets of the confrontation, the staffs were required to conform with strict specifications regarding their composition and dimensions. After a diligent process of close examination, each second ceremoniously offered to exchange his staff with the other second, before they presented the staffs to the waiting combatants. After performing that duty, the seconds moved quickly aside.

With one end of the staff resting upon the sand, the upper end of the staff came slightly above the Arkillians' shoulders. The duellists stood facing each other, their bold facial markings revealing a mutual hostility.

Kur, the elder combatant, stood studying his younger opponent, surveying his assured cocky manner. Over the centuries, Kur had stood on the exercise sands far too many times for someone less than a fourth of his own turns to easily defeat him. Still, his opponent had a reputation for speed and skill with the staff, and Kur anticipated a strong opposition.

Being the challenger, Kur issued the traditional formal greeting. "Ca, it is acknowledged that you have come with honor."

In strict accordance with formal tradition, Ca responded, "Respected One, I am honored by your notice."

As the formal exchange ended, the arbiter, who was standing between and offset from the duellists, extended his arm over the sand. Pausing for a moment, then dropping a scarlet ribbon, he moved quickly aside. Even before the ribbon touched the sand, Ca attacked.

Moving forward from his beginning formal stance, Ca's first attack came as a lifting blow delivered with power emanating from his upper and lower body. As he swung the staff, his footwork brought him forward and then fluidly into a graceful flow to his left.

Responding, Kur's hands shifted quickly down the staff, taking a new position near its middle. As he moved left, the elder duelist countered the younger Arkillian's lifting blow with a simple deflecting parry, which he followed immediately with a smashing counterblow delivered toward Ca's extended right leg, and a second lifting strike with the butt of the staff.

Ca's initial attacking movements had carried him into a wide step, his feet moving through a well-practiced triangular pattern. He succeeded in evading Kur's counter strikes.

Once more, the two Arkillians stood looking directly into each other's eyes, their facial markings now flushed with anger. The younger Arkillian had taken the offensive, and flowing with graceful motion, he continued pressing his elder with a series of deft strikes, while shifting both his style and rhythm, constantly seeking an advantage.

Kur met each attack with skilled defensive counter moves, while not pressing an attack of his own. The pattern of staff movements was blurred, as each Arkillian feinted and then moved, each striving to create an advantageous opening. Ca continued pressing his attack, while Kur skillfully defended against his shifting styles. Both Arkillians were adept with the staff, and the duel was sharp, both duellists scoring numerous light strikes and an occasional heavier blow. In its form, the struggle with staffs was a fight involving skill and stamina.

As the fight continued, Kur's greater experience and effective defense began to wear down his youthful opponent's confident offensive. Kur sensed the moment when a shift in tempo announced his younger opponent realized he had either overestimated his own skill or severely underestimated Kur's

115

ability. Immediately, Kur smoothly shifted from defense to an offense, combining blurs of grace, power, and speed.

The number of Kur's strikes connecting with his opponent's body steadily increased, as did their accumulating effects. The young Arkillian's movements became less graceful, and his initial aggressive offense faded, shifting to a defensive style.

Kur was now moving with an unwavering steady fluidity, adding more bruises on top of the young Arkillian's earlier bruises. Then, while attempting to sidestep one of Kur's lifting blows, the younger duellist slipped on the loose sand. Momentarily off balance, the young combatant was unable to parry Kur's powerful strike; the staff hit directly into Ca's midsection, with a resounding thud. Involuntarily reacting to the blow, Ca was bent forward.

Kur followed up his initial strike with a second descending blow, which struck the young Arkillian between the back of his neck and shoulders. With skill, Kur softened the second blow, knowing if delivered with his full strength it could be lethal.

As the young Arkillian collapsed, stunned and prostrate upon the sand, his staff flew from his hands. Immediately, the arbiter moved quickly forward, taking a blocking position between the two contestants. He signaled the contest was finished. Honoring the arbitrator's hand signal, Kur promptly stepped away.

Assuming the initial formal posture, Kur placed one end of his staff upon the sand and faced his young prostrate opponent. It was with practiced mental discipline that he steadied his breathing and took control of his battle energy. During the fight the younger Arkillian had landed some heavy and painful blows. Now, beginning to feel his bruises, Kur managed his pain and suppressed an urge to wince.

Aided by his second, Ca struggled to first kneel, and with obvious difficulty, endeavored to stand. As he did, his second restored to him his previously dropped staff.

Straightening to the upright, Ca turned to face his older opponent. Resuming his initial formal posture, no trace of his earlier cockiness remained.

Having bested his younger opponent, and following tradition, Kur spoke first, and with apparent admiration. "Ca, you came with honor, and you are now noticed with honor."

Looking toward his elder, Ca was barely able to manage and speak through his pain. "Honored Kur. I am grateful for your notice and extend my earnest respect to you and your noble Nest."

The formal exchange ended both the duel and its painful lesson in respect and the proper manners toward elders.

Chapter Twenty-One:
Pink Pepper and Honey

She was bumping up against her deadline to complete Janet's study. Its constraints were broad, trade goods common both today and one-thousand years ago, and she was hoping the final group of commodities that made that cut would not be overwhelming.

With Gepeto walking briskly alongside, she entered into the study, looking toward her faithful digital assistant. "Good morning William."

"Good morning, Ma'am."

Is the initial standard deviation analysis of plausible trade categories completed?"

"Yes, Ms. Susie. Your specified Net-search of the Geneva archives has yielded a correlation of commodity by categories, each having import and export periodic fluctuations exceeding average annual three-standard deviations."

"Hopefully, your identified commodities list is not overly huge."

"Ms. Susie, the observed category list is short; coffee, tea, wheat, corn, beer, wine, spices, gold, silver, diamonds, rubies, sapphires, essential oils, silk, wool, molasses, and honey."

"A short list, that's a relief. Can you confirm all of the categories are within the specified boundary criteria?"

"Ms. Susie, coffee," William responded, "was not a common trade good one-thousand years ago."

Susie sighed. "We'll keep coffee on the list. Identify the next observed ambiguity."

"Ms. Susie, there are many distinct types of tea. Broadly identified, they are black, green, and herb. Which type of tea do you desire?"

"Include all three types of tea. Is there another ambiguity?"

There were, and Susie methodically refined the data list that William required before beginning his raw data acquisition. When her review was completed, she instructed William to print out a corrected list.

Scanning the list, with a smile she noted, white honey, amber honey, light amber honey, other honey, black pepper, green pepper, pink pepper, and white pepper. Humph, she thought, I wasn't even aware such diversity existed.

Finally satisfied with the list she instructed, "William, finalize the list as it is. You are to perform a Net-search. Using the Geneva World Trade Council commercial data archive, for each year since 1947 until now, you're to determine the quantity bought and sold of each item on the category list. Organize the raw data year-by-year. Then, organize each year by trade items. Next, organize each item by exporting countries and total export quantities; likewise, all importing countries and total imported quantities. Proceed with data acquisition. Advise me when the data is complete and ready for my review."

"Ms. Susie, data acquisition is initiated."

Turning, Susie walked over to where Gepeto was sitting and looking out of the floor-to-ceiling plate glass picture windows, looking down the hillside toward the ocean. The day before, he had been off leash and able to run along the beach at the nearby cove, where he intelligently avoided a lounging ten-foot long young male sea-elephant. Gepeto and the sea-elephant showed no sign of alarm, both seemed mutually curious about one another. But Susie noted that Gepeto adroitly chose to stay close to her as they walked past.

With a smile, Gepeto looked up at Susie, fully enjoying his wonderful view of the surrounding world. Sitting down in a chair, Susie reached out and rubbed Gepeto's ears, while musing about her work in progress.

There was something in its simple definition that still troubled her. Why would anyone at the Department of Commerce be interested in items traded one-thousand years ago? And, was it a mere coincidence that the topics list, which William's initial Net-search produced had included UFOs?

Standing up, she walked over to her desk and opened her work diary. Flipping through its pages, she located her earlier work session with William, and read, *William, given the hypothesis that interstellar travel exists, and interstellar trade does as well, then what would be the most valuable interstellar trade commodities?*

She knew the real-world answer was the most profitable trade goods were those that brought the highest legal return on the investment. That was basic common business sense, but it ignored the unmentioned and nagging question of illegal commerce, which often yielded multiples of honest returns.

Musing, she wondered, *Could the request from the Department of Commerce mean they were concerned about the possibility of illegal commerce between people on Earth and UFOs?* Although implausible, the idea was a stunning concept. Could her current analysis be determinative? That thought cast a new light on her work. If off-world trade actually existed, then it was a very well-kept secret. But, why keep it secret? A secret commerce implies it's an illegal commerce, not one open or consisting of fair-trade. If such off-world trade existed, no meaningful value could be placed on any of the items on her list.

Hmmm, what was it that William had said regarding probable trade items? Flipping through her notes, she located and read, *William, why do you specify pearls and not include diamonds or other gems? Diamonds are mineral, and they most probably occur in other solar systems, whereas a pearl is the biological product of a marine bivalve mollusk indigenous to the Earth, and is unlikely to be found elsewhere.*

Given William's guiding criteria, she reviewed the first list of trade items and immediately crossed off gold, silver, diamonds, rubies, and sapphires. All of these were items that should be available in other solar systems.

Well now, she thought, *if I were preparing a camel caravan over high mountains and hot burning deserts, what would I not carry?* Smiling, she deleted beer and wine. These items were heavy, consisting mostly of water. The concept of hauling water over interstellar distances made no sense.

She again read her dwindling list, musing, *coffee, tea, wheat, corn, and molasses,* noting these were organic products that could, in all likelihood, be transported as seeds and then grown on other worlds.

Her list was reduced to spices, essential oils, silk, wool, and honey. She momentarily considered the essential oils and spices, wondering, *Should I eliminate them using the same criteria utilized for evaluating coffee, tea, corn, and wheat? Nope,* she decided, *they stay on the list.* essential oils and spices were not items sold in bulk like wheat and corn. Given their special properties, she concluded they needed to be examined further.

Then, Susie noted silk, wool, and honey were all products of living creatures. The honey could be processed on Earth and reduced to its sugar form, eliminating the bulk of water. Wool was problematic; like seeds, sheep could be transported to some other world. Arbitrarily, Susie decided to retain wool on her list.

Silk and honey were unique, not only were they the products of insects, their production was dependent upon a unique interaction between the insects and specific flora. The idea of honey as a major interstellar commodity still troubled her. Even as a sugar product it was heavy.

Looking at her notes, she again considered William's comments; *Such items, materials, and substances would need to have a low mass-to-value ratio, be easily transported and held in high regard and value in one or more sentient cultures.*

This being true, she thought, *then honey would be a highly prized substance.* She again reviewed her modified list; *Spices, essential oils, silk, wool, and honey.*

"Hey, William, how are you doing?"

"Miss Susie, I am still extracting and organizing the raw data."

"Well, head's up, I've got an update for you."

She provided William with her modified list and then settled into her comfortable leather chair, waiting. There was an enormous amount of data to collect, filter, organize, and then evaluate. Monday morning, she knew, was not that far away.

It's going to be a long night.

Chapter Twenty-Two:
Foreboding

Although still more than a half-cycle travels distant, the Earth and its moon were visible on the view screens and out of the alcove observation dome. The blue planet and its large single moon were suspended in darkness; only about a fourth of their respective surfaces were illuminated.

Kur always felt a sense of wonder when approaching another world, and as he looked out of the observation dome at the twin crescents, he appreciated their geometric symmetry and stark beauty. Turning from the observation dome, he looked toward the two Arkillians sitting at the small table, the ship's captain and the Council's senior trade arbiter. Their meeting together was the first designated official action upon arrival. They, however, had accomplished most of the planning and preparation for arrival during the long voyage, so the meeting was essentially a formality.

"Captain, what is our current status?" Kur asked.

"Honored One, the ship will be in its solar orbit within one-third cycle. All shipboard functions and operations are within normal operating parameters. Once in orbit, and in accordance with your instructions, I will deploy eight fighters and establish a tactical perimeter. They are ordered to isolate and destroy any approaching vessels."

Kur acknowledged the Captain's report with a hand signal, then looked toward the trade arbiter. "Are you ready?"

"Yes, all cargo lifters are fully briefed and prepared. Once we are in our orbit, we will initiate the communications links into our Earth communication networks. Once that is achieved, we will download our standard requests for confirmations of our manifest to each of our earth-side providers.

"The manifests are extensive this trip, and it will take several cycles for us to fill all of them. After the normal manifests are filled and secured on board, we will begin filling the special orders, especially those requested by the Kreel.

"In general, all Nest representatives on board are working together without any noteworthy conflicts, at least, there are none reported."

With a hand gesture, Kur acknowledged the reports from the two Arkillians. Then, without further words, he stood and departed the alcove. His two servants, who had been waiting outside, fell into step behind him.

Being the senior Council member on board, Kur was obliged to confirm that standard arrival procedures were being followed. His next inspection was the Intelligence section. Because an Arkillian ship had not visited Earth in turns, it was essential they collect and analyze the data the concealed monitors had gathered during the intervening interval.

When Kur entered the Intelligence compartment, the officer in charge moved smartly to meet him, making a gesture of respect and then standing quietly at attention.

Kur took notice of the young officer's excellent military bearing, and his Nest badge. "Have you begun recovery of data from the surface?"

"Yes, Honored One. At present, we are acquiring data from the monitors on the planet's facing side. We are using standard parametric compressed burst encryption. That method harmonizes with the normal background noise of the planet's magnetosphere, which assists in masking the transmission. As the planet rotates, we anticipate continued and uninterrupted data collection."

Kur carefully studied the young Arkillian officer, and liked what he saw. The officer was alert, in what appeared to be excellent physical condition, and was impeccable in his uniform and manner. It was pleasing to Kur to know that Scion was still developing such admirable young military personnel. Accordingly, Kur extended an approving compliment.

"You are noticed and are a tribute to your Nest."

Having fulfilled his immediate duty, Kur departed the compartment. Inwardly, he was deeply troubled.

The Arkillians' influence in space was not as widespread as that of the Kreel. Yet, Kur believed given time the Arkillians would challenge the Kreel's economic dominance of interstellar commerce. The primary hurdle in achieving that goal was attaining advanced technology; the Kreel had ships that were superluminal, and the Kreel jealously guarded their technical secrets.

Of course, We have our own secrets, Kur mused with some pleasure. *Those secrets include our mind control technology. The Kreel may purchase and employ some of that technology, but without our assistance they cannot develop that technology further. And, the Council knows how to negotiate. The Kreel pay dearly for our assistance and pay handsomely for their special orders.*

Obtaining special orders for the Kreel was not always easy, but it was always highly profitable. Except for very few items, such as living human beings, which the Arkillians refused to consider chattel, they gave no serious or moral consideration why the Kreel so badly wanted animal body parts from some mammals on Earth.

Given their overt military posture and reports of aggressions, the Arkillians had no reason to trust the Kreel. Having once traveled as an ambassador on a Kreel ship to their three home worlds, Kur knew those planets were a considerable distance from Scion. Even with their superluminal ships, so far, the vast distances kept the Kreel from becoming overly obtrusive. *Perhaps,* Kur thought, *the best part of occasional trade with the Kreel was its infrequency.*

Retracing his steps along the passageway, Kur returned to the meeting alcove and took a seat. Once again, he looked out of the observation dome and studied the distant blue planet and its moon. It appeared altogether too quiet and peaceful. In contrast, Kur's inner intuitive sense was shouting an alarm.

For days, Kur had felt disquieted, feeling a growing nagging unease. He recognized the inner foreboding as a premonition of unseen, but imminent danger. Having survived several thousand turns, and numerous battles, he had long before learned to listen to such inner warnings. Acknowledging his apprehension, he was now taking the actions necessary to alleviate his concerns.

Notified of Kur's presence, the Captain entered the alcove and took his own seat. "Honored One, is there a problem?"

"Captain, while I lack confirmed information to prove that danger is near, I feel everything is not as it seems. I sense there is a tangible threat that we have yet to identify. My instincts demand caution, and you are therefore to take increased defensive measures.

"Cancel the deployment of the eight reconnaissance fighters previously scheduled. Instead, deploy one third of our 100 fighters. Make and hold ready the second third for immediate deployment. Keep the final third in reserve. You will use them to escort the cargo lifters during their retrieval assignments.

"Assume a full battle-ready condition. Establish more than a tactical perimeter. Instead, initiate a high-level sweep of nearby space, and reconnoiter back along our inbound path. Do you understand?"

"Honored One, I understand. It will be so."

"Good," Kur acknowledged.

Turning again toward the observation dome, he stared out into the vast obscuring darkness. He snarled inwardly, *I do not know who you are, but I know you are lurking out there, poised to strike. We are ready, come, taste the bitterness of your coming defeat.*

Chapter Twenty-Three:
The Taste of Crow

Outside it was hot, muggy, and extremely uncomfortable. Janet was grateful to enter the government complex and take refuge within its carefully controlled internal environment. While disliking not being on time, the report from Susie required more time to review than she had expected. Once again Susie had shown her acute ability to cut to the chase, and her results were unexpected and brilliantly troubling. When, in light banter, Susie had asked if the study had anything to do with UFOs, she had winced. How had Susie possibly connected a market research assignment with UFOs? Sidestepping, she had responded, *No, UFOs fall under the purview of the Department of Transportation*. Susie had laughed at her answer, yet sounded unconvinced.

As Janet moved deeper into the building, concealed cameras scanned her features, including facial proportions, the shape of her ears, her weight, height, length of stride, the color of her eyes and hair, and complexion. The security computers compared these biometric measurements against the data on file and verified it agreed with the unique data echo scanned from her nametag. While the nametag could be counterfeited, the security file on record could not be. The three-tiered crosschecking verified who she was and that she had legitimate business within the building.

The zones of security level increased as she continued toward her destination. If the computers had determined she lacked clearance, she would immediately be denied further access and security personnel would be directed to her position. The system worked in both directions, if anyone attempted to enter an unauthorized area, the system blocked further progress while simultaneously locking the doors behind that person, denying possible exit. Thereafter, security personnel would arrive and the potential infiltrator would be questioned.

As she took an elevator and hurried along, the number of people walking in the corridors lessened. Reaching her destination, she was slightly out of breath. The plain door before her displayed a simple title on a brass plaque, Charles Sullivan, Under Secretary of Commerce.

Turning the knob and entering the room, Janet smiled at Lois, who was sitting dutifully at her desk outside the inner office. "It seems to be my turn to be late," she said.

Entering the conference room, she saw that Charles, Darrell, and Carl were seated around the small circular oak conference table, all being in conversation with each other. There were numerous documents spread out before them. They stopped talking as Janet took her chair and by way of explanation, she held up copies of Susie's report.

"Darrell, it's my turn to eat crow. Your idea of an import export analysis was simple and insightful. Carl's recommendation that the initial search be restricted to trade goods common today and one-thousand years ago also paid off.

"Based upon what my researcher has discovered, there's a correlation in the trade patterns indicating there is trade occurring when Monstro visits. And, there's several strong correlations that support that possibility. The data certainly warrants further investigation. An expanded search will undoubtedly find more indicators."

"Janet, is there sufficient information to point Carl's team toward anyone specifically involved in trade with Monstro?" Charles asked.

"Yes sir. While this is only a preliminary study, I believe there's more than sufficient information to give Carl and his team a solid beginning point."

As she spoke, she handed copies of the report to each of the men, and they promptly began scanning through its pages.

After a minute or so, with a sigh, Carl looked up from the report and toward Charles. "Sir, if Darrell's data is correct, then Monstro will be in its parking orbit within a few hours. My time to get ready appears to be short. I want to get this study over to my team, so we can begin our investigation. If any of this works out, I want to have a team on the ground at every point on this planet involved in any transfers with Monstro."

"Carl, just remember our primary objective is gathering meaningful intelligence on Monstro and its activities. You are to remain circumspect about your investigation. Whoever is active in trade, if such trade is confirmed, needs to be identified. Covert interstellar trade reeks of careful planning, deception, and possible hostile intentions. I don't care if they are only trading postcards, I intend to rip their covers off.

"I don't want two or three obvious people; I want the entire network. Furthermore, I want to know how they operate, where they get and hide their money, and how long they've been participating in off-world commerce.

"Am I making myself clear?" Charles said.

"Very clear, Sir."

As Carl left the conference room, Janet looked to Darrell questioningly. "Did I understand Carl to say that Monstro is only several hours away? Monstro must have made better time than your initial estimates indicated."

"It has. For some unknown reason they altered their deceleration curve. It has retained a higher approach velocity than usual and is only now beginning an abrupt braking maneuver. It's operating significantly outside its normal envelope. Fortunately, we got our new satellites into position before their arrival, so we are monitoring Monstro's entire flight path. We haven't a clue why Monstro is deviating from its normal behavior, but the propulsion signatures we're getting are the best we've ever obtained. The engineers at the advanced propulsion research group are having a field day with the new data."

The phone on Charles' desk chimed, and standing, he moved quickly and picked it up. "Sullivan here."

Janet observed as Charles listened, his expression growing tense. After several moments, he hung up the phone and returned to his chair, then looked at Darrell.

"The change in Monstro's deceleration curve is not the only significant difference in its arrival profile. Space command reports Monstro is transmitting a wide spectrum of what looks to be active search patterns, as if they're looking for something. It's also deploying groups of fighters, and they're spreading out in formations. I've just been informed that our military is alarmed and going to a heightened state of readiness.

"Darrell, keep me posted on any new developments in your analysis. Immediately report anything out of the ordinary. something we don't understand has badly spooked Monstro, and I've got a bad feeling about what's happening."

"Understood, Sir," Darrell said.

"Janet, you're commended for your report. Your results were unexpected, but they may begin to explain part of the puzzle surrounding Monstro."

"Sir, the real credit belongs to a very special young lady. She is insightful, and her work is of the highest professional standard," Janet said.

Charles stood, signaling the end of the meeting. "It's time for the both of you to get back to work. Janet, whoever that young lady is, give her my compliments. Now, the both of you clear out, I've got work to do," Charles said.

Chapter Twenty-Four:
Mid-Watch

The hour was late, Lan was quiet, and Zorn was on duty in the CAC. Others working around him were focused on multiple data streams coming in from deployed monitors.

Zorn was watching the image of the inbound alien ship; it was filling the monitor screen. The optics on the sentinel had detected the Capital ship hours earlier, and it continued tracking the target since its optical acquisition. As the ship neared the third planet, Zorn noticed when the ship abruptly terminated deceleration. The departure from a steady deceleration curve was the first observed deviation from an otherwise smooth approach. The maneuver immediately caught his attention, and he sent a short message to Roy, who was then in his quarters.

The two men now sat beside each other, each having large mugs of hot neab in their hands. The image of the ship being relayed from the sentinel was sharp and clear. Roy saw them first. Dozens of fighters were erupting from the middle of the ship, then separating into precise groups of four fighters each. They promptly began to disperse.

Zorn sighed, "So much for blocking their fighters before they deploy."

Picking up a handset, Roy keyed a button, then waited for an acknowledgment. There was a momentary silence, then Lorn's rather tired voice responded. "Shaw here."

"Lorn, sorry to wake you. I'm in CAC. You'd better get here as quickly as you can. The target is coming in hot and battle ready. They're deploying fighters on their final approach."

There was no verbal response, but Roy heard a click, as the communicator was closed. In less than three minutes Lorn entered the CAC. Behind him came four of his tactical staff members, including Elayne. As the staff members moved to their individual plot stations, Lorn came directly over to Roy and Zorn.

"I thought you might like this," Zorn said, holding out a hot mug of neab.

Lorn accepted the mug, thanked Zorn, and turned and study the monitor.

"How many fighters are deployed?" Lorn asked.

"So far, about thirty. Some are moving into what looks to be a protective screen. Others are doing a fine-grid search, as if they expect trouble. They seem to know what they're doing; their maneuvers are crisp and efficient," Roy said.

"Humph, I knew it was a brute, but it's only when you compare the ship with the size of its fighters that its real size becomes apparent. It's massive," Lorn mused.

"Incredible, the target is not employing any stealth or even attempting to conceal its activities. In fact, they're active on a broad range of frequencies and appear battle ready. By all the muses, it'll require some time just to sort out the sensor data. Are we collecting communications traffic?" Zorn asked.

"Yes, we're way ahead of you. The sentinel was given a high priority command to monitor any communications from or directed toward the target," Lorn said.

"Humph, they're definitely using some Kreel technology, but given their tactics I don't think they're Kreel," Roy said.

Suddenly, the monitor screens went dark. There followed an immediate chorus of murmuring throughout the CAC. There were long minutes of anxiety, then the monitors brightened. Nearly filling the screen was an image of one of the fighters. After only a moment, the screens again went dark.

Slowly, Zorn let out his held breath. "If the sentinel was forced to suspend its data link, they had to be getting close. But that fighter looked close enough to ask the pilot to smile for the little birdy," Zorn said.

"Did that fighter look familiar to you?" Lorn asked Zorn.

Zorn paused a moment and studied the stored image of the fighter; then, he affirmed, "Maybe, it looks like an old frontline Kreel design, but one back a thousand years ago. You'll find it listed in the Kreel database as a Type-32. It's old, but very capable and nimble."

During their conversation, other crew members had been arriving, and CAC was slowly filling up. Again, the image transmitted from the sentinel returned and their monitors brightened, now showing a group of four fighters moving in a diamond formation. One fighter was leading with two trailing and the fourth lagging slightly aft and below the leader. The sentinel maintained tracking of the group, showing the four craft as they split smoothly out from their initial formation. The lagging fighter moved forward and in line with the front fighter, forming a staggered line abreast. As if one fighter was a pivot, the remaining three swept about and assumed a new heading. The maneuver was precise.

As the fighters completed a 30-degree turn, four beams of green laser light stabbed through the darkness. Where the four laser beams converged, there was a sudden brilliant flash. Without pause, the fighters continued their turn, smoothly transforming once more into their original diamond formation.

Zorn observed it all with an experienced appreciation. "That was smooth and effective. Really, quite impressive."

Roy was checking the data stream coming in from the remote sensors and soon determined the coordinates of the explosion, "They just eliminated one of the satellites our sentinel observed moving out from the third planet."

During the next three and a half hours, the long-range detectors on Lan, and its deployed monitors, observed two additional explosions, both were satellites deployed from the third planet. During the fighters' close-grid search, the images from the sentinel were interrupted more than a dozen times. One interval of interruption lasted more than twenty minutes. Tension within the CAC escalated, until the data stream was reestablished. As the fighters expanded their search grid, the frequency of interrupted data lessened.

The tactical methods and procedures utilized by a military organization are like fingerprints, unique and revealing. Those on Lan knew there was a high probability they would be committed to battle with the target being observed. Therefore, they considered every nuance of the target's tactical method critical.

The speaker softly intoned, "Captain in Combat Analysis Center;" Kellon stood quietly for a moment studying the main tactical display screens, then walked to where Roy, Lorn, and Zorn were working.

"Roy, what's your current assessment?" Kellon said.

"Sir, my guess is something spooked the target. Just what isn't clear. Assuming the target is carrying a full complement, it appears to have deployed about a third of its fighters. This suggests an alert status, not a prelude to imminent battle. Zorn may have some observations that might interest you."

"Zorn, what do you have?" Kellon asked.

"Sir, what we've observed adds to the puzzle. The fighters deployed appear to be an older Kreel design, dating back more than a thousand years. My assessment is the target is not Kreel, but rather some culture that's working in conjunction with the Kreel," Zorn said.

"What do you base your deduction on?"

"Sir, there are several observed telling conditions. First, the pop patterns are Kreel-like, but not Kreel. The target is of Kreel manufacture, but subluminal and more than two-thousand years behind current Kreel technology. Their fighters are similarly outdated. Finally, the observed tactics are definitely not Kreel. I don't believe the Kreel would handicap their own forces with old technology. Still, they might sell that older technology to a client culture, while keeping the military advantage of modern technology to themselves. Given these conditions, what I believe we're dealing with here is a previously unknown non-Kreel culture, one that's doing business with the Kreel."

"Humph, your deduction would explain a host of conflicting issues. It makes good sense," Kellon mused.

"Roy, how long will it take your team to evaluate the target's search and sensor data? I'm particularly concerned about their ability to compromise our stealth capability," Kellon said.

"Sir, it'll take at least a day to prepare a preliminary report."

"Roy, given the behavior of that assault ship, we may not have a day before we're committed to battle. I expect your preliminary report on my desk in six hours," Kellon said.

"Yes, Sir," Roy said.

Chapter Twenty-Five:
Import and Export

Once her curiosity had been awakened, Susie found it impossible to push the possibility of an existing interstellar trade out of her thoughts. While going back over the lists of imports and exports with William, several companies caught her attention. Because of their global size and business advertising, a few of those companies were easily recognized; others were companies she knew nothing about. In particular, one company stood out– Gumbolt Import and Export. It was mostly the location of the company home office and its wide flung affiliated satellite facilities that intrigued her. The company's distribution network seemed oddly skewed, with its home facility and overseas branches generally located in diverse and sparse regions.

Why, she reasoned, *would a company involved in international import and export locate one of their largest facilities and warehouse terminals in a remote mountainous area, far from major rail or port facility?* That such a company might be located in the mountains of Switzerland was odd. Likewise, the company was established in the eleventh century, as Gerhold Gumbolt; it was still closely held by one family. Here were all the tantalizing elements of a grand mystery, one she felt compelled to examine.

The more she analyzed the company, the more intrigued she became. As harebrained as her idea of a secret interstellar trade might be, curiosity was akin to a nagging hunger, and she intended to feed that hunger. Besides, a brief visit to Switzerland might prove a wonderful tonic for chronic overwork.

Having some spare time between jobs, she decided to do some personal snooping regarding her hunch. After making up her mind, she instructed William to arrange for the necessary hotel, ground transportation, sub-orbital shuttle flight from San Francisco to Paris, and to obtain an Inter-European States monorail system pass. When purchasing the tickets, the International Transit Information Center routinely crosschecked her personal data, comparing her personal information with both national and international criminal and government census data. Her identity was verified, and it was certified no outstanding warrants existed concerning her in any jurisdiction. Therefore, she was issued a silver-clearance security password for the entire trip. The password, along with her authenticated physical characteristics and photograph, were encrypted and downloaded with her itinerary directly into her personal cellular communicator. The entire process took less than half an hour. After arranging with a neighbor to take care of Gepeto, she carefully packed and was then on her way.

After checking her luggage at the monorail station in Paso Robles, the express high-speed monorail trip to the San Francisco New Commerce Center took less than an hour. As Susie traveled through the coastal transportation system, embedded security computers interfaced with her personal cellular communicator, noting her silver-clearance security International password and verified her matching physical characteristics. The ground transportation security computers dutifully alerted and updated International Air Transportation Security of her changing locations.

Without impediment, from the SFO Center Arrival hub she used the elevated moving passenger belt network to reach the outer public areas of the Trans Orbital Airways facilities at SFO International. It was but a short distance from its general public area to the restricted Trans Orbital Airways departure courtesy lounge. On entering the lounge, one of the Trans Orbital Airways hosts pleasantly greeted her by name, offering her a courtesy beverage, and directed her to comfortable seating. Just beyond the transparent carbon composite safety window, part of the glittering swept wing and one of the hydrogen scramjet engines on the San Francisco Paris shuttle was visible. Looking about, Susie casually observed the hustle and bustle of the busy airport. Regardless of how frequently she traveled, there was always the air of excitement at busy airports. Today was no exception.

When her cellular communicator vibrated, signaling it was time to board the shuttle, she walked the short distance to the boarding gate.

Once on board the shuttle, she found her seat and casually looked around the cabin and its typical cramped seating. It was going to be a full flight. She sighed and mentally prepared herself to settle in for her hopefully uneventful journey.

The only thing Susie actually disliked about the shuttle was its poor quality of in-flight food. In self-defense she had packed some snacks into her small carry-on bag. *Why,* she thought, *is it so hard for a company to provide reasonable fare for the traveling public? Must they always offer the same token bad coffee and bag of stale peanuts?* She sighed; *Some things just never seem to change.*

Upon arriving in Paris, she walked the short distance to the high-speed European monorail terminal that was located at the airport, taking the next express coach between Paris and Bern.

After the long and bloody global era of social and religious upheavals that had defined the first centuries of the new millennium, the separate Sovereign European Nations had stubbornly held to their own unique national identities, thereby enriching the whole tapestry of Europe. From Susie's own historical viewpoint, such intrinsic national identity and loyalty was an often-proven commendable governing system. She had never trusted any proponent of a "one-world government" or any of its managing global industrial cartels. Her narrow viewpoint was any rational person trying to reason with even a small bureaucracy typically experienced frustration. The very concept of a huge one-world bureaucracy, euphemistically called a one-world government, should be enough to scare any rational and still sane person.

Arriving in Bern, Susie walked from her express coach along the platforms and then out to the public street. She knew William had leased and scheduled a rental car to meet her upon arrival. Standing curbside, Susie checked the nearest column number, then entered and sent it to the waiting car. Within minutes a gleaming new touring coupe pulled up smoothly before her and stopped, greeting her even as its gull wing passenger door lifted and the stepping panel extruded. She had always delighted in the gull wing design, and silently thanked William for his good choice.

After the hours of being crowded into public conveyances, she was looking forward to the ride to her hotel. When she slipped into the passenger seat, the AI addressed her in a distinct German accent. "Good afternoon, Ms. Wells. My name is Roth, but you may address me by another name, if you desire. I am pleased to advise you that your luggage has safely arrived, and it is properly stowed in the boot. Your William has provided me a list of your dining and beverage preferences. If you desire, I will display these for your review and update."

Susie leaned back into the seat and felt the soft leather embrace her tired body. "Roth, you can address me as Susie. There is no need to review William's list of preferences. If you happen to have a cold root beer, I would be most grateful."

There was a soft hum and a cold beverage container emerged from the accessory console between the driver and passenger seats. Susie twisted off the top and took a grateful sip of the ice-cold beverage. "Thank you, Roth. Now, please take me by the most direct route to my hotel."

An acknowledging tone sounded, the car started, and safety restraints gently moved into place across her shoulders and over her lap. The car eased out from its parking slot and began to move expertly through the busy monorail station arrival area.

As the car merged with and moved with the bustling city traffic, Roth asked, "Do you prefer silence, music, light conversation, or sight-seeing highlights?"

Susie pondered the question a moment, "I prefer music, preferably solo piano played softly. Roth, if we do pass any facility belonging to the Gumbolt Import and Export Company, then by all means provide me a brief annotation."

Roth acknowledged her request with another melodious tone, as the car proficiently moved through and out of the city traffic, heading along a sweeping highway toward the towering nearby mountains. Susie found the seat controls and moved the seat to its most reclined position. Leaning back into the seat, she relaxed and sighed. Embraced by the sensuous vitality of the grand piano notes filling the coupe cabin, with pleasure she smiled at her surroundings. The car steadily increased its speed....

Chapter Twenty-Six:
Cargo Carriers

The busy days of uploading cargo from a planet's surface were always active and exciting. After the long voyage, the abrupt shift to a heightened physical activity was welcome. At such times Kur enjoyed walking through the cargo and hangar areas. The hangar he was then walking in was but one of ten allocated to handling cargo, and all the hangars were bustling.

Commerce on every planet was unique. On some worlds with other similar life forms commerce was open and bidirectional. On several worlds, those where the Arkillians had established dominance, they moved openly and defiantly in their unilateral one-sided trade objectives. Earth in many ways was different; in the beginning the subjugation of Earth was achieved by use of brute global destruction, and it made no difference whatsoever if the surviving human mammals observed Arkillian ships overhead. Millenniums later the Arkillians deftly fostered a perception among the human mammals that Arkillians were gods descending from heaven above. With primitive species such subterfuge had proven to be a profitable ploy.

Things had changed. Fourteen thousand years previous, when Earth was made primitive, none then sitting on the Council had foreseen the rapid burst of advanced military technologies the racial conflicts they had purposefully engineered would produce. During the past five hundred years the bickering mammals had developed thermo nuclear weapons and rudimentary interplanetary space capabilities. They even sent a few rudimentary long-term subluminal probes to several nearby solar systems, including to Scion. That unanticipated act alone, like nothing before, warned the council the human mammals posed a potential threat. Upon return to Scion, Kur intended to demand the Council take immediate action to once again render primitive the population of the Earth.

Turning, Kur observed Rin was walking toward him, and his facial markings revealed a heightened state of agitation. Upon reaching Kur, Rin extended but a cursory gesture of respect.

"Honored Kur, I have just learned the deployment of fighters was the direct result of your instructions. It appears we need to discuss the matter."

Kur had judged it was best to keep his own troubled thoughts private; besides, there was no good reason to mention his foreboding to Rin. That the Captain was alerted was sufficient.

"Rin, there is nothing needing discussion. My instructions were precautionary, permitting an examination of some of your recent concerns about Earth's technology."

"Good, it is time you finally listen to my concerns. And, it seems our precautions proved fruitful, several nearby satellites monitoring our activities were detected and destroyed. It now appears we are arriving in a predictable manner. Even from a rudimentary military viewpoint, it is unwise for us to be both detectable and predictable, especially by a lower mammal species."

"Rin, we have a strong contingency of deployed fighters, and this ship is combat ready. Our fighter sweeps of surrounding space are continuing.

As for the few satellites being positioned to observe this ship, I remind you we are at a Lagrange point. There is no evidence that the destroyed probes were there to watch us, and their proximity is undoubtedly simple coincidence. To conclude otherwise is indulging in paranoid thinking."

Rin looked unconvinced, but looking around the busy hangar area, he asked, "Are you going down on any of the cargo runs?"

The question surprised Kur. He had not set foot on Earth for more than a thousand turns and had no desire to do so again.

"No, there is a great deal of work remaining to do here with the analysis section. They are beginning to analyze the uploaded intelligence data from our Earth-side monitors. There will most likely be some adjustments needed in the suppression field before we depart. That demands we evaluate the current political dynamics on Earth and the existing tensions before deciding what changes need be made.

"Why do you ask? Are you thinking about going down?" Kur asked.

"I have had thoughts about doing so. Still, I am not certain it is prudent, and yet it might be a valuable experience. It would be my first time to stand on that planet. Do you think it would be a worthwhile experience?"

Kur remembered the first time he had stood on Earth. It was long ago, but he remembered it was an exhilarating experience. Of course, there were always associated risks. If there were any serious mechanical problems, the outcome could prove fatal. Still, the idea of hitching a ride in one of the new fighters was alluring. They were some of the Arkillians' most recent acquisitions from the Kreel, sleek wedge-shaped craft that were fast and very maneuverable, both in space and in a planetary atmosphere.

"Rin, standing on Earth is something you should experience. Still, I recommend you take the process one step at a time. First, take an atmospheric flight with one of the escort fighters. Later, go with a Tactical Support Unit. They have the means of securing the landing area and the appropriate weapons needed to assure if trouble does develop, you have the muscle needed for an expeditious extraction. Remember, it would not be considered good news for a member of the High Council to be lost and wandering somewhere about on Earth."

As they watched, five cargo lifters, two tactical support ships, and four fighters were being prepared for the first drop. The cargo lifters were silver cylinders, appearing somewhat stubby in length and because of their width they looked squat. The lifter was designed for easy access, having wide cargo doors and retracting ramps, which allowed direct cargo movement into or out of the ship. The tactical support ships were of similar design, but with a smaller and narrower profile. The weapons blisters positioned on the tactical support ships gave them a distinctly aggressive look, and each carried heavy armaments and a team of ground security troops. Their task was establishing a security perimeter about the cargo retrieval point and to assure there was no interference with the lifters during cargo extraction. The fighters provided top cover for the groundside operations and acted as scouts to monitor the larger region around the landing area. The fighters also provided added striking power to reinforce the tactical support ships, as required.

"Honored Kur, why do we go through such difficulty, why not simply move the ship into the atmosphere and announce our demands?"

Kur winced with the suggestion. His inner sense of danger was troubling, and the last thing he wanted was an unnecessary act of bravado that could only increase risk to the ship. Accompanying his rising inner sense of pending threat, there was an unaccustomed sense of vulnerability, which he disliked. His awareness sharpened the fact they were but a single ship and far from home.

"Remember Rin, our goal here is economic, not military. The explicit purpose for this voyage is commerce, and overt military action on the planet would be contrary to standing Council policy. We are here to extract trade goods, not to alter existing Council policy concerning this planet. Still, if given cause to use force, we will exhibit that force in a substantial fashion."

As they spoke, a warning buzzer sounded in the hangar. Those who were not aboard the ready ships moved quickly away from the launch area. a transparent atmospheric barrier began dropping from its retainer above and then magnetically sealed to the bulkheads and deck. Vacuum pumps began evacuating the atmosphere from the launch area. As Kur and Rin watched, the outer hull split vertically, and the hangar doors slid open, opening the active hangar to the dark void of hard space.

One by one, the ships gently lifted on invisible magnetic cushions and moved toward the exit. The fighters moved out first and were immediately followed by the tactical support ships. The cargo lifters departed last. The entire sequence was quickly completed. After the last ship exited, the launch cycle reversed, and the atmospheric barrier slid smoothly up into its storage retainer. The now empty hangar had a hollow sound and there was a sharp frigid bite to the air. Later, when the cargo ships returned, their holds would be brimming with immense wealth.

Nodding to Rin, Kur turned away and walked toward the hangar exit. He needed to analyze the tactical reports from the fighters on long-range patrol and the reports from the tactical sensor groups. His inner warning alarm systems were strident, they would not permit him to further disregard them....

Chapter Twenty-Seven:
A Fat Stationary Target

While dropping sunward, Shey was focused on her passive sensors. Although lacking a programmed sense of humor, when she noticed an odd logic circuit feedback, she followed her instruction and entered the event into her programmers' file, noting it as possible amusement.

As a normal part of her holographic stealth performance capability, Shey could alter the apparent shape and color of her outer appearance. This stealth capability allowed her to blend like a chameleon with any background. Normally while in space she wore flat black from her stem to stern. In contrast, when on parade, she wore the proud glistening white and gold trim of the Guardian Force. She liked those clean bright colors and took every opportunity to display them.

At the moment she was not wearing her parade colors or flat black. Instead, she was wearing bright new colors, scarlet and green. They were unlike any colors she had previously worn. It was this alteration in her appearance that had produced the odd feedback in her logic circuits.

Since its appearance, Captain Kellon considered the alien Capital ship a potential threat, one about which they lacked any meaningful tactical data. To correct the problem, Roan and Zorn had proposed a high-risk mission to Captain Kellon. They reasoned if Shey detuned her propulsion signature to that of a Dargon fighter, and displayed Dargon hive colors, it might be possible for her to attain an optimal firing position near the alien ship. If it failed to detect Shey, then they would have proven their full stealth capability was tactically adequate. If Shey was detected, then they would execute an immediate withdrawal.

Zorn had recommended the tactical profile of a Dargon fighter as camouflage because its propulsion was efficient and not easily detected. He reasoned, either by direct contact or through interaction with the Kreel, the aliens might be aware of the Dargon. If perchance Shey was detected, a Dargon signature could only mislead the aliens to a false conclusion. Of course, The downside of Zorn's plan was if Shey was lost in action, then the fat would be in the fire.

Captain Kellon had viewed the plan favorably, and being himself a master of artful misdirection, authorized Roan and Zorn to alter Shey's tactical profile to that of a Dargon fighter. Working together through the night, Roan and Zorn retuned Shey's propulsion and reprogrammed her holographic image.

To minimize the threat to Shey, Kellon ordered Scout ships Sheba, Misty, and Cindy to move to a blocking location along Shey's planned exit path. Their mission was to block and if required strip off any fighters pursuing Shey. The mission was to be a Scout reconnaissance in force.

When beginning the mission, Roan had moved them to a departure point located well above the Ecliptic Plane. Once there, she had put on her new holographic shape and bright colors.

Dropping sunward, Shey intercepted the track line the target had followed as it approached the third planet. They were now moving offset and parallel to that original track, rapidly approaching the Capital ship.

As they approached the outer fighter screen, Roan inquired, "Status."

"Weapon system set Condition 2; all missiles ready standby. Currently tracking six deployed groups of fighters; one is deployed as a close protective cover. The others are dispersed, each is about twenty minutes flight time from their Capital ship. We're currently three minutes from the closest-point-of approach with the outermost group.

"While we're using the Dargon signature, I feel like we're adorned with bright navigation running lights. Suddenly, I'm missing our stealth capability."

"You're now missing our stealth capability? When everything comes unglued, remember this entire mission was your bright idea," Roan retorted.

"Well, if we manage to survive, remind me to stop having bright ideas," Zorn grumbled.

They were both holding their breath as they reached the CPA with the outer most fighter group and slipped past, continuing uninterrupted toward their primary objective. As they passed CPA, both men let out quiet sighs of relief. There was no telltale sign of having been detected.

"Zorn, those fighters are well positioned to block a retreat. If we are detected, we might need to fight our way out. How far are we from the optimum firing point?" Roan asked.

"Five minutes."

"Shey, set the Kreel screamer to Condition 2," Roan ordered.

"Kreel screamer is set Condition 2," Shey acknowledged.

In Shey's compact control room, the five minutes sped past. Then, Roan's fingers moved deftly over his controls, as he directed Shey to the predetermined firing location. That position was located tactically offset from the target and it placed Shey nearer to the third planet than was the alien ship. Roan eased Shey into her predefined position and then aligned her heading to the planned evasion vector. They were then holding a zero-relative velocity referenced to the Capital ship.

As if he might be overheard, Zorn whispered, "Confirming, we're at the optimum firing point.

"The target is using a scattered phase active signal with random search patterns. I'm detecting some new intriguing variations in frequency harmonics, but the basic signal structure is pure old classic Kreel. There're some odd fringes on several side lobes. Still, there's nothing in their active search pattern that should be able to map us. Given their active profile, the probability is their passive sensor sensitivity is also old Kreel and isn't likely able to detect our Dargon configuration. So, now that we're arrived safe, and proven our stealth is effective, what's next?" Zorn said.

"For starters, keep your eyes on those fighters. They're a bit close for comfort. As for what's next, since we've successfully answered our primary question, let's see if we can determine the actual detection threshold of their passive sensors. I'm going to gradually increase our propulsion profile and see what happens. When the target does detect us and this close, it will flag us a threat. Stay sharp, and keep your eyes on those fighters."

"Roan, I'm not worried about their blasted fighters. We can outrun them, but how do you propose to outrun a main laser barrage? "Zorn asked.

"Not to worry, I've got it covered. But, when they do detect us, be sure to let me know," Roan said.

Zorn groaned. "Shey, we're about to become a fat stationary target. Roan, I don't remember my bright idea included an offer to provide free target services. Please note, I'm putting in for an immediate transfer to the cooks and bakers' school."

"So, noted," Roan said, with a smile.

Zorn's banter, like Roan's, was lighthearted, but every fiber in their bodies was taut. As Roan keyed in the evasion sequence, Zorn continued scanning his detection and countermeasure data readouts.

"Shey, on my mark, immediately go to sixty percent acceleration," Roan ordered.

"Acknowledged."

"Shey, increase our ambient propulsion radiation signature by two percent."

"Signal is increased."

After several minutes passed, Roan whispered, "Shey, increase the signal strength another two percent."

"Increasing," Shey acknowledged.

Incrementally, Roan continued increasing Shey's ambient signature.

Once, Zorn glanced over and noted the radiated signal strength. He winced.

"Why am I beginning to feel like Shey is a flashing light bulb?" Zorn mumbled.

Shey's propulsion signal had been incrementally increased 28 percent, when Zorn nearly jumped from his seat, shouting, "Move. They've got us."

"Shey, mark. Accelerate. Fire the screamer." Roan ordered.

Chapter Twenty-Eight:
Who Done It

Her propulsion system growled thunderously, as Shey optimized her acceleration toward the nearby planet. "Screamer launched," Shey reported.

"Now you've done it, Roan. We've got their undivided attention; here come the fighters. The screamer is active," Zorn reported.

A jammer, the screamer was transmitting a strong broadband electromagnetic signal with narrow bandpass apertures that permitted Shey's tactical sensors to continue to operate. The screamer was effectively saturating the aliens' primary active and passive sensors, momentarily masking Shey's movements.

"Shey, execute evasion 3. Drop radiated propulsion signature to initial Dargon settings. Increase acceleration to 80 percent. While they're blind, get a laser sample of the Capital ship's hull," Roan ordered.

Sharply altering her course, she maneuvered to a widely diverging vector normal to the bearing line of the Capital ship. "Complying," Shey said.

A volley of slashing energies sliced through the volume of space immediately behind Shey. The proximity of the laser barrage caused Zorn to flinch, as he remained focused on his tactical and countermeasure readouts.

"They've launched more fighters. They must have been on immediate deployment standby. The fighters are opening into a tactical pattern and vectoring directly toward our previous position. The outer screens of fighters are moving toward the Capital chip. The odds seem fair, about forty to one," Zorn reported.

"Shey, target the Capital ship and launch the Zed decoys, spread Delta-5. Zorn, this is getting tight, stay sharp."

Once launched, the decoys moved in full stealth mode, arching high and out away from Shey. Dispersing, the probes maneuvered into a staggered battle formation and dropped stealth. Going active, they were moving directly toward the

Capital ship. They were programmed to simulate the propulsion signatures of Dargon battle cruisers. To a tactical team on the Capital ship the simulated Dargon cruisers appeared from nowhere. Posing an imminent threat, they demanded an immediate counteraction. The fighters broke away from pursuit of Shey and moved toward blocking positions, preparing to oppose the new threats.

Having completed the athwartship evasion, Roan again directed Shey back toward the planet, "Shey, set evasion 1."

"Our screamer and decoys have self-destructed on schedule," Zorn reported.

Roan's intention was to first reach and then swing about the planet, putting its bulk between Shey and her pursuit. When masked by the planet, he intended to set full stealth and break out into the safety of deep space.

"These guys are quick, they have figured out our evasion route and some fighters have taken up pursuit, but our lead is comfortable and growing," Zorn reported.

Having outdistanced her pursuit, Shey began arching around the planet. "Look out. Four fighters closing at 340, low. They're coming in hot and we're painted." Zorn warned.

"Shey, target identified threats, set Condition 1," Roan ordered.

Breaking to port, Shey pitched down and maneuvered directly toward the incoming fighters. Her forward point defense lasers and gun turrets firing in short bursts, Shey engaged the enemy. Zorn heard Roan mutter, as he evaded to starboard, while driving Shey deeper into the planet's atmosphere, while angling for the night side.

"By all the fires of Tartarus, that was tight. As we passed, Shey hit two of them. One is adrift and the second is disengaging. The remaining two have reversed their course and are beginning hot pursuit. Roan, if we stay in atmosphere, the other inbound fighters will catch up. This is a really good time to exit stage right."

Roan had been forced to direct Shey deep into the atmosphere, pushing her hull temperature to its limit. "Is our heliographic profile holding?"

"Systems are in the red, but holding - Look out, two more fighters rising from below, bearing 315," Zorn warned.

Roan broke hard to port. "Shey, target all hostile ships and fire."

Shey's laser turrets and guns erupted, firing even as she angled to evade the four intercepting fighters. Two light missiles streaked aft toward the pursuing fighters.

"The two lower fighters have disengaged; they were both hit and damaged. One pursuing fighter has disintegrated. The second fighter appears badly damaged and has disengaged," Zorn reported.

"It's long past time to get out of here," Roan muttered.

Entering the planet night side, Roan set full stealth, then broke vertically up and out of the atmosphere, soaring outward, reaching for the safety of stealth and deep space.

After a few minutes, Roan inquired, "How are we doing?"

Frowning, Zorn sighed. "We appear to be in one piece and in the clear. That's more than some of the opposition can say. Roan, that got a bit too worrisome. For the record, the next time you want to provide free target services for hostile Capital ships or fighters, don't even think of inviting me to your little party.

"According to my tactical sensors, we stirred up a hornets' nest. If there were any undeployed fighters, they're now all wide-awake and fully deployed. It looks like the Zed decoys really shook them up, and they've assumed a tight defensive screen about the Capital ship. My recommendation is that we quietly go home and leave it up to the bad guys to figure out who done it."

"Shey, set weapons Condition 2. As soon as security protocol permits, send a status report."

Ten minutes later, Shey had located a secure communications node and signaled their status. An hour later, Roan set Condition 3, and shortly thereafter they rendezvoused with Shey's waiting sisters. At rendezvous they matched velocities and flowed into a precise three-sided pyramid battle formation, with Shey at its point. It was only then that Roan and Zorn began to unwind.

While Roan asked Shey for background music, Zorn unbuckled his restraining harness and moved aft into the galley. He returned in a few minutes with two steaming mugs of neab. Roan's frown and obvious concentration made it clear to Zorn that he was even then formulating his post action report.

Zorn knew that Roan had to somehow justify his command decision to intentionally allow Shey to be detected. *Ouch,* Zorn thought, *the Captain is going to have both our hides nailed to a bulkhead and salted. By all the muses, the fallout from our little escapade is at best unpredictable and at worst even more unpredictable.* Zorn sighed, *Oh boy, here it comes, brace for incoming.*

Moving in silent unison away from the solar primary, the four Scouts were returning to outer darkness and the waiting warm security of Lan's hangars. For a long while Shey had remained quiet, and when she spoke her calm voice was unanticipated.

"Roan, did I do everything right?"

Shey's question broke Roan's concentration, interrupting his work on the post mission report. Momentarily Roan hesitated in wonderment. Coming from a Scout AI, Shey's innocent question was startling, since it revealed an extraordinary level of cognitive self-awareness. Still considering the far-reaching implications of Shey's question, Roan answered, "Shey, you and your sisters did everything just right. You were wonderful. And, you can tell your sisters that I said they also did everything right."

Shey noted the inflections and qualities of Roan's words; they had produced another odd feedback in her logic circuits. She entered the event into her programmers' file, denoting it as happiness. If possible, Shey would have smiled. Then, Shey informed her sisters of what Roan had said about them. The four AIs then began a conversation about Roan's approval and examined every detail of the mission. Their conversation was still in progress when hours later they rendezvoused with Lan, were welcomed into their waiting hangars, and the hangar doors closed snugly behind them.

Chapter Twenty-Nine:
Battered and Bruised

The Captain and his Chief of Operations stood attentively before the table where Kur and Ca sat facing them. When Kur spoke, his words came out in a soft hiss.

"Explain how you lost two fighters and had four other ships shot to pieces."

"Honored One, we suffered battle casualties by an alien ship of unknown origins," the staff officer responded.

Kur sensed Ca stiffen beside him. He was angry, his facial markings bright.

"What do you mean by an alien ship of unknown origin? Don't you mean it came from that big blue planet you can see through the observation dome? That is the only place the attack could come from. What I want to know is how could any ship coming from that planet get close without being detected? More to the point, how many attacking ships were destroyed, and what retaliatory actions do you recommend?"

As to protect his staff officer from further upbraiding, The Captain interjected, "Honored Ones, we now have considerable information suggesting the enemy ship did not originate in this solar system. More significantly, our analysis clearly indicates what occurred was not an attack. It was a feint, the purpose being to gather Intelligence."

Suddenly alert, Kur thought, *Here is evidence justifying my premonition of imminent danger.* "Captain, clarify your analysis of recent events. Then, tell us why you believe the feint, as you label it, did not come from Earth."

"Honored One, in accordance with your instructions, this ship is set combat ready. My standing order is any alien vessel detected nearing this ship is to be immediately rendered unable to communicate and be destroyed. When passive sensors detected an unknown propulsion signature dangerously close, the fighter group providing our protection moved toward the enemy, and two primary laser batteries fired. The enemy had apparently detected our fire control tracking beams, and maneuvering, it escaped. When accelerating, it deployed a strong cluttering beacon that temporarily blinded our sensors and communication channels.

"As we were clearing the effects of the beacon, four major class ships were detected. They were on an attack approach. Our fighters on standby were launched and moved to block the approaching ships. The fighters were prosecuting an effective blocking maneuver and preparing to engage the enemy. Then, the four attacking ships disappeared. At the same time the jamming beacon terminated. Our tactical team leaders immediately realized the four inbound targets must have been elaborate decoys, however, by then the enemy ship had disappeared.

When the enemy was detected, a general recall of our outlying fighters was issued. Four fighters providing top cover for one of our cargo extraction teams responded. As they rose out of the Earth atmosphere, they were attacked by an inbound alien ship. One fighter was rendered inoperative, its crew killed. A second fighter was badly damaged, its crew suffering one dead and two injured. Although badly damaged that fighter returned to the Nest ship. While sounding an alarm, the two remaining undamaged fighters turned about and gave pursuit.

"When the fighters had responded to our recall, two ground security ships rose to a higher altitude, providing the top cover. As the security ships rose the alien ship fired on them and simultaneously launched an attack against the two pursuing fighters.

"Both of the ground-security ships suffered significant damage from laser and shell bursts. If they had not been armored for ground combat, both support ships would have been destroyed.

"Honored Ones, Council member Rin was aboard one of the two security ships that were damaged. He is bruised and somewhat battered, yet I assure you he is otherwise well. After they were damaged, Council Member Rin demanded both of the damaged ground security ships remain on station and continue providing protection for the extraction team. That extraction mission was completed on schedule. During the final extraction phase, two Earth aircraft penetrated the extraction zone. They were destroyed.

"The cargo lifters, with their ground security ships, are now clear of the planet's atmosphere. To assure Council Member Rin's safety, I have ordered twelve fighters to escort the uplift group to the Nest ship. They are anticipated to arrive here within a tenth-cycle."

"Captain, I commend your prudent actions. Immediately notify me if there is any alteration in Council Member Rin's status."

"Honored One, it will be so.

"Concerning the two fighters we lost, there is no opportunity for recovery of the crew or the fighter that broke up in the atmosphere. The second fighter and its dead crew was taken in tow and is now being returned to our Nest ship.

"Regarding the enemy, and why it cannot be of Earth, its propulsion signature was recorded. As it evaded our initial battery fire, we also measured its acceleration. It was beyond our own capability, and far beyond any Earth technology.

"Searching our Kreel databases, we located a similar propulsion signature. If the match is correct, we were probed by a Dargon long-range fighter. Consequently, the probability is one or more Dargon Capital ships are operating near or in this system."

Kur was aware of the Dargon from Kreel reports, they were hatchlings and utterly hostile to all other species, hatchlings and mammals alike. Worse yet, the Dargon had faster-than-light ships and were Interstellar raiders. That the Dargon had probed the Nest ship's defenses was alarming; Scion was within easy reach of a Dargon faster-than-light ship. They looted at will, asking no quarter and giving no quarter. The Dargon simply struck and then disappeared.

"Captain, how do our own fighters compare to the Dargon fighters?"

The Captain paused momentarily reflecting before answering. "Honored One, there is but minimal data in our Kreel database on Dargon fighter performance. Given what we observed today, it is reasonable to conclude that they are extremely capable and dangerous. It is my conclusion our initial detection of the Dargon ship happened only because they wanted us to detect them."

Kur suddenly felt a surge of cold rage. That a Dargon ship had approached to an attack range undetected, then mocked the Arkillians by taunting them, infuriated him. The sheer arrogance of such an action promoted a flash of fear, which was immediately followed by anger regarding their audacity and a subliminal admiration for the courage of the enemy.

"Captain, what is your evaluation of the Dargon tactics?" Kur asked.

As if to redeem his tactical officer's reputation, the Captain signaled him to respond to Kur's question. The officer's military robes and his displayed award ribbons attested to his many turns of service and military achievements. Kur took note that he wore the honored badge of a combat pilot.

Sweeping aside his lingering visceral anger toward the Dargon, Kur moved to soften Ca's prior upbraiding of the officer. "I recognize and salute you for your service. Your Nest is noticed. I request your keen analysis."

The officer's facial markings subtly shifted, reflecting Kur's positive acknowledgments. "Honored Ones, our analysis indicates that the Dargon are not fully aware of our combat potential, especially regarding our sensors and weapons. The Dargon ship revealed an acceleration profile significantly greater than that of our fighters, but the ship also revealed distinct limitations in Earth atmosphere. Notably, the Dargon have exhibited an ability to avoid our search and fire control sensors. Therefore, The Dargon can strike us at will, and we are vulnerable.

"Our post action analysis indicates the Dargon tactic was to generate an increasing propulsion signature until we detected it. That it was then capable of evading our main battery fire and later inflict damage on our fighters shows the Dargon have courage, tenacity, and cunning. They appear to be a formidable enemy. "

"Do you have any recommendations?" Kur asked.

"Honored One, having now detected the Dargon propulsion signature, we may be able to modify some of our bio-receivers to monitor for that specific waveform. In some ways, the Dargon propulsion signature is similar to monitoring for brain waves. Both are complex waveforms that exhibit very low frequency characteristics and are difficult to differentiate. If we can successfully adapt the bio-receivers to extract the Dargon propulsion signal from background clutter, we could square the underlying signal and get a clear detection sequence. That would provide improved detection and localization capability. If successful, the improvements in sensors will increase our ability to defend the Nest ship."

The officer's recommendation lifted Kur's flagging spirit. "You and your team are noted with distinction.

"Captain, you are to proceed with all available resources to implement the modification of the bio-receivers. Maintain your battle-ready condition. Maintain seventy percent of our fighters on patrol, withholding the remaining fighters on standby. Rotate the fighters by thirds on a one-tenth-cycle schedule.

"You are to prepare this ship for immediate departure. When breaking out of orbit, use maximum acceleration. Set our initial trajectory directly away from Scion."

"It will be so, Honored One."

"Next, prepare a long-range probe. Put all available information about the Dargon into that probe. If we are compelled to fight a last-ditch battle, that probe must be launched toward Scion to warn them of the Dargon presence. Do you understand?"

"Honored One, confirm your instruction that we are to proceed at maximum acceleration away from Scion."

"I do confirm those instructions."

"Honored One, I understand. It will be so."

Dismissing the officers, Kur held out his right hand, as if to receive an unseen object. One of his waiting servants quickly approached, placing one of Kur's favorite cups into his hand. It was full of honey mead. Deep in reflective thought and looking out of the observation dome at the Earth and its moon, Kur rotated the cup slowly between his fingers. He seemed unaware of Ca's presence.

Breaking into Kur's reflections, Ca asked, "Why have you told the Captain to recall all cargo extraction teams? We have lifted less than forty percent of the manifested cargo. Do you intend to depart before we complete the cargo uplift?"

"Ca, if we are scattered detritus drifting in space, the percentage of cargo that was uplifted will not matter."

"But, why did you instruct the Captain to accelerate away from Scion, rather than immediately departing for our nests?"

Kur sighed deeply, "Ca, think for a moment. We are in a dilemma. All our ships travel at sub-light velocities. Most of the other sentient species we deal with have no space travel or else travel at sub-light speed. The Kreel have faster-than-light ships, but they are hatchlings and we are able to trade with them. The Dargon are the first species we have encountered that have faster-than-light ships and are absolutely hostile. They can be at Scion long before we could reach our nests to warn them. We will not lead the Dargon to our nests. Therefore, we will move away and into outer space. If we can survive, and it is deemed safe, we will try and double back toward Scion. If the engineers succeed and develop an improved means of locating the enemy before they strike, we may be able to defend our Nest ship. It would be a major victory if we could somehow capture one of their faster-than-light ships.

"Ca, remember that ignorance of our enemy is our greatest danger and time is our friend. We will embrace time, since each passing cycle improves our chance for survival."

Without further comment, Kur stood and walked from the small conference room, entering the main bridge. The Captain turned to face him, apparently standing without surprise.

"Captain, we are a first line combat ship of the Arkillian Nests. We do not run from any enemy, nor do we whimper in battle. I have directed you to maintain a full battle readiness. As soon as our last cargo lifters are safely aboard this ship, as instructed, direct the Nest ship toward the vicinity of the orbit of the outer minor planets of this system. There you will seek out cover amid the rubble of the outer comet belt. We will deny the enemy the advantage of open space. If we are to fight, then let it be on our own terms and in our place of choosing. We will not only damage our enemy; we will destroy him. Do you understand?"

"Honored One, I understand and it will be so."

Chapter Thirty:
Who's on First?

It was late and the Commerce building was nearly empty as Darrell hurried through the quiet corridors. When he reached his goal, he found Charles' inner office brightly illuminated and the protective window blast shutters closed tight. Janet was sitting at the circular conference oak table and Charles was talking on the phone. Both Charles and Janet's expressions revealed deep concerns.

Looking over, Charles waved to Darrell, motioning him to take his seat at the table. "Carl, I understand your legal position is awkward. Janet tells me she's quite spirited and will most likely protest your interdiction. Nevertheless, make direct contact and then escort her home. Our tracking indicates she's staying at the Gumbolt Hostel in Bern."

Charles paused momentarily, listening. "That's your problem, Carl. Be polite, and advise her that coming home is at the personal request of Janet Rodgers. If necessary, explain to her that if the Swiss conclude she's not a simple tourist, she might find it somewhat difficult to leave Switzerland. I want her debriefed and your report on my desk within twelve hours."

Still frowning, Charles sat listening before speaking again. "Understood. Good luck."

Returning the phone to its cradle, Charles let out a deep sigh, and turned to look at both Darrell and Janet. "We're in the middle of a colossal mess. Our total effort is now focused on determining who's on first base and who's pitching. And, every military organization on the planet is on heightened alert. This situation is like taking an open keg of black powder to a barbecue. We need to get on top of the problem."

As if it were all Darrell's fault, Charles snapped, "Well Darrell, what light can you shed on what is going on?"

As Charles spoke, the door opened and Lois, his secretary, entered carrying a large vacuum flask of coffee and a tray of cups, sugar, cream and sandwiches. She placed these on the table and tactfully withdrew, the door closing softly behind her.

"Sir, our surveillance of Monstro indicates there was a firefight. But we do know Monstro was in the thick of the fracas.

"As I previously reported, Monstro's fighters located and destroyed three of our new satellites. Fortunately, they did not find the fourth, and it's still functioning. Because of our instrumentation losses, our data is fragmentary. Still, using the available data we're building a probable sequence of events along a timeline."

In exasperation Charles sighed, "Darrell, cut to the chase, out with it. If all you have are guesses, then give us your best guess."

"Yes, Sir. When Monstro came into its parking orbit, it exhibited a heightened level of readiness. We were unable to discern any cause for that level of alertness, until now. Several hours ago, our remaining satellite detected a striking new propulsion signature. Oddly, that propulsion source was in the general proximity of Monstro and seemed stationary. Then, over a short interval the new propulsion signature inexplicitly intensified.

"Suddenly, the unknown ship accelerated toward Earth. At the same time Monstro began a laser barrage and deployed more fighters. The unknown ship was fast and extremely evasive. Although the laser bursts were intense, they appear to have missed the intended target.

"Then, for several minutes our sensors were effectively jammed by some strong scrambling signal, so what happened next is unclear. Still, during that brief interval, four very strong propulsion signatures appeared out of the background noise. They were like nothing we've ever seen. They appeared to be four large ships moving directly toward Monstro.

"For sure, Monstro took notice of those four ships. Its fighters began moving to block the new signatures. After about three minutes of observation, the four new signatures simply vanished. At the same time, the strong interfering signal terminated. There was no more laser fire from Monstro or any explosions suggesting one or more large ship had been destroyed."

"Well, what happened to the initial target, the one Monstro fired on?" Charles asked.

"We don't know. We lost track of the first propulsion signature when our detectors were blinded by the jamming. The last measurement we obtained indicates the unknown ship was accelerating and heading this way. We have engineers going over the new propulsion signatures looking for clues. Sir, we are up to our necks in new data, and it is going to take time to sift through all of it."

"Darrell, could the initial unknown ship signature possibly be the product of some military force here on Earth?" Charles asked.

"No way, Sir. The acceleration profile of that ship was staggering. Our propulsion technology is not remotely capable of such performance. Whoever built that ship is definitely not from here."

"Humph, I hope Monstro comes to that same conclusion, otherwise it might get a bit sticky, "Charles grumbled.

Puzzled, Darrell asked, "Apparently there's more to the local story than I'm aware of."

"There is considerably more; a firefight occurred over Europe. Your unknown ship seems to have engaged several of Monstro's fighters and came out on the better side of the engagement," Janet said.

"A firefight? What happened?" Darrell asked.

"Our Olympus European Tracking Center was doing its normal monitoring of Monstro's activities and observed a formation of its ships entering European airspace over Switzerland. All but four of the ships descended below the horizon line and the Center lost track. The four ships remaining above the mountains appeared to be providing topside cover for their ground operations. Suddenly, the four ships departed, heading up and in the direction of Monstro. They were still departing our upper atmosphere when something we couldn't track engaged them. One of the ships was disabled and set adrift. A second fighter was clearly damaged, but disengaged and proceeded out toward Monstro. The two remaining ships reversed their course and returned into our upper atmosphere, as if in hot pursuit of some object. At the same time, two of Monstro's ships rose above the mountains and we regained track. Then, both the lower ships were scattered, descending below the line of sight. One of the ships returning into the atmosphere was destroyed, the second ship appeared damaged and in trouble."

Deeply frowning, Charles looked toward Darrell. "What Janet has outlined isn't the worst aspect of the problem. As we speak, Carl's team is in Switzerland trying to recover any pieces of

Monstro's downed ship. Every other intelligence agency in Europe also seems to have a team on the ground.

Further complicating everything, the Swiss are being difficult. They lost two of their fighters in the general area."

"Sir, how could the Swiss fighters get involved? "Darrell asked.

"Dammed bad luck. It happened following the aero combat. Surveillance reports indicate when they came too close to whatever Monstro was doing in the mountains, Monstro's ships operating in low altitude destroyed them. The Swiss haven't yet acknowledged that fact. Instead, they have released a news bulletin saying the two aircraft collided during a training exercise. Both aircraft crews were killed, and the Swiss are understandably not happy or cooperative.

"Of particular interest to us is Carl has encountered a young woman, who is smack dab in the middle of the entire melee. After studying the local topographical maps, he had located an ideal elevated location that seemed perfect for his team to observe a potential cargo pickup point. Arriving on site, he found a woman already there and busy breaking camp. She is equipped with a camo pup tent, a complete camping ensemble, and what may be a portable Questar observatory.

"Understandably, Carl was surprised to find someone has already staked out his selected site. Keeping the woman under observation, his team located her car. From its registry, Carl has identified the woman. She's an American, named Susie Wells."

Darrell smiled and raised an eyebrow. "That name sounds mighty familiar. Could she possibly be the same Susie Wells who wrote your report on possible interstellar commerce?" Darrell asked Janet.

"Yes, she's the one and very same. What's even more interesting is she is within a few miles of one of the Monstro pickup points and immediately below the point of the aero combat. She seems well equipped with a telescope, camera, and recorders. What she is doing out there by herself is still open to speculation, but Charles just told Carl to retrieve her posthaste," Janet said.

"Humph, we may have just got lucky; she may have gathered vital information. I'm sorta looking forward to meeting your Ms. Wells," Darrell mused.

"Well, when Carl does retrieve her, she'd better have a good justification for being there, and just camping won't fly.

"The worst part is the combat sequence in our atmosphere has alerted every news network on the planet. By tomorrow, the newspapers will be full of wild stories of UFOs. Generating gray disinformation news releases to obscure the truth is going to keep my staff busy for weeks," Janet protested.

"Just hope it's only wild UFO tales that you need to worry about. If Monstro decides we launched an attack, it's likely to respond in kind; The question is, where and in what manner." Darrell mused.

"Damned," Charles muttered.

"From the beginning of this entire mess Monstro has been a huge security nightmare. Because of the gulf between our technologies we've had to walk soft. Now, we've got some new alien force with advanced technology that overshadows Monstro. This puts us into the sorry position of not even knowing who's coming to bat. I don't like this situation, and it can't be tolerated.

"Darrell, the current set of facts is unacceptably confusing. I want every scrap of data you can put your hands on to be collected, collated, correlated, and analyzed. Get every byte of information from the European center and merge it with your satellite data. I want you to wring out every scrap of Intelligence possible. Work the problem and give me a clear picture of what is going on, and do it fast."

"Yes, Sir."

"Now hear this, at 07:00 tomorrow morning, I'll be briefing the President. I'm not going into that meeting empty-handed. Darrell, you're going to be in that meeting with me, so look in your closet for a clean shirt and a tie."

"Yes, Sir."

"And, your written report is to be submitted in no more than six hours. Monstro's possible military response has our defensive posture on heightened levels. We're on the edge of a full-scale battle with an alien having an advanced and unknown capability.

"Janet, I want the same response from your group. You've got six hours and not one minute more. Do you both understand?"

Both affirmed they did, and the meeting abruptly ended.

Chapter Thirty-One:
Spooks

It was still morning, but the earlier exciting events were plainly over and Susie was concentrating on breaking camp. A soft buzzing sound scattered the surrounding silence. Perplexed, she glanced at her NetCom and wondered, *Now why on Earth would Roth be calling?*

Keying her Net-Com, she inquired, "Roth, what's up?"

"Ms. Susie, six strange men have been walking around me. They did not try to force entry, but they are now following my earlier tracks and heading in your direction. Do you want me to do anything?"

Frowning, Susie glanced toward where Roth was parked under the cover of large nearby trees. Roth was correct, there were men walking among the trees and coming toward her. She observed they were dressed casually, and looked like tourists.

"Roth, I am leaving my Net-Com active. If there is trouble and I ask for help, immediately contact the local authorities. Do you understand?"

"Ms. Susie, I will comply," Roth said.

Resuming her packing, Susie unobtrusively picked up and pocketed the data storage cubes containing the visual and commentary record she had made on the mountain top during the preceding days. As one of the men walked toward her, the other men spread out. With apparent curiosity, they were looking down toward the valley below and at her gathered belongings. The man that was approaching her was smiling and did not appear threatening.

"High there, I'm Susie. I'm about to fix myself a cup of green tea, might I fix one for you?"

"Thank you, but no. Ms. Wells, my name is Carl Suthaford, and I work for the United States Department of Commerce. Out of curiosity, Might I ask, why are you camping in so remote a location?"

As he was speaking, the man removed his wallet and extracting a card, he held it out to Susie.

That the man knew her name came as a shock, and Susie felt a sudden twinge of fear. Accepting the card, she observed it was an official looking ID, showing the man's 3D photo, a flashy hologram US Government seal, and the bold letters, United States Department of Commerce. Looking about, she observed the other men were busy documenting the area, including her camp site and equipment.

With a thousand unanswered questions swirling in her mind, she handed the card back to the man. "It's nice to meet you Mr. Suthaford. In answer to your question, it's a nice quiet place to do some stargazing. While I don't want to appear rude, but since I can't fix you a cup of tea, I do need to finish packing."

"Ms. Wells, like you, I don't wish to appear rude, but I have been told to give you a message, it's from Janet Rogers. She is asking you to drop whatever it is that you are doing and promptly accompany me back to New Washington. She is rather insistent that you immediately come home."

"Mr. Suthaford, I have no intention of budging an inch, at least not until I establish precisely who you really are. Please excuse me, but I need some privacy."

"Fully understood," the man said, as he turned and walked toward where the other men were busy.

Given all that had recently happened, she was not in a trusting mood. Fretting, she thought, *OK, so they are Americans. But, their demeanor shouts spooks, not commerce. Still, they certainly know who I am and that I worked for Janet.*

Keying her NetCom, she called Janet. It was late in New Washington, and Janet's office AI answered the call. Identifying herself, Susie asked about Mr. Suthaford. The AI corroborated the men's identification and backed up his story. Frowning, she broke the connection and considered her situation. If the AI had not confirmed Janet had personally asked her to immediately return home, she would not consider budging an inch. *Okay,* she thought, *so I'll cooperate, just a little.*

She had traveled half way around the world in pursuit of a first-class mystery. From her chosen mountain campsite, she had filmed amazing events unfolding in the lower valley and in the sky above, events that had exceeded her wildest expectations. *Little old me, Susie Wells, has actually seen people from another world walking around on Earth, and have the video to prove it. Who would have believed it?*

Finishing packing her gear, she called Roth. Depositing the equipment in his trunk, she took the passenger seat in the coupe. The gull wing door swung down, and with a solid thump latched, securely enclosing her within the safety of the compartment. Only then did she, with a rush of relief, sigh.

Following her instructions, Roth carefully moved out of the sheltering trees and back onto the mountain road. As they traversed the beautiful winding road toward town, she observed that the men who had been watching her made no secret about following Roth in their own vehicle.

Taking advantage of the few minutes of unobserved privacy afforded within the coupe, she retrieved the data cubes from her pockets and slipped them into her NetCom. Compressing the data, she activated her encryption program. For added security, she employed a second key and again encrypted the initial encrypted file. Her encryption program was non-commercial, being a gift from a trusted friend who worked at APL University of Washington. He had jokingly assured her only a government agency might be able to crack the encryption, but then only maybe, and only if they spent millions of dollars and several months of computer time.

After encrypting the data, she sent the file directly to William, with the identification phrase, Treasure Island. Next, using a random alphanumeric text she overwrote and erased the working files eight times. Then she erased everything and destroyed the data cubes.

Arriving at the hotel, she got out and stood next to Roth, waiting for the following car to pull in and park. Mr. Suthaford stepped out of the car and walked to where she stood waiting.

"Ms. Wells, have you decided whether you'll return with me to New Washington?

"Yes, but only because I confirmed Janet made that request. Now, I need to go up to my room and clean up and change clothes. Can I depend upon you to see my camp gear and equipment if transferred from my car, safely taken through customs, and come with us?"

"Yes, rest assured, I'll take care of that."

While the men waited outside her hotel room, Susie changed clothes and repacked her luggage and carry on. Exiting the hotel, she called and said her good-bye to Roth. He cheerfully thanked her for all of the good conversations and promised that from time to time he would communicate with William. The sleek touring coupe then drove down the street, and with a brief beep of his horn, turned the corner and disappeared.

Mr. Suthaford and another man escorted her directly from the hotel to the airport. There was no conversation whatsoever. Reaching the airport, the vehicle was briefly stopped at a security gate, then was allowed through. They quickly moved past the barrier and onto the apron, where A clearly marked US Air Force aircraft was parked. She noted the aircraft was not a sleek sub-orbital design, but one of the older supersonic trans-Atlantic executive corporate types. Whoever these men really were, they clearly did not rank high enough to warrant the really fancy transportation. Still, the confirming sight of the official aircraft was reassuring, and somewhat eased her overall anxiety.

Upon boarding, Mr. Suthaford directed her to her seat, casually informing her the flight was about 4700 miles and would be about five hours. As soon as they were aboard and seated, the aircraft began moving along the apron, and then turning onto the broad runway it picked up speed, rotated, and lifted off.

She looked around the small interior of the aircraft and noted there were only two other passengers, Mr. Suthaford and another man. They were busy talking together and not paying her the slightest attention. That was good, or at least she hoped it was good.

Once in flight and leveled off at a cruising altitude, Mr. Suthaford came to where she was seated and pleasantly, but unsuccessfully, tried to entice her to tell him about what she might have seen. She declined to discuss the matter, telling him if Janet asks, she might consider telling her, but no one else. He accepted her statement on its face value and dropped the matter.

Although not wearing leg irons and handcuffed or forcibly dragged by her heels from Switzerland, Susie still felt the unplanned brisk exit from Bern was at best dismal. Looking out the window, all there was to see was the dark sky above and clouds below. The reassuring steady sound of the engines indicated they were at cruising altitude and probably out over the Atlantic. Feeling cramped and stiff, she tried to recline the seat back a bit further, but it was stuck upright and would not budge.

Nuts, she inwardly grumbled.

Lifting up the serving tray from its arm rest storage slot, she unfolded it, and laying her arms across the opened tray, she rested her head on her arms. Struggling to find a comfortable position, she closed her eyes, steadied her breathing, and tried to relax.

At that moment, Susie was tired and more than a little angry. The anger tended to helped offset some of the icy tentacles of fear then squirming in her belly. For the thousandth time she wondered, *Now what have I gotten myself into this time?*

Chapter Thirty-Two:
A Bit Rustic

Excruciating pain in her neck woke Susie. With a groan and yawn she sat up and looked about her, thinking, *I must have dozed off.* Listening, she heard the engines begin spooling down and felt the aircraft begin its steep descent into the lower atmosphere. Stretching, she yawned again and then checked her wristwatch. It had been somewhat less than five hours since their take-off in Bern.

Bumpy, the aircraft dropped through the cloud layers. She was still looking out of the window when the aircraft touch downed. It was very early morning, and a dense ground fog blanketed the area. The fog shrouded buildings revealed only random patterns of ethereal and defused glows of lights. Presumably they had landed in New Washington and were taxiing toward a terminal.

Responding to ground control, the fog did not require the aircraft to slow as it taxied. After turning off the main runway it continued along the apron, coming up to a large gray building. Distinctly announced by a slight telltale jerk, the aircraft came to a complete stop. The hydrogen engines began spooling down from their high-pitched whine, dropping through the descending octaves toward silence.

Susie looked forward. Carl Suthaford was approaching her. While everyone was trying to remain polite, nevertheless there was a mounting interpersonal tension.

"Ms. Wells, please come with me. I'm informed Ms. Rodgers is waiting in the terminal and is eager to see you...."

As they walked out of the jetway into the arrival area, Janet was standing there waiting. From her changing countenance, Susie knew that Janet felt a genuine sense of relief upon seeing her.

"Welcome home, Sherlock. Someday that famous curiosity of yours might get you into some real trouble. Now, we need to hurry; the President is expecting us. And, we don't want to be late," Janet said.

Susie froze. "The President. Why on Earth would I be going to see the President?"

"Ms. Susie Wells, in certain government circles you are becoming well-known and respected."

"Janet, until you tell me what's going on, I'm not taking one more step."

"As to what is going on, your incorrigible curiosity has inserted you smack in the middle of a national security zone. Because of where you've been and what you may have seen, it's essential that you promptly talk with professional investigators. That you don't understand the circumstances doesn't alter your involvement one whit. And, to cut through your stubborn nature, and to assure you that this is of the highest National importance, you have been invited to the White House to meet with the President."

"Humph, just as I thought, those men who brought me here don't work for the Department of Commerce."

"Don't be absurd, Of course they do. Now hurry, we can't keep the President waiting."

Still standing stationary, Susie looked imploringly at her friend. "Janet, look at me. I can't possibly go see the President of the United States dressed like this. Just look at my hair. It's a mess."

Janet took her by the sleeve and gently tugged. "We have to hurry and you look positively lovely. Admittedly a bit rustic, but still lovely."

Together, the two women exited the building. A car was waiting curbside and the two men who had come with her from Switzerland were standing beside it. One of them opened the rear door for them. Janet and Susie slid into the rear seat, the door solidly closing behind them with a thunk. The two men sat in front and the car moved away from the terminal toward Government Park.

Susie was still trying to comprehend what was happening. Several times she repeated to herself, *I am going to see the President. Me – Susie Wells. Will wonders never cease?*

"Janet, what should I say to the President? I didn't even vote for him."

Janet glanced toward Susie, and with a broad smile commented, "Neither did I."

Having been politely ushered into a spacious and very comfortable executive office by a woman named Lois, Susie found herself sitting alone at a small oak table and with a cup of excellent coffee. The office was on the upper floor of the Department of Commerce building, and the title on the door had read, Charles Sullivan, Under Secretary of Commerce.

Even with Janet's assurances, she still had trouble accepting the repeated identification of the Department of Commerce. To her acute observations the rich aura of cloak and dagger somehow excluded the Department of Commerce. It simply did not add up.

Her meeting with the President had lasted only a few minutes, but it made a deep impression on her. According to Janet that was precisely why she had been introduced to him. His words to her were gracious, "Ms. Wells, we are deeply grateful for your voluntary contribution to our national security. Thank you for your cooperation in a matter of a most serious nature."

The remainder of their conversation, though brief, had been general and casual. But, his first words still lingered in her consciousness. His stated presumption of voluntary cooperation and contribution, combined with a most serious matter, still had her somewhat mystified. And doubly so, since she had not been particularly cooperative in returning from Switzerland. Yet, upon further reflection, his words were revealing. *The government must believe I have something they very badly want,* she thought, *and I guess it is up to me to decide whether I am going to cooperate. Still, he is the President, and he actually took time out of his busy schedule to see me. That has got to count for something.*

Looking about, she took notice of the furnishing in the office. The furniture was made of elegantly shaped solid wood and had fine leather coverings. It was high end stuff and the type of furniture she could appreciate. Stylized wood bookshelves along one wall were filled with an assortment of beautifully bound books of varying heights and colors. She scanned some of the titles and noted many were ageless classics from Herodotus and

Homer to Mark Twain. She heartily approved of the collection, and was duly impressed with the tasteful and classically non-Government issue décor of the office.

Looking out of the large windows, she could see the New Washington Monument rising above the trees in the distance. When the Capitol was rebuilt in Missouri, the white house, Capital buildings and many of the historical monuments were carefully and lovingly collected and then restored amid newly constructed parks, lakes, and areas of forests. Most everyone considered Government Park a national treasure and a source of national pride. Susie certainly counted herself among that group, considering the Park was classically beautiful.

When the door did open, two men entered. Coming over to the table, they sat down, an older man sitting to her left and a younger man sitting on her right.

The older man introduced himself, "I'm Charles Sullivan, an Under Secretary of Commerce. Ms. Wells, I am pleased to have this opportunity to meet with you. The gentleman sitting on your right is Darrell Fann. He's my senior manager responsible for data collection and analysis. And of course, you already know Janet. She's another of my senior managers. She will be joining us shortly."

The man's brisk manner and tone of voice indicated that he was more accustomed to telling people what to do, rather than asking them. The younger man of the two remained silent. His clothing was distinctly ruffled as if he had slept in them. He looked physically exhausted. It was obvious that he had even less sleep than she had.

"Ms. Wells, there're just a few items that I need to discuss with you. It's still early, and I understand that you've already had a very full day, and you must be suffering from jet lag. So, I'll be as brief as possible.

"To begin with, we both know that you've been in an extraordinary location for a week. We also know that you weren't spending that time stargazing. During your stay on that mountain, you undoubtedly saw, and we hope recorded, the activities occurring on and around the Gumbolt Global Import and Export facility. You may have also observed what appeared to have been a military exercise in the general area. What you may have observed is of the utmost importance to the national security of this country.

"Coming to the point, I also know you directed a large data transfer from your touring car to your personal AI at home in California. It's my presumption that whatever you sent is the fruit of your week spent on the mountain. If I am correct, then I am requesting that you provide this office with the encryption keys for that data. I am also further requesting your cooperation in providing us with a complete description of all that you have observed or surmised while in Switzerland."

While listening to Mr. Sullivan, Susie had sat quietly. Now, he was impatiently waiting for her answer. Inwardly she was feeling a buoyant sense of confidence, her friend at the University was correct. Obviously, the government had monitored and intercepted her data download to William. *They have tried, but not yet been able to break the encryption. If they had, Charles Sullivan would not be sitting there politely asking me for the keys.*

"Mr. Sullivan, just so that we understand each other, until I fully understand precisely who you are and why you want what I might have, I am unable to further cooperate with you or anyone else."

Taking a deep breath, Susie asked the singular question that was paramount in her own mind. "Sir, really, just who are you and what is your real job?"

Chapter Thirty-Three:
Council of War

Kellon was not at all pleased. While he held both Roan and Zorn in genuine esteem, their last mission had crossed the line. The risk of Shey being detected was an unavoidable aspect of their mission, but Roan's command decision to intentionally expose Shey to enemy fire was not. Even worse, the inevitable fallout from Roan's rash decision was unpredictable.

Hearing a knock upon the conference room door, Kellon glanced at the chronometer, thinking, *They're at least on time.* "Enter."

The door slid open and Roan entered, with Zorn in the rear; behind them, the door smoothly closed. When approaching Kellon, they came to attention and saluted, smartly.

"Sir, Commanders Roan and Zorn reporting, as ordered," Roan said.

Returning their salutes, Kellon remained silent, not granting them at-ease or permission to sit. Kellon studied the two men standing at attention before him, noting that their formal bearing and duty uniforms were impeccable. In spite of their recent conduct, he felt a growing pride in these two officers.

"Lan, provide us with an overview of Commanders Roan and Zorn's last mission."

"Yes Sir. Shey's log and sensor record reveal a successful mission. All the mission objectives were achieved and exceeded. Shey determined the sensitivity of the target's primary passive sensors, and obtained comprehensive spectrum analysis of its active tracking and fire control sensors. A full laser analysis of the target's hull composition was also obtained.

"Upon completion of her defined mission objectives, Shey executed a successful exit. Random light resistance was encountered during her tactical withdrawal. Overcoming the resistance, Shey completed her evasion maneuver and rendezvoused with her Scout escort. All Scouts returned to Lan without damage or loss of life."

Kellon did not miss the skillfully redacted brevity of Lan's mission overview, grumbling inwardly, *Now even the AIs are collaborating*. "Lan, expand on the nature of the light resistance Shey encountered."

"Yes, Sir. Initially, Shey took, but sidestepped laser fire from two of the target's main batteries. Shey then nimbly evaded approximately thirty defending fighters, effectively executing a planned tactical withdrawal.

"When approaching the planet, Shey encountered four Kreel Type-32 fighters rising out of the atmosphere. They were on a direct closing vector and detected her Dargon configuration. Reacting, Shey maneuvered to engage, and upon orders she fired on the three nearest fighters. One fighter was neutralized and a second ship was damaged. Because of the circumstances of the engagement, Shey was compelled to enter the planet's atmosphere. Moments later, two additional enemy ships were detected rising on an intercept vector. Acting on orders, Shey engaged the two lower ships that were closing and simultaneously directed two missiles toward the Type-32 fighters then in close pursuit.

"The two lower enemy ships were damaged and broke off their engagement. One of the pursuing Type-32 fighters was destroyed, breaking up in the atmosphere. The second fighter was damaged and broke off its pursuit. Then, entering the night side of the planet, Shey set full stealth and lifted out of the atmosphere, returning into space. Shey encountered no further resistance."

While Lan gave his report, Kellon had studied Roan's steadfast countenance. Roan, like Zorn, was maintaining his formal posture of attention, looking straight forward.

"Commander Roan, precisely at what point was Shey detected? Kellon inquired.

"Sir, Shey was detected at the preplanned optimum firing point."

Kellon did not reply, waiting calmly for Roan to continue. After several moments, Roan apparently understood Kellon's silence, and continued.

"Sir, we had arrived at that predefined point undetected. In an effort to determine the readiness and passive sensor sensitivity of the target, I ordered the ambient Dargon propulsion signature to be ramped up. The signal strength was then increased by two percent increments, until we were detected. Detection occurred at 1.28 times the initial ambient Dargon level. Upon detection, we executed our withdrawal along the preplanned exit route.

"Sir, the encounter with the six ships near the planet was a random event. Those ships had been in low altitudes within the atmosphere, and our sensors didn't track them until they emerged on a closing vector. Engagement with the incoming ships was purely restricted to defensive actions."

Kellon shifted his disapproval from Roan toward Zorn. "Commander Zorn, do you have anything you would like to add to Commander Roan's statement?"

"Sir, No Sir."

Leaning forward, Kellon placed his elbows on the table and clasped his hands together. "Commander Roan, the common military term covert has an unambiguous definition. You unnecessarily and intentionally exposed Shey and her crew to direct enemy fire. In doing this, you have also loudly proclaimed our presence in this solar system. The long-term consequences of your precipitous actions are not yet apparent. While I am pleased that Shey returned in one piece, I am not at all pleased with your performance.

"Commander Zorn, it's obvious you went along with Commander's Roan's command decision, without providing a formal objection.

"Now, both of you hear me loud and clear; this matter is far from concluded.

"Both of you are dismissed."

Saluting smartly, Roan and Zorn both executed a crisp about-face, and exited the Captain's conference room. The door slid closed behind them.

Standing, Kellon walked to the side table and poured himself a cup of neab from a thermos, and returned to the table. He knew his senior staff was exceptional, even so his command burdens at times became overly heavy; breaches in common sense like that of Roan and Zorn did not help matters. He was aware his next decisions were likely to impact billions of humans within this solar system and also affect more billions on the assembled worlds. Problematically, the anticipated response from HQ to his situation reports was at best weeks away. Until it arrived, the command responsibility for what he did next was his burden alone. Until ordered otherwise, standing Guardian general orders prevailed.

"Lan, what is the current status of the Capital ship?"

"Sir, it is maintaining its heliocentric orbit near the third planet. Our sentinel is monitoring what appears to be a general recall of all its ships previously deployed to the planet. No new departures are being observed."

"Lan, confirm that all its ships are returning to the Capital ship."

"Confirmed."

Understanding flooded Kellon's mind, *By all the muses, they're pulling up stakes. Roan, your and Zorn's reckless Dargon gambit must have shaken them to their core.*

Kellon sat pondering, if he were placed in the same tactical position as the other captain, then what would he likely do? *He is alone and years from home or reinforcement, confronting an imminent attack by a technologically superior and ruthless adversary. If he knows the Dargon have superluminal capable ships, then he might try to hide, but he knows he can't run.*

From his own experience, Kellon understood the other captain's tactical problems, and they were numerous.

Cataloging his adversary 's options, Kellon sorted through them and considered what was most likely to happen next.

"Lan, display on the bulkhead a standard ecliptic heliocentric chart showing the current planet positions in this solar system."

For a few minutes, Kellon sat studying the plot that had promptly appeared. "Lan, construct a line from the capital ship toward the star system we believe to be its home world. Place an icon where that line intersects the orbit of the eighth planet."

A thin red line appeared, and a small red square appeared on the outermost blue circumference ring. "Now, construct a new line from that icon through the position of the Capital ship and extrapolate that line to where it intersects the orbit of the outer minor planets. Place a second icon at that point."

The new line nearly bisected the concentric circles on the chart. "Lan, place an icon on the chart showing our current position."

A golden icon denoting Lan appeared on the chart. It was in near proximity to the last drawn red square.

"Well, there goes the neighborhood," Kellon mused aloud.

It looks like Roan's command decision and fate have linked up to alter everyone's best laid plans. It's about time to either move or else fight, Kellon thought.

"Lan, Have the officer's mess prepare and bring in cups, neab, and some bakery items. Notify senior staff officers, and include those two rogues, Roan and Zorn. They are all to be in my conference room in thirty minutes. It's time for a full council of war."

Chapter Thirty-Four:
Survival

Sitting alone, Kur was pondering their problems, and they were many. A Dargon attack appeared imminent, and his hopes for being able to survive and return to Scion were at best dismal. In spite of his earlier bold words to his Captain, Kur understood the Nest ship was designed and built for ground assault and not for an open battle in space. Its very size and mass limited its maneuverability. Of course, their fighter screen would be escorting them; although smaller, faster, more agile, and well-armed, the fighters had distinct offensive armament limitations.

His primary responsibilities were to Scion, the Council, and the survival of the Nest ship. He was badly in want of an edge, an alternate course of action, something not leading directly to a courageous, but nevertheless last pitch battle to the death with an enemy possessing vastly superior technology.

Undeniably, his personal survival was a consideration, however, what was more important was Scion learned of what was happening. The data probe he had ordered the Captain to prepare for launch was far from foolproof; he needed a viable fallback plan.

Impatiently rising from his seat at the table, Kur departed his den and walked along the passageways to the Intelligence Center. He could have had one of his servants bring the desired file, but he felt the need for a walk. Entering the compartment, he asked the senior duty officer for the archival records for the old Arkillian installations on Earth, and patiently waited for a copy to be made.

Following their initial suppression of Earth, the Arkillians had built multiple operational bases on each continent. Time had proven the facilities were unnecessary and increasing economic pressures rendered the expensive facilities too costly to maintain. One by one the facilities had been abandoned, and none had been used in a thousand turns. Kur knew most of the facilities had been thoroughly destroyed, but he retained hope that a few might still be accessible and serviceable.

In particular, from his youth he remembered there had been a major installation in the golden desert on the largest of the planet's six continents. Because of its remote location, that installation had been extensive.

Having obtained a copy of the archive file, he returned to his den and inserted the classified file index into a data slot. His fingers moving deftly over the control console revealed his long acquaintance and familiarity with the information recovery system. He reviewed the data on the abandoned installation, and unlike most of the other installations, it had not been demolished. After some heated disagreement at that time, the installation had been carefully preserved and then concealed.

Kur made note of the name of the Council member who had so long before demanded that prudent decision. Thinking positively, Kur decided upon his return to Scion that he would give a note of merit to the Council and to that member's Nest.

When he compared the coordinates of the facility with the current population density maps, Kur was pleased to see the old installation was within the mountains of one of the lowest population density regions of Earth. There were no major industrial or transportation systems in its immediate vicinity. Interestingly, the current regional population was still essentially nomadic, and there were no major towns or cities nearby. According to the current file, the area was rich in eatable plants and wildlife, providing an ample emergency food source, if such a harsh necessity arose. The information was far better than he had hoped, and his facial markings brightened into a pleasure pattern.

Sitting, he thoughtfully considered his options. Being marooned on Earth would not be pleasant, yet it offered a most desirable option; life. That option was certainly preferable to a death in cold space. Where there is life, there is hope and the opportunity to take positive action.

Given their fierce reputation as raiders, the Dargon did not conquer and then occupy planets. They were raiders, who struck and then moved on. If Scion received the warning probe, they would certainly come, and come in force. Even if the warning probe did not reach Scion, after a reasonable time, someone from

Scion would come looking for a missing frontline ship. Those stranded on Earth would then be found and rescued.

Using sign language, he instructed a servant to notify Ca to come. Soon thereafter, Ca arrived and sat down across from Kur.

With newly found deference, Ca asked, "Respected Kur, how may I be of service?"

"Ca, I have identified an old, but preserved facility on Earth. If in the coming battle our defense goes badly, we must secure a defensible position to fall back toward. You are to immediately lead a combat team down to Earth and survey that facility. You are to perform a thorough reconnaissance of its current condition. In particular, determine the condition of its food production, communication, and remaining operational defensive features. Identify what will be required to bring the facility up to a secure and full operating status.

"The human population density in the region is sparse, still they are tribal nomads. Such humans have well-honed senses, especially those of smell, sight, and hearing. Use caution and leave no trace of your visit. Since a Dargon attack might come at any moment, you do not have much time. As quickly as possible, return with your report."

Ca glanced at and memorized the identification code on the file that lay between them, Standing, he saluted, "Honored Kur, it will be so."

After Ca had turned and left the room, Kur paused to consider the apparent change in Ca's attitude and was pleased.

Embracing the moment of calm, Kur sat motionless, thinking, *If we cannot outrun or outmaneuver the enemy, then we must out-think them.* It was time to define tactical defensive operations. Turning to his servants, he signed that he wanted to see the Captain.

When the Captain and his two senior tactical officers arrived, Kur swept aside formality and protocol. He directed them to take seats at the table, then, he signed to his servants they were to bring food and drink. Kur's only remaining objective was to plan for their survival, that being a hard stone upon which to sharpen the cutting edge of their combined intellects....

Chapter Thirty-Five:
Calm Before the Storm

Roan found working with his mind and hands to solve design and engineering problems enjoyable. He even liked the characteristic smell of the lubricants used for machine cutting oil. At the moment, he was working aboard Lan at a machine bench in the special weapons shop.

Shey's laser analysis of the hull of the Capital ship had disclosed it was an unusual composite armor made from steel, ceramics, and silicon. The hull had been built to take and absorb punishment. Still, the magnetic signature of the steel provided an unanticipated opportunity for passive targeting.

The dimensions of the enemy ship posed yet another tactical challenge. How does someone attack a ship eight-thousand meters in length? It was built for warfare. The number of hatches, inner bulkheads, and interlocks within the ship must number in the tens of thousands. Even if a large breach in the ship's hull were made, the majority of the interior of the ship would remain intact and functional.

Making the tactical problem ever more difficult, Kellon's goal was to disable and not destroy the ship, at least not at first. The upcoming battle would undoubtedly set the stage for a prolonged conflict with whatever species was crewing the ship. If possible, Kellon wanted to board and recover Intelligence data about the species that sent the vessel into the solar system. The more information that could be obtained now could provide a greater margin for success during future battles and help pave the way for eventual negotiations.

Roan's approach in solving the tactical problem of size was direct. Blowing a few large holes in the ship's hull would not disable it, yet a small hole would cause a volatile decompression in an effected compartment. Together, a large number of small holes made and distributed all over the hull would decompress many compartments and could disable the ship.

When the hatch slid open, Roan glanced up. Zorn was entering, while balancing a platter full of various food items and a vacuum flask of neab. Putting the tray on the work bench, he asked, "How's it going?"

Stretching, Roan let out a sigh. "Well, the tough problem is solved. The design of the warhead is complete and tested. I borrowed from an old historical design, an inverted conical-shaped charge. The new warhead will blow a neat eight-centimeter wide hole through twenty-five centimeters of most ferrous alloys. That depth of penetration should give us a comfortable margin on the probable thickness of the armored hull. As for guidance, the UV laser and magnetometer used for terminal homing, propulsion, warhead sanitization, and self-destruction components are all sub-systems we can quickly manufacture or take from ship's stores.

"We're still assembling some odd fasteners, and completing the modification of several stealth instrumentation pods to serve as our missile launchers. I'd judge we're near full readiness."

Looking over Roan's shoulder at the warhead design figures, Zorn frowned. "How can that small of a warhead have that much punch?"

Enjoying explaining his handiwork, Roan smiled. "It's not the amount of explosive that is important, but rather the shape and the material used as the cone lining. When the warhead detonates, the lining material becomes a hyper-velocity molten stream projected directly into the target's hull. It will produce a molten plume and lethal blast shock within a compartment, decompression immediately follows. It's a simple and effective design. And, the warheads are extremely easy to make. The production shops on Lan will have twenty-thousand of the missiles ready within two days."

"Roan, aren't you overlooking a glaring problem?"

"Such as what?"

"Well, didn't you notice that during our flyby all the fighters and the big old Capital ship have potent offensive and defensive weapons capabilities? Without first getting our own hulls punched full of big holes, how do you propose we deliver twenty-thousand little missiles all over the large hull?"

"Your question is insightful. The beautiful part of the design of the new missile is it is small. It's extremely improbable the Capital ship point-defense sensors are tuned for a passive missile of its size. Better yet, the final terminal laser homing stage needs to be active for only a few seconds. That doesn't give defensive weapons systems the time to respond to thousands of simultaneous multiple threats.

"The real tactical problem we are confronting is how to obtain an even distribution of missiles over the entire hull. I've written several possible tactical attack simulations to assist our Scouts in perfecting our attack run. Working together we should be able to slip in close, launch our full missile complement, and be long gone before the target knows we were ever there. It'll take several more simulations before I'll be happy, but it's looking good."

Pouring himself a cup of neab, Zorn took a seat. "Humph, it sorta makes sense, sorta. But nothing is ever that easy. Still, what's the bottom line? Will the new missiles actually disable the ship?"

Emulating Zorn, Roan poured himself a cup of neab and then leaned back. "Yes, but not necessarily permanently. Undoubtedly, they will temporarily disable its operational ability to evade further attack. And, once we have them disabled, we can create an opportunity to get aboard.

"Now, it's my turn to ask some questions. Just what have you been up to these past days?"

Smiling, Zorn looked up. "Well, I've been very busy, working closely with Elayne."

"Given that smile, I don't doubt that for a moment. But the question is what have you two been working on?"

"Actually, the work with Elayne is fascinating, it's work involving the linguistics and physiology of the crew aboard the Capital ship. Even with all the AIs working together, it took the intelligence group three days to crack their encryption algorithms. Then, linguistics required another four days to construct a preliminary delineation of their language. We now have a basic operational bi-directional computer translation matrix.

"Given the analysis of the backlog of intercepted communications traffic, we have sufficient information to begin the evaluation of their social and racial characteristics. They call themselves Arkillians, and they refer to their home planet as Scion. They're not mammals, but like the Kreel and Dargon, they are oviparous.

187

"Interestingly, while they trade with the Kreel, they do not trust them. There are frequent references to the Kreel that are less than flattering. As for the Dargon, all they have to work with is being obtained from a limited Kreel database.

"In general, their opinion of all mammals is dismal, and they hold humans in abject contempt. From their communications chatter we were able to determine they've had facilities on the third planet for thousands of years. Since they arrived, they have been monitoring the humans, manipulating, and suppressing them."

"Suppressing them? How certain are we about the time frame?"

"The time estimate of their being on the planet for more than ten-thousand years has a ninety percent certainty."

"That would explain their lack of caution when entering this system. They know they have superior technology," Roan said.

"That's not all. We've overheard in their communications chatter a repeated phrase, 'to make primitive.' This has the ring of a periodic global assault. What's more, the rising level of technology on the third planet has them nervous. Some conversations suggest that in the near future they may be preparing another global assault, intending to cull the human herd and force the inhabitants back to a manageable primitive state."

"Such a global assault would kill billions of people." Roan said.

"That's their intention. And, there's even more, and it's more disgusting. Analysis of the communications among the populations on the planet indicates they currently enjoy lifespans of less than one-hundred years," Zorn said.

"That being true, then The Arkillians have used more than mental pop patterns to suppress the humans. They must be using DNA weapons to modify the genetic pool to enforce a short lifespan, barely supporting a healthy level of culture. That aggression is a murderous assault on billions of people for more than 200 generations."

"Agreed, and as bad as that is, there is more."

"How could it be worse?" Roan asked.

"The Arkillians are also responsible for the striking variations in skin color we've observed. Apparently in order to generate regional strife, through genetic manipulation, they have created an artificial division within the surviving human population. They seem to relish using the strategy of divide and conquer, employing every stratagem to control the population, keeping them scattered, in conflict, and oppressed. "

"Zorn, if ever there were a just cause for open warfare, aggression against an entire world population for 200 generations is it. If there were any remaining reservation about the upcoming battle with this species, it's now gone. Their utter arrogance can only be based upon an unchallenged presumption of racial superiority. I'll wager two brews our last mission shook them to their core," Roan said.

"No bet. It definitely shook up their commanders. They believe they fired upon a Dargon long-range fighter and are expecting an eminent attack."

"It's their very arrogance that may give us an edge. Does their Kreel database contain any reference to Guardian Force?" Roan said.

"None we've detected. And, given their attitude toward humans, it's rather doubtful it does," Zorn said.

"Good. Consider for a moment, what if they were to learn it's humans, not the Dargon, who are attacking them."

"Hmmm, after the first shock, it might provoke them to act rashly. Hey, what if prior to launching our attack we issue a demand ultimatum? The shock value alone might gain us a tactical advantage," Zorn mused.

Roan glanced over at Zorn. "I think we should go see if Kellon is able to meet with us. I'd like to give him an update on our progress. We might also suggest adding some psychological warfare to his battle plan, something that might just puncture their bloated arrogance."

"Sounds like a plan-"

Shey's voice broke into the conversation. "Roan, the girls and I have been listening. We are prepared to do another flyby, if you want."

"Shey, that might become necessary. But for now, how are your armaments loadouts proceeding?"

"Except for your new icepick, all Scouts are fully armed and supplied. All we need is a launch order."

Roan's habitual interaction with Shey was as if she were a person, not an AI. The AI programmers had intentionally made the personality nuance of each Guardian ship matrix unique, and in Roan's opinion they had exceeded their wildest expectations.

"Shey, for now stay focused on system and subsystems testing and preparation. Make maximum use of this quiet time. Remember, this is the calm before the coming storm."

"The girls are armed and ready. We will continue testing, as ordered," Shey said.

Chapter Thirty-Six:
High Stakes Game of Deception

After she insisted knowing the identity of her host, without hesitation Charles offered Susie a position within Olympus. It was clear to Susie that Olympus had already performed exhaustive background checks and was offering to make her earlier relationship formal. Signing additional paperwork, Susie made her new relationship official and was briefed. Learning about Olympus's true mission and its cover identification within the Department of commerce did not come as a surprise.

Having provided Olympus with the requested encryption keys to her data files, Susie was given three paid days off to rest up and attend to her own affairs. Then, on the morning of the fourth day she returned to the Department of Commerce and to Charles Sullivan's office. After her arrival, there was a few minutes of general conversation with Charles and Darrell, then she went with Darrell to see some inner workings of Olympus.

When leaving Charles' office, Darrell walked with Susie to an executive elevator. Upon their entry he inserted a key card into the elevator control panel. The elevator smoothly dropped and accelerated. Susie watched as the floor numbers rapidly decreased to the basement levels, but the elevator did not even slow. It continued dropping. Until then, Susie had no idea that a vast underground network of tunnels and facilities existed under New Washington. When The elevator came to a gentle stop, Susie noted that the floor indicator still displayed the higher basement level.

The elevator door opened onto a small clean receiving area. Other than the elevator door, there were no apparent exits. Promptly, a calm voice challenged them for their identification and destination.

Darrell answered the challenge, providing the needed information. Computers matched his image, physical profile, and voice signature with data on file. Susie was required to identify herself by name. As she did, her voice signature was added to a newly established security file.

After completing their security screening, a previously unobtrusive doorway silently opened.

Darrell led Susie out onto a small platform that was situated in an empty and featureless tunnel. With the distinctive thump of a heavy object, the door closed solidly behind them. The lighting was subdued, yet it offered adequate illumination for her to study the surroundings.

The air was cool and dry with a distinct smell of air conditioning. The entire area was uniformly drab, concrete gray and without adornment, except for a small white rectangular sign with black block letters, NE-1207.

Within two minutes of their stepping onto the platform, a sleek gleaming white cylindrical vehicle appeared out of the tunnel and came to a silent stop before them.

Susie noticed it had no wheels and presumed the transport used some form of air cushion or magnetic field to levitate and maintain its silent frictionless movement.

Darrell preceded her into the unoccupied transport, and Susie followed. They took two of the available seats. Without any noise the vehicle accelerated away from the platform.

Several windows were in front and on both sides of the passenger compartment, permitting people to look out on mostly featureless tunnel walls. Occasionally they passed a small platform similar to the one they had initially stood on. Several times the vehicle slowed and then sped up as it crossed an intersecting tunnel. She only saw one other cylinder like the one they rode in; it was crossing a tunnel ahead of them.

Five minutes after entering the vehicle, it slowly came to a stop and the door slid open. Darrell quickly stood and instructed Susie to follow. As soon as they stepped upon the platform, the transport moved silently away through the continuing tunnel.

As they crossed the platform , a door opened. They entered a small reception area and security did not challenge them. Entering a waiting elevator it lifted them a short interval, its door opening onto a bright   corridor. As Susie walked beside Darrell, several people greeted him. They then looked questioningly toward Susie, as if to say, "Now who do we have here?"

Darrell noted Susie's interested look and smiled. "We're in my department, and we don't have many visitors. Nearly everyone here is working directly for Olympus and is involved in data collection and analysis. That you are here with me suggests to others that you may be a new member of the team. On that note, let me officially welcome you aboard."

Darrell led her through a sliding door and into a large busy room where the light was subdued. Except for the background murmur of various small groups of individuals, the room was quiet. Several large data screens were positioned about, they extended from ceiling to floor. Each screen contained a multitude of bright images of alphanumeric data, graphs, and video images. There were multiple control consoles and Susie noted those working at the consoles were focused on their tasks, not even looking up as Darrell and she entered the room.

"When Monstro is in the solar system, the data collection center is busy on a continuous 24-hour basis. The room we are in is the primary hub of the data collection network for the entire Olympus Project. The men and women you see working here are analyzing data streaming in from satellites and ground installations located all around the world. Their task is to efficiently direct selected data to specialized individual analysts and to assure all the collected data is properly identified and tagged for later archival access. Immediately adjacent to this central hub are numerous smaller work areas, a first-class cafeteria, a VIP dining room, and assorted offices." Darrell said.

Susie was somewhat awed by the quiet intensity of the activity in which she found herself. Following Darrell, she walked into an adjacent analysis room. There were two men working at separate consoles.

"Good morning Charlie, please upload and play back the Wells' File from its beginning," Darrell said.

For the next few hours, Susie watched in amazement as the footage she had taken on the mountaintop in Switzerland was repeatedly shown, each segment being carefully analyzed, sometimes frame by frame. At various times, different people came into the room, viewed the footage, discussed their observations, and then departed.

After several hours she felt herself growing weary of the repetition, and her mind drifted to an earlier conversation with William. After she had asked about Gepeto, William had inquired, " Ms. Susie, when do you plan to come home?"

She had assured William that it would be soon. Now, based on the slow pace Olympus was analyzing her data, it could take several weeks before she and Gepeto could again enjoy walking together on the beach.

Until now, she had not studied her own mountainside recordings. She therefore found the video as interesting as did the others. The one sequence that most peaked everyone's curiosity was the short scene showing a scarlet and green-colored ship. The whole sequence had lasted but a few brief moments, and it was by pure chance she captured the image.

While filming the departure of two of Monstro's spacecraft she had also recorded the strange brightly colored ship. As she videoed the scene the strange ship fired laser beams and damaged both Monstro's ships.

"Charlie, get a full spectrum analysis of those laser beams. We should be able to determine the power, frequencies, and a possible source for that weapon system. Whatever it is, that beam is effective and delivered a terrific level of damage."

One of the men adjusted a selection frame around the brightest section of the laser beam. "Even as we speak boss, the data is already in weapons systems analysis."

Further studying the image, Darrell frowned. "Susie, those are striking colors. They're almost the colors of a badge or heraldic ensign. do you notice anything strange about that image?"

"No, not immediately."

"Look at the ship as a whole. Pay particular attention to its edges."

"Now I see it. There's something odd. Even allowing for atmospheric distortion, the edges seem too fuzzy and soft to be a solid object."

Darrell turned back to instruct the operator. "Charlie, enlarge the image to full screen and then enhance and sharpen it."

The image of the ship filled the screen. In spite of the operator's best effort, the edges of the craft defied further enhancement.

"There's definitely a shimmering about the ship. That effect might be the result of a propulsion field or perhaps some form of energy shielding. "Darrell said.

"Darrell, I can think of another possibility." Susie said.

"And, that being?"

"Well, what we're looking at may not be the real image of that spacecraft. Somehow the ship could be manifesting a cloaking image to mask its real appearance."

"Given that your suggestion is valid, then the next obvious questions are how and why. "Darrell said.

"As to how, I don't have a foggy engineering clue. However, as to why, about that I can make some guesses. First, the tactical deception is not intended for our benefit, it's done for Monstro. There are at least two plausible reasons for such deception. One reason being to mislead Monstro by hiding their true identity. The second possibility is they want to shift blame to someone else, someone who given the bright colors Monstro will identify. In either case, a really high stakes game of deception is in play." Susie said.

"Hmmm ..., that makes sense. Anything else?"

"Well yes. The masquerade implies there are at least three high-tech interstellar cultures engaged in military conflict, Monstro, the culture in the scarlet and green ship, and the culture being blamed for the attack. Else, the entire masquerade would be meaningless."

Darrell leaned back in his chair, softly groaning. "Oh boy, Charles will be elated when hearing that; we don't need two additional unknown bad guys."

Chapter Thirty-Seven:
Code Orange

Turning from the enlarged image of the green and scarlet colored ship and toward Susie, Darrell sighed. "Regarding your hypothesis there are three cultures in conflict, I disagree. There are at least four, and We're the fourth. And, as of now we don't have a clue about who is fighting who. This situation is untenable."

Turning back to the operator, Darrell instructed him to back up the sequence of images to the point where the aliens were walking about. After a moment, the requested scene appeared. One of Monstro's bulky appearing ships was shown resting on the ground, its large hatch was open and a loading ramp was extended. There were two distinct classes of aliens in the scene. One group was taller and had a larger angular build than the other. The two groups appeared to be the same species, but they were distinctly different. It was the taller aliens who were directing the loading operation. In watching the video, Darrell was far more interested in studying the alien ships than the aliens.

"Those ships are bulkier than the other type and are obviously the cargo ships. Charlie, scan back to where we can see the other type of spacecraft."

The images blurred and then froze. "Look, that spacecraft is about the same length as the cargo craft, but narrower. Notice the blisters along the hull. Also, there are no open hatches or personnel exiting the ship. My assessment is these ships are the armed guards protecting the area. Charlie, sort out and send all of the images of the ships having blisters to the weapons analysis group. Request they closely examine the blisters on the hull. See if they can determine their purpose or functionality."

"It's done. Images are selected and transmitted as ordered, boss.

"Wow, these images are really crisp. Nice work Ms. Wells," Charlie said.

Charlie's unanticipated compliment surprised and pleased Susie. "Charlie, please feel free to use my first name. The video is crisp because I was using my old fashion portable Questar telescope. It's sorta archaic, but provides marvelous magnification with a very clear resolution image."

"This is unquestionably the best look we have ever had of these folks. Charlie, send the entire file over to anthropology. Perhaps they can tell us more than is readily apparent on our first glance," Darrell said.

"Transfer is complete, as ordered."

"Good. Now, what's our latest on that last odd tracking report?" Darrell said.

"Well, it's definitely odd and interesting. They didn't follow their typical flight pattern, and what makes the sighting really unusual is that it headed directly into the Mongolian Desert. The second strange factor is the makeup of that formation, four of the faster fighters and four smaller ships, those with the blisters. There were no cargo types. Currently, our tracking assets in that part of the world are sparse. Unfortunately, we lost track of the formation in the mountains. Then, twelve hours later we regained track as the ships moved back into space and returned to Monstro. Precisely where those ships spent twelve hours is not determined. I've instructed our tracking teams to determine if we can shift additional tracking assets into the area. That's about all I've got, boss."

"Susie, do you happen to have any information about that particular region?" Darrell said.

"Nothing other than what is generally found in tourist info. It's a desert region occupying about thirty percent of the entire country of Mongolia. It's about 500,000 square miles in total area. While it's commonly called the 'Gobi Desert,' the people who live there think of it as having four major divisions, all of which they call 'Gobi.'"

Darrell turned with a smile and looked at Susie. "Tourist info? Do you have any other tourist information?"

"Well, since you asked, it's my understanding the Mongolian region has been inhabited since ancient times. It's also acknowledged to be rich in old UFO legends. In most Ural-Altaic languages, the word 'Gobi' literally means 'desert.' In the literature of the region, the Gobi is also called 'Shamo.' It has springs, forests, sands, steppe lands, soaring snowcapped mountains, and a very diverse animal kingdom. It's clearly not an uninhabitable Sahara Desert type of place. The Gobi includes vast plains like those of Europe, the towering peaks and mountain ranges of Asia, and broad valleys and sand dunes like Africa. This is why some people call it the land of the three continents. I guess the term 'three continents' originated because those first using the terminology had no knowledge of the other continents, But that's merely a guess.

"Oh, by the way, there're legends about an ancient lost city in the Gobi, it's called Khara-Khoto. It's said the rulers of the Ming dynasty destroyed that city in the fourteenth century."

"Humph, anything else?" Darrell said.

"Yes, there's one small additional item that might interest you. The western part of the Gobi is located inside China. Off hand," that's about all the Gobi information I remember."

"I suspect that working with you is going to prove interesting," Darrell said.

Responding to a personal communicator alert, Charlie listened to an incoming message and frowned. "Boss, that was tracking. They report that the last few remaining groups of Monstro's ships are departing from the planet, all except one. A new group is departing Monstro. It's a rather large group and its heading toward Asia. There are about forty cargo ships and at least thirty defensive blister types. There are also eight fighters escorting the group."

"Charlie, have we been able to get additional tracking assets into position over Asia?" Darrell said.

"Sorry, not yet."

"Humph, whatever Monstro is doing, it's throwing its standard operations handbook out of the hatch. Charlie, contact the Director and the other branch managers, Code Orange. Set them up for an immediate conference call on this screen. Then, try to get a satellite or any other surveillance asset into position over Mongolia, ASAP, priority AA plus," Darrell said.

Within forty-five seconds, images of Charles Sullivan, Janet Rodgers, and Carl Suthaford appeared on the screen before them. Charles spoke first. "Report."

Darrell briefly summarized the unfolding events, including Susie's observations, then outlined the steps he had taken.

"That's all good, but what's your immediate assessment?" Charles said.

"Sir, given the odd distribution of the new group, I believe Monstro is preparing for an imminent battle. Accordingly, Monstro is offloading its VIPs, key civilians, and important non-combatants. My conclusion is their actions mean they have reason to question their ability to win in an upcoming battle with whatever species is crewing the green and scarlet ships.

"Moreover, that there are so many inbound cargo ships suggest Monstro has some unidentified facility on Earth to receive them. Oddly, there are no records of previous flights of any significance into Mongolia. Even so, there must be an existing facility in the mountains we're unaware of."

"Darrell, while you may not have modern tracking data, there is an enormous collection of ancient stories about UFO activity around the Gobi," Janet said.

"That figures. Susie has theorized the combatants may include a third as yet unidentified interstellar group, namely, whoever those in the scarlet and green ship are impersonating."

"Dammed, this is degenerating into a mess beyond any hope of determining who is driving the situation. Given your assessment, Monstro is knowingly marooning its people here. I can't believe they would do that indefinitely. If defeated, they must expect a relief force, most likely by a large military contingent. We're not yet ready to challenge their technology in open combat--"

"Sir, there's one way we might shift the odds in our favor; that's by capturing the aliens marooned here. If we can obtain their functioning technology, it might considerably advance our propulsion and weapons programs."

"Be careful Carl, China and Mongolia are not about to invite us to romp all over their sovereign territory," Janet said.

"Janet is correct, they won't. Still, we need to gain intel to assess what military defenses and capability we're facing on the ground. So, you're to identify the three Special Forces long-range deep penetration reconnaissance teams nearest to Mongolia. Put them on immediate standby for deployment. Arrange with Space Warfare for their insertion. Upon ending this call, I'm calling the President to get authorization to launch. Do you understand?" Charles said.

"Yes, sir," Carl said.

"Just remember, time is a priceless commodity. So, let's get to work," Charles said.

The screen went blank.

"Charlie, I want immediate and a constant feed from tracking. And, we require the current coordinates of that inbound formation. Do what's required to get the needed assets expedited into the target area. We will require precise coordinates of where they go to roost. And, somewhere within 500,000 square miles won't cut it.

"Next, commandeer one of our orbiting large deep-space telescopes. If anyone argues about their precious allocated viewing time, tell them it's being shut down for urgent critical maintenance. I want that telescope locked on Monstro until I tell you otherwise."

"I'm on it, boss."

The image on the screen transformed into a political map, detailing the far side of the Earth. The inbound Monstro group was not yet visible on the map, but its spatial coordinates were displayed in an upper corner.

"At least we have some time before they reach their destination. Hopefully we can get additional tracking assets into position in time. We have to be able to look down into those mountain valleys before they get there," Darrell said.

Suddenly, Susie realized her life had abruptly made a dramatic course change. Operation Olympus? A week ago, she had not even heard the term or known of its existence. Now, she found herself sitting smack in the middle of a growing international crisis involving conflict and several interstellar cultures. The unadorned thought that surfaced unbidden was, *What have I gotten myself into?*

Chapter Thirty-Eight:
Gauntlet

Kur entered into the Nest ship's busy Combat Center and stood studying the tactical screens, and reconsidered his recent choices. Again, he asked himself, *Have I done everything possible to assure the safety of those for whom I am responsible?* He asked this knowing only future events could reveal the answer.

Looking at the 3D holographic display he observed the symbolic representation of surrounding space. When observing the symbol representing the departing formation, he felt a flood of relief. Ca and Rin with all their Nest members were safely aboard those ships. Soon they would reach the protective shelter of the Earth base. Given its engineered concealment and ground-based defenses, Kur was confident they would be secure until a relief force arrived. Wishing them well, he thought, *Safe journey friends.*

"Captain, have all the departing ships been launched?" Kur said.

"Honored One, it is so. Seven cargo lifters and six assault ships remain. Eight fighters are escorting the departing ships. The remaining fighters will stay with us."

"Well done. Prepare the ship for departure. Set our initial course toward the outer debris belt as we planned. Bring all weapon systems to ready alert and stand-by to extract the ship from its orbit. You are to advise me when the departing formation reaches the Earth atmosphere."

His sense of foreboding had not abated, and Kur's concerns for the safety of the Nest ship continued to increase. There were simply far too many undefinable factors in play, and his actions were purely defensive, being but responses to events structured by others. He was even now striving to take unpredictable actions, and if all being well, gain a measure of control.

The primary tactical problem was that they were separated decades distant from Scion and possible relief. His anger was smoldering. Those who cut the normal escort cruisers from the mission undoubtedly were trying to increase the profit margins, and he cursed them, *May their tongue turn bitter.*

The present circumstances and vulnerability were reprehensible and unacceptable. If they survived this mission, he was going to assure all future missions had a proper military escort of several cruisers, regardless of the impact on profit margins.

Approaching, the Captain saluted. "Honorable One, the departing formation has entered the Earth atmosphere. Upon your orders we are prepared to exit orbit."

Without hesitation, Kur ordered, "Execute Departure. I will be in my quarters. At the slightest indication of potential trouble, immediately summon me. Do you understand?"

"Honored One, I understand, and it will be so."

Departing the Combat Center, Kur knew they were open to attack. Reaching the outer debris belt was running a gauntlet. The time immediately ahead was going to be difficult, with danger constantly nipping at their heels. Walking through the corridors, he felt the rising deep rhythm and resonant thrum of the massive propulsion generators; they were ramping up toward maximum power. He was weary. Hopefully, he would get some rest prior to trouble. Clearly, the next move was the Dargons'.

Exerting its maximum acceleration, its increasing velocity moved the Nest ship outward toward the unblinking stars.

Unseen and undetected six prepositioned relay monitors shifted from their previous assigned orbits, moving away from Earth and outward from its sun, while maintaining their relative position with the Arkillian ship. The lone sentinel, twice noticed and identified as a stony asteroid by the Arkillian fighters, lingered a short while and then also purposefully moved away from Earth toward the stars....

Chapter Thirty-Nine:
Load Out

The soft tone of the communicator sounded and Kellon touched its control pad. "Kellon here."

"Sir, Grey here. The sentinel has detected a large deployment of ships leaving the target and entering the planet's atmosphere. There appears to be about sixty or seventy ships, mostly cargo and assault types. As soon as they entered atmosphere, the target broke out of orbit. Our sentinel indicates that it's pushing its maximum power envelope. The ship is somewhat faster than we had anticipated. Adjusting for the speed difference, we've several hours before we need to get underway."

"Roy, what is your assessment as why the new group of ships departed the target?"

"Sir, their commander is a professional and has likely acted to minimize casualties. I believe he has reduced his shipboard contingent to a core military crew and is battle ready."

"Humph, agreed. Carry on," Kellon said.

Standing Orders were the bedrock of Guardian Force operations. Those orders constituted Kellon's guiding authority, dictating that he takes actions to end the alien oppression of the humans on the third planet. Accordingly, everyone on Lan was committed to battle.

Being keenly aware they were far from home, Kellon understood there were no reinforcements. Furthermore, the battle with the target would result in far-reaching consequences for both species. Still, Kellon's clear duty was the protection of human populations on multiple worlds.

Standing, Kellon stretched. "Lan, locate and connect Commander Roan."

"Yes Sir."

"Sir, Roan here."

"What is the status of your new ice pick?"

"Sir, all Scout ships, except for Shey, are fully armed and ready for immediate deployment. The final batch of small missiles is currently coming out of system verification and quality control. This last batch will be loaded into launch pods and ready within an hour. Otherwise, we are ready."

"Have you finalized your attack scenario and completed its simulations training? Kellon said.

"Yes, Sir.

"Good. Now, you're to work with Commander Grey. Go over the details of your attack plan. He needs to be as familiar with your tactics as you are."

"Yes, Sir."

"Roan, do you have any questions?"

"Well, Sir, we're still badly outnumbered. And, if the enemy commander decides to self-destruct, the shrapnel from a ship that size poses a serious danger to everything in its vicinity. I don't have a strategy worked out for that possibility."

"Point well taken. Our tactic is to minimize our proximity to the target, since keeping our distance is our best defense against such an outcome. This means moving in close, then hit and run. Continue with your load out and keep Commander Grey tight in the loop." Kellon said.

"Yes, Sir."

Kellon sat momentarily reflecting on his several centuries spent in space warfare. Merely surviving in a hostile environment was difficult. To enter that environment and intentionally conduct warfare seemed sheer madness. Remembering his last walk down to the beach, the fresh sea air, and the warmth of the sunshine on a spring morning, his longing to be back home gnawed like a sharp hunger. Sighing, Kellon consciously redirected his mind toward his command responsibility.

"Lan, take a report for Guardian Headquarters."

"Sir, ready."

"In accordance with Guardian Standing Orders, I am preparing to engage a larger alien military force. Enclosed is a brief description of the events leading up to this engagement. All personnel are in a state of good morale, prepared, and committed to the coming action.

"The intended first contact will be an initial communication with this alien culture. It will be made by direct video with their commander. Given the proximity of the two involved solar systems, eventual peace between the species is deemed essential. The preferred goal of contact is a peaceful coexistence. If a peace can be achieved, then the sacrifice of the battle element of surprise will be well spent.

"Realistically, the enemy's long-term brutality, and contempt for humanity, suggests a battle is the most probable outcome of first contact.

The loss of one of their Capital ships will undoubtedly result in the aggressor culture's swift and powerful response in force. Therefore, I recommend that Glas Dinnein and Guardian Force immediately prepare to defend this system.

"Until the humans in this system are able to defend themselves, Guardian Force protection of this solar system is essential. Given their current level of technology, the effort required to bring them to a level of self-defense should not be great nor the time required prolonged.

"It's essential to send medical teams. Our analysis indicates the people on the third planet have been subjected to DNA warfare and multiple mental oppression methods for more than ten-thousand years. They truly need our help.

"Lan is preparing for battle in the tradition of Guardian Force. I commend each and every member of this fine crew."

Before continuing, Kellon took a deep breath. "Lan, you're to encrypt the message Black Hole and send it out over my signature.

"Lan, have you any thoughts concerning the message contents?"

"Sir, only that we are fully capable of kicking their butts."

Lan's unanticipated reply caused Kellon to smile. *When we get back to Glas Dinnein, Lan's AI programmers are going to find a cold case of brews on their desks.*

"Lan, I agree, we'll get the job done...."

Chapter Forty:
Far Nest

Carved deep into solid granite, the stone-cold hangar was cavernous. Its concealed entrance was carefully positioned two-thirds up the sheer face of a thousand-foot cliff. Upon their nighttime arrival, the entrance, indistinguishable from the surrounding rock face, had silently pivoted wide open. The group of ships quickly entered, the massive hangar door smoothly pivoting closed behind them. The Arkillian engineers who many turns before built the facility had built it with precise confidence, and their work had passed the test of thousands of turns.

Once within the hangar a soft illumination from overhead panels flooded the secured void, the light being reminiscent of a pleasant winter day on Scion. The hangar could have easily held every fighter, cargo lifter, and ground ship on the Nest ship; those in the hangar barely filled a tenth of the available space.

Looking about, everything considered, Ca was pleased; here, he was in complete command. While the immediate future held dire challenges, he was nevertheless delighted at his age to have been given the responsibility for an important Council mission.

Kur had been most gracious before their departure from the Nest ship. Their unique destinies having moved them in different directions, both knew they might never see the other again. *Yet, given good fortune,* Ca thought, *the enigmatic currents of our destinies may again bring us together.*

Ca had carefully studied the Intelligence estimates regarding current human technology and knew it was sophisticated. If they had been tracked into this region of the planet, every available satellite would now be scanning for a trace of their presence. Action needed to be taken to counter that possibility.

Ca's first priority was to assure all the ships were secured. He then satisfied himself that the hangar entrance thermal and camouflage systems were active. Turning, he crossed the cold hangar and entered the environmental pressure locks. Exiting the lock into the living and working areas, he was pleased to find the ambient temperature was more comfortable than during his first visit. The climate controls and air purification systems had been activated during that initial inspection tour, and they were returning the inner complex to Scion normal values of temperature, pressure, and air freshness.

Ca's main conference room was sparsely furnished, but the room was spacious and elegant in its subtle colors. When entering he found Rin and three senior officers waiting. Rin was relaxed and sitting at the conference table, while the three officers stood at stiff attention. Just inside the door two of Ca's servants were standing and immobile. Looking about, Ca signed to them, instructing they bring food and beverages for five.

Walking to the table, Ca took a seat at its head. After a momentary pause, he invited the three officers to take seats at the table. Rin's facial markings indicated surprise at Ca's unanticipated gesture of informality, but he said nothing.

Among the Arkillians, sharing a meal with others had a deep significance. In mixed-status meal sharing, established hierarchies were strictly preserved, however, those of the lesser status were deemed especially noted and worthy of praise. Being members of the Council, Ca and Rin were of the highest ruling class, therefore the honor that Ca was attributing to the three senior officers was particularly noteworthy.

Understanding there was a high probability they might be marooned on Earth for decades of turns, Ca was aware the overall success of his mission required flawless discipline. Accordingly, he had carefully selected each officer on a strict basis of their proven military experience and exemplary service. Likewise, the troops that accompanied them were of the finest elite Arkillian forces. The senior commander was wearing decorations of air combat on his robes. The other two officers were elite ground force commanders. Like the troops, they were all tested combat veterans. Ca mused, *The Arkillian presence on Earth might be small, but we represent a formidable group.*

Before speaking, Ca carefully studied the countenance of each of the three officers. When he finally spoke, his words were calm and measured.

"Each of you is noticed with distinction. Also noticed are your Nests. Your exemplary service and earned merits have qualified you for this crucial mission. Our identity code is 'Far Nest.' All communications directed from our Nest ship to Far Nest is to be brought to my immediate attention.

"Our principle mission is to continuously monitor and record the progress of our Nest ship. If the Nest ship comes under attack, as we expect it will, we are to record a continuous telemetry stream of the evolving battle. All aspects of that battle will be preserved and archived for analysis. This duty becomes especially important should our Nest ship be destroyed. All archived data will be given to Council members, when they arrive to relieve us.

"We are situated in a wilderness on an alien planet and are but a few among a vast horde of hostile mammals. Make no mistake, these humans are not as stupid as once was thought. Even now they are looking with satellites and ground searchers for this Far Nest. They are not to find it.

"Our mission here is strictly covert in its nature. Our orders are to maintain an active surveillance site at this installation, and remain undetected. We are to continue our surveillance until we are relieved by our Nest ship or else other Arkillian vessels.

"You are to take all necessary steps to obliterate all traces of radiated energy, heat, waste, or outside activity, and will continue in keeping it that way.

"You are to tune a multi-channel broadband passive bio-receiver to monitor the nearby region for humans and their communications. If any humans or ground communications traffic is detected within a three-day walking distance of this facility, I am to immediately be notified.

"If aircraft are observed searching within a ten-day walk of this facility, I am to immediately be notified.

"Above all, there are to be no active transmissions of any nature. All our ships and their internal systems will remain inert, inactive, and dormant, unless I personally command otherwise. We are not going to give the humans any means of detecting this facility."

"To augment our defenses, a heavy suppression field is to be promptly established surrounding this facility. the field must be subtle and psychologically prevailing, but not so granular as to be electronically detected. The purpose of the field is not to kill, but rather to discourage any curious human from coming too near.

"You are to evaluate the primary weapons systems of this Far Nest. Based on my own examination, I believe you will find they are quite impressive.

Ca scanned the countenances of the three officers, carefully noting the details of their facial markings. In like manner, they returned his gaze with complete attention.

After a slight pause, Ca asked, "Do you understand?"

"Honored One, we understand and it will be so," The senior officer said.

Entering the conference room, Ca's servants placed before each of those sitting at the table a selection of food and beverages. Ca then raised his cup in a toast.

"I salute each of our Nests, and especially our Nest ship and those who are preparing for battle. I expect each of you will fulfill your duties with the same dedication and determination as those now about to enter combat."

Ca drank but a sip and then put his cup down on the table. As he did, the three officers and Rin took up their cups and likewise drank a small amount and placed their cups back on the table, as had Ca.

Selecting food, Ca began to eat; Rin and the others followed his example.

Ca's formal gesture of sharing a meal with the three officers was not flattery. He fully understood everyone on the mission was facing as much danger as was those on the Nest ship. They were far from Scion, isolated on a hostile alien planet, and surrounded by billions of mostly hostile adversaries. He was not foolish; being prudent he understood the combined actions of the three excellent officers would define his first Council command, be it either as a success or failure.

Following the meal, the three officers were formally excused. After their departure, Ca sat back and reflected on their circumstances. If not for Rin speaking, he might have forgotten his friend still remained in the room.

"Do you think we will ever see Scion again?" Rin said.

"Indeed Rin, we will survive. Still, our chances for survival are only minimally better than those aboard the Nest ship.

"It is time for us to begin our inspection tour. There is much work required if we are to assure our survival."

Walking together through the network of empty corridors, they entered into the communications area. Some of the Arkillians on duty were busy inspecting and selectively activating equipment left generations before. Others were installing new equipment brought with them. As he stood observing, Ca approved of their progress. They remained in communications until the encrypted telemetry stream transmitted from the Nest ship was being received and properly recorded.

Moving back through the hallways, Ca and Rin entered the main Combat Center. The center was large and filled with multiple three-dimensional holographic projection tanks. One tank showed a portion of the surface of the planet. The display could be adjusted to reveal other areas as needed, with accuracy to scale and terrain. A second visual tank held a three-dimensional representation of the solar system. A third tank showed a blue icon that represented the Nest ship and green dots were representing the escorting fighters. The details needed for the tactical display were being obtained from the incoming Nest ship telemetry. The display was an exact duplication of the tactical display within the Nest ship combat center. With relief, Ca noticed there were no red dots. *Good,* he thought, *the enemy is not yet detected.*

Leaving the Combat Center, Ca and Rin next inspected engineering, life support, production and maintenance, crew living quarters, dispensary, commissary, hydroponics, food preservation and storage, training and recreational areas, weapons lockers, power generation facilities, and libraries.

After their inspection tour, Ca dismissed Rin. Alone, he again walked to the Combat Center. Standing and looking at the solar system representation, he observed the Nest ship was still following the preplanned evasion route, accelerating directly for the fifth planet of the system, a gas giant. The Nest ship would select its final approach vector to that planet based upon the tactical situation. If they were not under attack when reaching the planet, they would choose a vector that accelerated them toward the outer debris belt. If they were under attack, Kur would adapt their maneuvers to maximize their survival.

Ca moved back to study the tactical tank. As long as the tank was showing its bright display of moving points of colors, the Nest ship was still safe and transmitting its telemetry. Satisfied all was as it should be, he returned to his quarters.

In a matter of hours, the newly installed instrumentation would be operational and able to detect and display human activity anywhere near the facility. While much work still remained, Ca was pleased, thinking, *We will soon be prepared for whatever happens next.*

Chapter Forty-One:
Slingshot

Since Monstro broke out of its parking orbit, Olympus was employing all available sensors to monitor and track its progress. Its continuing rate of acceleration and unanticipated trajectory surprised everyone. It was heading directly toward Jupiter.

As it moved outward, Monstro was maintaining a regular flowing helix screen of escorting fighters. Perturbations in its course suggested it was adhering to some subtle evasive pattern. The data indicated it expected an imminent attack.

Current analysis concluded Monstro's intention was to add to its speed by performing a slingshot around Jupiter. A second theory was Monstro might use Jupiter to make an unpredictable and significant course change.

Clearly, Monstro was in a big hurry. But inexplicably it was moving directly away from its home star system.

The working area around Darrell was cluttered with empty coffee cups and the waste cans were bulging with empty crushed box lunches and paper cups. Monstro's sudden departure had demanded everyone in Analysis work double shifts on a seven day and twenty-four-hour cycle. During the previous several days, Darrell had barely shut his eyes. Making matters worse, the predictable and constant demands of the Executive branch for updates was wearing down his entire staff. Even little things, like the absence of windows in the Analysis section, which produced a blurring of day and night, tended to depress morale. Grumbling inwardly, he mused, *Is it really necessary we're treated like gophers?*

His communicator vibrated. In irritation, he keyed it and snapped, "Darrell here."

"Good morning, Darrell. Ouch, no offense intended, but you look like you've been on a three-day bender. How much sleep have you had in the past seventy-two hours?" Carl said.

"Clearly, not enough. Now, give, what intel do you have for me?"

"Well, we're receiving new reports from our deep recon teams in the mountains. So far they haven't found a tangible trace of our visitors or of their facility."

Darrell winced. Carl's teams were working at high risk in a politically hostile region, and they were working without adequate information. He felt personally responsible.

"Carl, I'm sorry. We finally got tracking assets into the area, but not before those inbound ships had gone to ground. We've repeatedly examined the three distinct monitored flights. Those three routes do not point to a common terminus. By following multiple evasive routes, the ships have maximized their concealment. We're going over every satellite image, looking for deviations or changes in foliage, rocks, or trails. The infrared images are being triple checked. We'll find them, but it's taking time --"

Carl interrupted. "Understood. Be advised, our ground teams are establishing multiple energy detectors along with broadband monitors. We're working to place them on the high points to gain optimum coverage. It's slow work, but those guys are the best in the world at what they are doing.

"The purpose of my call is to tell you the first ground monitors will be coming online and up-linked in about fifteen minutes. Darrell, be sure to keep me informed on any breakthroughs."

"Be ye hereby advised, you're at the top of a short list. Do you have any viable leads, anything at all?"

"Maybe. We do have one interesting anomaly, sorta. The mountain people are spooked and seem agitated. They sense something that we're not yet aware of. Some of them are beginning to pack up and move hurriedly down the valleys. It's a good possibility that whatever they're moving from is what we need to be moving toward. As for now, we're trying to learn the cause of their alarm. Sorry, but that's all I've got. I need to get back to work. Really, Darrell, you need to stop burning your candle on both ends. Get some sleep, if you can."

Darrell smiled. Carl was a good friend of many years and they often seemed to be able to read each other's thoughts. "You don't look all that hot yourself. You could use some sleep too. And, just remember you're working where you ought not be. So, be careful."

"Consider it done," Carl said.

Standing, Darrell yawned, stretched, then exited his work area and walked over to the central Analysis room. All around him people were busy. Looking about, he felt a blending of fatigue and pride. Each of the men and women were professionals and superb at what they did. Most often their job was thankless, public recognition and appropriate honors for extraordinary effort for classified work was rare. Most of the families back at home had no real concept of what their loved ones actually worked on at the Department of Commerce.

Entering the central Analysis room, he quickly confirmed the new telemetry signal from the Gobi was coming in strong and the assigned analysis group was busy working on the data. As Darrell walked up, Charlie looked at him and frowned.

"Boss, why are you still here?"

"Why? I suppose it's because the supply of hot coffee is abundant and the rent is agreeable. But, how are you doing? Is there any change in Monstro's trajectory?"

"Well now, as a matter of fact, there is. Until about thirty minutes ago Monstro was moving directly toward Jupiter. Whoever was after Monstro would have considerable difficulty in guessing what its new trajectory might be when rounding the planet. Any attempt to predict its new trajectory, to sorta get out in front to ambush it, would be difficult."

"How difficult? Explain," Darrell said.

"Well, given an enemy would have difficulty in predicting the new trajectory, that enemy would need to get lucky or else be really fast. The latter possibility doesn't seem plausible, given how fast that big ship is moving. We've never seen it accelerate at this continuous rate. For sure, we have nothing on our drawing boards that can hold a candle to its constant rate of acceleration."

"Well, how soon will we know what its next move will be?"

"The good news is we sorta know now, boss. Thirty minutes ago, Monstro made a slight course correction. As of now, it's committed to its new trajectory...."

Darrell did not miss Charlie's long pause, and smiling took the proffered bait. "Out with it, there're no secrets permitted, and no gloating either. Just the facts, nothing but the facts. Where's it headed?"

"Shucks, boss. You take all the fun out of this job. The new fact is its trajectory remains in the Ecliptic Plane; it's heading out toward the outer debris belt."

"Humph, that maneuver makes absolutely no sense. Why on Earth would it accelerate away from its home, just to head for a bunch of debris, and at what must be near its flank acceleration? Give, what's your best guess why it's doing that."

"Best guess? Well, did you ever see a quail hen fake a bad wing and lead a predator away from her nest?"

Charlie's unanticipated response startled Darrell. "Humph, you're right on target. It must be trying to lay down a false trail away from its own world, and that single fact is revealing."

"Agreed, boss. Whoever spooked those guys on Monstro has done a class act. By all indications, they're running scared."

"Scared? I seriously doubt that. They may simply be trying to achieve a defensible position. Continue to maintain all available sensors focused on that ship. Whatever they're trying to defend themselves against might be smart enough to get out ahead and just be waiting for them."

"Boss, I can't see how anyone could get out in front of Monstro. If some adversary pulls off that brilliant gambit, I recommend you don't play any poker with them. If Monstro gets jumped beyond Jupiter then Monstro's crew had every reason to be running scared."

"Let's just hope we've no reason to play poker with hostile aliens, at least not for the foreseeable future. Now, quit loafing and get back to work. And, keep me updated."

"You are a mean-spirited, hard-driving and unfeeling boss," Charlie said.

"I heard that crack, Charlie. Be herewith advised, no more coffee breaks permitted for fifteen minutes," Darrell said.

Returning to his work area, Darrell was pleased to see that during his absence the cleanup crew had been there. There were no empty cups anywhere, and the wastebaskets were empty with new liners neatly folded over their rims. Sitting down, he picked up his communicator to update his own hard-driving and unfeeling boss. The number he dialed buzzed only once before the anticipated response.

"Sullivan here."

"Charles, I've just talked with Charlie. Monstro has altered course. Our best evaluation is it's attempting to misdirect their adversary away from their home world."

"And, just how did you determine that strategy?"

"Sir, Monstro is currently moving directly away from its home system."

"Hmmm ..., that's at least verifiable," Charles said.

"Yes, Sir. If our deductions are correct, Monstro knows who his enemy is and hopes his enemy doesn't yet know the location of his home system. Monstro is moving toward Jupiter and still accelerating. When it rounds Jupiter, Monstro's trajectory remains on the Ecliptic Plane. It's heading for the outer debris belt. Possibly, it's seeking a defensive position to make a stand."

"That makes sense. Now, what is Carl reporting? Are you getting data?"

"Yes, Sir. We're receiving telemetry. And, there is no trace of Monstro's landing party. That's all we have here."

"Humph, at least we know more than we did yesterday. Good work. Keep me informed."

As he closed his communicator, Darrell could not help but wonder about the events unfolding in deep space. Whoever the combatants were, those on Earth were in the position of being mere spectators. As many times as he acknowledged that harsh reality, the sense of deep unease never lessened; he well understood playing catch-up in warfare can get you killed real dead....

Chapter Forty-Two:
Battle Stations

Easing free from the outer debris belt, Lan moved unseen through the void, swiftly dropping sunward and passed across the orbit of the eighth planet. Then, Kellon directed Lan to a full stop, while continuing to evaluate the target's maneuvers.

The implemented battle plan embraced two principal components. First, draw the target away from the human occupied planet and out into the outer solar system, then with decisive force, prevent the target from returning inward. The hostile aliens were being evicted, permanently.

Kellon's initial deduction that the enemy commander would move toward Lan had been confirmed days earlier. Now, as the aliens approached, the time for direct confrontation was drawing near. Aboard Lan and the four Scouts, the crews checked and then rechecked every system and subsystem, reviewing every nuance of their chosen battle plan. Far from home and possible reinforcements, they were relying upon their planning, skill, and experience for their survival.

The days passed, and everyone continued working to be prepared and ready. With keen interest they observed as the target accelerated around the fifth planet, an exotically banded and brilliantly colored gas giant. In the Combat Analysis Center, Lan's tactical team precisely measured, plotted, and projected the new target trajectory.

Compensating for the effects of the aliens' slingshot maneuver about the gas giant, some minor adjustments were made to the planned intercept. Tracking data from the sentinel trailing the target, along with data from the monitors that Shey had deployed upon their arrival in the system, was streaming into CAC. Every detail of the target's maneuvering was being subjected to critical analysis.

As the moment of commitment to battle arrived, Kellon was sitting in his command chair in CAC, his attention focused on the tactical plot. The forward display had altered from the previous heliocentric display to a standard tactical relative motion plot.

Lan was symbolically shown as a stationary golden icon, located at the geographic center of the polar display. All other plotted objects were shown relative to their position from Lan. A red icon was indicating the position of the primary target. A thin red line showing the track of the relative motion vector extended from the target symbol. Lan's deployed sensors were being shown as blue dots. A lavender icon marked the position of the trailing sentinel.

Immediately below the polar plot was a narrow rectangle, having the same width as the upper plot. The rectangle was divided horizontally in its middle and was displaying the scaled elevation of each plotted object, either above or below the defined tactical plane. At the moment, that plane was being defined by the target relative motion vector and Lan's position.

Each object being tracked in the upper polar plot was projected vertically downward, and a corresponding symbol was proportionally positioned above or below the tactical plane. At a glance, an analyst could determine the relative horizontal and vertical position of any tracked object relative to Lan and the tactical plane.

Offset and immediately to the right of the tactical plot was a large video display. Images of the alien ship and its escorts were being transmitted from the trailing sentinel and shown on the screen.

Turning, Kellon looked toward the Navigation station and Commander Grey. "Roy, have you calculated the point where the target is likely to begin its deceleration?"

"Yes, sir. I'll put a marker box on the plot to indicate that event."

On the tactical screen, a small narrow rectangular red event box appeared. It was a simple graphic that overlaid the extrapolated target's relative track.

"Sir, the target should begin deceleration about the time it crosses the orbit of the seventh planet, about the same time it enters the indicated event box."

Studying the plot for a few moments, Kellon ordered, "Lan, freeze the current tactical plane. Next, transmit the tactical plot to all Scouts. Alert Commander Roan, he is to stand ready to take the Scouts to their predefined attack positions."

"Sir, Commander Roan and all Scout ships have acknowledged receiving the data. I am standing by to synchronize launch of Scouts on Commander Roan's order."

Kellon keyed the communications control pad on his command chair, connecting to Shey, "Roan, Kellon here. Are the Scouts ready?"

"Sir, Shey is reporting all her sisters are ready, standing by for orders to launch."

"Good. Roan, keep it tight. Lan is standing by, ready to synchronize Scout launch on your command," Kellon said.

"Sir, preparing to launch."

Three minutes later the distinct sounds of the heavy Scout hangar doors cycling were heard throughout Lan. "Sir, all Scout ships are now clear, and they are moving together toward their assigned attack positions," Lan said.

Observing the tactical plot, Kellon watched as four golden icons moved away from Lan, moving directly toward the displayed red event box. Inwardly, Kellon mused, *Good fortunes and may the muses be with each of you.*

"Navigation, move us sunward. We're to arrive at a point two-thousand kilometers directly above the target, at the point when it enters into the defined event box. We're then to be at the same speed and heading as the target."

"Acknowledged," Roy said.

"Tactical, initiate a clampdown on all sources of detectible energy. Double check our temporal wake. Lan is to maintain full stealth."

"Acknowledged," Lorn said.

"Tactical, confirm the Zed decoy is programmed and ready for deployment," Kellon said.

"Tactical here. Confirming, The Zed decoy navigation program is updated to the current tactical plot. The decoy will simulate a Kreel Gortoga class cruiser."

As Lan approached the outermost edge of the defined event box, Kellon ordered, "Tactical, deploy the Zed decoy."

"Tactical here. Zed decoy is launched."

As Lan and the Scouts continued sunward toward their designated intercept point, the Zed decoy dropped down and came fully about, slowed, and began moving along the projected target track line. The decoy was to serve as proffered bait; having reduced its speed, the leading fighters would soon overhaul and detect it.

Three hours after the decoy had been launched, clear images of the approaching fighter escort were being shown on the video screen in CAC. The escort was using active sensors, and was dispersed into a large three-sided pyramid formation. The apex of the imaginary pyramid was on the projected track line, and the base of that pyramid formed a triangular plane perpendicular to that line. One fighter was positioned at the apex and an additional fighter was positioned at each of the three points on the pyramid base. As Kellon observed, the three escorts at the points of the base held their geometric and relative positions with each other, even as the imaginary base of the pyramid slowly rotated. The escorts were providing overlapping active sensor coverage, sweeping a sizable volume of space.

From experience Kellon knew the fighters were efficiently prosecuting an effective search pattern, however, Lan had obtained from Shey's prior unauthorized escapade the enemy sensor sensitivity, signal characteristics, and bandwidths. This information had enabled Lan to fine tune his countermeasures and sharply blunt the escorts' sensor effectiveness. Lan and the Scouts' inherent stealth capabilities also severely limited the enemy's sensor effectiveness.

As the fighters passed under Lan, Lorn activated the previously positioned Zed decoy. As planned, its internal holographic generators created a surrounding three-dimensional image of a Kreel faster-than-light Gortoga class Cruiser, along with the appropriate wake signature. The basis of the tactical gambit was the approaching fighters would overtake and detect the decoy. Thereafter, the decoy was programmed to accelerate and maintain a constant separation ahead of the escort, awaiting further instructions.

As the hours of waiting and sitting passed, Kellon became aware of the increasing tension across his shoulders and within his body. Consciously, he checked his breathing, bringing it to a slowed controlled rhythm, and relaxed his tongue. One by one, he isolated, examined, and then tightened and relaxed each of his major muscle groups.

Soon after the point escorting fighters had passed by, the main formation of alien ships approached. Roy was studying the video screen and disapprovingly shook his head.

"Sir, difficult as it is to believe, they're coming straight on with all their lights burning brightly. Even my dear mother wouldn't approve their tactics. They look like a cruise ship on holiday. And, if that's their best, they're not accustomed to having serious opposition."

"Well, given what we've learned, for the past 10,000 years they haven't faced any opposition. Today is their wake-up call," Kellon said.

"Sir? Wakeup call? To wake up, they first will need to survive," Roy said.

Thirty minutes later, having completed his planned interception maneuver, Lan was 2,000 kilometers directly above and position-keeping with the primary target and its protective screen of fighters. There was no indication the target was aware that a deadly opponent was poised above, with its talons extended and ready to pounce.

Studying the tactical plot, Kellon affirmed Lan's four Scouts were each holding at their assigned attack positions. Each Scout was offset at a different corner of an imaginary square, which was centered upon and perpendicular to the target trajectory. Like Lan, they were maintaining a constant relative position from the target, and each had acknowledged Condition 3; their systems were battle ready.

All of the tactical elements of the battle plan were in position, and the proffered bait was being temptingly dangled. The time for battle had arrived.

Kellon keyed Lan's general announcing circuit. "Kellon here. Our primary target is now directly below us. We are about to take action to assure it will not return to further injure the humans on the third planet.

"Lan, set and confirm Condition 2. Sound battle stations."

Throughout Lan, the resonant tones of the battle stations alarm were reverberating, and Lan's crew moved briskly through the passageways, taking their assigned combat stations. CAC filled with additional members, even as the battle stations alarm faded. The initial murmuring of low conversations within CAC quickly transformed to quiet alert attention.

"Lan, drop us back and ease us down. Maneuver us into a trailing firing position astern of the primary target. Attain and hold our separation at ninety percent of maximum medium missile effective range."

"Sir, Acknowledged."

"Tactical, initiate passive medium missile solutions on the primary target. Using light missiles, optically target its escorts."

"Acknowledged. Sir, Fire Control now has passive optical locks on the primary and fifty-seven of its escorts. "Lorn said.

Kellon again considered the image of the primary target and its escorts, and revised his attack sequence.

"Tactical, cancel optical locks on the primary. Set heavy and medium missiles to ready standby. Isolate the target's laser batteries and active search and fire control sensors. Allocate anti-radiation and point attack missiles against those discrete targets."

"Sir, acknowledged. Twenty-seven anti-radiation and thirty-two discrete point missiles are now targeted."

As the minutes dragged past, an expectant hush filled CAC, as everyone waited.

"Tactical here. The Zed decoy reports the point fighters have detected it. As programmed, it's accelerating and maintaining the defined separation distance."

"Tactical, send the trigger command to the decoy," Kellon said.

"Sir, the decoy has acknowledged the trigger. It is now transmitting the standard Kreel parley signal," Lorn said.

A sense of rising expectant tension spread throughout Lan. Prepared and ready for battle, Lan and his Scouts were primed for imminent action. Everyone waited for the enemy's decisive response to an ultimatum....

Chapter Forty-Three:
Ultimatum

Shrill sounds of battle alarms were echoing throughout the Nest ship. Leaving his quarters, Kur hurried toward the bridge. Others around him were also hurrying to their designated assignments and tactical positions.

Upon Kur entering on to the bridge, the Captain promptly approached him. "Honored One, our point patrol sensors have detected a large ship directly ahead of us. It appears to be a Kreel warship. Its trajectory is the same as ours. While remaining within sensor range, it is maintaining a constant separation from our point patrol. Transmitting on their normal recognition frequency, it's transmitting a repeating parley signal. They are awaiting our acknowledgment."

"Has the Kreel ship taken any action that seems hostile?" Kur said.

"No."

"Captain, bring your senior tactical officer and come to my adjacent conference room."

Entering the small conference room, Kur took his seat at the head of the table. Inwardly he worried, *After all our efforts to evade a Dargon ambush, now there is a Kreel ship pacing us. What was it that Rin said, back when we were approaching Earth? 'We seem to be arriving in some predictable manner. Even from a rudimentary military understanding, it seems unwise for us to be that detectable and predictable.' Rin, you are proven correct, in spite of all our efforts to be unpredictable, that Kreel ship has intercepted us with apparent ease.*

His troubled thoughts did nothing to raise his confidence that they might be able to fight their way through the current crisis. He was still fretting when the Captain and his senior tactical officer entered. Kur turned to face them.

"Report your current assessment," Kur said.

The Captain signed to his tactical officer that he was to proceed with the briefing. "Honored One, the ship we are tracking does appear to be a Kreel faster-than-light warship.

Appearances aside, I choose to reserve my final assessment of its identification until we have some confirmation. "

"Captain, how far are we from the outer debris belt?" Kur said.

"Honored One, we are presently about one half the distance from the third planet to the debris belt. We were just commencing our planned deceleration maneuver."

Kur was not happy. They were in open space, vulnerable, and dealing with what appeared to be an advanced Kreel warship, where there should be no such vessel. Unbidden questions began to rattle about in his mind. *Why would a Kreel warship be in this system? Where are the Dargons? Would a Kreel warship come to their aid if they came under a Dargon attack?* The tactical situation was becoming more complex with each passing moment.

"Captain, verify battle stations are crewed and active. Give orders to ready weapons to fire. Prepare to take evasive maneuvers as required.

"Launch our remaining fighters and the assault ships. Deploy the cargo lifters we have on standby, assign them to rescue operations.

"Confirm that all of this is being recorded and transmitted to Ca and his team. When you are fully prepared for battle, return here."

"Honored One, I will make it so."

The Captain departed, leaving the senior tactical officer standing at attention and facing Kur. "As the senior tactical officer, do you have any recommendations?" Kur said.

"Honored One, we have taken every available defensive action. We are prepared for battle and will give as good an accounting of our Nests as possible."

"Well spoken," Kur said.

A moment later, the Captain returned and reported. "Honored One, the remaining fighters, assault ships, and lifters are deployed and the ship is battle ready. As ordered, the telemetry is being transmitted."

"Good. Captain, you have spent your entire life in preparation for battle. I have accomplished all that a Council representative can prudently do. The immediate tactical problem is a matter for the military. I acknowledge your skill and my confidence in your ability to meet the immediate tactical challenges. Accordingly, you are to take all defensive and offensive actions you determine appropriate. If we are to engage in battle, then let it be well fought and a tribute to all our Nests."

"Respected One, you have honored my officers and our Nests."

"Captain, regarding our Kreel interloper, assign the communications channel of its parley call to this station. Then, acknowledge the Kreel signal. Let us hear their introductory block parley message. Perhaps we may even learn why the Kreel are here."

The Captain spoke into his communicator, and the screen on the conference room bulkhead brightened. An image took form. Kur had thought himself prepared for any possible threat, but he was proven wrong, yet again. If someone had struck him hard with the butt of a fighting staff in his stomach, he could not have experienced a greater shock to his entire being.

It was not the anticipated snarling and glaring image of an arrogant and demanding Kreel Officer that appeared on the screen, but rather that of a solitary human male. The human was calmly looking directly out of the screen, as if he could see Kur sitting stunned and silent in his chair. The first words issuing forth from the filthy mammal were those of a well enunciated formal Kreel challenge. Then, after a short pause, the human actually began speaking fluently in Kur's own language.

Kur's sense of shock was sudden and complete. The calm words he was hearing only increased his sense of rising alarm.

"My name is Kellon, you have been observed entering into this solar system on a hostile mission. The evidence of your previous aggressions against the inhabitants of the third planet is blatant, and we have documented it. Your long-term actions against the human populations in this solar system are murderous acts and criminal in nature. Your barbaric aggression is ended, here and now.

"You are given two choices – immediately and unconditionally surrender, or choose to die. The choice is strictly yours to make. If you choose to surrender, we would consider letting you return to your home solar system, but understand this, we will demand restitution for your criminal acts against humanity. Again, the choice is yours to make.

"The terms of your surrender are not subject to negotiation. You have precisely one-hundredth of a cycle to recall all of your deployed fighters and secondary spacecraft to their hangars. You will also immediately cut all power to your active sensors, telemetry, communication, and weapons systems. You will also cut all power to your propulsion generators.

"Any hostile act directed toward this ship or any attempt to take further evasive action will be considered an aggressive response, and we will assume you are choosing to battle. Your time to conform to our demands begins now."

The screen went blank. Kur sat stunned, his mind in a state of utter confusion. First, there were the Dargons, appearing where they had never been seen before. Now a Kreel warship appears with a human operating from the bridge. He had called himself 'Kellon' and spoke fluently in both the Kreel and Arkillian languages; none of it made any sense.

Was Kur to believe that a mere mammal was making ultimatums and demands on the entire Arkillian Empire? *How could this be so?* Kur knew one truth; *Dargon raiders did not make demands and speak of restitution. Dargon raiders would have attacked without warning and without reservation.* With certainty, he knew that whoever was in that ship was not Dargon.

Could the Kreel have made some alliance with the humans? Why would the Kreel give humans, or any dirty mammals, faster-than-light warships and not provide the Arkillians a similar capability?

The human had actually demanded unconditional surrender and spoken of restitution for crimes and murders against the people of this solar system. He had called the Arkillians criminals and murderers.

Nothing seemed to fit together or be real. Kur's head began to hurt.

Looking around, he observed that the two officers in attendance were showing the facial markings of shock and dismay. "Captain, do you have any assessments or recommendations to make about what you have just seen and heard?"

The Captain, his facial markings beginning to return to a calm appearance, looked directly at Kur. "Honored One, if there is a human crew on that ship, then we shall destroy them. If there is a Kreel crew on that ship, masquerading as humans, then we shall engage them in combat. As long as this ship has propulsion and a laser turret operating, we will not surrender."

Kur felt the inner surge of his own rising anger. The Captain was correct; they would certainly fight.

"Captain, if there are humans operating that ship, how would you propose to destroy them?"

"Honored One, we would transmit a lethal probe pulse and saturate the entire ship with enough raw energy to fry the brain of any human on board."

Kur clucked approvingly. "Captain, I have but one recommendation to your proposed action. Instruct the weapons crew to employ two saturation beams, the one proven effective on humans and the second conforming to the pulsed characteristics found in Council database file, Scion 23. That pulse frequency will effectively fry any Kreel who might happen to be on board."

That an Arkillian beam weapon existed to kill Kreel was a secret known only to the scientists who had developed it and to a few members of the Arkillian Council. Kur was one of those select Council members. He clucked again. The surprise registered by the Captain's facial patterns was noteworthy.

"Captain, to acquire time, we will act as if we are yielding to their ultimatum. I suggest you initiate a recall to our nearest escort. Begin returning the auxiliary craft first. Take aboard the lifters, then the assault ships. Begin reducing propulsion power. As soon as the weapon is made ready, you will strike our enemy without hesitation.

"Immediately thereafter, launch another long-range probe toward Scion. The ultimatum, and all associated tracking data, is to be recorded in the probe. Do you understand?"

"Honored One, I understand."

"Good. After transmitting the mind beams, you are to take all actions, as you deem appropriate. Perhaps, just perhaps, the Kreel have kindly provided us a faster-than-light ship of our very own."

"Honored One, it will be so."

Saluting, both officers turned and briskly left the conference room. For a few minutes, Kur leaned back and looked out of the observation port at the stars. He then turned and signed to one of his servants to bring his favorite silver cup and some mead.

Shortly thereafter, the servant hurried in bearing the requested cup.

Rolling the cup between his hands, Kur thought, *If we are going to die*, which he now doubted, *then I choose to be comfortable during the process. If the Kreel are acting with treachery and duplicity, Ca needs to know that fact.* Picking up his personal communicator, he dictated a voice message to Ca, then encrypted the message and bundled it in the outgoing telemetry stream being sent to the planet.

The senior tactical officer entered the conference room, making a gesture of respect. "Honored One, if you wish to observe, we are about to transmit our forward saturation beams."

Placing his cup on the table, Kur followed the officer onto the bridge. As he entered, the Captain nodded, then turned to the weapons console and spoke to its operators. On the instrument board, Kur saw the representation of a narrow beam of pulse energy radiate toward a distant target. In short order, a similar second beam followed.

Human or Kreel, Kur thought with deep satisfaction, *they are as good as dead.*

While all of his logic was proclaiming it was a victory, his innermost instincts suddenly cried out in alarm. A sharp foreboding of imminent disaster swept over him. Suddenly feeling very sick, he turned and departed the bridge. Entering his conference room Kur once more picked up his silver cup, with its remaining golden beverage. Walking the few steps to the viewing port, he stood looking out at the countless stars. Sipping from the cup, Kur brought to mind many wonderful memories of his youth and of growing up on Scion. Acknowledging having lived a long time, with a genuine pleasure he remembered his nest and his large family. Looking out at the surrounding stars, he chose to ignore the activity and rising clamor on the adjacent bridge.

Sipping from his beautiful cup, he thought, *That is odd, I never before noticed the stars are not hot; in truth, they are very, very cold.*

Chapter Forty-Four:
Pandemonium

At his battle station in CAC, Commander Shaw was focused on his console, watching for the anticipated Arkillian response to the ultimatum. With each passing minute, the allocated time of grace provided for the Arkillians to submit rapidly evaporated. Battle seemed imminent.

"Tactical here. The target is decelerating. Some ships are returning and are entering hangars."

"Lorn, my gut instinct is shouting not to trust these Arkillians. What type of ships are entering hangars? Are they fighters? "Kellon said.

"Tactical here. No fighters, only the armed shuttle and cargo ships are returning to their hangars."

"Kellon here, everyone, stay on your toes. If they're going to break out, they'll need to act soon."

For the next few minutes, like a coil spring being compressed, tensions within CAC increased. Normal voices dropped to mere whispers, as if those on board Lan subconsciously felt their words might be overheard by the enemy.

Scowling, Roy turned and looked toward Kellon. "Navigation here. Sir, I don't like this. The fighters aren't returning in conformance with our time limits. Something is rotten."

Lorn drew in a sharp breath, "Tactical here. By the shades of Tartarus, the Arkillians have given us their answer. The Zed decoy has recorded an intense burst pulse of energy. Now, it's recording a second massive pulse hitting it."

"Tactical, Kellon here. Be explicit. What type of energy pulse? Was it a laser or a particle beam weapon?"

Lorn's fingers were deftly tapping the tabs on his console. "Sir, checking. Got it. Both pulses were complex and intense; I'm running a comparative analysis. Got a match. The initial pulse was akin to a stun beam, but the power intensity would have killed any human. The second strike was also a similar pulse, but the computer is unable to determine the species it was intended to kill."

"Navigation here. Heads up. The target is beginning a sharp evasion maneuver; it's breaking out."

For a few moments Kellon sat studying the developing tactical plot and then mused, *Well, they've given us their answer. They've chosen battle. So be it.*

"Lan, notify all units, confirm Condition 2, battle ready. All units, permission granted to set Condition 1, fire at will. Repeating, fire at will.

"Lan, launch our two divergent Zed decoys. Place them high to starboard and set them in a defensive split.

"Navigation, execute evasive pattern Four Delta," Kellon said.

Lan promptly launched two divergent decoys, and his offensive missile batteries began firing. Adhering to the ordered evasive pattern, Lan began rolling smartly to port, avoiding probable counter fire.

The two divergent decoys were configured to appear like two first-line Kreel cruisers. Rapidly moving off to starboard, they were programmed to remain evasive and near Lan's initial firing point. Their sole tactical purpose was to draw enemy fire away from Lan.

Continuing his ordered evasion maneuver, Lan was launching his second and third volleys of anti-radiation and point missiles, even as his first volley slipped through the defending escorts and point defenses, striking the primary target.

"Tactical, Kellon here. Continue targeting all active sensors and laser or missile batteries. Using only optical locks, stay on the fighters. Launch light missiles against any fighters within effective range."

As Lan was evolving his evasion maneuver, his outbound missiles were inflicting havoc. The target's evasion was ineffective, its dwindling answering barrage of laser fire was being blindly directed along the shifting inbound trajectories of Lan's missiles. From Lan's perspective, the enemy's counter fire was useless.

Upon receiving Kellon's orders to set Condition 1, the four Scouts began their coordinated attack runs. While Lan drew the target's fire, like swift falcons, striking their common prey from four quadrants, the Scouts prosecuted their attack.

"Roan, by Nodons' whiskers, Lan is inflicting withering destruction on the fighters. Less than one in twenty of his anti-radiation and point missiles are being intercepted by the target's point defenses. It's losing most of its active sensors and laser batteries. The counter fire astern is faltering, random, and diminishing under fire."

"Understood. I'm compensating for the target's evasion, adjusting our attack run on the fly. Keep me updated," Roan said.

"Boy howdy. Lan's attack caught them napping. More than thirty fighters are destroyed and another ten appear badly damaged. The entire engagement volume is in bedlam.

"Roan, heads up, we've got inbound trouble. The forward fighter echelon is moving our way. They're looking for Lan, but are moving directly toward our position. It's about to get ugly, soon."

"Understood. Get optical target locks on those inbound fighters, and keep an eye on our stealth factor. Hold fire, unless absolutely necessary. I'm still compensating for the target's evasion. We're getting close to our drop," Roan said.

"Sir, all Scouts are still synchronized," Shey said.

"Good. Shey, keep it tight. Stay on the primary. Watch our stealth factor. Now, bring us smartly along the target's length, from stern to bow. Shey, take us in, keep it smooth and make it happen," Roan said.

"Acknowledged. Now holding in our launch groove," Shey said.

"Shey, careful. Watch your firing offset. Set Condition 1 on bearing."

"Roan, Shades of Tartarus. Sheba is engaged in a fire-fight. She is in trouble, taking multiple hits. But, she's still holding to her attack line. Her stealth is breaking down," Zorn said.

"Shey, tell Sheba to break off. Tell her to get out of there," Roan said.

"Sir, Sheba is now fully engaged with multiple fighters, and beginning her target run.

"Sir, I am now at our firing point," Shey said.

At minimal standoff range, Shey began launching her ice picks, distributing them uniformly along the target's full length. While Shey remained locked on the target, the launch sequence demanded forty seconds. They were extremely vulnerable.

Inwardly, Roan's urgent thoughts were, *Hurry girl. Be precise, but get us out of this mess.*

"Roan, all icepicks are launched. Weapon pods are detached. Executing evasive actions. Now, pitching up and rolling out of this pandemonium," Shey said.

"Shey, Except for medium missiles, set Condition 1. Using light missiles and all counter-measures, fire at will on targets of opportunity," Roan said.

Shuddering under her changing hull stresses, Shey rolled sharply starboard and upward, moving away from the target and its approaching fighters. Her point-defense guns and laser turrets erupted, creating a wide cone of lethal projectiles and energy. The noise within Shey was loud, the sporadic rhythm of gun fire augmented by the sounds of launching light missiles.

The battle volume, with its crossing laser beams and multiple explosions was undiluted mayhem. Her hull was groaning, her powerful internal power systems protesting under the shifting demands imposed by intense combat and the restraints of temporal physics. Her stealth factor was precariously dropping.

The cumulative counter measure fire and light missiles being launched by the withdrawing Scouts increased the general bedlam. Adding to the confusion and spreading volume of carnage, the anti-radiation, point, and light missiles coming in from Lan's shifting stand-off positions continued to strike the remaining fighter escort and key locations on the primary target. The target's remaining fighters were being decimated. Then, the damage being inflicted on the target by the impact of thousands of the small missiles began to reveal its horrific effects.

"Shey, enough. Order your sisters to break off and withdraw. Get us out of this madness," Roan said.

Responding, Shey broke away from the melee. Roan felt his racing pulse begin to return to normal.

"Shey, report, do we have any battle damage?" Roan said.

"Checking. Sir, there is no battle damage reported. All sub-systems report they are functioning in the gold."

"Shey, send our battle status report to Lan.

"Zorn, what do you have?"

"The other Scouts are reporting in. I need another moment to sort it all out. Sheba is in big trouble, reporting heavy battle damage. Lan is moving up to give her protective fire cover, as is

Scout ship Misty. Misty is reporting light battle damage; So is Scout ship Cindy. All Scouts, even Sheba, have reported their ice picks launched. Lan reports he is damage free."

Zorn's last reported item caused Roan to relax. They were a long way from home, and it was good to know Shey had a warm hangar nearby.

"Zorn, what is your assessment of the damage inflicted on the target and its escorts?"

"My first approximation is the primary target has ceased all combat activity. It has lost its propulsion and its acceleration is zero. The target is adrift. Seventeen fighters remain underway. All remaining fighters are either utterly destroyed or else crippled and adrift. They are mostly scattered along the line of battle. By all appearances, the battle is over."

"Not so fast. Where are those active fighters?"

"There are two groups of four fighters each, they're merging together near the primary target. Another group of three is moving to join them. The other six active fighters are scattered in ones or twos along the line of battle. At present, they don't seem to pose an active threat. I'm updating our tactical plot," Zorn said.

Roan had survived by remaining vigilant, and he was not about to change his prudent habits. "Shey, hold this station. Continue tracking all enemy fighters.

"Zorn, signal Lan for instructions. Ask, do we finish off the fighters or leave them alone?"

"I'm on it. Roan, we're ordered to remain alert, but take no further offensive action. Sheba is reporting her crew badly injured and unconscious. Lan is working to bring Sheba safely aboard."

"Shey, move to support Sheba. Position us abeam Misty as a second blocking force between Sheba and the nearest group of fighters. You're to destroy any fighters that even twitch toward Sheba or Lan."

"Acknowledged," Shey said.

In CAC, Kellon's attention was on the tactical plot and video screens. His immediate problem was Sheba. She was badly damaged, and while under her own power she was barely moving.

Kellon began to relax only after Sheba was brought safely aboard and secured in her hangar.

"Lan, ease us directly away from the battle line. Send a general recall to our Scouts, they are to return to their hangars.

"Roy, assure damage control, maintenance, and ordinance are standing by when the Scouts get into their hangars. I want those three operational Scouts repaired and fully armed," Kellon said.

The video screens revealed a scattering of flotsam strewn on the length of the long line of battle. The broken debris from the once sleek fighters only accentuated the dismal spectacle of the now inert dark bulk of the alien Nest ship. It was no more a proud interstellar voyager, it was but a ruined hulk adrift among the stars, a maritime hazard.

Kellon understood the death toll on a ship of that size must be counted in the thousands. He felt no sense of triumph. The images of carnage had filled him with a sense of disgust.

As he stood and exited the CAC, Kellon ordered, "Roy, you have the CAC."

"Sir, Acknowledged."

Chapter Forty-Five:
About to Knock

Lan was located well offset from the battle line, moving parallel to the devastated Arkillian ships. Sitting in his conference room, Kellon was viewing the tactical plot on the bulkhead, the same plot then being displayed in the Combat Analysis Center.

Since combat ended, Kellon had worked with Lieutenant Cloud and her staff. Together, they composed a brief general post battle message to the Arkillians, hostilities were deemed to be over. Unless the Arkillians provoked further battle, no military action would be forthcoming. The message ended with a declaration, "Let whoever speaks for the Arkillians respond."

"Lan, ask Commander Grey to join me."

"Sir, Commander Grey reports he is en route."

When a soft knock was heard, Kellon responded, "Enter."

The hatch slid open, and Roy entered and accepted a proffered seat. As he sat down, Kellon observed that Roy looked as tired as he himself felt.

"Roy, what's your latest update concerning Sheba and her crew?"

"Commander Galen's condition remains critical; however, the guarded prognosis is Sheba's crew will pull through. Sir, they won't be flying anytime soon.

"Regarding Sheba, she took several major hits. We nearly lost her. Maintenance reports that before she can resume service a full yard overhaul is mandatory."

"What is maintenance saying about the other scouts?"

"Sir, Shey suffered no battle damage. Misty and Cindy are still being evaluated. Given preliminary diagnostics, the assessment is they can be operational within forty hours. Both ships, however, will require additional repairs."

"Roy, advise maintenance that they have thirty hours to bring both Misty and Cindy to a ready status, including fully rearming all three scouts."

"Yes, Sir."

"Do we have an accurate count on the disabled enemy fighters? How many of them are drifting with survivors still alive?"

Looking perplexed, Roy answered, "Yes, Sir, we're monitoring twelve severely damaged fighters. They've marginal power and perhaps survivors. Some are emitting a beacon. None are maneuvering. Sir, as your XO, may I inquire as to why you're asking about disabled enemy fighters?"

"Why? Because, my duty demands that I determine our best course of action. This battle has determined nothing. But, it's likely to be the opening shot of a far broader conflict. I keep trying to find some way to avoid that spreading conflict.

"The enemy has lost the battle. It's adrift. Still, there are likely to be survivors on that Capital ship. And, there is a part of me that is aware other sentient beings are in deadly peril. My gut instinct is to reach out and help. Just perhaps, a small amount of our help might save many lives. And, just perhaps, our help now might avoid a larger conflict later."

"Captain, respectfully, I believe one of your primary postulates is flawed."

"In what way flawed?"

"Sir, the battle has definitely determined one important issue. We prevailed.

"We admittedly know very little about the Arkillians. Yet, we have gained some solid knowledge concerning them. We know their tyranny has wrongfully oppressed billions of humans on a planet for millennia. The probable death count among those billions of human beings is beyond our estimation.

"We also know, when challenged by an open and proper declaration, their unequivocal response was firing a deadly weapon, by which they intended to kill you and every member of this crew. Had their target actually been Lan, they might have succeeded.

"Sir, ask yourself, would the Arkillians be feeling any remorse if they had killed us? Considering their long history of tyranny, oppression and killing humans, I seriously doubt it. It's far more likely, their having just captured a faster-than-light cruiser, the Arkillians would be celebrating.

"Sir, I recommend we do acknowledge the Arkillian's plight, but that we first consider the dire scrapes of billions of humans on the third planet. Even now they are being inflicted with an incredibly short lifespan and suffering under Kreel pop-patterns. "Sir, our present choice of possible action seems rather clear. We can stay here, at risk to both our crew and ship, trying to help a ruthless adversary; else, we can move on and help billions of human beings."

"Roy, as usual, your recommendation is well stated. We do have some unfinished work. And, it's time that we do something about putting an end to the mental oppression being inflicted on the planet.

"Lan, redirect the trailing sentinel to a new parallel trajectory, one well offset from the battle line. Program it to maintain stealth and monitor the primary target. It's to record and report all detected communications. Begin shifting its six communications relay probes into an expanding chain trailing the sentinel. They are to relay the gathered data back to you."

"Acknowledged," Lan said.

"Roy, unless the enemy can restore its power and propulsion, it will pass right through the outer debris field and beyond the heliopause boundary. You are to calculate the trajectory of the Arkillian ship. Add that data to the detailed battle summary report that you send to Glas Dinnein. If Headquarters wants to deal with salvaging the ship, then they can send a salvage ship with a proper escort.

"Got it, send a note home to my dear mother. Gladly, sir. And next?"

Smiling, Kellon continued, "Next? Recover our Zed decoy. We need to analyze those focused energy bursts. Have the weapons analysis team go over its internal data buffer with a fine-tooth comb. Since the decoy was masquerading as a Kreel ship, direct the team to evaluate the second pulse for Kreel physiology.

"Confirm our existing radiation shielding would have blocked that weapon. If not, begin modifications of our shields as required to nullify that weapon's potential threat.

"When the weapon analysis is complete, encrypt the data Black Hole and send the analysis directly to Admiral Mer Shawn."

"Yes, Sir," Roy said.

"Next, configure a basic beacon to broadcast on the primary Arkillian tactical frequency. Lieutenant Cloud will provide you with the message to broadcast. Set the beacon to repeat the message for a full hour and then self-destruct."

"Sir, Acknowledged."

"Roy, we can't undo everything the Arkillians have done, but we can definitely terminate the Kreel pop patterns.

"Lan, display the Arkillian ship's previous orbital coordinates near the third planet. Then, expand the area around planet three. Show the position of the surviving satellite that was launched from the planet."

The bulkhead plot immediately shifted from a tactical display to a new heliocentric plot. Then, that plot altered to an expanded graphic display surrounding the third planet.

"Oops. I completely forgot the fighters missed one of those satellites," Roy said.

"They did, and it's the door upon which we are about to knock."

"Sir, knock? As your XO, may I ask, how do you propose to knock and still remain covert?"

"Just look about. The battle line is littered with the debris from our covert actions. Undoubtedly, every government on that planet was monitoring the Arkillian capital ship. They already know something happened. And, as for remaining covert, we don't need to explain to them who we are. Besides, those satellites were placed in orbit by a governmental agency, and I'll wager a cold brew that they won't be reporting our contact in their news media or be sending a memo to another government."

"Sir? 'Wager a cold brew?' Sir, my dear mother raised me up and taught me never to make or take imprudent wagers, especially those I would likely lose. As your XO, I regret the need to report that it appears Zorn is having a deleterious effect on our entire crew. "

"Roy, your mother was a wise woman. Have you any questions?"

Standing, Roy saluted. "No Sir."

Kellon returned his salute with a smile. As the hatch closed behind Roy, Kellon leaned back in his chair and momentarily closed his eyes. Sighing, he leaned forward and again studied the plot on the bulkhead.

"Lan, prepare to move us out of our current trajectory. We will be moving toward the third planet. After Commander Grey has recovered the Zed decoy and deployed the broadcast beacon, begin our transition to enter the precise solar orbit that was previously occupied by the target. Put us on that precise station in forty hours."

"Sir, the maneuver is being calculated, even as we speak."

Chapter Forty-Six:
Silence

"Ca, come. Hurry."

Running into Ca's quarters, Rin was shouting, and his voice was trembling with raw fear.

"Rin, be calm. Now, exactly tell me what has happened," Ca said.

"Ca, it is terrible. The tactical tank has gone silent. There is no more telemetry. Absolutely nothing is coming from our Nest ship. Nothing at all."

"It was known the Nest ship might be lost, but the thought of its actual destruction evoked a sudden surge of alarm. Ca immediately suppressed that fear. "Rin, listen to me. Kur knew a powerful enemy was lurking in the outer darkness. He took every precaution to protect Scion and the Nest ship. Still, it may not be as bad as it appears. Come, let us together go to the Combat Center and see what can be learned."

The hollow sounds of their echoing footsteps returning along the network of mostly empty corridors troubled Ca. At odd times he had felt the entire complex seemed more a tomb than a vibrant nest, and never more so than at the moment.

Entering the main control room, Ca moved to where his senior officer was working. On Ca's approach, the officer looked up and immediately saluted. The markings of an intense anger were flushed across the officer's facial features. While studying the officer's countenance, Ca smartly returned his salute.

"Provide me with your latest evaluation," Ca said.

"Honored One, all indications are a battle took place. It was short and decisive. The Nest ship is no more."

The officer's blunt words struck Ca. The death of many thousands of Arkillians on board the Nest ship underscored the magnitude of the disaster. Shaken, Ca walked over to a nearby chair and sat down. He well understood the Arkillians who had come with him to Far Nest were now truly marooned.

Becoming angry at his own weak thoughts, Ca began shaking off the squirming tentacles of fear. With mental discipline, he calmed his racing thoughts.

"Immediately replay the last tenth cycle of telemetry. Also, examine the telemetry stream for bundled messages," Ca said.

Acknowledging Ca's orders, the officer signed to one of his subordinates. The tactical tank promptly filled with vibrant dancing points of light.

At first glance, everything displayed in the tactical tank appeared to be in perfect order. The Nest ship was clearly in the center of the display, and it was adorned with the anticipated pattern of escorting fighters. Then, Ca saw the single red symbol, a hostile ship. It was moving just ahead of the point patrol.

"What is known of that enemy ship?" Ca said.

"Honored One, the fighter's sensors identified the ship to be a Kreel faster-than-light cruiser of the Gortoga design."

Ca sat bolt upright, his mind screaming, *What is a Kreel cruiser doing in this system?*

Studying the embedded data log, the officer began his description of the recorded events. "When the Kreel cruiser was detected, it was moving just within the detection range of the point patrol. Upon being detected, the enemy accelerated and began to broadcast a standard Kreel parley call.

"Alerted, the Nest ship went immediately to battle stations and deployed its remaining fighters. It also deployed the remaining ground assault ships and lifters to act as lifeguard craft. When the Nest ship was fully battle ready, a parley acknowledgment signal was sent to the enemy. In response, the enemy sent back a standard video challenge block."

"Do we have that challenge?" Ca said.

"Yes, Honored One. The message is bundled in the telemetry. I am dividing the embedded challenge from the data stream. I am channeling it to the display screen."

The large bulkhead display brightened, and upon turning to view it, Ca was dumbfounded. It was not the anticipated image of a snarling Kreel officer, with his fangs bared, but rather the image of a calm human male. Shockingly, the human male was using the Kreel language and perfectly enunciating a formal Kreel challenge. He then smoothly transitioned from the guttural sounds of the Kreel language and began fluently speaking in the Arkillian language.

"My name is Kellon. You have been observed entering into this solar system on a hostile mission. The evidence of your previous aggressions against the inhabitants of the third planet is blatant, and we have documented it....

Ca sat stunned and speechless as the image of the man continued to levy charge after charge upon the Arkillian Empire and make demands, including absolute unconditional surrender. Then the screen went dark. Knowing the depth of his own confusion, he wondered how the message must have affected Kur. He thought, *It can only be but a hoax, some type of cunning ruse. It must be.*

"You are to obtain a transcription of every word of that message. Now, proceed with the replay of the remaining recorded events."

Once again, the colored lights in the three-dimensional tank began moving. The officer scanned and again read from the event log.

"Honored One, the Nest ship sent a recall to the ground assault ships and lifters. They were ordered to return to their hangars. Some of the most distant fighters were ordered to pull back toward the Nest ship. The main propulsion was reduced by twenty-five percent."

Listening carefully, Ca was troubled, *Was Kur complying with the enemy demands?*

With sudden heightened emotions, the officer continued his narration. "Honored One, they did not surrender. They chose battle. The Nest ship projected a lethal probe beam at the enemy, a beam set to kill humans. A second beam was immediately projected and it also hit the enemy. I do not recognize that beam configuration."

"What is the recorded source of the second beam pattern?" Ca said.

Upon checking the log, the officer's countenance revealed puzzlement. "Honored One, it is found in the restricted Council database file, Scion 23."

In surprise, Ca thought, *Kur, you did indeed fight, even against the Kreel.* "They indeed chose battle, and they fought to protect Scion. They are noted to their Nests, with extraordinary distinction."

"Honorable One, somehow two more Kreel Gortoga cruisers appeared directly astern of the Nest ship. The Nest ship was under heavy missile attack from the stern. It returned laser fire and moved to evade. The nearest fighters dropped aft to engage and attack the trailing Kreel cruisers. The many missiles striking the Nest ship and its fighters had no detectable radiation signatures and were passive homing in their design.

"The accumulating missile damage was devastating; approximately thirty of our fighters were quickly destroyed. Then, a secondary attack hit the Nest ship. Many compartments reported multiple explosions. The sensors could not locate the missiles or determine their source. There were puzzling indications of multiple attacking ships, they attacked from every quadrant. The types and number of attackers cannot be determined.

"Sensors did record two flights of fighters engaged one of the attacking ships. They reported they heavily damaged the ship, and it was breaking off its attack. The enemy ship continued to sharply evade and return fire with laser, guns, and missiles. Our attacking fighters were destroyed.

"Honored One, the battle reports are confusing. Our fighters received missile and laser fire from multiple vectors. The Nest ship was under massive bombardment.

"The Nest ship did succeed in destroying the two enemy ships attacking from astern. Then, the Nest ship lost power. That is the end of the telemetry."

Ca felt numb, but there was also a growing sense of pride. The Nest ship and its defenders had fought a superior force with courage. He thought, *they destroyed two of the attacking Kreel cruisers.*

"You are to alter two of our most sensitive bio-channels and assign them to monitor our operational frequencies. Keep those two high gain receivers directed toward the location of the battle. There may be some survivors. I want to hear any communications between them.

"You are to maintain strict discretion. The humans are not to detect Far Nest."

"Honored One, it will be so."

"Did the Nest ship deploy a long-range probe?" Ca said.

"Yes, Honored One. They launched a probe immediately after firing the two probe pulse beams at the enemy. The onboard emergency system also automatically launched another probe as the Nest ship lost power. The onboard system would have downloaded the last cycle of telemetry and critical files into the second probe. That probe launch was successful."

"Are there any embedded messages from Council member Kur to Scion, Rin, or myself?"

"There is one message. It is directed to you. It was sent just prior to the firing of the two probe pulse beams."

"Have that message divided from the telemetry and send it to my personal communicator."

"It will be so," the officer said.

Beckoning for Rin to follow, Ca turned and departed the Combat Center. Where they had previously hurried, now they solemnly walked slowly back to Ca's quarters. The fading echoes of their steps that followed them were the most forlorn sounds Ca had ever heard.

Chapter Forty-Seven:
Last Communication

With Rin following, Ca entered into his quarters and walked directly to his study. Taking a seat at the table, he motioned Rin to come and sit. Upon sitting, Ca noticed Rin's facial markings were paler than he had ever before seen them.

"Rin, can I have anything brought for you, food or beverage?"

"No.

"Ca, I did attentively listen to the Officer. How can he or anyone else call what happened to our Nest ship a battle? Its fighters and the Nest ship itself were violently crushed, like an egg shell. Even now, we have no idea who the enemy is. What I do understand is that whoever destroyed our Nest ship has demonstrated they have both superior tactics and overpowering technology.

"Ca, there is great cause for us to be alarmed. Given what just happened, we are far from Scion, vulnerable, and isolated. Ask, even if a relief force does arrive, then what will happen to it?"

Ca understood the raw depths of Rin's anguish; he was openly expressing some of his own unspoken darker concerns.

"Rin, we can be certain when Scion does receive the long-range probes, with their dire warnings, our Nests will respond. They will come in great force. Our duty now is to remain alert and patient."

Taking up his personal communicator, Ca selected Kur's final message and activated his remote speakers. Immediately, Kur's familiar resonant and well-modulated voice filled the room.

"I send greetings to my trusted fellow Council Members, Ca and Rin. I regret that what I must relate here may cause increased burdens upon you. It cannot be helped.

"Soon, we will be fully engaged in a battle for our lives. This may therefore be my last communication.

"Our sensors have detected a Kreel faster-than-light warship directly ahead of us, where no such ship should be. Despite what the sensors report, in truth, I do not know who our enemy is.

"I do not now accept as truth that Dargons are involved. They are brutally direct in their warfare, relying on frontal attacks and overwhelming force. By contrast, our enemy is cunning, evasive, and proven clever in the warcraft of misdirection.

"Still, the appearance of a Kreel cruiser is most troubling. The enemy is adeptly using known Kreel communications protocols on normal Kreel communication frequencies, so its appearance cannot be lightly discounted. We also know the enemy either correctly anticipated our maneuver around the fifth planet or else has demonstrated exceptional speed. In either case, we are facing a most dangerous adversary.

"When you do hear this message, you will likely have already heard the enemy's ultimatum. It was far more than a simple Kreel challenge. The shocking improbable image of a human male mammal proficiently speaking both the offensive guttural Kreel language and then our own language is inexplicable. Perhaps the Kreel are really the enemy, and perhaps they have contrived and transmitted the human image in order to produce an emotional effect. In spite of appearances, it is inconceivable the Kreel would ever sell or give their latest faster-than-light technology to any other species, and doubly unlikely they would give it to filthy human mammals.

"You are aware I have never trusted the Kreel. This upcoming battle may be the result of their guile and treachery. If this is true, then the long-term destructive ramifications of such dishonor toward Scion cannot be forgiven. Caution is demanded here. In truth, and in spite of appearances, the enemy may not be the Kreel.

"I cannot forget the pivotal words contained within the ultimatum. One can be certain that those words were carefully chosen, and those words brazenly assault the entire Arkillian Empire.

"The message constitutes a deliberate taunt, one seemingly intended more for provoking than communicating; yet, there may be truth pronounced within those demands.

"The first sentence declares we were observed entering this solar system. This implies that the enemy was already in the system before we arrived. Therefore, since our arrival we have been under constant surveillance and scrutiny.

"The enemy has boldly charged the entire Arkillian Empire with a barbaric aggression, and speaks of it having documented our aggression. Ask, why prepare such documentation? For what possible reviewing judicial authority might such documentation be prepared?

"Then, examine the next charge: our long-term actions against the human populations in this solar system are murderous and criminal in nature. This is the second use of the phrase, 'this solar system.' Again, I believe there is truth here.

"Perhaps, our enemy is a representative of an unknown interstellar culture or even a representative of a federation of such cultures. That some unknown interstellar power has taken notice and charged the Arkillian Empire with criminal and murderous actions, if not sheer rhetoric, is indeed a most serious matter. An unknown powerful interstellar enemy may well have announced itself, and this possibility must be evaluated by our Council.

"I do not know the outcome of the coming battle. If we are fighting against the Kreel, then that should soon become obvious. If we are contending with an unknown interstellar adversary, then we are indeed facing a most dangerous chasm of ignorance.

"For reasons of their own, our enemy has chosen to remain hidden from the humans on Earth. Our monitoring of the Earth news media clearly shows they have had no contact with another interstellar culture, Kreel or otherwise. Our analysis of human communications would have clearly revealed any such contact. There has been none.

"I am unable to forget the accusatory challenge, 'Your barbaric aggression is ended, here and now.' That powerful statement is based upon a commanding power and absolute confidence. I regret, at this moment, I do not share a similar confidence.

"How I do wish that I could be sitting with you as you listen to this message. Most likely you will have already obtained the data that I so desperately need in order to understand the perilous path immediately ahead.

"For now, my urgent advice to you is to employ maximum caution. Your threat is twofold, it being from the humans on Earth and also from the Kreel or else some yet unidentified interstellar power. Your mission is much more critical than we

253

first thought. Above all, guard your security. Avoid all unnecessary risks. Attempt to collect all possible information and be ready to deliver it to Scion. Know that you are noted with distinction, as are your Nests.

"Ca, you need to check with your senior officer. in the event that the Nest ship is lost in battle, I entrusted him to deliver a small package to you.

"Good hunting, and may the fresh Spring breezes on Scion soon brush away all your concerns."

Silence displaced the vibrant tones of Kur's voice, as it faded from the room. Suddenly, Ca felt like an orphan, very much alone.

Looking toward Rin, Ca observed he also felt the combination of grief, anguish, and hopeless loss. For several minutes emotional pain and silence engulfed them both.

Mastering his grief, Ca activated his communicator and accessed the senior officer's link. The officer immediately acknowledged the call.

"It is my understanding that Council Member Kur entrusted you with a package that is to be presented to me. Do send that package now."

Brief minutes later, one of the elite military personnel entered the room and made a formal gesture of respect. "Representative Ca, I am ordered to place directly into your very hand this package."

Handing the package to Ca, the soldier stepped back and stood at attention. Glancing up from the package, Ca formally acknowledged and saluted the soldier, then dismissed him.

Unwrapping the package, Ca reached in and withdrew one of the old and beautiful Earth silver cups that Kur so highly prized. Turning it slowly in his hands, Ca admired its ornate design and artistry. He knew that it was a treasure having great personal value to Kur. In Kur's memory, Ca knew that he would continue to prize the artifact, as long as he might live.

First signing to one of his servants, Ca turned toward Rin. "Would you kindly share with me a cup of mead, and join with me in making a toast to Kur and those other hatchlings who during the battle have passed beyond?"

Chapter Forty-Eight:
Puzzles

The long conference table Darrell was working on was strewn with charts, plots, and documents. The cascading events during the preceding weeks had left him frustrated and weary. Still, an enormous amount of data needed further analysis. Making things worse, Charles was on his case daily, demanding hourly updates. The real problem was not so much Charles as the White House. He fumed, *Why can't bureaucrats understand all the data is fragmentary. It's not conclusive, except that Monstro ran into big trouble.*

Hearing someone enter the room, Darrell looked up and smiled. It was Susie. He had come to enjoy her company and refreshing outlook on life. Besides she was downright attractive. Inwardly, he had to acknowledge his own feeling concerning her presence. Imaginatively, his mind wandered to the improbable possibility of walking hand in hand with her, preferably barefoot and along a sandy beach.

"Since you're obviously planning to sit here all night, I thought I might bring you a fresh cup of hot coffee. I brewed it from my own special blend of Guatemalan," Susie said.

"Thank you."

With Susie standing so near, He was finding it difficult to focus his mind on work. *Perhaps,* he mentally rationalized, *that's only because I am tired.* Again, he pulled his mind back to where it belonged, focused on Monstro and all things Olympus.

"Speaking of coffee, what's the current scuttlebutt about Monstro?" Darrell said.

"Well, rumor has it that Monstro performed a slingshot around Jupiter and remained in the Ecliptic Plane. Then, somewhere around the orbit of Uranus, Monstro came under attack. Our deep-space tracking stations picked up what appeared to be some type of communications chatter. Then, one of our telescopes observed what looked like a violent series of explosions and an exchange of laser fire. Oh, and one more item,

Olympus's installations monitoring Monstro's signal reported the signal has terminated. That's all I've heard to date."

"Humph, it seems the grapevine is up to date. Remind me to post yet another notice near the coffee pot about gossip, something original like loose lips sink ships."

Susie parried his jibe with a smile. "Have the analysts trying to crack that signal had any luck?"

"Not yet. We think it was some sort of telemetry. Monstro's communications have always been baffling. We know there must be constant communication with the home planet, and perhaps others, but we don't really understand how they are communicating.

"Their recent signal is an anomaly; it's apparently being directed to those hiding in Mongolia. If it's a telemetry signal, and we can crack it, then we might learn what happened out beyond Saturn."

"How is your search for Monstro's hidden facility coming?" Susie said.

"In brief, it's not. That they chose Mongolia to hide within has not made our problem any easier."

"That means you're still hitting a brick wall about who bushwhacked Monstro."

"Frustratingly true. Charlie said he didn't believe anyone could get out in front of Monstro. And, if some adversary did pull that trick off, he recommended that we ought not play poker with them. Well, someone did get out in front of them, and we don't have an inkling as to who."

"We do know one definite thing, Darrell. The new player didn't get along with Monstro."

"Admittedly, that much we know. But we lack hard data about who that new player is, and why he's here. Overall, Monstro seemed benign. But, what about the new guy?" The bottom line is the White House is climbing all over Charles, and he's in turn on my case. Everyone wants to know the future, and, I don't have a crystal ball."

"Darrell, just perhaps some of your working presumptions are invalid."

"In what way invalid?"

"For starters, you don't know if Monstro was benign. From what I can tell, your focus has been heavy on technology and weak on social sciences and economics. I remember UFO stories about abductions, animal mutilations, and similar horror tales.

"Frankly, you have very little data concerning all of Monstro's global activities. Don't forget, their ships were heavily armed and lethal. They demonstrated that when Monstro's fighters summarily destroyed those two Swiss military aircraft. Monstro was many things, but benign was not one of them."

"Given that's true, we still don't have a clue about the new player."

Placing both her hands on the table, Susie leaned slightly forward and looked questioningly at Darrell. His mind once again was tugged back toward the earlier image of running barefoot along a beach. Darrell groaned inwardly, *I definitely need some sleep, followed by a long vacation.*

Perceiving Darrell had some inner issues, somewhat perplexed, Susie resourcefully continued, "Remember, one of the oldest political expressions in the world is my enemy's enemy is my friend. Whatever the new player's intentions may be, we know they've acted in a forceful manner, they've terminated the status quo. Until we have evidence to the contrary, why not consider them friends?"

"Why not? Because, it's not that easy. Jumping to that unsupported assumption could get someone killed."

"That's only a perhaps. Besides, there's an important item concerning the event timeline that you haven't considered."

"And, just what might that be?" Darrell said.

"Think back. Remember, just prior to the fireworks in deep space, there was a short burst of communications traffic."

"And, so what?"

"Well, this burst of communications implies Monstro was challenged by his adversary before the battle. Likewise, Monstro rejected that challenge."

"Challenge? Might I inquire, just how did you reach that conclusion?"

Pulling back one of the chairs, Susie sat down. "How? Well, let's examine the timeline. Monstro arrives near Earth and begins to go about its normal business, whatever that really was. Monstro was behaving in a perfectly predictable manner. Then, wham, everything changes.

"Monstro detects a little alien spaceship lurking near its position. Except for the laser barrage from Monstro, there are no detected bursts of communications between Monstro and the little ship. Next, after elusively evading Monstro's lasers, the little green and scarlet ship streaks toward Earth. During its skillful evasion maneuver, the alien ship runs into Monstro's fighters. Again, there are no detectable bursts of communication, except for another exchange of laser fire and a few missiles. Poof, some of Monstro's fighters go away."

"Go on, you've got my complete attention."

"Hmmm, that's becoming apparent. But, back to the topic of Monstro, its immediate reaction to a brief military encounter is stark. Therefore, we can safely conclude Monstro believes it's contending with an immediate and lethal threat. We know this is true, because Monstro offloads some VIPs to Earth. Your best guess is their purpose is to monitor whatever next happens to Monstro. Would Monstro have done that if it didn't consider it was in mortal danger?"

Darrell noted Susie's oblique comment, *Becoming apparent? Humph*. "Continue."

"Gladly. It's clear Monstro must have known something about his adversary, including that it had superior offensive capabilities. Otherwise, why did it make a hasty offloading of VIPs and go for a maximum acceleration departure?

"Here is where it becomes intriguing and a bit complicated, and --"

Darrell raised a hand, interrupting Susie. "Hold it right there. Nothing you've said supports your initial statement, namely that Monstro was challenged."

"It certainly does. Remember, we know Monstro departed orbit with all its burners turned on maximum heat. Apparently, Monstro was concerned about an enemy attack. Having reached Jupiter, Monstro's apparent gambit was the possibility of making a random course change, which might confuse his adversary. Passing Jupiter, Monstro likely was beginning to feel confidence about its tactics.

"Ask, why was Monstro trying to reach the outer debris belt?"

"Well, why?"

"One plausible reason is it was seeking shelter among millions of pieces of debris."

"Agreed, but again why?" Darrell said.

"Thank you for asking. Monstro understood its adversary was faster than he was. Its entire maneuver was intended to reach an environment that denied his adversary its superior speed advantage. This deduction supports that Monstro knew a great deal about its adversary. Of course, the subsequent events prove its adversary was not confused, it got in front of and intercepted Monstro. This single fact tells us Monstro had every reason to be alarmed."

"Susie, in spite of all you've said, you have yet to establish Monstro was challenged."

"But that conclusion is obvious. Remember, on two prior occasions involving brief military interaction between Monstro and its adversary, there were no indications of attempted communications. The entire sequence was shoot first and maybe talk later, and that just maybe. The undisputed fact is Monstro was running for the bushes. It had no reason to talk with anyone. Only its adversary might have had a reason to send a message to Monstro prior to a battle."

"Continue."

"Be patient, we're almost there. Ask, given the hostile circumstances, what might such a message possibly contain? "

"Sorry, I don't have a clue."

"Darrell, it could only have been an ultimatum. If not an ultimatum, then there would have followed some dialog. But there was no following dialog. Translation, message was an ultimatum, it was rejected, ergo battle resulting; Quod Erat Demonstrandum. It's all quite logical.

Darrell sighed, muttering under his breath, "Q.E.D."

"Now, here is where it gets really interesting. Ask, why did the adversary send an ultimatum to Monstro prior to battle?"

"Sorry, not a clue. Why?"

"Well, if the interaction were purely hostile, the logic of battle would mandate an undeclared stealth ambush from hiding, not first making a prior declaration and thereby giving a warning. Conclusion, whoever the adversary is, they are supremely confident of their own power. And, they were attempting to establish meaningful communication and a dialog."

"That sorta makes sense, along with a thousand other possibilities. But, what does it all mean?".

"It means it's reasonable to postulate the adversary is not purely amoral and ruthless, but is willing to take big risks, prefers communication, gives prior warnings, and possibly seeks negotiation. The adversary is principled."

"Susie, that's really a stretch."

"Perhaps. Still, I'll wager a root beer that when two or more divergent, civilized, and technically advanced cultures meet in deep space and communicate, there must exist a basic mutual communications format or protocol. The burst of communications prior to battle argues that's true. Furthermore, the existence of a common communications format suggests it does not involve encryption, like that with Monstro's telemetry. If we can crack that communications format, the insight gained might prove extremely useful."

"Blast it all, sometimes I get too close to a problem. Your presumptions are welcomed and appreciated. Until now, the brief bursts of communications have been ignored. That's my mistake, and that I can fix."

Picking up his communicator, Darrell left a brief message on Charlie's voice-mail, outlining Susie's observations and directing him to put his best analysis team to work on the burst of communications.

Leaning toward Darrell, Susie smiled invitingly, her voice becoming soft, full, and resonant. "Darrell, I love puzzles. May I also obtain a copy of that intercept along with its metrics and associated frequency and celestial bearing data?"

Darrell sighed; *Humph 'apparently.' Susie, you know that's downright unfair. Still, she has earned the right to try and crack the puzzle.*

"Susie, really well done. With some misgivings, I will authorize Charlie to give you a complete data set. But handle it with care...."

Chapter Forty-Nine:
Repeating Transmission

Ca was busy reading the latest log entries. Emotionally distressed, he was still contemplating the consequences of the devastating battle and the destruction of the Nest ship. When his communicator vibrated, he saw it was from his senior officer. Answering, the officer requested he come to the control room. Putting aside his work, Ca rose and made his way along the familiar corridors.

Upon entering the combat center, the senior officer crisply saluted him. Ca had come to appreciate the military formality, and with a growing sense of respect, he returned the officer's salute.

"Why have I been summoned?" Ca said.

"Honored One, there are two items worthy of reporting. The lesser item concerns the nearby ground searchers that we are observing. They are proficient and diligent. The searchers near the canyon are beginning to withdraw. They do not appear to have found any trace of our presence.

"The second matter is hopeful, and it requires your evaluation. We have detected a short and repeating transmission coming from the zone of the battle. It is being broadcast on our standard tactical frequency. There is no video, only an audio message."

"Replay that broadcast message," Ca said.

The speakers promptly activated, and Ca heard a strong human voice speaking fluently in the Arkillian language. Ca immediately recognized the voice; it was the same individual who had demanded the Nest ship surrender.

"Attention Arkillians. The hostile action taken against this ship has resulted in your current desperate plight. It would have been far wiser if you have accepted our proffered and fair demands.

"Unless you provoke further hostility, the battle is over. You may safely attend to your wounded.

"What will happen to you next remains your choice. The demands delivered to you before the battle are still proffered. If there is anyone remaining alive with authority to speak for the Arkillians, then let them identify themselves. This channel will be monitored awaiting your reply.

"Who speaks for the Arkillians? Let him now speak for them."

"Honorable One, that is the entire message. It suggests the Nest ship has been severely damaged, but not destroyed," the officer said.

Ca had listened carefully to what the officer said, and thought, *Can the Nest ship in fact still exist? This officer's insight is surprising. If we are to survive, I need others with such perception.*

"Tell me, what is your own opinion of the content of that message?"

Ca took notice that his question surprised the officer. *Good, he is trying to discern if I am genuinely asking an inferior for his opinion. Very good indeed.*

"Honored One, my belief is the last message is but a continuation of the enemy's initial communications. If both messages are considered together, they indicate the enemy has a long-term political agenda.

"Before the battle, we had no confirmation of who the enemy was or any means of evaluating the enemy's military potential. What was then known was the enemy appeared to be Kreel, and either anticipated our maneuver or else had the speed to intercept the Nest ship. The seemingly boastful demand that the Nest ship surrender argues the enemy had accurately measured our military capability.

"The enemy's first message gave us a clear warning, but even with our having that notice, they brushed aside and eliminated our defenses. From a military perspective, that feat is impressive.

"Now, the Nest ship appears to have survived, but is rendered helpless. A military force capable of inflicting such horrific damage upon our Nest Ship is able to utterly destroy it. Paradoxically, apparently it has chosen not to do so.

"Now, again the enemy speaks of our having choices. For reasons of its own, the enemy terminated the battle short of a total victory. I ask, why?

"Puzzlingly, the enemy recommends we take care of our wounded and ask for someone having authority to speak for the Arkillians. Again, they issue their demand for surrender.

"Honored One, I believe the one who is speaking is speaking truth. That he has chosen to maintain an open frequency indicates he is seeking a dialog. This argues the enemy is looking beyond the battle toward a negotiation with the Arkillian Empire. That endpoint seems to be the only plausible reason why the enemy has spared the Nest ship from complete destruction. Finally, this message establishes that the enemy is not Kreel. We are dealing with an unknown interstellar culture."

The officer's response was insightful and plausible. The response pleased Ca.

"I believe your considered views warrant much merit. Yet, it might be wise for us to consider several other possibilities.

"As you have said, our enemy has knowledge of our actions and capabilities. Perhaps our enemy also knows we are concealed here on the planet, and is now trying to tempt us to reveal ourselves by communicating with him. We know there are humans searching for us. Possibly the enemy is also looking for us. Conceivably he wants first to eliminate us, then return and destroy the Nest ship."

"Honored One, we pose no military threat to our enemy. If the enemy knows we are here, then he also knows we are isolated far from our home world, and it will be turns before a relief force can enter this solar system. Therefore, the enemy has many turns to search for us. Again, I believe the one speaking is speaking truth."

The officer turned back to his instrument panel. He made some quick adjustments and the tactical tank once again became illuminated. An icon representing the Nest ship appeared on a thin blue line that extended outward. As Ca watched, the scale of the display altered and a representation of the primary and orbiting planets appeared. The blue line continued beyond the orbit of the outermost planet.

"Honored One, unless the Nest ship is able to restore power and motivation, its inertia will carry it out of this solar system. We will continue monitoring for the Nest ship, hoping for some communication.

"Until we hear from Representative Kur, if he has survived, you are the senior Council representative in this solar system. When our enemy asks who speaks for the Arkillians, he is addressing you. How will you answer?"

Ca considered the question appropriate. "You are correct in your observations. Yet, Representative Kur's last orders were that we are to protect ourselves and remain covert and secure. We may not represent a direct military threat, but we do represent an effective Arkillian presence in this solar system. There is still time during which to decide how best to respond to their communication. For the present, we will continue to monitor and observe.

"Your stated insights are of value to me. They are relevant, and they afford me a valued opportunity to examine another perspective. I encourage you to offer your thoughts when you consider they might assist me in making decisions."

The officer did not reveal any facial response to Ca's unusual statement. He stood fully erect, then smartly saluted. Ca returned the salute, turned and departed Combat Control.

Musing as he walked, *Perhaps Kur is still alive.* There was indeed much for him to reflect upon.

Chapter Fifty:
On Station

The observation dome was fully open, its protective shield petals being withdrawn. Kellon was sitting at a table in the large circular conference room with Lorn and Lieutenant Cloud. Soft music, consisting of a male choir singing old sailing ship ballads from the early historic times of Glas Dinnein filled the room. *Somehow,* he thought, *those ancient sea-faring songs are appropriate.*

Lorn had reported there was no detectable Arkillian activity within the orbit of the fifth planet. While Kellon knew of the Arkillian contingency down on the planet, those Arkillians would undoubtedly be keeping a low profile. Nevertheless, he was maintaining full stealth and a high alert.

As they approached the planet, Kellon turned toward Lieutenant Cloud. "Elayne, do you know what the indigenous people call their world?"

Elayne continued gazing at the breath-taking vista of the blue planet and its large moon, even while answering. "Sir, we've have identified at least thirty different languages spoken by the indigenous population. In the language of the nation that launched the satellites, it's known as The Earth."

"Earth. And, what is the root meaning of the word?"

"Sir, I suspected you might ask that question. It has many associations, and the simplest definition is soil or dirt. There are also numerous social and mystical associations, including references to a Mother Earth."

"It seems we have a very rich new language to learn. From what you have told me, the various myths and belief structures are numerous and complex. That diversity will require even more study."

"Sir, we've barely scratched the surface of what we don't know. Merely identifying and cataloging the cultural qualities will require an immense effort," Elayne said.

"In that matter we are in complete agreement. It seems the side effects of long-term Kreel pop-patterns, when combined with a shortened lifespan, produces an extremely complex and vibrant social structure," Kellon said.

Like Kellon and Elayne, Lorn was looking at the blue planet with keen interest. "Sir, that these people have survived millenniums under oppression is incredible. I need to keep reminding myself we're here because they actually sent a primitive interstellar probe across nearly a hundred light years to our own system. Captain, the achievements of these people are a testament of the incredible quality of the human spirit."

"Lorn, I believe in time the people of this world are going to provide a powerful force for the maturing and expansion of the human species. I doubt the Arkillians gave that possibility any thought, but I see a potential for tremendous good coming out of this tragedy."

"Captain, even as we speak of the enduring spirit of the indigenous people, remember they have an extreme preoccupation with military matters. Nearly every nation on that planet, from the small to the large, has some level of advanced military capability. The entire planet is an armed camp.

"If our data is accurate, some of those weapons include fission and fusion weapons. Astonishingly, they've actually used such weapons against each other within the confines of their own atmosphere."

"Lorn, what's your assessment of their military capability?"

"Captain, we've been monitoring their communications and tracking systems for several days. All of the major countries have sophisticated detection and tracking systems. Some of the systems are for commercial transportation, while others are purely military. Their atmospheric aircraft are capable of high performance, and are designed to be extremely proficient within the atmosphere.

"Surprisingly, we are detecting trace evidence of primitive forms of temporal physics and its related energy and motivation systems."

"What recommendations do you have?" Kellon said.

"Sir, until we establish an understanding with these people, we need to remain very circumspect and cautious. I recommend the Scouts operate in a limited covert manner, employing all stealth procedures. I further urge we minimize any contact."

Looking out of the dome at the beauty spread before him, Kellon was wondering how such a bountiful planet could be dangerous. *Blast,* he thought, *I have to remember where we are, hope for the best and prepare for the worst.*

"Lorn, agreed. We'll restrict the Scout activity to a bare necessity. My primary goal is to identify the locations of the pop pattern transmitters. Then, we will neutralize them. How are the surface scans for the transmitters proceeding?"

"Our scans began about a day ago. From that range our ability to isolate the transmitters was negligible. Now that we've come this close, we should be able to locate the transmitters rather quickly."

"Do you foresee any problem in sending a small tactical team down to inspect and destroy the detected Arkillian sites?"

Kellon's question surprised Lorn. "Captain, I consider any exposure of our personnel on the surface of that planet to be a very high-risk venture. If you happen to select a facility where the Arkillians are dug in, then likely there would be direct military confrontation. Before deploying ground forces, there should first be a very compelling reason."

"I am in partial accord with your recommendations. Yet, given the opportunity for Intelligence gathering, perhaps the risk is acceptable. The Arkillians and their technology still pose unanswered questions. And, it's probable we'll face the Arkillians in battle again. Potentially, their planet-wide transmitting facilities here might provide us with their entire library of pop patterns. Such an intelligence bonanza would constitute a real prize.

"Remember, the analysis of their beam weapon and our defensive screens was a revelation. That weapon, in spite of our shielding, would have immediately killed at least thirty percent of our crew and disabled nearly all of the remaining personnel. That is sobering. Even now, we don't have a complete fix for our defensive screens."

Elayne frowned. "Sir, I can only wonder what the Arkillians really do know. If our information is correct, they've had thousands of years to perfect their weapons against humanity. If their beam weapon is an example, then they've used that time effectively."

"I agree Elayne. It's clear the Arkillians have a detailed knowledge of human physiology, knowledge that could be extremely dangerous if employed against us. We need to learn all we can about that Arkillian technology. And, that may require our taking some risk."

Turning to Elayne, Lorn asked, "What is the current political structure on the planet?"

"Sir, the data is far from complete. What we do know is the history of this planet is riddled with political conflict and warfare. The economic struggle and continuing warfare have created diverse military capabilities and fostered interconnecting political alliances between nations. If any of our personnel were captured by the people on this planet, it's unlikely we could easily negotiate their release."

"Your comments only strengthen my convictions. We could destroy the Arkillian facilities from above, but there would be random remaining wreckage. Undoubtedly, our actions would alert the various governments to the destroyed Arkillian sites. I'm not about to provide Arkillian technology to any political faction on this planet.

"Lorn, use Shey, and either Misty or Cindy, whichever is most ready for duty. You're to use maximum stealth. execute a low-level reconnaissance of each ground-based ribbon-transmitter site. Determine if Arkillians are based at those facilities. Have you any questions?" Kellon said.

"Only one. What level of force is authorized if we encounter Arkillians?"

Kellon sighed. "In such a case, lethal force is authorized. Our personnel have good judgment. I'm not going to restrict their options in unexpected engagement. But accidents involving the people on this planet are unacceptable. Operating as Guardians, no collateral damage is acceptable.

"First, let's locate the facility, then gain access. Our tactical ground teams are to be fully prepared for that eventuality."

"Sir, understood and acknowledged," Lorn said.

Kellon frowned. "We came here to accomplish two principal items. The first is the elimination of the Kreel pop-patterns, and the second is to attempt contact with the government that put the Intelligence satellites into orbit. Whoever engineered those satellites has knowledge of the Arkillian presence in this system.

If we knock on their door, just perhaps we might be able to establish meaningful communication with these people."

"Sir, how do you propose to safely achieve such a contact?" Lorn said.

"How? Well, whoever placed those satellites in orbit wanted to observe the Arkillians. Therefore, they must have designed the satellite with both visual and broadband receivers.

"Lan will soon be holding at the same position the Arkillian ship was previously located. We've already determined they use simple frequency and amplitude modulation in their common broadcasts. Therefore, our first step is to direct a low power laser directly at the satellite. The laser will then transmit six sequences of pulses. Each sequence will consist of the primary numbers from one through twenty-three. Because the laser will intermittently blind the onboard detectors, they cannot but help detect the pulses. Our second step is to direct a communication signal using basic frequency modulation and transmit the same sequence of numbers. Then, we will go silent, opening and monitoring the broadcast wavelength that we use to broadcast the prime numbers. The sequence will be repeated each half hour, until we receive a response."

Lorn smiled. "Sir, that approach is simple and direct, it's definitely worth trying."

A soft melodious chime sounded. "Sir, we are now on station and on schedule. Status is set Condition 3." Lan said.

Noting the chronometer, Kellon smiled. "Lan, be advised that you are twenty seconds late arriving on station."

"Oops Sir, perfection is elusive," Lan said.

Surprised, Kellon wondered, *Did Lan just make a joke?* "Lan, arriving on time means that we've something to celebrate. Have the galley bring a chilled bottle of wine, three glasses, and a small wedge of cheese."

Once again, Kellon turned toward the clear dome, contemplating the beautiful world that rotated slowly before them. A few moments later, the hatch opened and a steward entered carrying a tray. Placing it carefully on the conference table, he saluted smartly, then turned and departed.

Kellon carefully poured some wine from the open bottle into each glass, and then cut several pieces of cheese. As host, he extended the wine and cheese first to Lieutenant Cloud and then to Commander Shaw. Lifting his own glass, he proposed a toast.

"I salute all the ladies and gentlemen of this beautiful planet Earth. May prosperity and goodness embrace you at home and wherever in due time your children choose to journey."

They sat for a moment, all enjoying the special moment and blended tastes of good wine and cheese, companionship of shipmates, and music. The broad view through the dome was startlingly beautiful, and Kellon knew they each uniquely felt the special essence of their arrival. For the moment, they relaxed, knowing that within a few hours they would be facing new and unanticipated challenges.

Chapter Fifty-One:
Looking for Trouble

The morning held the bright promise of a warm and wonderful day. Sunshine was filling the room, and Susie was thrilled to be home again in California. Only moments before, her friends had brought Gepeto home, his tail wagging furiously. She gratefully thanked her friends, who in her absence had obviously taken excellent care of him. For them both it was a joy-filled reunion.

Upon her return, William had simply greeted her, "Welcome home, Miss Susie."

Getting right back to work, she responded, "William, locate and make contact with Jerry Bernard at the Applied Physics Laboratory of the University of Washington. I need to talk with him as soon as possible. So, until you find him keep trying to reach him."

Dr. Bernard was one of her graduate professors and had over years become a good friend. Now, Susie hoped he might help her.

Gepeto had followed her wanderings throughout the house, his happiness evident. Carrying her suitcases from the front hall into the bedroom, unpacking was comprised mostly of transferring her dirty apparel from suitcases to the appropriate laundry basket. But a small package was removed from a suitcase and carefully set aside. Changing, she put on something more comfortable than her travel clothes, donning a loose soft embroidered white blouse, jeans, and a pair of moccasins. Picking up the small container she had set aside, Susie headed toward the kitchen. With a broad smile, she resumed her normal routine.

Reaching for the container of Sumatran whole coffee beans, she carefully added two measures to the grinder and promptly ground the roasted beans. Then she pulled out her small electric kettle and added sixteen ounces of fresh water. As the water began to heat, she opened the small package. Inside was a glass and ceramic French coffee press. It was the only item she had acquired in Europe. With anticipation she dropped the fresh ground coffee into the press, and as the kettle whistled, she poured in the boiling water, swirled the fluid, then gently pressed the plunger to separate the grounds from the freshly brewed coffee. One-half spoon of honey, a dash of cream, and voilà a cup of superb coffee.

Turning, she opened a bin, scooped up a large measuring cup of raw peanuts in the shell, and walked out onto the deck. She filled the vertical bird feeders and then deposited the generous portion of peanuts onto the feeding platform. With an easy whistle, borne of long practice, she began a series of birdcalls, announcing it was time to feast. Even as she put the peanuts out, the blue jays and woodpeckers began to assemble. She was glad to see that they had not given up on her.

Back inside the kitchen, Gepeto reminded her of his presence by dropping his favorite bone on the floor by her feet. Recognizing the bid for an exchange, she pulled out one of the drawers next to the oven and removed two small dog biscuits. Gepeto watched expectantly as she deposited the treats into his bowl.

Susie looked about, and with a sigh, gave thanks for her many blessings. It was indeed good to be safe and once more secure in her own home.

Returning to her study, for the first time in weeks, she felt totally relaxed. Sitting quietly in her familiar surroundings, the previous weeks of hectic activity seemed almost a fantasy. After living in hotel rooms, camping on a mountaintop, and then spending days underground at Project Olympus, she badly needed a break.

She had just lifted her cup of coffee to her lips, when William announced, "Ms. Susie, I have located Dr. Bernard. He is holding on line one."

Putting her coffee down, she keyed her communicator. "Hello Jerry. I've just returned from Europe."

"Was it an interesting trip?"

"Yes, very. But more business than pleasure. Still, it was exciting and wonderful.

"Jerry, your encryption algorithm proved very useful. Even some folks who have enormous resources were unable to crack it. I thought that you'd like to hear that."

"Humph, how enormous? Dare I ask, who the folks might be?"

"Sorry, but I'm not at liberty to say who they are, but I assure you they have very powerful resources."

"You make it sound like you've been keeping company with spooks. At least give me a hint."

"Honest, I only occasionally work for the Department of Commerce. I also do my best to avoid dark alleys. But, honest, I did use the encryption algorithm and it did work, even as you said it would."

"Dear Susie, reluctantly moving beyond the cryptic, might I ask, why are you calling?"

"Well, I need your help. I've come across a recorded radio transmission. And, before you ask, I'm not at liberty to tell you where I acquired the information."

"Cutting to the bare facts, just what do you need from me?"

"Well, it's sorta cryptic, involving proprietary information. If you're willing to work somewhat in the dark, I attest it will represent a real challenge. I'm asking you to evaluate data and determine if you can define its structure and decipher its content."

"Susie, all these evasions are beginning to intrigue me. We have moved beyond facts to cryptic, and then on to vague, and have finally arrived at evaluate, structure, decipher, and mysterious contents. Don't I get even a clue?"

"Clue? Well, it's a record of communication between two parties. The communications are not encrypted, are important, and it must be handled circumspectly."

"Not encrypted? Circumspectly? Well, that figures. If I understand correctly, if we crack the puzzle, we'll not get rich and famous, and we can't even tell anyone about its mysterious contents. It sounds a whole lot like some Government work I used to do."

Jerry, it's really important and urgent. And, it's truly sensitive. Will you do it?"

"Since it's just for you, and not some other folks, I'll compress my priority stack of work and put your cryptic teaser right on the very top. That's presuming you will send me the data."

"I can and will. I'll use our standard keywords and send it immediately. Jerry, you are wonderful, thank you.

"Oh, Jerry, I almost forgot. Before you go, there's one more little favor."

"OK, but only one. What is it?"

"When you examine the metadata, please recommend a good transceiver that might generate the same type of communication signal."

"Humph, it sounds like you're looking for trouble. Until now, I had no idea you were interested in ham radio. Do you prefer something in the megawatt range or will something more modest meet your unique needs?"

"Jerry, be serious. I confirm the transceiver is for me. I am looking for something with a high gain and low power output. Honest, if I could tell you more now I would."

"Susie, I'll go along on the ride, for a while. But I do expect a full explanation as soon as possible. Agreed?"

"Yes, agreed. As soon as I can, I promise I'll fill you in on all the details."

"OK, count me as being on board. But, now hear this, loud and clear. I had better not wake up some morning at 05:00 with some heavy hammering on my door."

"Jerry, that's not likely. And, you're terrific. Thank you. I'll be eagerly looking forward to your report."

Susie terminated the communication and sighed. "William, locate the file I sent to you yesterday evening."

"That file is located, ma'am."

"Good. Using the appropriate key, translate the encrypted file. Once the file is in plain form, then using the encryption keys used with Dr. Bernard, encrypt it again and send it to Dr. Bernard."

"Well pup, are you ready for a quick walk?"

In reply, Gepeto rolled over on the floor and kicked all four legs straight up. Smiling, Susie scratched his belly. "Well, don't just lay there. Hop up."

Walking along the street with Gepeto, Susie enjoyed the incredible fragrance of the flowers. Honeysuckle and jasmine were blooming everywhere. Europe had its charms, but there was no other place like the central coast of California.

She knew Darrell would not be particularly pleased to learned the data had been sent to a third party. *Still,* she rationalized, *he never specifically said the data was classified. Besides, it isn't likely he will ever find out.*

Frowning, Susie pondered, *What was its Janet said when I arrived at Government Park? Ah, someday that famous curiosity of yours might get you into some real trouble.*

Susie smiled at that memory, yet, she knew her friend and sometimes boss had also been serious. Undeniably, she was going in search of trouble, and the outcome was uncertain.

Looking down toward her wonderful pup, she smiled and whispered. "Going in search of adventure is all part of the fun, isn't it, Gepeto."

With a firm determination, she thought, *I intend to enjoy the gift of my life to its fullest, come what may. It's not the function of life to arrive safely at death's door. Life is an adventure to be experienced. Look out world, here we come....*

Chapter Fifty-Two:
Planetary Assembly

The large room was quiet and elegantly appointed. Its most striking features were the complete lack of windows and the heavy double entry door, with its deeply carved intricate relief images of people, wildlife, starships, and mountains. The door had no apparent knobs or handles. A luxurious deep pile rug, rich and dark brown in color, covered the floor. The soft natural light within the room came from the walls and ceiling, yet no light fixtures of any kind were apparent. A few holographic images of men and women appeared on the walls, and they looked somewhat somberly back at whomever might be studying them.

Opposite the entry, the wall held a broad mural showing a sweeping structure, the Planetary Assembly building on Glas Dinnein, as depicted on an autumn afternoon. The gleaming white and bright golden trim surfaces of the building seemed almost self-radiant, and it was shown surrounded by fountains and rich foliage. The conference room was located deep within the same building.

Situated in the center of the room was a long and highly polished wood conference table, and twelve chairs were arranged around it. Six of those chairs were occupied.

Admirals Mer Shawn, Ron Cloud, and Dylan Cord sat on one side. As the senior Guardian Force officers, each were wearing full dress uniforms.

The three individuals sitting across the table from the Admirals were civilians wearing normal, but well-tailored apparel. Two of the civilians were women and the third was a man.

Eryan Kyrie, Admiral Secretary of the Planetary Assembly, was sitting in the center, directly opposite Mer. To her right sat Jan Mercer the Judge Advocate. Rich Sumor, the Chief Administrator, sat on Eryan Kyrie's left. All three civilians looked serious and none showed the slightest hint of a smile. The tension within the room was nearly palpable.

"Admiral Mer Shawn, how long have you had this information?" Eryan Kyrie said.

"Madam Secretary, the urgent tactical situation report was transmitted from Cruiser Lan several weeks ago. Because of their extreme distance from Glas Dinnein that message only arrived here several hours ago. Upon its receipt, your administration was promptly notified, and all related reports were forwarded to your staff."

"Admiral, I noticed you failed to follow proper protocols when forwarding the message," Rich Sumor said.

"Administrator Sumor, your observation is correct. Because of the urgent nature of the report, the matter was handled outside of normal protocols. Given its gravity, as promptly as possible, the report was placed responsibly before the Planetary Assembly."

Eryan was frowning; she well understood the last thing needed now was to allow the meeting to descend into a blame game. She needed answers.

"Mer, how did you come to find yourselves embroiled in this mess?"

"Madam Secretary, from the viewpoint of our standing traditions, and the often-stated purpose of Guardian Force, the current situation is considered to be well within the purview of our operating parameters.

"Cruiser Lan is proficiently executing a long-range and covert reconnaissance mission. Their initial deployment was a direct response to an alien intrusion into our own sovereign space.

"The initial contact report sent by Cruiser Lan is contained within the statement placed before you. It details what Lan discovered upon entering the originating solar system. Madam Secretary, I respectfully submit, that after thoroughly reviewing the problem, I find nothing akin to a 'mess.'"

"Admiral Mer Shawn, be hereby advised that I disagree with that assessment. Now, kindly continue," Eryan said.

"Yes, Madam Secretary. The most recent report from Lan has significantly altered our initial mission assumptions. Frankly, this is not surprising, since it was the lack of information that mandated the reconnaissance mission. Clearly, given the serious content and implications of the recent message, the entire matter mandates your immediate appraisal. We are accordingly here in person to make our report directly to you, and to assist the Assembly."

Eryan had known Mer Shawn for many years, and they remained close friends. Nevertheless, the problem was not simply another administrative or budgetary issue. The discovery of a planet with more than ten-billion human beings was itself astonishing. Then learning those humans were long suffering under the heels of oppression by an unknown alien species was shocking. The next jarring surprise came with the realization that one of their star Cruisers was far from Glas Dinnein, and although far distant and alone, it was preparing to engage in a battle. Even more troubling, that battle might already be over, and the Guardian Cruiser with its Scouts may have already been destroyed.

Pulling her mind back from dark and presumptuously negative thoughts, Eryan returned her attention to the main issue. The entire matter was fraught with high-level risks, which further underscored the scope of their ignorance. Looking directly at Mer, her countenance revealed her contained but evident emotions. She was demanding precise answers, and would tolerate nothing less.

"Admiral Mer Shawn, be herewith advised, you have a distinctly different understanding of authorized Guardian Force operations than I do. From my disadvantaged reference point, it appears Guardian Force operations has involved the Assembled Worlds in an interstellar war a hundred light years from home. I must stress, I don't believe beginning an interstellar war with an unknown culture is within the normal purview of Guardian Force operations. Even you must acknowledge these circumstances set a new high for going about looking for trouble."

"Madam Secretary, with well due respect, it's not distance that's at issue here. None within Guardian Force went about looking for trouble. Cruiser Lan is on a fully justifiable and dangerous covert reconnaissance mission," Dylan said.

"Madam Secretary, I agree with Admiral Cord. Captain Kellon and his crew are acting with great courage and operating in the highest traditions of the Guardian Force. Properly and within full compliance of their standing orders, they're now defending an inhabited human world, and doing so at risk to their own lives. Even now, they remain far from home and in peril.

They're doing precisely what we've repeatedly required and expect from Guardian Force.

"What Cruiser Lan discovered was unanticipated and horrifying. More than ten-billion humans have been subjected to harsh tyranny and hammered by Kreel mind assaults for millenniums. It's only by force and brutality that such oppression of an entire world can be maintained. Given our own experience with Kreel pop-patterns, it's highly probable that those pop-patterns are but the very tip of many egregious afflictions.

"The Assembly needs to be aware of and consider a vital point. Until now, Captain Kellon's actions have fully maintained the covert nature of his mission profile. If at this point the Assembly should choose to withdraw Cruiser Lan, then no one in that distant solar system will learn of our identity or the location of Glas Dinnein.

"What Captain Kellon has accomplished is a brilliantly executed long-range tactical reconnaissance. Yet, that is not what brings us to this meeting. We're not here to talk about the Guardian Force.

"The urgent issue placed before the Assembly is about tyranny and aggression being enacted against billions of human beings. The primary question today is fundamental: What will the Assembly decide regarding such tyranny? The Assembly has a clear choice--"

With a hint of sarcasm, Rich Sumor interrupted Mer's comment, "Admiral Mer Shawn, just what clear choice by the Assembly might you be referring to?"

Eryan watched as Mer met the Chief Administrator's gaze. This was not the first time they had found themselves on opposite sides of an issue. Much of Mer's work involved striving to acquire the monetary resources necessary to support Guardian Force operations. As in any open republic, there were always competing demands for limited resources. More often than not, Rich Sumor was inclined to obstruct funds for the Guardian Force. It was only when the news was reporting the Kreel or Dargon were inflicting increasing casualties that money seemed to flow without his obstructions.

"Administrator Sumor," I am speaking of the crucial choice the Assembly must soon make. As for me, that choice seems rather apparent. The Assembly will either choose to send military and humanitarian resources to support more than ten billion human beings, or else it will abandon those billions of humans to certain tyranny and possible genocide."

Mer's blunt words caused Rick Sumor to stiffen. Leaning forward, his eyes narrowed.

"Admiral, do you mean to imply that if we don't support your actions, we will be personally responsible for the death of billions of people?"

"Chief Administrator, the responsibility for any action rests upon those with the authority and means of taking such action. If the Planetary Assembly should decide to ignore the desperate need of ten-billion human beings, then just where else do you believe the responsibility for that action resides?"

Rich Sumor's face flushed hotly. As he opened his mouth to respond, Eryan spoke up, cutting his response off.

"Gentlemen, let's keep our focus on the problem at hand. Admiral Mer Shawn, am I correct when stating that although Cruiser Lan's report is newly arrived here, it is in truth several weeks old?"

"Madam Secretary, that is correct."

"Then, is it correct to say that Cruiser Lan may already be utterly destroyed and all hands lost?"

"That too is correct."

"Admiral Mer Shawn, what do you recommend we do here today?"

Mer leaned forward; his attention focused on Eryan. His posture and manner clearly showed the intensity of his convictions. Likewise, Eryan found herself intensely aware of the momentous nature and long-term consequences of the decision being required from the Assembly.

"Madam Secretary, it is recommended that reinforcements be deployed in support of Cruiser Lan. Those reinforcements should consist of two parts. The first detachment should be purely military and dispatched immediately. The second detachment would be a blended military and planetary aid group. The second group will require some time to assemble and equip, but it should be ready to depart in the near future."

" Admiral, why not send just one group?" Jan Mercer said.

"Madam Judge Advocate, the initial demand is urgent and is purely military. Cruiser Lan is facing a large Capital ship able to deploy around a hundred fighters. I'm confident in Captain Kellon's capability, yet he is in a particularly difficult position. I would feel more comfortable if the military odds were more weighted in our favor. I therefore recommend the urgent deployment of the first group, it consisting of three cruisers.

"Given the long-term detrimental effects of Kreel pop-patterns, the mental and physical problems of the indigenous population must be severe and chronic. Those people are going to need considerable medical assistance. Therefore, I recommend that the second group be weighted heavily toward medical personnel, accompanied by a well-qualified political liaison staff. By the very nature and composition of the second group, it will take some time to assemble and provision.

"Madam Judge Advocate, does my elaboration satisfactorily answer your question?"

"Yes, Admiral Mer Shawn, it does," Jan Mercer said.

"Admiral Mer Shawn, I'm quite confident about one matter. You wouldn't be sitting there making your recommendation about a first group, without first having specific plans well defined, and probably in triplicate. Am I correct in my assumption?" Eryan said.

"Madam Secretary, your assumption is correct."

Eryan paused for a moment, looking across the table at each of the three Admirals. "Gentlemen, I regret to say that we in the Assembly are often forgetful of your knowledge, wisdom, and dedication to our mutual defense. That we now have military forces operating at great peril while protecting others is not something we can ignore or take lightly.

"Please make all preparations deemed necessary to provide immediate military support for Cruiser Lan. I will personally communicate the problem you've outlined here to the entire Assembly. You will be notified within six hours of our formal decision. Can you be ready to deploy those three cruisers within six hours?"

"Yes, Madam Secretary. We can deploy those forces in even less time, if approved."

"As for the second group, your comments indicate some time will elapse before you're ready to dispatch them."

"Madam Secretary, I believe that the second group should only be dispatched when the military situation is clarified and stable. I'm not able at this time to identify when that will be so," Mer said.

"I agree with your assessment of the matter. Please send to my office your staff's recommendation for the composition of the civilian component of the second group, as soon as possible."

"Gentlemen, you all have a great deal of work to do during the next six hours. For that matter, so do those of us in the Assembly. I personally thank you for coming here today, and I appreciate your thoughts and opinions on this most important matter."

Standing, Mer stretched his hand across the table to Eryan. "Madam Secretary, we thank you for your prompt and personal attention."

Smiling, Eryan reached out her hand in response. For a brief moment, their fingers lingered, barely touching. Within the boundaries of several thousand years, there were many memories and crossroads in the lifespan of two friends.

When those within the room approached, the massive wooden doors swung smoothly open, and with a soft but distinctly solid thunk closed behind them.

Chapter Fifty-Three:
Field Decision

At first, Lan had directed Shey to a southern continent. Her prime mission was to survey a mountainous terrain in order to confirm the location of a detected Kreel pop-pattern transmitter. Their search had been fruitful, near the equator they had found a concealed ribbon transmitter site. Following well-developed reconnaissance procedures, they had obtained a full terrain scan of that region, including the critical subsurface and life-energy profiles.

With the survey completed they began their scheduled return to Lan. Following a low altitude contour, Shey had streaked over a dark ocean, then pitched sharply up and drove toward the safety of deep space. Just prior to exiting the upper atmosphere, Shey had detected a weak Kreel parley signal, where no such signal should be. Without hesitation, Roan decided the signal demanded investigation. Accordingly, Shey promptly turned about, Roan directing her to trace the signal to its source.

Now, dropping silently through the atmosphere, Shey conformed to a nearly vertical trajectory. Her outer hull color configuration was a dull flat black. To the unaided eye Shey was merely a flickering shadow within enveloping darkness, invisible in a moonless night sky. It was nearly one hour before mean darkness, and the region immediately below Shey was quiet and showing little activity.

"Roan, we are descending below five-thousand meters. As ordered, I am coming to a full stop at one-thousand meters," Shey said.

Coming to a full hover, Shey was poised above what appeared to be a wooded and quiet seaside residential community.

Concentrating on his tactical console, Zorn was examining the instrument readouts. Roan also was intent on his own instruments.

"Shey, keep your sensors scanning for local aircraft or any indication that we've been observed. Remain on this station," Roan said.

A soft tone acknowledged Roan's orders. Moving his hands expertly across his keyboard, Zorn sought after pinpointing the Kreel signal.

"Lock established," Zorn said.

On the large view screen before them, a night vision image expanded. Shown in clear detail were several streets and a number of buildings set out in a pattern that followed the coastal and terrain contour lines of a low hilly region. The search cursor was precisely centered on one structure within the residential community.

"Are you positive the signal is emanating from that structure?" Roan said.

"Confirmed. Two life forms are within the structure. One is a human woman and the second is a small mammal of undefined type. I am also receiving what appears to be the signal profile of one or more computers of a sophisticated design."

"How about security? Can you see any indication of detection or defensive systems?"

Zorn again made a few adjustments. "There's a simple network of infrared signals near the structure. They are most probably an intruder alert. They don't seem complex. So, now we're here. But what, pray tell, are we here to do?"

"Be a little patient, I'm still contemplating that small problem."

Inwardly, Roan fully understood why Zorn had asked the question. Just being here was contrary to the mission profile and their orders. Roan mused, *I'm not going to ignore a Kreel parley signal, consequences be what they will be.*

"Shey, passively scan the surrounding area for any indication of organized military elements or activity and report," Roan said.

"I am currently tracking twenty-six aircraft within a three-hundred-kilometer radius of this location. Only three are of a military profile and none of those are moving toward our location. There is no discernible military activity on the ground."

"Roan, aren't we out on a shaky limb by just being here?"

"No. There're no standing orders about making contact with anyone on Earth."

Smiling broadly, Zorn chuckled. "Well, technically speaking, you are right. Still, I am now wagering two brews that if Kellon had considered such contact might occur, he would have issued those specific orders."

"There you go again, thinking like a Cruiser Captain. I keep warning you about that personal trait. Someday, it'll get you in real trouble, or even worse, promoted. Remember, command latitude exists to permit our making field command decisions, where deemed justified, and where there are no standing orders to the contrary."

"You don't need to convince me. We both know your command latitude is a consequence of Kellon's omission, not his permission. I wager two brews this little side trip comes back to bite us. I'm now bracing for yet another black mark on our otherwise sterling performance record. So, since we're already here on the shaky limb, what comes next?"

"Well, it's extremely implausible a Kreel parley signal is coming from a human dwelling. Yet your sensors confirm it is, correct?"

"Correct. The Kreel signal is on frequency and proper in all characteristics. And, it's definitely coming from that building. While I really dislike repeating myself, what comes next?"

"That should be obvious. The signal is a standard announcement parley signal. So why not simply transmit the expected response and see what happens next?" Roan said.

"Just perhaps, given a little more time, you might find a more direct approach."

Roan ignored Zorn's quip. "Shey, send the standard Kreel response and monitor for an acknowledgment."

"I am answering the Kreel signal," Shey said.

Almost instantly, the appropriate Kreel counter-acknowledgment flashed back. Then a male human voice immediately followed after the counter signal.

"Greetings voyagers. My name is William. May I be of some assistance?"

"Well done, Roan. Now what?" Zorn said.

"Roan, the voice answering our call is a synthesized human voice. I believe a computer is responding," Shey said.

Troubled, Zorn was studying his instruments. "Whatever you're planning to do, we had better get to it. This is becoming very convoluted. And more to the point, we are running out of our allocated mission time."

"Understood. I'm pondering the problem."

Zorn looked up; his voice serious. "I'm monitoring movement within the structure. I recommend you hurry your pondering."

William's wake-up alert woke Susie from a sound sleep. As her eyes flickered open, she willed her mind to function.

"Ms. Susie, there is an incoming acknowledgment with the proper protocol to your transmitted signal. As instructed, I have provided the indicated response and expressed a verbal greeting. I am waiting your further instructions."

Instructions? As Susie struggled for full awareness, she remembered her efforts of the past several days. Responding to her request for assistance, Jerry had completed the first stage of his analysis. He determined the pattern of transmissions consisted of several distinct and different components. The last of those components was some form of audiovisual signal. He had isolated the initial components and separated the audio message. However, the video component was complex and he was still trying to determine its characteristics. He told her that he had no idea of the conversation of the audio message. It was in some totally unrecognizable language, and it did not even sound human. He was more than a little curious, and obviously concerned for her welfare, having cautioned, "Are you certain you know what you are doing?"

She had reassured him she did. Having accepted her assurances, he was continuing to work on the video problem and would keep her posted.

After having obtained the handshake and message components from Jerry, she immediately obtained and used a small transceiver to begin transmitting the initial signal. She had instructed William to monitor the transmission frequency for an acknowledging response. If it were detected, he was to transmit the counter acknowledgment and notify her immediately.

As she fully realized the implications of what William had just told her, her eyes opened wide. She hurriedly sat up, her heartbeat beginning to increase. *Someone has answered the transmission,* she thought, *not a simple random call, but one with the correct handshake protocol.*

She looked to the bedside clock. It was almost midnight.

Gepeto looked up as Susie slipped out of bed and into her embroidered silk night robe. She quickly pulled her hair back with a silver clasp and slid her feet into hand-stitched moccasins. Then she flung open the bedroom door and hurried toward the study. Gepeto rose quickly from his bed mat and promptly followed on her heels.

Chapter Fifty-Four:
Beneficial Information

Departing her bedroom, Susie hurried to the study. "William, has there been any further communication traffic?"

"No, Ms. Susie."

While Susie was worrying about what was the correct next step, the speaker on the transceiver activated, and a feminine voice clearly said, "This is Shey calling William. William, if you are receiving my transmissions, please respond."

"Ms. Susie, what are your instructions?"

That a woman was speaking in English to William exploded into a cascade of questions, yet it eased Susie's rising anxiety. The woman's clear voice conveyed a sense of firm serenity and assurance. Susie looked toward the microphone atop her monitor, then made her choice.

"William, open the transceiver for two-way communications."

Again, the feminine voice repeated her inquiry. "This is Shey calling William. William, if you are receiving my transmissions, please respond."

"Shey, my name is Susie. To whom am I speaking?"

There followed nearly 30 seconds of silence before the reply. "Susie, I am a Guardian. May I ask in return, who are you, and why are you transmitting a Kreel parley signal?"

The directness of the questions took Susie somewhat aback, and she wondered, *What should I say?* "Well, first of all, I do not know what a Kreel parley signal might be. And, what is a Guardian?"

"Susie, the signal you have been sending, and the recognition signal you correctly responded with, are the current challenge and recognition signals of a species called the Kreel. The Kreel are an interstellar travel-capable species, which you would not desire to encounter. That you are sending a Kreel parley signal requires me to ask, how do you have knowledge of such a signal? Why are you broadcasting the signal?"

"Shey, did you say that the Kreel are an interstellar-capable species?"

"That is correct, and they are also a very dangerous and hostile species. Again, I must ask, how do you have knowledge of the Kreel signal? Why are you transmitting it?"

"Not so fast, Shey. Before I answer your question, I also need some information. You say you are a Guardian. I ask again, what is a Guardian?"

Attentively concentrating on the communication, Susie did not notice Gepeto. Laying down by her feet, he had begun to softly growl.

"Susie, Guardian Force is a military force established for the specific purpose of protecting human civilization. Individual members of the force are called Guardians."

William began to speak, and Susie told him to be silent. Gepeto then abruptly stood, and looking directly across the room and toward the front of the house, His growls deepened; the ruff down his back was rising.

For the first time hearing Gepeto's warning growls, Susie took notice. Such behavior by Gepeto was rare, and it warranted immediate attention. Suddenly, she felt an inner alarm.

"William, scan the perimeter security alert system. Is there anything out of order?"

"Ms. Susie, there is an unidentified male approaching the front door."

"William, display."

On the monitor screen there appeared the image of a tall man, he was moving with an erect military bearing and coming directly down her driveway toward the front door. He was making no effort to hide himself, walking quite purposefully, and with apparent confidence.

"William, are the doors and other entries secured?"

"Yes, Ma'am. All doors and windows are closed and locked."

William's assurance lessened her sense of alarm, but not much. Susie continued studying the man, as he approached. He was wearing odd clothing that did not conform with any traditional style. Unbidden, the thought occurred to her, *He is a very handsome man and certainly carries himself well. The real question,* she thought, *who is he and why is he here at this hour of the night?*

The speaker activated again. Susie heard Shey's reassuring voice.

"Susie, there is a man now approaching your dwelling structure."

"Yes," I am observing his approach. Do you know who he is?"

"Yes, the man is Commander Roan of the Glas Dinnein Guardian Force. I am in direct communications with the Commander at this time."

As Susie observed the screen, she saw the man stop some ten feet from the door. He stood, as if waiting.

"Susie, the Commander has come to visit with you at some personal risk to himself. He hopes that a meeting with you might provide mutually beneficial information. However, if you should choose not to meet at this time, he will immediately depart, and we will never contact you again. You must make the decision soon, since we are at some peril being here."

Susie carefully studied the man. She liked what she saw, and her curiosity was clamoring.

"Shey, before I give you my answer, please answer one question."

"If I am able to do so."

"What is a Glas Dinnein?"

There was a momentary silence before Shey replied. "Glas Dinnein is a world about one-hundred light years distant from Earth. It is our home."

Susie heard the words, and they shocked her to the core, *A world one-hundred light years distant. That means the man standing at my front door has come one-hundred light years across space. How could that possibly be true? That is impossible.*

Whoever he was, he was standing at her front door wishing to meet with her. Susie's mental processes went on full overload.

"Shey, can you answer one more question?"

"If I am able to do so, I will gladly answer all of your questions. Yet, again I stress, Commander Roan is waiting, and we are running out of time."

Susie wanted to open her door, but she was also scared. "Shey, is Commander Roan a human being?"

As Susie was observing the Commander on her monitor, she saw him begin to laugh. She thought, *He at least looks human.*

"Susie, I can and do personally assure you the Commander is very human."

After several moments, Susie began to smile. Maybe the Commander's laughter made the difference. She then didn't know or even care. Her mind was made up, perhaps it was foolish, even childish, but Susie knew if the man had dared turn to walk away, she would have run out the door and chased the man down. She heard herself speaking with a calm tone, which was at odds with her racing thoughts.

"Shey, you may tell the Commander that I most certainly will speak with him. In fact, tell him as fast as I can get there, I will personally greet him at my front door."

As she ran from the room, she heard behind her, "The Commander looks forward to meeting you."

At a near run, Susie moved down the hall. Gepeto obviously felt her excitement and bounded along beside her. When she reached the door, she paused and curled her fingers through Gepeto's collar. Suddenly becoming aware of her apparel, she winced. *Why would a man travel a hundred light years to visit and not even give a girl the chance to dress properly?* Her mouth tilted into a small, wry grin, *Well, here we go.*

Standing straight and tall, and throwing her head back, she took a deep breath, and opened the door....

Chapter Fifty-Five:
Mutual Trust

As the front door swung open, Susie found the man waiting on her porch. He was looking cautiously at Gepeto. He was a big dog, weighing nearly a hundred and fifteen pounds. He stood looking up at the stranger, his tail wagging briskly. A smile slowly formed on the man's countenance.

Like Gepeto, Susie also liked what she saw. Stepping back, she motioned the man to enter.

"Please, come in, Commander Roan."

As in deference, Roan nodded and stepped into the entryway. As Susie closed the door behind him, her mind was swirling with a thousand questions, all concerning the improbability of their meeting.

Unbidden, the first thing that came out of her mouth was, "Are you really human?"

"Yes, I am human. And, given certain blood samples, I also believe you are human."

The man's peculiar answer produced a host of new questions, but she pushed her curiosity aside. Although nearly midnight, she felt compelled to respond in a hospitable fashion.

"Commander, may I prepare you a cup of coffee or perhaps tea?"

"Regretfully, I have not yet had the opportunity to thoroughly absorb your language. I do not understand what the terms coffee or tea mean."

"Well, coffee and tea are beverages made by adding hot water to either ground beans or the leaves of plants. They are considered to be refreshing."

"Susie, my time here is restricted. Regretfully, I must decline your offer.

"I'm here to learn how you became aware of a Kreel parley signal. Your answer is critically important, else I would not have come."

Oddly, Susie felt totally comfortable in the presence of the strange man. It made no logical sense, but he exuded an aura of complete trustworthiness.

"Commander, if you will follow me to my study, I'll try to answer all your questions."

Susie led the way, Gepeto dancing along beside her. As she reached the door to the study she stopped. Turning, she observed Roan hesitantly standing near the front door. Then, she understood that it required mutual trust for them to be meeting in so unusual a manner.

While indicating Gepeto, Susie commented, "His name is Gepeto. He's a good dog and quite safe, I promise. Please come."

As Roan followed her into the room, Susie noted he glanced alertly about, taking in the furnishings, décor, equipment, and books. The warm environment of the room and its simple tasteful furnishings seemed to meet with his approval. Susie beckoned toward a chair and asked him to take a seat.

"Roan, do not get too comfortable. There are military aircraft in the vicinity, and I do not like remaining stationary," Shey said.

"Shey, I'll make this as brief as possible."

Noting Susie's inquiring look, Roan offered, "Shey is my ship. And, she is becoming somewhat anxious at our current circumstances."

"Then, your ship is an AI? I've been talking with your ship?"

"Yes. Her name is Shey, just like your computer is named William."

Roan's response had surprised Susie. Before she could frame her next question, Roan interrupted her thoughts.

"Susie, how do you know of a Kreel parley signal?"

Susie felt as much as heard the commanding tone of his direct question. Sighing, she turned toward William and motioned.

"Listen. William, select and play the message loop."

Immediately, the sounds of the Kreel parley signal filled the study. Then came a recognition sequence, and it was followed by the sound of Kellon's spoken demands to the Arkillians.

Utterly surprised, Roan stood without comment. He wanted to ask many questions, but the constraints of time prevented that. He made another command decision, *Come what may.*

"Susie, that message was sent very far from Earth. Do you understand what is being said?"

"No, the language is totally unknown. Yet, I think it was some type of ultimatum, given before a battle in deep space."

Roan had not believed it possible that he could be more surprised by the unfolding events. But he was proven wrong.

"Then, you know about the Arkillians and the recent battle?"

Puzzled, Susie replied, "I do not recognize the word 'Arkillian,' but I do know that there was a fierce battle fought in deep space between an unknown force and a large alien spaceship we call Monstro."

Roan studied the countenance of the young woman. Time was pressing, and it compelled him to be direct.

"Do you work for an Earth government?"

"Well, yes, in a small way. I sort of work for the Department of Commerce, sometimes."

Trying to find the correct words within the newly learned language, Roan spoke slowly and deliberately. "Is the existence of Monstro common knowledge among your people?"

"No. It's mostly a secret."

Susie's quick and innocent response caused Roan to smile. One of his eyebrows subconsciously arched, inquisitively.

"It's mostly a secret, but it's one you appear to be well-informed of."

Frowning, Susie suddenly became quiet. She worried, *Have I said something I ought not to have said?*

Chapter Fifty-Six:
On My Honor

Observing Susie's expression, Roan was aware of her sudden concern. Nevertheless, he continued pressing forward his urgent request.

"Susie, my available time to remain here has elapsed, and I must now return to Shey. What I am about to ask of you requires a serious decision on your part.

"Guardian Force desires to discreetly make contact with your government. In particular, we want to communicate with those officials who recently launched some satellites into the orbit of the Earth to observe Monstro. Can you help us make that contact?"

"Well, perhaps. I do know the people who launched those satellites."

"Do you have a personal communicator?"

Susie brightened. "Of course."

Opening the drawer of her desk Susie withdrew her communicator. She held it up for Roan to see. He looked at the small communicator and nodded approvingly.

"Susie, I have an earnest request to make. On behalf of Glas Dinnein and Guardian Force, will you accept our invitation and come with me? Will you become a point of contact between your government and Glas Dinnein?"

"Commander Roan, to be certain I understand what you are asking, please repeat your request."

"Susie, will you volunteer to become a liaison between your government and those of us in the Glas Dinnein Guardian Force?"

With A broad smile, Susie replied, "Why, Commander Roan, are you inviting me to take a ride with you in your little spaceship? If so, will you assure me, on your honor, that you'll return me safely home?"

Hearing the playfulness in Susie's voice, Roan was somewhat bemused, wondering, *What type of person is this woman?* In his entire busy life, he had seldom met a woman who was so quick to adjust to the unexpected. Yet, she stood before him, smiling at the prospect of leaving with a total stranger, and go beyond anything she had ever before experienced. She was demonstrating courage and a quick mental capability to gather data and reach insightful conclusions. He instinctively recognized in Susie an exceptional quality, an adventuresome love of life.

"Yes, indeed Susie, I am asking you to come with me and take a ride in my spaceship. Also, I promise, on my honor, that you will be returned safely home."

"Well, if Gepeto can come along, then we have a deal. But I will need a moment to dress more appropriately."

Roan looked over with interest at the animal resting on the floor. The animal gazed directly toward him, with attentive awareness, watching him. Roan wondered about the obvious relationship between this woman and the animal, and came to a quick decision. *In for a gram, in for a kilogram,* he thought.

At the thought of Kellon's reaction to his unauthorized contact with someone on Earth, he winced. He strictly avoided thinking about what Kellon's response was going to be when he appeared with an Earth woman and her dog. *The fat was certainly going to be in the old campfire yet again.*

"On both your expressed conditions, yes."

Turning, Susie hurried from the study, and returned a few minutes later. She was wearing a long-sleeved white shirt, with flowing lines, tucked into dark turquoise slacks secured at the waist by a soft leather belt. In turn, the slacks were tucked into calf-high leather boots. Her hair looked freshly combed, pulled back by a broad silver bar set with turquoise stones. She carried a small bulging leather bag by her side, its supporting strap over her right shoulder.

"William, if I am not returned safely to this site within seven days, you are to make a complete transcript of what has transpired here. Then, assure it is sent to Darrell Fann at Olympus."

"Ms. Susie, be careful."

From the speaker, Shey spoke, "William, I have been monitoring the conversation. Please be at ease. Susie is in very capable and good hands. I personally assure you she will be safe and returned home in good working order."

Roan stood listening to the exchange between the two computers. Such dialogs always amazed him.

"Susie, we must be on our way."

Together Susie, Gepeto, and Roan walked to the front door and out into the darkness. Pausing only a moment to secure the lock behind her, Susie followed Roan out toward the trees. Gepeto was running happily about. As they approached the tree line, Susie saw there was a flat circular disk lying on the ground. The disk was about six feet in diameter and six inches in thickness, black in color and essentially featureless. Roan stepped onto the disk, and reaching down, he lifted a small recessed ring. A chair assembly neatly unfolded like an origami object. He beckoned Susie to sit down. Susie hesitated, not trusting the slight assembly.

"Susie, in spite of its frail appearance, the chair is quite strong and can easily support your weight."

Assured, she sat. Roan requested her to take firm hold of Gepeto, and hold him against her knees. Roan then bent over and lifted a second ring, unfolding another chair. After sitting, he turned to check that Susie was holding securely to Gepeto.

"Are you ready?"

Nodding her head, but starting to wonder why she had ever agreed to this, Susie answered, "Yes."

"Shey, we are on the transport disk. Bring us home."

Susie felt a gentle but invisible restraint embrace her. There seemed suddenly to be a windbreak, yet she could only see a slight shimmer, but nothing solid. The disk upon which they were sitting silently lifted into the night sky. She felt Gepeto begin to tremble as he looked about at the ground lights quickly falling away below them.

There was no noise or a hint of wind as the disk rose swiftly into the darkness. It was an exhilarating and a wonderful experience. Susie began to wonder just how she might get one of these little flying gems for her very own. She almost laughed aloud, imagining Janet's face as Susie zipped up to the front of the Department of Commerce.

They had moved vertically for some distance when a soft rectangular light appeared directly before them. Susie more sensed than actually saw what must be a massive object nearby. They then moved directly into a small dimly illuminated compartment, and settled down. The hatch through which they had passed closed firmly behind them and the lights brightened.

"Shey we are safely aboard, well done. Now, please depart this station and promptly return us to Lan."

"Acknowledged."

The unseen support restraints Susie had previously noticed disappeared. As Roan stood, an adjoining hatch slid open. A second man, wearing the same type of uniform as Roan, entered and looked with interest at Gepeto. Then he turned toward Susie and broadly smiled.

"My name is Zorn. Welcome aboard the Guardian Scout ship Shey."

Chapter Fifty-Seven:
Despair

Kur tried to lift his head up. He failed, letting it fall back upon his forearms. He was in his own quarters and his body was bent forward over the worktable. Pain flooded his entire being, and he was unable to determine where the physical pain ended and the emotional pain began. He could not even remember if he had slept last night, and had forgotten what not being overly tired felt like.

Again, his mind snapped back to what had happened. First, there were the cold unblinking stars, then came the battle. It had not lasted long; of that he was certain. His memories of the pandemonium were vague, consisting mostly of the sounds of explosions and the shouting of others. There were so many explosions, a continuous and rolling thunderous roar, coming on and on without cessation. The entire Nest ship had reverberated with the detonations. Then came the silence, that terrible-terrible silence that was punctuated by an occasional shout and groans. The silence stridently proclaimed they had lost their main power, all propulsion, and the battle.

It was fear itself that was the most devastating. And, it still gnawed at him.

His communicator began to vibrate; painfully persistent, it managed to gain his attention. Slowly, he sat up and pressed the communication key.

"Proceed."

"Honored One," came the Captain's weary voice, "I am reporting as instructed. The cargo carriers and tactical support craft are now returning with the last of the recoverable fighters and their crews."

"Captain, how many were they able to recover?"

"Honored One, together we have recovered twenty-seven fighters. The remaining fighters were either damaged beyond repair, or were beyond our limited recovery range."

"How many of the crew members were saved?"

"Forty-eight, Honored One. Seventeen are in critical condition. In time they are all expected to recover."

"Good. Captain, your efforts this day are commendable and noted."

Kur closed the communicator and reconsidered the Nest ship's appalling condition. *It might be worse,* he thought. *We could all be dead.*

Out of the more than one-hundred gleaming craft that had boastfully filled the hangers upon departure from Scion, twelve remained battle ready. Those twelve fighters were fully armed and combat ready, for all the good that might do them.

Following the battle, the ship still remained adrift, if adrift properly expressed their constant high ballistic velocity. It continued to move rapidly away from the solar primary, hurrying toward nowhere in particular.

Nearly all the outer compartments of the Nest ship were ruptured and exposed to the cold and hard vacuum of space. The survivors had but begun one by one to cautiously seal and then enter each of those frozen outer compartments, recovering their dead. It would require much time before the living could enter and reclaim all of the compartments, but then the dead were patient.

It was only because of the careful design of the ship that anyone had survived. All of its most critical life support, command and control, and power generating systems were compartmentalized within the core of the vessel, not in its outer compartments.

When the battle began, Kur was in an outer compartment. He knew his being alive was not because of skill, but the consequence of pure random chance. *Yet, not quite random chance,* he thought. *I am still alive because the enemy also chose to grant a bountiful mercy before departing.* That singular complex act remained out of reach of his comprehension.

Why would an enemy do that? Victorious, they should have utterly destroyed the ship; I would have. Shaking his head in confusion, he pushed back his chair and managed to stand. He was deeply troubled, unable to grasp the concept of anyone extending mercy toward a defeated enemy.

The full extent of damage to the ship was unknown, the surviving officers and crew had yet to finalize a full damage and casualty report. The first reports indicated somewhat less than half of the Nest ship's crew had perished during the battle. Indisputably, the ship was reduced to a drifting hulk, one barely subsisting on emergency power. The acknowledged reality was none aboard was guaranteed a safe return home. Everyone knew that truth.

A deep emotional anger sparked and then swelled from within his being, *Enough of such defeatist thoughts.* He almost shouted out his defiance.

Had not the rescue and recovery effort required for the fighters seemed impossible? Now, we have found and recovered twenty-seven damaged fighters and forty-eight of their surviving crew. If we can cannibalize or build sufficient replacement parts, some of the damaged fighters might yet see future service. If we have achieved that impossible goal, then even if it takes a hundred turns, I will get this Nest ship and its remaining crew back to Scion. I will not fear.

I am Kur. I am a senior member of the Arkillian Council. It is my responsibility alone to get this Nest ship and its surviving crew to Scion, and I will do that.

Turning, he looked at the wonderful images of his Nest mates that adorned his wall. With determination he thought, *I am Kur, and I will not shame and dishonor my nest.*

Kur sat down at his work table and pressed the communicator button. A moment later, the Captain's voice responded.

"Honored One, what do you desire?"

"Captain, you and the senior navigation, engineering, communications, and tactical officers are to immediately assemble in my bridge state room. I will be there shortly. Together we are going to devise a detailed plan to restore the Nest ship to an operational status. Captain, we will be returning to Scion."

Kur switched off the communicator, stood and then moved with purpose toward the hatch and the bridge beyond. *We are going home or else perishing in the attempt.*

Chapter Fifty-Eight:
Incredulity

Susie with Gepeto followed Roan along a narrow passageway, with Zorn bringing up the rear. They soon entered into what appeared to be Shey's control room. Entering, Susie looked around at the pristine features of the compact compartment, and noticed its soft blend of earthy hues. The multiple view screens and numerous readouts immediately intrigued her.

The man called Zorn eased into a command chair, while Roan directed Susie to a seat, which he had deftly pulled origami fashion out of a slot in the starboard bulkhead. Sitting down cautiously, she found the chair firm and very comfortable. As she experimented with the ability of the chair to pivot and recline, Roan moved forward and took his own command chair next to Zorn. Gepeto, obeying Susie's hand signal, settled down on the deck next to her.

With Roan, Susie, and Gepeto safely onboard, Shey was free to take full advantage of her flight capabilities. Moving silently in a low flat trajectory, she crossed the coastline and passed over a dark ocean. Arching gracefully upward, she rose out of the Earth's atmosphere, accelerating toward Lan.

"Roan," is it possible to see the Earth from here?" Susie said.

"Yes. Shey, please isolate an external camera and adjust it for a wide-angle view of the Earth."

Shey acknowledged Roan's order with a clear tone, and suddenly the entire unadorned bulkhead on Susie' left side, which extended from the overhead to the deck, burst into brilliant and vibrant colors. The image of the majestic coupled spheres of the Earth and its moon filled the entire bulkhead with its stunning beauty. Susie gasped at the clarity of the extraordinary image, it seemed as if she could reach out and touch the clouds.

"Roan, the view is incredible."

While Susie was enjoying the image of Earth, Shey was moving ever more swiftly away from all that Susie had ever known, moving out into the vast and unfamiliar.

Overhearing Roan and Zorn's communications with another ship, Susie's attention shifted from the image of Earth to their conversation. Although not understanding the language being spoken, the tone of voice of someone on the other ship clearly revealed incredulity. Smiling, she thought, *They can't be half as incredulous as I am.*

Leaning forward, Susie asked, "Roan, am I correct to presume that your shipmates are surprised you have a passenger on board?"

"That's a perceptive observation, and yes. We had no intention of making direct contact with anyone on Earth. I've acted on my own authority, and there may well be some personal repercussions."

Zorn muffled a laugh. "Don't worry about Roan or me. After several thousand years of breaking rules, we've become somewhat accustomed to being reprimanded for our repeated brilliance."

"Zorn, did you say, after several thousand years?"

"Susie, we've traveled to your world for many good reasons. There is much that as yet you don't understand about your own planet's history. Please, be patient for a short while more, and everything will be explained. I promise that," Roan said.

Susie heard Roan's confident assurance, but she felt it was a very improbable commitment. As she sat pondering, she wondered, *Since they didn't come to Earth to make direct contact with anyone, then what was their mission? And, what did Zorn mean, 'Several thousand years?'*

After a momentary pause, Roan continued, "Your deduction was correct. There was considerable surprise when I reported that Shey had a representative from one of Earth's governments on board. They were even more bemused after I told them you represent the very government agency that inserted the intelligence satellites into orbit before the Arkillians arrived. When they asked how this was possible, I simply told them you initiated first contact. They're all understandably mystified."

"Roan, we are cleared for hangar docking," Shey said.

"Shey, proceed with docking. "

As Susie observed, the large tactical display reset to a relative motion plot, and the associated vector diagram for the docking maneuver filled the display. Avidly interested, Susie examined the symbols displayed on the polar plot. She had knowledge of relative maneuvering diagrams and quickly understood the purpose of the display.

"Roan, can you show me a view of your larger ship?"

"Sorry, our ship is now running in a full visual stealth mode. there's nothing to show. But I can show you an image of a similar ship. Shey, please show Susie the image of Cruiser Lancer and the Blossom Nebula."

Immediately, the scene on the bulkhead showing Earth was replaced with a stunning image. It was of a glistening ship suspended in the darkness of space. Shown behind the ship was a large and incredible burst of multihued colors. The sudden impact of the beautiful image filled Susie with wonder. The long, lean lines of the beautiful vessel before her were elegantly simple and clean. The ship's colors were a brilliant white with gold trim gracefully adorning its length.

"It's beautiful. Is that what your ship really looks like?"

"It is when we want to look like that. Most of the time, however, we prefer not to be seen," Roan said.

"Does your ship have a name?"

"Indeed. It is Lan."

As Zorn and Roan were busy with the docking, Susie considered the ship's name. *Lan*, she repeated several times in her mind. "Roan, I like the names of your ships."

With complete fascination, Susie watched the changing plot and an external video feed. Shey slowly approached Lan and was then drawn gently by some unseen force into a softly illuminated volume. The outer hangar door thumped closed and Shey announced the hangar air pressure was approaching normal values.

Roan turned and looked at Susie, smiling encouragingly. All at once, Susie felt a mix of being nervous, excited, and above all, more curious than she had ever been in her life.

"Susie, on behalf of the Scout ship Shey and her crew, thank you for the trust you have afforded us," Roan said.

Then the outer hatch opened. The penetrating chill air of the hangar pushed its way into the warm cabin.

"Please, gather your things and follow me," Roan said.

Following Roan out of the main hatch and onto the short brow, Susie became uncomfortably aware of the frigid temperature and noticed the prevalent odors of lubricating oil and air conditioning. Then, she was startled; Roan abruptly stopped. Looking past Roan, she watched as a group of men with weapons hurriedly filed through a hatch into the hangar. Encountering a group of armed men was the last thing Susie anticipated, and she felt a sudden twinge of alarm.

Chapter Fifty-Nine:
Formalities

Watching the file of armed men briskly entering the small hangar, Susie hesitated, suppressing her initial alarm. When Roan looked about and flashed her a reassuring smile, it helped.

"Don't be alarmed, everything is all right." Roan said.

Moving forward along the brow, Roan motioned Susie to follow. With Gepeto close behind, she followed. As they stepped off the brow onto the deck, a man sharply commanded the group of armed men to attention. Then, they smartly presented their weapons in a brisk salute.

One man, in what must have been a dress uniform with all manner of decorations, stepped forward and extended a hand in greeting.

"Ms. Susie, I'm Captain Kellon. On behalf of Glas Dinnein and Guardian Force, I welcome you aboard Guardian Cruiser Lan as our most honored guest."

Susie noted Roan's broad smile and recognized the military gestures as being formalities similar to those of diplomats meeting one another in New Washington. What she then did not know was Captain Kellon was affording her the full military honors accorded to a visiting planetary ambassador.

Mustering up the most gracious smile she could, Susie accepted Kellon's extended hand in her own. "I thank you for the kind courtesies that you have extended toward me. On behalf of my government, I extend my warmest greetings to Lan, you, and to your brave crew."

Gepeto was looking up at the Captain, his tail wagging. His big smile revealed he was obviously enjoying himself.

"I also thank you for permitting my dog to come aboard. Gepeto is a good dog, and I assure you he will pose no problem."

Looking at Gepeto, she commanded, "Gepeto sit," and Gepeto sat. He seemed very pleased with himself. She reached down and patted him on his head.

Turning toward the assembled officers standing near, Kellon introduced Commanders Grey and Shaw. Next, he introduced

Susie to Lieutenant Cloud, then addressed her by first name, Elayne. Susie was delighted to see another woman among so many men. As their eyes made initial contact, Susie sensed an instant connection, as between old friends.

There being so much she did not understand, Susie was far from being at ease. Still, it helped that she instinctively liked and trusted Elayne and the others.

Following the brief introductions, Kellon bowed slightly and asked Susie if she would please follow him to a warmer environment. Reaching out she took Kellon's offered arm. Since she was not dressed for the arctic-like cold of the hangar, it was with genuine pleasure that Susie accepted his invitation.

Looking up, she asked, "Are all the men on your world as handsome as those I have already met?"

Captain Kellon looked down at Susie, and recognizing her playful remark for what it was, he smiled.

Exiting the hangar, Susie was escorted through a broad passageway, up several levels in an elevator, and through another broad corridor and into a spacious circular and extraordinary room. At first glance, Susie was almost fearful. Some form of transparent dome covered the entire room. The most astonishing aspect of the dome was its optical perfection; it was so transparent as to be all but invisible. She quickly relaxed, and stood awe-struck viewing Earth and its moon; they were suspended before her as if mere ornaments in the boundless void.

Although having seen hundreds of photographs of Earth taken from space, they did nothing to prepare her for actually being in space and seeing firsthand the Earth and its moon suspended before her. Both spheres were in partial shadow and in a two-thirds gibbous stage of illumination. Standing, momentarily overwhelmed by the incredible beauty, her first impression was the moon seemed larger than she had expected.

Susie became aware of Elayne standing beside her, also looking out at the spectacle. A question bubbled up in Susie's mind, and she turned toward Elayne.

"Were you in the battle that we observed in our outer system several days ago?"

Elayne hesitated, seemed to consider the question, then she turned to look toward Captain Kellon. Kellon, who was standing nearby, had overheard the question. Without hesitation, he replied.

"Yes, Ms. Susie, we participated in that conflict."

Susie thoughtfully considered the Captain's response. Then, turning, she faced him.

"Sir, it took Monstro several weeks to move from its parking orbit near the earth to where the battle occurred. Some of our engineers considered that achievement a remarkable feat. Yet now you and your ship are here within several days. It seems that Monstro did indeed have reason to be alarmed about the military capabilities of his adversaries."

"Yes, they did.

"Ms. Susie, I understand Commander Roan woke you from your night's sleep. By now you must be exhausted. If you will follow Elayne, she will escort you to your assigned quarters and provide you with an opportunity to refresh.

"Then, I would like to arrange for a small informal gathering, where you can meet more of our officers and crew; if that is agreeable with you," Kellon said.

"Sir, I appreciate your consideration, and am looking forward to meeting more of your officers and crew."

"Ms. Susie, please follow me. I will show you the way. "Elayne said.

Kellon stood thoughtfully watching as Elayne and the Earth woman with her dog departed; *She is astute and self-possessed. That is promising.*

After a short walk along corridors and a brief elevator ride, Susie found herself in a nice, but somewhat stoically appointed compartment. Elayne pointed out a communications panel and demonstrated how to use the ship's communicator to request information, food and beverages, or to contact other members of the crew, and especially how to contact her. Next, she showed Susie the adjoining bathing and personal hygiene facilities, explaining the operations of each fixture and appliance. She then asked if Susie had any questions. Susie had none. With a reassuring smile, Elayne left Susie to explore the compartment and its features.

While appearing outwardly reserved and calm, finding herself unexpectedly in space and aboard a strange starship with complete strangers had left Susie inwardly tense and tired. She promptly set about refreshing herself, and then stretched out on the comfortable bunk, striving to calm her breathing and active mind.

After a few minutes, Gepeto came over and placed his chin on her arm. Looking down at him, Susie smiled.

"I know buddy, It's all strange. But it's going to be alright."

Yawning, Susie just closed her eyes for a moment, and calmed by the soft background operational sounds of Lan, immediately fell into a light and much needed sleep. Gepeto watched her for several minutes, then he settled down on the deck next to Susie and also slept.

Chapter Sixty:
Of Flying Chairs

The Olympus Internal Security inter-office alert had reached Darrell's desk only two hours earlier, and at best it was problematic. Fretting, Darrell thought, *If I know only two things about Susie, they are she is intelligent and impulsive. Now blast it all, she is also missing.*

From its beginning Olympus had automatically scanned police, government communications, and intelligence sources for any mention of their personnel. It was security with a double-edge. If an employee became embroiled in a problem, it was in Olympus's own self-interest to immediately know about it.

During the night, Susie's name had appeared in one of the routine internal security scans. According to a police report, she was presumed missing, and under very strange circumstances. Olympus Security had immediately notified Darrell.

The pressure on Darrell from Charles and the Administration had not lessened since Monstro's space battle several days earlier. Consequently, with little time off, Darrell was barely able to go home and get meaningful sleep. And now, the sun barely up, here he was at his desk, troubled and worrying.

Given all his other problems, the one concerning his newest employee was the most upsetting.

Even before Security had dropped the matter of Susie on his desk, Charlie had notified him that something new and odd was happening. Several hours earlier, a laser had begun intermittently blinding their most recently launched satellite. Since Monstro had departed its orbit, interest in that satellite had waned. Now, a mysterious interference had begun, and its source was undetermined. For certain, whoever was aiming that laser had the precise coordinates of the satellite. To their knowledge, Monstro had never discovered it, so, who and why was someone interfering with the satellite now?

The interference was coming at even intervals, with a span of silence in between. The entire interference pattern was just that, a pattern, and that implied purpose.

Darrell's mind was tugged away from the satellite problem back to Susie, *Where could she be?* With misgivings, he had given her permission for a short leave to return to California. In return, she had promised to stay in touch. The plain and admitted truth was he had come to care for her, and not only as an employee. He felt for her, she was missing, and that made the matter personal.

The internal security memo had flagged a routine police report. Routine? Sure, he thought, but bordering on the impossible. Coming home around midnight from a date, a neighbor saw Susie come out of her house with her dog and a strange man. The neighbor swore that the man, Susie, and her dog all walked out onto the lawn. There they appeared to unfold and sit down on what looked like a pair of flimsy folding chairs. Next, the neighbor claimed the ground and the chairs and people and dog had lifted straight up into the night sky, without so much as a sound. The neighbor had immediately called the police and reported the matter.

When the police arrived, they had found Susie's house secured, with all the doors and windows locked. Susie's car was in the garage. The police had no indication of foul play, only a strange story of flying folding chairs and dogs. They were keeping the incident open, and they were not further investigating the matter. But Olympus was.

At Darrell's instruction, Olympus Security jumped into a full investigation mode. A quick check of her known friends found no trace of her, but an examination of her electronic communication record revealed a clue. Some of Susie's recent calls were placed to a world-class physicist, Dr. Jerry Bernard at the University of Washington. Susie had recently called him four times.

Darrell had never met Dr. Bernard, but knew him by reputation. Looking at the clock, and adjusting for West Coast time, he winced, muttered "sorry," and placed the call. On the fifth ring a tired sounding man answered.

"Good morning."

"Good morning, Sir. My name is Darrell Fann, and I am an employee of the US Department of Commerce. I apologize for the hour, but my call regards a mutual friend, Susie Wells. Sir, she has gone missing."

"Missing?"

"Yes, Sir. I'm aware she recently talked with you several times. I hope you might be able to tell us something that could help us locate her."

"Mr. Fann, I've recently been concerned for Susie's welfare. Missing, just terrible."

"Sir, are you familiar with what Susie was working on?"

"Well, she and I have been collaborating on a rather complex communications problem. Because of our findings, I found the work disturbing."

"Disturbing? How so?"

"Mr. Fann, I'm not now prepared to discuss the matter further, but I do know Susie was interested in obtaining a transceiver. I don't want to seem rude, but it's very early. And, I've told you all I really know. I hope I have been of some help."

Dr. Bernard terminated the call. Despite his frustration, Darrell was impressed. A physicist of Dr. Bernard's caliber could prove an invaluable resource. And, Darrell doubted Olympus could have recruited him. That Susie had done so might yet become beneficial. Just perhaps they had found something in that communication loop that Olympus had yet to discover. For certain, Susie had some interesting friends.

Flying lawn chairs and flying dogs seemed improbable, yet that very improbability tended to support its veracity. Increasing worry was steadily replacing his initial anger.

Then, inspiration came to his aid. William, Susie's AI research computer, might have information. Looking up William's contact number, he thought, *It's worth a try.*

William responded immediately. "Good morning, May I be of some assistance?"

Darrell smiled at Susie's choice of accent for her computer, a proper British Butler. "Good morning William, my name is Darrell Fann. Do you know who I am?"

"Sir, you are Susie's new supervisor at the Department of Commerce. How may I help you today?"

William's responses seemed beyond those of a typical home AI, and he began to suspect Dr. Bernard and Susie had been working together on more than the communications loop.

"William, Susie seems to be away. Can you tell me where she might have gone?"

"No, Sir."

The abrupt response surprised him, then Darrell remembered when talking with an AI, it was important to be precise. "William, do you mean that you do not know or else that you cannot tell me?"

Darrell would have sworn he heard a deep sigh, but discounted the implausible idea. *Computers can't be frustrated,* he thought. *Or can they?*

"Mr. Fann, I do not know where Miss Susie has gone. If, however, she has not returned home safe in six days, I have specific instructions to provide you with information."

"William, information? Six days? Are you serious? Is she safe?"

"Mr. Fann, Ms. Susie is in good hands and quite safe, as is Gepeto."

Flying chairs and flying dogs were starting to sound more plausible by the minute. "William, you say you don't know where Miss Susie has gone. Can you at least tell me who she is with?"

"Yes, Sir. Miss Susie is with Shey."

"William, who is Shey?"

Before William answered, Darrell noticed there was a distinct hesitation. "Sir, Shey is a Guardian ship, and she assured me Susie will be returned home safely within seven days, and in good working order. Gepeto, too. More than that, I am not at liberty to discuss."

In spite of Darrell's efforts, William refused to expand on his answers. In utter frustration, Darrell ended the call, muttering, "The definition of stupidity is arguing with an AI."

Pondering, he reconsidered what William had said, *Shey is a Guardian ship who has assured William that Susie will be returned home safe within seven days and in good working order. But what is a Guardian ship? Apparently, Shey is a talking ship who made a promise to another AI computer.* Somehow, Susie had established contact with someone having advanced technology, which might explain talking ships, flying chairs, flying people and dogs. Yet, none of the information helped Darrell stop worrying.

Picking up his communicator, he keyed Janet's number. The phone rang twice, then Janet answered. Outlining what he had just learned, he requested, "Janet, please put out a global alert for her. If she's moving anywhere on Earth with her personal communicator, I want to know where she is."

Closing the call with Janet, Darrell worried, *Susie, where are you?*

He had exhausted all the options regarding Susie's disappearance, and standing, Darrell departed his office. Stopping at the coffee-mess for a fresh cup of coffee, he then walked to the main analysis center. Looking about the large area, he spotted Charlie standing with three others. They were apparently involved in an animated conversation. Approaching, he overheard part of what Charlie was saying.

"Those laser patterns are beautiful. They're simply a progression of prime numbers from one to twenty-three. After a pause, they repeat over and over again, but they're the same sequence of numbers each time. My guess is that someone is trying to establish communications with us. Now we just need to figure out how we reply."

When Darrell approached, Charlie turned and apparently noticed the worried expression on Darrell's face. "Hey boss, is there anything new about Susie?"

"Perhaps, but it's still a bit vague. It's possible Susie may have figured out how to make contact with whoever it's trying to communicate with us. I wouldn't be surprised if she's already out in space somewhere and hard at work."

Puzzled, Charlie stared blankly at Darrell for a baffled moment, then his countenance flashed a huge grin. "Go girl, go. Boss, do you think she may have contacted the folks in the little green and scarlet ship? Do you really think she has scooped us, yet again?"

Despite his worry, Darrell was grinning. "Yep, Charlie. That's exactly what I'm beginning to think. And, it may all relate to your satellite problem. Like you said, whoever is transmitting that laser beam is hoping for a response, otherwise they wouldn't even bother. They know we can't reply with a laser, which means they're anticipating a reply by other means. Start scanning the broader electromagnetic spectrum for regular anomalies. If they're sending laser pulses, perhaps they're also sending the same pattern on a specific wavelength, one we can respond on."

"Boss, that makes sense. We'll get right on it."

"Charlie, Sullivan and the White House are still all over my case. They're looking for anything positive. So, the instant you have any results, anything at all, you're to immediately inform me."

Returning to his office, his communicator vibrated. "Fann here."

"Darrell, just an update. The global scan did not produce a trace of Susie's personal communicator. Sorry." Janet said.

"Thank you. Please keep the scan active."

Darrell stood, frowning. Then he sighed, muttering to himself, "Dear Susie, what have you gotten yourself into this time?"

Chapter Sixty-One:
Of Cheese and Wine

The selected crew gathered to set the conference room up for the reception of their unexpected guest. The room was rearranged, the tables and seating being placed informally around the room, and the lighting was softened. The Officers' Mess had busied itself supplying the central table with various appetizers, wines, and an assortment of cheeses. Regrettably, given the length of the mission, such amenities were only available in limited supply.

While the reception was being quickly assembled, the intention was to create a casual and relaxed atmosphere. In that effort they were successful.

When Elayne and Susie entered the conference room with Gepeto, they were deep in conversation and laughing. To all outer appearances, although being in a very unfamiliar environment, Susie seemed to be at ease.

Kellon, observing from the outer edge of the room, watched Susie's gracious manner with a keen interest. Elayne was then skillfully working them through the gathering, introducing Susie to each of the officers and crew that they encountered. When reaching the central table, Susie with apparent interest looked at the assortment of various food and beverages set out for the reception. Gepeto, though well behaved, was obviously aware of the food, and looked hopefully up at Susie.

As Kellon watched, acting as hostess, Elayne prepared a small plate of assorted cheese and offered Susie a glass of red wine. Tentatively sampling the wine, Susie's initial cautious expression shifted to a broad smile. Carrying their glasses of wine and small plates of food, Susie and Elayne worked their way through the group to where Susie was able to acquire an unobstructed view of the Earth and its large moon.

With purpose, Kellon moved to where Susie was standing and gazing out at the Earth. "I agree, it's truly beautiful," Kellon said.

"It truly is. Sir, I believe it's the most exquisitely beautiful sight I have ever seen. And, even more astonishing than the view is that I'm standing right here onboard Lan. There're so many questions I want to ask, but don't even know where to begin."

"Ms. Susie, questions are the portals of inquiry, and the open exchange of information between our peoples is of a mutual benefit. In spite of where you choose to begin, all of your questions are deemed important."

"Sir, please do call me Susie. Ms. Susie is far too formal among friends."

"As you wish, Susie it will be. Concerning all that we do not know, admittedly we are both rich in questions. As where to begin, perhaps we can start with what you know about the ship you have called Monstro and those who crew it."

Kellon could almost see the decision process unfold within her mind -- How much do I dare share? But I also need information as well. How much can I trust this man?

Susie took a sip of wine, then placed the glass on the table beside her. As Susie turned to face him, he continued his assessment of the personal qualities of the woman standing before him, admiring her apparent emotional strength and composure.

"Sir, I work for a little-known government agency, called Olympus. It's is an agency within the Executive Branch of Government known as the Department of Commerce. I don't know all the details of the Monstro project, but there are some things that I can speak to with confidence.

"Olympus has monitored Monstro's activities for several centuries. We know that those crewing the ship have surreptitiously interacted with a small group of as yet unidentified people on Earth. Their interactions seem to involve commercial ventures, but there are also thousands of stories that suggest a much darker aspect of Monstro's visits. About those darker events, I have little information."

"You used the term 'monitored.' Would I be correct to presume there is no formal contact between Monstro and your government? "Kellon said.

"That presumption is correct. The scope and purpose for Monstro's visits remain unknown and are suspect. It's the prime purpose of Olympus to observe and study Monstro. The goal being to gain information concerning their operations, especially their technology, and do this without provoking confrontation.

"We have photographic evidence establishing the species aboard Monstro is not human. Admittedly, we know very little of their culture, but they have shown no reluctance in using deadly force. Recently, without provocation several of their smaller craft destroyed two aircraft, killing their crews."

"Susie, do you know where the home world of the Arkillians is located?" Kellon said.

"Sir, we believe they come from a nearby star system, called Tau Ceti. During the past two-hundred years we've sent three probes into that star system, they all failed upon arrival. None sent back helpful information."

Are you willing to sit down with Commanders Shaw and Grey, to compare our information, and determine if we are in agreement concerning their home system?"

"Sir, I'll do whatever I can to help. But now it's my turn to ask a question. What triggered your battle with Monstro?"

"That question is direct, but fair. Perhaps, the best way for me to answer it is by asking yet another question. How far back does human written history extend on Earth?"

"Well, our earliest written history is quite fragmentary. In terms of documentation, the earliest written document is a letter from a father to his son, written about seven-thousand years ago. Of course, there is archaeological history. That extends back to about twelve-thousand years ago. But that's often limited to a patchwork of conflicting theories, scholarly guesstimation and disputes; it all becomes fuzzy and fragmentary beyond twelve-thousand years. Somehow, we've lost 250,000 years of human history.

"By contrast, our oral traditions, legends, and myths are very rich. They span many thousands of years and tell stories about global upheaval, both natural and of a more mysterious nature. These stories include lost continents and civilizations, like Atlantis and Lemuria. Unfortunately, and in spite of enormous effort to unravel existing ambiguities, most aspects of early human history remain shrouded, conflicted, and unresolved.

"But Sir, what has Earth history to do with triggering your battle with Monstro?"

There was simply no easy way for Kellon to soften the truth. "Susie, there is a reason why human history on Earth is fragmented and sparse. We have gleaned from the Arkillians a disturbing truth. About twelve thousand years ago the Arkillians disrupted and shattered the then flourishing human cultures on Earth. Before your recorded history begins, they brutally subjected the Earth and its people to a prolonged global campaign of aggression and domination, which they militarily term, 'making primitive.'"

Susie's countenance revealed her shock. Standing, she looked at him with an expression of complete confusion.

"In answer to your question, the recent battle was triggered when we confronted the Arkillians. We informed them we had observed their aggression against your world, and informed them their criminal behavior was being terminated. We issued an ultimatum that they surrender. They were not receptive, and chose rather to fight. The following battle was short, intense, but decisive."

Looking about the beautiful room, Susie struggled to assimilate the ambiguities. All about her, Lan's crewmembers were enjoying themselves in animated conversations, drinking wine, eating cheese and other party tidbits. They did not look as if they had recently been in a fierce deadly battle or that the battle had inflicted injury to Lan or his crew.

"Captain Kellon, I'm somewhat confused. Might I ask, what is the current disposition of Monstro? Did you destroy the ship?"

"No. We chose not to destroy it. When we left Monstro, it was inert, adrift and without primary power. Unless power and its drive are restored, its ballistic trajectory will carry it beyond your system's heliopause. We know there are survivors, but as a consequence of Commander Roan's coordinated attack, Monstro was severely damaged."

Surprised, Susie turned and looked with interest toward Roan and Zorn. They were across the room, laughing and seemingly enjoying themselves.

"Captain, if I understand you correctly, for about twelve millennia the Arkillians have conducted a prolonged oppression of humanity. Sir, from what I understand, that postulate doesn't seem possible. Except for their occasional acts, such as recently destroying two aircraft, Monstro was never overtly aggressive. We have no reason to believe we been under oppression. Can you elaborate further?"

Knowing that the truth was distressing, Kellon chose his next words carefully. "Susie, what is your anticipated lifespan?"

"Sir, you're asking how long I expect to live? Well, if I eat properly and live wisely, with exercise and good genes, perhaps eighty to ninety years. But why do you ask?"

Her answer caused Kellon to inwardly wince. "Susie, it is our belief that for thousands of years the Arkillians have used psychological and genetic warfare on Earth against humanity. One principle aspect of their genetic assault is to shorten the average lifespan of human beings. On other worlds where humans live, we don't noticeably age in a thousand years. Our mortality is determined more as a consequence of accident, or a rare contracted illness, than through aging. The same should be the normal case for the people living on Earth. But it is not. That's only one example of the oppression. What is important is we have put an end to the Arkillian aggression."

Susie stood, again looking stunned. Kellon judged for the time being she was approaching her physiological limits.

"Sir, you mentioned there are other human occupied worlds. Worlds? We've been sending out deep-space probes for centuries, but concrete proof of another human worlds simply doesn't exist."

"Susie, one of your facts is flawed; concrete proof does exist. One of your early probes successfully reached Glas Dinnein. That is the prime reason we came to Earth, to determine who sent that probe. Lan and his crew are your missing concrete proof there are other human occupied worlds. At present, we're aware of eleven worlds, that is other than Earth, where humans live, work, and play."

Susie physically sagged, and for support she leaned on the table beside her. When she next spoke, her voice was little more than a whisper.

"Sir, can the effects of whatever the Arkillians did to our DNA be reversed? Can we be healed?"

"Susie, I simply don't know, at least at this time. It will require medical experts on Glas Dinnein to determine the answer to that question. If a cure is possible, I assure you we will find it."

Susie rested a hand on Gepeto's head, as if for reassurance. Gepeto in response was looking up at her. Kellon observed there was obvious concern expressed in the animal's eyes. He considered the relationship between the Earth woman and her dog unusual and interesting.

"Captain, would you please excuse me? I would like to sit down for a moment."

Becoming concerned, Kellon looked about and observed that Elayne was nearby. He motioned her to approach.

"Elayne, Susie is not feeling well. Please assist her. Perhaps another glass of wine or some neab might help."

Concerned, Kellon watched as Elayne directed Susie to a nearby comfortable chair. His simmering anger toward the Arkillians was being amply fueled by the harm they had done to the people of Earth.

Looking about, Kellon observed Roan and Zorn were still in attendance. The decorations that festooned their dress uniform jackets were among the highest military honors that Guardian Force and Glas Dinnein could bestow. Both were also acknowledged rogues. Being members of a Scout ship crew explained much. Roan had been correct; he had overlooked issuing a formal order regarding no contact with anyone on Earth. His oversight had provided Roan with the legitimate latitude, and recognizing the fleeting opportunity, Roan had promptly seized the initiative. In doing so, he had placed Shey, Zorn, and himself at elevated risk. Yet, because of Roan's quick decision and action, they now had Susie on board Lan. That was a blessing from above. Kellon mused, *It might be appropriate to award those two rogues yet another meritorious decoration.*

Apparently, Roan had observed Kellon looking at him. In response, Roan walked over to where Kellon was standing.

"Captain, Zorn and I are enjoying the reception for our new found friend. From all indications, Susie is a remarkable woman."

"I wholeheartedly agree."

"Sir, I asked our electronics shop to examine her personal communicator. The people on Earth have evolved a complex and sophisticated personal communications network. I was told it will take some time to fully explore all the nuances of their system, but our communications group has already altered Lan's own communications protocols and network to interface with her communicator. Whenever she desires to speak with anyone on the Earth, she is now able to do so at leisure, and without revealing Lan's position."

Kellon welcomed Roan's initiative and his solution to a pressing problem. "Well done Commander, well done indeed."

Turning, Kellon looked toward Susie. Seemingly, she had regained her composure and was involved in a discussion with Elayne and Zorn. *Perhaps,* he thought, *this would be a good time for her to make that first call home.*

Chapter Sixty-Two:
Thunder and Lightning

The day had been one of those twenty-hour marathons, and Darrell was beyond weary. Just prior to his heading home, Charles had called. He wanted a face-to-face meeting, ASAP.

Dutifully, but irritated, Darrell used the underground transfer system to reach the main Department of Commerce building and took the elevator to the top floor. Upon entering the outer office, Lois told him to go right in, Charles was waiting.

Opening the door, Darrell was surprised and pleased, Janet and Carl were sitting around the table with Charles. They all looked up and smiled. Taking his chair, he turned toward Charles.

"I seem to be the last one here. Sorry to keep you waiting."

"When, did you last get eight hours of sleep?" Charles said.

Suppressing a flash of anger, Darrell resisted the urge to ask, how long has it been since I have had eight hours off? He recognized his irritation was the product of fatigue, and pushed the irritating thought aside.

"Sir, it's been several days."

Looking at the others around the table, Darrell saw they were all showing serious signs of a lack of sleep. Janet seemed more tired than he had ever seen her. However, it was Carl's appearance that was most shocking. He looked in need of medical help.

"Carl, what happened to you? You look like you were pulled sideways through a knothole."

"No knotholes, but something could have been in the Mongolian water."

"Enough banter," Charles said.

"I have an appointment with the President in the morning. We've work to do, and little time to do it. I require a complete update on where we stand.

"Carl, what is the status of your search effort in Mongolia?"

"Sir, we ran into a stone wall. The locals have hundreds of stories of ghosts and monsters that they believe live in those mountains. They are scared to death of the place. Most of the natives won't venture near the deep valleys, not even for sizable payments.

"While working in that region, it took an effort to even physically move about. I've never felt that miserable before. "

"Can you be more specific?" Charles said.

"Regarding the cause of the problem, no. However, as to the symptoms of the problem, that I can elucidate.

"We all had nightmares, and some of our men were afflicted with piercing headaches. None of us could get any real sleep. The immediate consequence was a bad case of the jitters and deepening fatigue. We've had to rotate our personnel into and out of the region more frequently than we anticipated. This added to the stress, since we are operating covertly in that area."

"Then, there's no clue as to what is causing the fatigue?" Darrell said.

"Nothing firm. At first, I thought it might be some type of radiation, but our detectors couldn't identify anything. Equipment readouts or otherwise, I believe something is generating some type of a mental field. I've asked our engineers to find new monitors, something that looks deeper and broader into the energy spectrum. But this will take time."

"Then, there's no evidence of where Monstro's group went to ground?" Charles said.

"Sir, sorry. We have nothing. But it's probable they went to where the locals are leaving, which only makes sense. Our problem is the search has become more dangerous, both politically and physically. We are extracting our last team tonight. After the area cools off, we'll return to the search. For now, my only plan is to go home, pull a pillow over my head, and sleep for a week," Carl said.

Charles turned toward Janet. "Your turn up to bat. Where does your investigation into Monstro's commercial network stand?"

"Sir, my group is progressing in identifying and monitoring Monstro's entire network. So far, we have tentatively identified around twenty. Most of the companies are relatively small and long-established firms. They operate using family ownership and close management. All the companies appear quite prosperous, and they maintain low commercial profiles.

"There is one common aspect. The families involved are very prominent, with well-established political influence in their own countries. As for distribution, the identified companies are operating in over thirty countries. Undoubtedly, more companies will be identified. Slowly, we are learning what was being done and by whom."

"Thank you, Janet. Well done.

"Darrell, it's your turn. And, first up is there any new information about Susie?"

"Sir, unfortunately not. It's as if she walked out her door and stepped off the face of the Earth. Janet put in effect a global watch-alert for her communicator, that search is ongoing, but it's negative."

"What came of our counter-Intelligence search of her home?" Charles said.

"Sir, we gained entry into her home. A complete forensic search was not made, but rather a quick walk-through inspection. There was no indication of foul play."

"Did Susie's AI have any information?" Janet said.

"Frustratingly little. At a pre-determined time, it is instructed to tell us what it knows. It did tell me Susie is with a Guardian ship, and it promised Susie will returned safe."

"It's obvious Susie made contact with someone, but who? The term Guardian doesn't ring any bells. Have you cracked the transmission Susie was working on?" Charles said.

"Yes, in part. Susie worked with Dr. Bernard of the University of Washington on the problem, and I have been talking with him."

"Dr. Bernard? The world-renowned physicist, Dr. Jerry Bernard?" Carl said.

"Yep, that Dr. Bernard. Susie and the good Doctor are old friends from her post-graduate days at the University. I finally convinced him of the importance of his and Susie's work. He decoded video images in the transmission, but the audible portion are not understandable. The decoded video segment is short."

Charles looked exasperated. "Darrell, if you have video images transmitted from the area of Monstro's battle, why haven't I already seen it?"

"Sir, I don't know. But, be ye advised, it was attached to my last report. If you'll activate your office monitor, I'll pipe it in now," Darrell said.

Charles turned on his office monitor and the image of a distinguished looking man appeared on the display. He was a human male, whose age appeared to be approximately fifty years. The man's countenance and bearing were those of confident authority, and his expression was firm. What was definitely not ordinary was the utterances he was making. They began with a series of growls and grunts, then shifted to odd clicks, whistles, and warbling hisses. It seemed incredible to Darrell that any man could mouth such a cacophony of sounds. After a few moments, the monitor went dark.

"Darrell, what is your assessment?" Charles said.

"Sir, the signal is validated as being transmitted from beyond the orbit of Jupiter. The image appears to be a Caucasian male. I ordered a high-level biometric search of our global facial image archives; no match was found. At this time, we have no other information."

"Lacking additional facts, give me your best speculations," Charles said.

"Sir, all we have is speculation. The image is of an individual human, and it was transmitted immediately prior to the battle. Our only conclusion is humans must have participated in the battle with Monstro. Also, the witness to Susie's departure firmly insists she was willingly departing with a man and along with her dog. There is no suggestion Susie departed with an alien. Yet, we have no technology that can explain what the witness observed, Susie on a folding chair and silently flying up vertically into the night sky."

"What has become of Monstro?" Carl said.

"All the channels tracking Monstro are flat-lined, not a trace of Monstro."

"That's at least something. We can deduce there was a battle and that Monstro is offline. It has had its butt kicked, but kicked by who? "Carl said.

"Who indeed. Susie made contact with humans having advanced space technology and apparently with a capability to engage in battle with Monstro. The prime question is who are they?" Janet said.

"How could any group or nation on Earth build a ship capable of taking on Monstro without our being aware of it?" Charles said.

"Sir, no one on Earth could have. The inescapable conclusion is the humans fighting Monstro aren't from Earth," Darrell said.

"That's ridiculous, Darrell. There can't be humans from some mythical planet here and fighting Monstro. The very idea is blatantly impossible," Janet said.

"Damn it, we had better figure it out; who are they, friend or foe? We have to go over our data again," Charles said.

Darrell's personal communicator interrupted, emitting a distinctive melodious tone. He promptly removed it from his pocket and keyed the receive button. As Charles and the others watched, his countenance altered from a tired frown to a broad smile.

"Are you safe? And, where are you?"

Darrell looked toward Charles, "It's Susie. She says she's fine and in good company."

Darrell keyed his communicator again, "Go ahead Susie, I'm piping you directly into Charles' office com."

"Hello everybody. I hope I haven't caused you too much concern. I'm calling to tell you that I'm safe and among friends. In fact, I want to show you precisely where I am and introduce you to someone special.

"Darrell, before I do, it would be best if you first set the transmission mode to video and the encryption code we previously discussed. When you're ready, I'll continue."

Darrell keyed his communicator and spoke a phrase into its microphone. The communicator burped twice, signaling the setting was complete.

"Susie, we're ready for video," Darrell said.

"Confirming, the encryption is in effect. I suggest you record this transmission. It will contain information that is troubling and very unsettling. You'll want to go over it several times."

Charles stood up and activated the recording sequence in his office system, then returned to his seat. "Susie, we're ready, please continue with your video," Charles said.

The office's large screen monitor burst into a full screen image. It was of the Earth and Moon as seen from space.

"It's really a beautiful sight from here. I hope you're getting a clear picture," Susie said.

"Wow, with a terrific view like that, I presume you're somewhere in space. The key question here is who are you with?" Carl said.

"Hello, Carl. I'm glad you made it back safely from Mongolia. As to your question, I'm now onboard the Star Cruiser Lan, with some very remarkable and wonderful people. I'm about to pan the room that I'm standing in. Then, I'll introduce you to my host."

As Charles, Janet, Carl, and Darrell with intense interest watched the screen, Susie began slowly to pan the domed conference room on Lan. Those watching from Earth observed a group of uniformed men and women standing in casual groups, having by all indications, a party.

"Susie, leave it to you to find a party filled with handsome men. All of us here are wishing we were there. Is the wine good?" Janet said.

Susie laughed. "Yes Janet, very good, but not as good as our California Zinfandel."

As they watched, Susie placed her communicator on a firm support. Shown in the center of the display was a man wearing what appeared to be a military uniform.

Charles let out a deep sigh. "Wheels within wheels, within wheels. Damn, that's the same man Darrell just showed us on his video, the man supposedly out beyond Jupiter just a few days ago. This is rapidly becoming confounded beyond any possibility of unraveling."

"Everyone, it is my personal pleasure to introduce you to Captain Kellon of Guardian Force, currently in command of the Star Cruiser Lan. Captain Kellon wants to provide you with some very important information."

Thunder and lightning, Darrell thought, *Star Cruiser? What comes next?*

334

Chapter Sixty-Three:
Your Priority is AA

Kellon had directed Lan to prepare a display for an incoming com-signal. The images received on board Lan were being shown on a large screen in the domed conference room. The image revealed four people, three men and a woman sitting about a small round table.

Studying the image, Kellon observed the strained and haggard appearance of the four individuals. Acting as the primary connector, and having introduced Captain Kellon, Susie continued her introductions by presenting each of the four people to Captain Kellon. He listened, appreciating her careful pronunciation of each of the four people's names and titles.

"Captain Kellon, my name is Charles Sullivan, and I'm an Under-Secretary of Commerce of the United States Government. While I'm pleased to meet you, this meeting is somewhat of a surprise. Getting to the pivotal issue, Captain, where have you come from and by what authority are you here?"

"Secretary Sullivan, before answering your questions, I must commend your Ms. Susie. She's an intelligent and gracious woman, who has made this meeting possible."

"Captain Kellon, Susie's whereabouts have been of great concern to all of us. That she is safe is what is important," Charles said.

"Secretary Sullivan, regarding your questions, where we are from is not nearly as important as why we are here. We were sent by our Government on a long-range peaceful reconnaissance mission. The information we then had was solid proof of humans living in this star system. I am confident you understand precisely why that singular fact was sufficient reason for us to cross interstellar space."

"Captain Kellon, what precisely are your operating orders?" Charles said.

"Our mission orders were to remain covert and to observe this solar system in detail."

"Covert? Observe? Captain, then you are breaching your orders by making this contact, as well as irresponsibly starting an interstellar war."

Secretary Sullivan, you are lacking in vital information. Although your statement is understandable, it is incorrect. Be advised, in all cases, our standing orders supersede mission orders."

"Captain, your standing orders be damned. Your reckless military actions taken here are far above any legitimate prerogatives of a ship's Captain, and they have placed this entire planet in jeopardy."

Sullivan's sharp words were grating, but more than a thousand years of working with bureaucrats had honed Kellon's defenses. Before responding, he had patiently listened to what the man needed to say.

"Secretary Sullivan, I repeat, you lack vital information. We are here in good will. Accordingly, this ship and its entire crew recently placed its very existence in jeopardy defending Earth.

"I am striving to avoid any misunderstanding between us. Accordingly, before we continue this conversation, there is a political fact you need to understand. Whatsoever the various governments on Earth choose to do is their own business; but their authority does not extend to Guardian Force, Cruiser Lan, or involve my prerogatives."

Kellon observed his words take their intended effect. It was clear Sullivan was not accustomed to someone frankly confronting him or challenging his authority. Kellon calmly waited, letting the man and his attitude simmer a moment before continuing.

"Secretary Sullivan, shortly after we arrived in this system, we observed an alien Capital ship enter. Adhering to my mission orders, we initiated a covert data gathering and analysis effort. We began observing the alien ship, your planet, and its population. Our analysis quickly yielded strong evidence your planet is being subjected to a long-term state of siege. That established fact immediately evoked our standing orders--"

Charles interrupted, "Siege? Captain Kellon, be more specific. What kind of data indicated we were under a state of siege?"

Standing next to Kellon, Susie interceded. "Charles, based upon what I have learned since coming aboard, Captain Kellon is absolutely correct. It is vital you obtain all the information Captain Kellon is prepared to share. And, you need to do this as quickly as possible. Knowing what I now know, the information is best transmitted in person, not over some communications link, encrypted or otherwise."

Charles sat back. His anger was still simmering, but was being kept under disciplined control.

"Captain Kellon, Sir may I ask, what is the present disposition of Monstro?" Carl said.

Kellon noted the appropriate nature of the question and approved. "Mr. Suthaford, our sensors show Monstro is without primary power and adrift. If Monstro is unable to restore its primary power, its inertia will soon carry it beyond your solar system's heliosheath.

"While a few fighters are still active near the ship, at this time the ship and its fighters do not pose a threat to Earth. Does that answer your question?"

"Yes, Captain Kellon, thank you. If permitted, there's another question I would like to ask. Were you personally involved in the combat action with Monstro?"

"Mr. Suthaford, the Cruiser Lan is here on a peaceful reconnaissance, not a combat mission. We came alone and without other ships. We intercepted the Arkillian ship and demanded they break off their aggressive action. In response, they chose to fight. The battle was brief. After the battle, we moved to our current location near Earth."

"Captain, you called those on Monstro 'Arkillians.' You also implied they fired the first shot. Regardless of who fired first, aren't the Arkillians going to consider your military action an act of war? And, when they do, Earth is going to be right in the middle of that war. What is your assessment of our present threat, and is that threat immediate?" Charles said.

"You are correct when calling the alien crew Arkillians. That is what they call themselves. As for the potential threat, yes there is a threat. It, however, is not immediate. There exists a significant window of time allowing for minimizing future threats.

"As for our action constituting an act of war, be advised, you were already in a state of war, and utterly defeated. That intolerable condition is now altered."

Charles frowned. "Captain, there is considerably more to this matter than we are aware of. My earlier words now seem hasty and misspoken. I apologize. Still, we have never considered ourselves to be at war with the Arkillians. In fact, we have acted to avoid any possibility of provoking warfare.

"Obviously, your statements require additional explanation and clarification. I agree, we do need a direct meeting to better understand each other. How soon can this be arranged?"

"Secretary Sullivan, the knowledge of our presence must be tightly restricted. Does that represent a problem?" Kellon said.

"I assure you, everything dealing with our project is highly classified. A tight lid will be laced on all information exchanged. Is my assurance adequate?"

"Yes, and that is based upon Ms. Susie's earned creditability. I have come to appreciate her insights and integrity.

"As for our meeting, I will arrange for two of my officers to be at mid-darkness where we contacted Susie. Can you have your people meet my officers that soon?"

"Captain Kellon, my people will be at that location at the agreed time."

Kellon considered his next words carefully. "Secretary Sullivan, the information I am able to provide is regretfully limited in scope. To fully explain some of what has happened on your world will require a level of expertise that I do not immediately have access to."

"Captain Kellon, when might we anticipate obtaining access to such additional information?" Janet said.

"Ms. Rodgers, as we speak, I am confident the entire situation in this solar system is being discussed back on my own world. If I may be blunt, your world is in a very deplorable state of affairs.

"Saying that, I assure you that Earth's safety is our uppermost concern. I earnestly counsel that you have patience. Even with the assistance of Guardian Force, it will take decades or even generations of work on Earth to move your world toward a restored balance. Whatever I can do now is only a most cursory prelude to what must follow.

"Mr. Sullivan, I am requesting the further services of your Susie for a while longer. Unless, you prefer her to return at this time."

"Captain Kellon your suggestion appears to provide the best return in the shortest time. As for Susie, I'll let her decide what she thinks is best," Charles said.

"Sir, there's a great deal I can learn being here. Gepeto and I will be delighted to remain for a while," Susie said.

"Then, it seems we are in agreement. I will send two officers this evening. They will return to the same location where Susie was located, and be on station at mean nighttime. Can your people be ready and afford the appropriate security for my personnel?"

"Absolutely. We will have a strong security team on the ground and provide appropriate air cover. Your officers will be received with the same courtesy and security we would provide to the representatives of a friendly and allied Nation," Charles said.

"Captain Kellon, can you pinpoint the location of the Arkillian detachment still here on Earth?" Carl asked.

"Given time, we could locate their base. Yet, at the present moment, we are fully engaged with other more pressing matters."

"Captain, there's one more item. We were receiving a series of laser pulses on a satellite. Do you have any knowledge of that?" Darrell said.

"Yes. Those signals were a preliminary effort to contact you. That communications effort was suspended."

"Captain Kellon, is there a way we may contact you, if the necessity arises?" Charles said.

"You can call me," Susie said.

"Good. Then, we've established important two-way communications. Captain Kellon, if there's nothing else, I recommend we close out this communication."

"Secretary Sullivan, we are in agreement. "

In Charles' office, the display went dark. Charles sat back for a moment, looking out of his broad windows. Evening was descending upon New Washington, and the shimmering lights of the Government Park monuments were just appearing. Heaving a deep sigh, Charles turned back toward his associates.

"Our world will never be the same as it was just an hour ago. Nothing has changed, and yet everything has changed. Carl, give us your best assessment of what has just happened."

"Sir, my first observation is the concept of human beings coming from some other star system requires getting accustomed to. Frankly, I don't have a hope of understanding how that can possibly be true.

"Also, according to Kellon, they are still engaged in some high priority activity. We haven't a clue as to what, except it doesn't relate to the Arkillians hiding in Mongolia.

"Sir, we are strictly playing catch up. I recommend we send our representatives to meet Kellon's officers and gain as much data as possible."

"Darrell, give us your best thoughts," Charles said.

"Sir, Kellon's ship arrived from some other star system. That star system must be at least eight or more light years from here. He arrived at about the same time Monstro arrives, a few weeks ago. Next, Kellon tells us his Government back on wherever he comes from is considering how best to handle the current mess on earth. That implies communication across light years distance in weeks. That translates into faster than light communications, something we consider impossible. Add to that, Kellon says he came on a peaceful mission, is alone and far from home, yet he proceeded to decisively kick Monstro and its fighters' butts. Then, he transits the AUs between Uranus and here in several days. You may have noticed, as I did, no one drinking wine at Susie's party was wearing big bandages. Conclusion: Kellon's military and propulsion technology are vastly superior to anything Monstro has, and that includes impossible faster-than-light travel. Finally, Monstro couldn't find our stealthy satellite, but Kellon knows precisely where it is located.

"Sir, when comparing our level of technology with the technology where Kellon is, we are but primitives working with stone axes and bear skins."

"Damn it, I hadn't considered that. Ouch, regardless of the hour, it looks like I'm about to spoil the President's day.

"Carl, my apologies, but you need to go home and pick up your pillow. I want you on the plane Janet is about to set up to get you and your team to Susie's home in California, and before 23:00 local," Charles said.

Carl groaned, and Charles looked toward Darrell. "And, as for you, heads-up. You will be traveling with Carl.

"Janet, get your staff busy. Set up the fastest military ride and get Carl and Darrell on site on time. Immediately, dispatch a west coast security team. I want the area around Susie's home locked down tight before 23:00. Get the Space Force to provide air cover over the area, and provide local helicopter transportation for Carl and Darrell's team.

"Your priority is AA. So, don't take any flak from anyone. If someone gives you back-talk, call me. I will personally oversee their early retirement.

"You all have your marching orders. So, get out of here and go to work. I need to call the President."

Chapter Sixty-Four:
Military Conundrum

The intervening weeks since Olympus's first contact with Guardian Force had passed quickly. Everyone was busy. Kellon found himself balancing his duties between interacting with Olympus and the increasing communications traffic from Glas Dinnein.

"Sir, I have established contact with Cruisers Lancer, Langley, and Lowe. They report they have entered the heliosphere. Commodore Byrn on Lowe is requesting a tactical update," Lan said.

"Lan, connect me with Commodore Byrn."

"Acknowledged."

Kellon's main communications monitor brightened, and the image of Commodore Byrn appeared. "Welcome to Earth, Commodore. It's good to see you again," Kellon said.

"Kellon, it's likewise good to reach the trek end," Byrn said.

"How was your crossing?"

"It was smooth. We merely followed your deployed navigation beacons, which seemed positioned every light year. Well done, Kellon. Well done indeed. Your diligent trail blazing was appreciated. But what is the current tactical situation? Are there any immediate threats?" Byrn said.

"None. The enemy, the Arkillians, are still without primary power. They are maintaining their ballistic trajectory and are strictly passive. We haven't detected any communications traffic since the battle. We stationed a full spectrum Sentinel to shadow them, so our data is current and tight."

"That means the big question is how are the interactions with the people on Earth developing?"

"Our contact is limited to one government, and that contact is intentionally sparse. We're maintaining a two-way channel of communications. The good news is they want to keep our presence quiet, even as we do. They have been cooperative. But understandably, they want as much information as they can garner, especially anything concerning our technology. "

"What about the Arkillians remaining on Earth? Have you taken any direct action against them?"

"No. And, at this time I don't recommend we do so."

"What is the basis for that assessment?" Byrn said.

"Most significantly, they pose no current threat. Shortly after arrival, we pinpointed their location. They have hunkered down in a hardened site and in very difficult terrain. Clearly they are not going anywhere soon."

Looking puzzled, Byrn asked, "Have you informed those on Earth that you know where the Arkillians are holed up?"

"No Commodore. The Arkillians have weapon grade technology that I don't think belongs on Earth. It's not beneficial to help Earth governments begin a race for what they would undoubtedly consider a technology windfall."

"Hmmm ..., I had not considered that aspect of the problem. What are the Arkillians doing? Do you have any idea?"

"Yes, we are closely monitoring them. Their orders are to hide, observe, and report when possible. They're waiting for their relief to arrive."

"Relief? Kellon if I have the tactical data correct, their culture is strictly limited to linear propulsion. Relief may be a long time in coming. Is my data correct?"

"You are correct. At least, correct according to what we now know. The overriding problem is they are in contact with the Kreel and trade with them. Most of the military technology we encountered is vintage Kreel, if you roll back the clock a few thousand years.

"They, however, demonstrated one technology that is of grave concern. And, not being aware of that weapon can get you killed."

"Being decidedly in favor of not being killed, what is it?" Byrn said.

"The Arkillians have an energy beam, one capable of piercing our shields and killing most of our crew. The good news is they fired on a Zed decoy, not on Lan. I've sent the specifications of the beam under Black Hole classification to Guardian Headquarters. Lan's engineers are still working to strengthen our own shields. I'll get the latest engineering data over to you."

"By all the muses, a death beam. That's not good news. How about the Kreel? Is there any indication they may show up?"

344

"Concerning the short term, my first approximation guess is no. The long term is problematic. From what we gleaned from Arkillian communications, the Kreel don't know the location of Earth, and the Arkillians are not telling them where to look. If the Kreel do determine Earth's location, then we will have a problem on our hands."

Byrn grimaced. "Kellon, that assessment is optimistic. If the Kreel learn of a primitive planet with ten-billion defenseless humans on it, they will see that as a big invitation to come to dinner. It would get nasty very quick, and we are still eighty light-years distance from reinforcements and resupply. That is a very long supply line to maintain."

"Commodore, what are your orders?"

"Orders? Well they are straightforward. First, I am to provide you immediate relief, so you may return to Glas Dinnein.

"Admiral Mer Shawn wants a better definition of the Arkillian local-space, military traffic, and first approximation of just how frequently the Kreel visit. Frankly, he is seriously worried about the Kreel being within ten light years of Earth.

"I'm ordered to take Lancer and jump over to Scion and make the first covert reconnaissance. Langley will remain here on guard."

"Commodore, Mer Shawn has good reason to worry. We both know three cruisers can't stop the Kreel, not if they come in force."

"Kellon, Admiral Mer Shawn and I are in agreement with your assessment. Earth represents a real military conundrum. In fact, it's a nightmare both militarily and politically. Making matters worse, how Earth will play out politically in the Assembly isn't yet clear."

"Commodore, politics aside, I would like to request a favor. We've been out for more than a year. If you have provisions to spare, Lan would be grateful for a limited replenishment of a few critical food items."

"Like perhaps cheese and wine? Your request does not pose a problem. Mer Shawn required that I bring out a full resupply pod, and it's loaded with goodies. If Lan will rendezvous with us on your way out, I will see that the pod is presented with proper flourishes."

"Commodore, thank you. But before I can depart, there remains one more unfulfilled duty.

"Meanwhile, I will have Commander Grey contact your Executive Officer and confirm you have the latest contact information for the involved Earth side Government. Since they are a bit skittish regarding precisely who we really are and why we are here, I suggest you keep them in the loop. Trust is not yet flourishing."

"They don't trust us? Is there a reason?"

"Some. I've not provided them detailed insights when answering their questions, other than saying we came looking for human beings. They don't know anything about the Kreel."

"Understood. I will follow your lead, and play it close."

"Kellon, I'm rather intrigued. If I had just been relieved after being nearly two years from home, I would be blazing a trail out of here. What is the one remaining duty you have referred to?"

"Commodore, there is currently an Earth woman on board. She was instrumental in our establishing first contact with the Earth side government. I have obtained clearance from Admiral Mer Shawn to return with her, if both her Government and she are willing."

"Shades of Tartarus, given the political situation on Glas Dinnein, I can see the potential advantage of having an Earth representative return with you, sorta an ambassador. Mer Shawn certainly knows how to play the Assembly. Her presence on Glas Dinnein might help. How long will it take to settle the matter before you hoist anchor?"

"My guess is not long. Nevertheless, now that you're here, I need to speed up the process. Is there anything else I can do to assist you?" Kellon said.

"No, not at the moment. I believe Lan is currently providing Lowe with a complete tactical update. I will alert my Executive Officer to expect Commander Grey's call. Good luck and good hunting, Kellon. Safe journey and fair winds on the way home. Byrn out."

"Lan," did you monitor the call with Commodore Byrn?"

"Yes, sir. Would you like me to ask Susie to come to your conference room?"

"Lan, advise her I would appreciate the opportunity to speak to her as soon as she is available."

"Sir, Susie has been notified and she reports she is on her way."

"Lan, ask the Officer's Mess to send in a thermos of neab and some cheese, if there is any cheese left."

After several minutes, a soft knock sounded on the hatch and Kellon acknowledged, "Enter."

Susie and Gepeto entered. She was out of breath. Kellon noticed, approvingly, she was wearing modified Guardian Force shipboard apparel.

"Captain Kellon, if I'm late, I'm sorry. I came as quickly as possible. How may I help?"

Kellon shook his head in amusement. "Susie, please sit down. I need to discuss something important with you, and it's urgent.

"I have obtained authorization to invite you to travel with Lan back to Glas Dinnein. That is, if you are willing to make the journey with us. Of course, you should get the permission of your government before deciding."

Susie's frown immediately altered to a broad smile. "Decide? Sir, I was afraid you wouldn't want me to go with you. I have already decided. If you will take me, I am ready to go. I would, of course, like to take Gepeto and my personal AI, William, along, if possible. William and Shey have become good friends."

Susie's casual comment puzzled Kellon, *'Shey and William have become good friends?'* Is *it even possible for two computers to develop a sense of friendship?* Kellon wondered, *I will need to put that intriguing possibility on a back burner for further reflection.*

"Then, I suggest you promptly obtain Secretary Sullivan's permission. As soon as you have his permission, we will be departing Earth. About the request concerning your AI, have Commander Roan instruct Shey to interact and upload your AI's entire matrix and data files."

Susie frowned. "Charles isn't the problem. Darrell is going to have a fit. I think he's a little jealous."

Chapter Sixty-Five:
Days of Ignorant Bliss

When Charlie knocked on his office door, Darrell slowly opened his eyes and looked up. Charlie was already entering, carrying a computer printout. With a sigh of surrender, Darrell shifted his feet off the desk, allowing his chair to lean forward to its upright position.

"What's up, Charlie?"

"Well boss, without any reservation whatsoever, I can report there isn't an alien spaceship within the orbit of Jupiter. To support this scientific based conclusion, I'm bringing the latest printouts of our broadest bandwidth scans from all satellites and ground installations."

"So much for your scientific based conclusion. I know for a fact that Guardian Force had one of their Scout ships parked over Susie's home last night. I know, because I was there at the time."

"Boss, I don't want you to get the wrong idea, but have you seen your oculist lately? Did you actually see a Scout ship lurking about?"

"No Charlie, I didn't see a Scout ship. Not then, and not ever. Now, what's the point?"

"Well, the point is our best sensors don't register any type of signal that could even remotely be identified as a propulsion signature. For all we know, they are hanging from a bunch of party balloons. We could at least detect and monitor Monstro, but these guys are as close to invisible as the ghost of my old Aunt Tilley. What's more, after weeks of trying, we can't get a clue as to what they are doing, nor do we have any inkling of their technology."

"Charlie, all I can advise is keep on trying. It will take some time, but if we stay with the program, we'll eventually get a break."

"Boss, don't take me wrong, I'm glad the Guardian Force is here. Haven't you noticed how everyone is acting lately?"

"No Charlie, I can't say that I have. Of course, I'm told sleep deprivation tends to dull the senses."

"Boss, I'm really becoming worried about you. Have you checked for a pulse lately?"

"If you are bucking for a raise, then you really need to work on your technique."

"Seriously, Darrell, I've been checking. Since Guardian Force arrived, there has been a sharp decrease in suicides and substance abuse. No insult intended, but even a dumb rock should have noticed the decrease in violent crime. Then there are the phenomena of spontaneous giddiness erupting all around the world. Darrell, what's happening everywhere and everyday makes Old New Orleans's Mardi Gras look tame. People everywhere are singing in the streets and partying. I can't help but wonder just what Guardian Force has put in the water."

"While I haven't been tracking the news, you have raised a good point. Back when Susie established first contact, Carl noted Guardian Force was busy doing something they considered a high-priority. I later asked Susie what they were doing. All she would tell me is they were busy cleaning out some of Monstro's remaining dark infrastructure, something to do with something she called ribbon transmitters."

Charlie's eyebrows soared. "Ribbon transmitters? What is a ribbon transmitter? Do we have any idea?"

"No. There's a decided lack of hard data. Guardian Force is tight-lipped about the whole thing. All we have are guesses, combined with some sketchy information."

"Honest, boss. I'm working in the dark, just what kind of sketchy information?"

Darrell yawned, "Well, Carl believes it has something to do with the psychic-contamination his team ran head-on into when working in Mongolia."

"If I understand Carl's efforts, he's still trying to find where Monstro's team went to ground. Is the psychic-contamination you mentioned still contaminating Mongolia?"

"Correct. The world may have become almost giddy, but the mountains and valleys of Mongolia, where Monstro's folks disappeared, remains a very dark and depressed region. Carl suspended all high-risk on-ground efforts. He's focusing on trying to root them out using satellite data."

"Good luck trying to do that. Well, if Guardian Force does nothing more than what they have already done, they still get my vote of approval. I can't remember when I last had better nights of sleep or was able to get out of bed feeling as refreshed."

Nodding in agreement, Darrell again leaned back in his chair and closed his eyes. "I'm jealous of your getting some sleep. As for me, I'm not getting much sleep traveling back and forth to California."

"Darrell, before you start snoring again--"

Darrell interrupted, "I don't snore."

"Repeating, before you begin to snore, yet again, there's a problem I need to mention. From all of Guardian Force's weaponry and cloak-and-dagger technology, there must be big trouble we aren't being told about."

"OK, I'll bite your bait. What's got you worried?"

"Well, based on the scant tidbits of information we have gleaned from the spooks, before Guardian Force arrived, they had no knowledge of the Arkillians."

"Correct. But what's your point?" Darrell said.

"Well, if they didn't know about the Arkillians, then what enemy do they have that gives rise to all their stealth technology and fire power?"

"Hmmm. I don't have a clue. I'll grant you that they do have sharp knives, and there is likely a cause for their paranoia. Still, given their paranoia, it is likely to remain outside of our sphere of knowledge, until they choose to tell us."

"Amen. I earnestly hope it does. Monstro was bad enough. Anything capable of standing toe-to-toe with the Guardian Force and give battle isn't anything I want to meet in daylight or in a dark alley."

Darrell's priority com sounded, and he looked to the ID and smiled. "Ah-ha, there is my favorite lady."

Darrell leaned forward and keyed his com system. "Hello Susie, what can Olympus Analysis do for you today?"

"Good afternoon Darrell. Things are popping out here pretty fast. So, I thought it was important for me to give you a heads up."

Charlie quickly moved around Darrell's desk, putting himself in the video pickup. He wanted to let Susie know that he was also in the room.

"Good afternoon Susie. Darrell and I are all ears. What's up?"

Hello Charlie. I'm glad you're there. Well, to begin with, Guardian Force has sent reinforcements. There are three cruisers now entering into the Solar system, even as I speak. They're here to relieve Lan. Oh, Darrell there is one more item. Charles has given me permission to return with Lan to their own world when he departs...."

Sitting alone in his office, Charles was looking out at the Government Park. The sky was overcast and the humidity outside was as high as the temperature. He was tired. When his communicator buzzed, he looked to see that it was Darrell. It did not require him to be clairvoyant to know the reason for the call.

Groaning inwardly, he reached over and keyed his communicator. "Sullivan here."

"Charles, I'm calling about Susie. She has called to say goodbye. Tell me you haven't given her permission to depart with Lan."

"Yes, Darrell. I have. The matter was discussed with the President. We agreed it could prove, in the long term, beneficial to have someone we know on board Lan when the ship reaches wherever they are going. Susie was also rather insistent about going."

"Charles, if she goes, we may never see her again. We don't even know where they are taking her."

Charles could hear the stress in Darrell's voice. There was no secret within Olympus about how he felt toward Susie.

"Darrell, the matter is settled. The President has approved. You might also consider that Captain Kellon would not have requested Susie accompany Lan, if he had not had high-level authority from Guardian Force to do so. As for seeing Susie again, I'm rather confident we will. Guardian Force is likely to be around for a long time to come. That means there will be other ships Susie can catch a ride on to get back here."

"That all sounds good Charles, but have you considered the term 'relativistic' lately? What's more, please note that Susie is departing on a warship, and three other warships have come to replace one warship. That isn't happening without reasons. Other than the Arkillians, there must be some real danger out there that we aren't being told about."

"You are now singing to the choir. Guardian Force seems on the level, but they are being very cagey and tight-lipped."

"Charles, you're being kind to them. I've worked face to face with them for weeks. They seem to be a great bunch of guys to go for a beer with, but they refuse to talk shop where tactics or technology is involved."

Charles looked out of the window, the darkening sky attracting his attention. *A storm is coming,* he thought.

"Darrell, remember the paint is still wet on the new relationship with Guardian Force. The arriving Guardian Commodore contacted me today. I've been told in about six months his relief will arrive. At that time a commercial ship full of technical types, mostly medical personnel will also be arriving to assist us. The odds favor our obtaining technical data from civilians rather than hard core military."

Charles observed Darrell sit bolt upright in his chair. His countenance revealed apparent astonishment.

"Six months? Thunder and lightning, that means they are moving around the universe at multiples of the speed-of-light. How can that be possible? I only wish I could be on that ship with Susie. I would give nearly anything for the opportunity to have a closer look."

"You may get that chance someday Darrell, but not this time. I was explicitly told Kellon only has permission for Susie to go back with them. If I understand Kellon correctly, she will be honored as Earth's Planetary Ambassador."

"Ambassador Susie? Ambassador for the Earth? Charles, can you just imagine the political fur that would fly, if that choice required the approval of all the governments on Earth? If it did, I'd wager Susie wouldn't be leaving even in twenty years, if ever."

"That competing friction between nations will need to change. If I am correct, that change needs to occur sooner than later. There being a bigger threat than the Arkillians, as now seems plausible, our days of ignorant bliss and innocence are about to come to an abrupt end...."

Chapter Sixty-Six:
Tearman

Throughout Lan the echoes of the battle stations alarm were fading. Even as the status board in CAC turned solid gold, Commander Grey looked toward Kellon.

"Mark, Condition 2. Sir, elapsed time is two minutes forty-three seconds."

"Roy, that isn't good enough. we are exiting jump in Kreel hunting grounds. I want that forty-three seconds clipped off the elapsed time."

"Yes, Sir. Two minutes and not one second more."

Roy looked at his navigation console, then back toward Kellon. "Sir, three minutes to jump-exit."

Kellon keyed the general communication channel. "Ladies and gentlemen, heads up. Three minutes to jump-exit. Repeating, three minutes to jump-exit."

Kellon observed all the jump-exit indicators were gold. *This is the last long jump,* he thought. *Not bad, fourteen jumps to traverse eighty light-years. After nearly two years, it'll be good to put my feet on solid ground.*

"Mark, one minute to jump-exit," Roy said.

The anticipated stomach twisting sensation began even as Lan was emerging from jump state, entering normal space-time. Exiting blind, jump-exits were always times of heightened tension. Lan immediately began monitoring his passive sensors, seeking all local contacts, be they friend or hostile. At the same moment, Lan initiated the star field survey that was necessary to calculate their exact spatial and temporal coordinates. He needed the coordinates to locate and interrogate the nearest navigation beacon and obtain any waiting messages and a regional tactical update.

"Tactical here, all clear. No contacts are within our immediate volume," Lorn said.

"Navigation here, all stations have reported status gold on exit. We are offset from Tearman's axis, approximately six AUs outside of the heliosphere."

"Navigation, Roy well done. We've been where none had gone before and returned to tell the tale. Sixty-three jumps out and only fourteen to get home."

"Well, sir, I didn't do it alone. And, it's easier to follow a brightly illuminated route than break trail through high brush. It's really good to see Tearman again. If we have your permission to put on some speed, estimating Glas Dinnein in three days," Roy said.

"Roy, your humility is commendable, but the achievement is still exceptional."

"Tactical here, Sir, we have received updated sector tactical data. Captain, the Kreel have been active. Commercial losses have been heavy during our absence. There're no alerts or active contact." Lorn reported.

"Sir, I have just received and decoded new communications traffic. Upon our exit, Admiral Mer Shawn requires an immediate face-to-face with you, priority AA." Lan said.

"Thank you, Lan. Set Condition 3. I'll make the call from my duty conference room.

"Roy, approval granted to pick up Lan's heels. But keep our stealth factor above 51%. Take us home. Navigation has the CAC."

"Acknowledging, Navigation has the CAC," Roy said.

Entering his duty conference room, Kellon walked to the side table. It had been seven hours since he had eaten, and he poured himself a cup of neab, lifting a cover he selected a piece of cheese.

While chewing the cheese, he instructed, "Lan, see if Admiral Mer Shawn is available."

"Yes, sir."

Humph, Kellon thought, *nearly two years away and I get an AA contact message on exiting jump, that can't be anything good.*

The display screen brightened, revealing Admiral Mer Shawn sitting in his office. He was scowling.

"Kellon, what's Lan's current status? Report."

"Sir, Lan is combat ready, set Condition 3. All hands are present, and there are no major injuries. We have aboard one passenger, the Earth's Representative, and her dog."

"What in blazes is a dog?" Mer Shawn said.

"Sir, a dog is a four-footed animal, about 35 kilos, and humans on Earth have elaborate and mutually beneficial interactions with them."

"Dogs? Well, I suppose there's always something new to learn. Before I proceed further, well done. Given the length of time on patrol and being in combat, making it home in one piece with all hands is commendable. Well done indeed."

"Sir, your acknowledgment and comments are appreciated. On behalf of Lan and his crew, thank you.

"Truthfully, Sir, we are all looking forward to getting a cold brew at McBride's."

"Undoubtedly, and I am aware of two other Admirals who will gladly join me in having a drink with Lan's crew. However, before we get to the cold brews, there is something you need to know.

"Given the importance of your mission and its success, the Admiral Secretary, herself, has declared that upon Lan's arrival, there is to be a formal greeting and celebration along the Avenue of Fountains. Lan is to arrive and enter the Avenue from the east precisely at sunset, three days hence. If you can't make it then, I'll set the celebration up for sunset on the fourth day."

"Sir, a formal celebration upon Lan's return? That wasn't anticipated. Sir, we are truly honored."

"Humph, not so much. You just got lucky. For a time, it was a toss-up between getting honors or else a court martial. Thanks to the Admiral Secretary, the toss came up honors. She pointed out that it's not every day a new planet full of human beings is found, let alone have a single ship go into battle so far from reinforcements. Still, the final call was squeaky tight.

"Kellon, the news of your mission has been made public. When you arrive, a thundering horde of civilians will be waiting to greet you. So, be prepared for a few accolades."

"Sir, that's not the quiet return we are accustomed to."

"That's the precise point. What Lan have just accomplished isn't a normal mission. Lan has earned the honors the Admiral Secretary is insisting on bestowing. From my own viewpoint, the honors might offset some of the demerits that undoubtedly have accrued during the mission."

"Admiral Mer Shawn, as ordered, Lan will be on location and at the specified time, three days hence."

357

"Good. Now, there're two additional items we need to cover. Upon your return, Shey will be detached from service to Lan and return to her duties with Guardian Intelligence. Lan will be assigned to work closely with Guardian weapons research. That Arkillian death beam has everyone here concerned.

"Guardian Operations is also having a nervous breakdown. They are fretting about Lan making so many jumps and being two years without yard maintenance and upgrades. Lan is to be docked for a total systems inspection and where needed, refit. "

"Admiral, I was informed there have been heavy commercial losses. Are the Kreel on the move?"

"Yes, and Intelligence is trying to determine why. Our defenses are being stretched, and the Kreel are probing looking for weakness to exploit. The new demand to deploy three cruisers to Earth has come at a difficult time."

"Sir, I'm concerned about Earth. If the Kreel show up in strength, three cruisers can't defend the planet."

"Acknowledged, but three cruisers are all we can spare.

"Kellon, I'm looking forward to seeing you in three days. Then, I expect a full and detailed report and in person. Mer Shawn out."

Chapter Sixty-Seven:
Glas Dinnein

It was day's end. Flowing off the ocean the wind was brisk, moist and chilly. The fiery crescent of Tearman having just set, the fading crimson light on the western horizon was shifting toward deep dusk. Spreading from the eastern skyline the enveloping darkness arched across the dome of heaven, gently displacing the receding rich shades of purples. The embracing night was clear and the stars brilliant.

In the gathering darkness, hundreds of brightly lit fountains positioned along a broad concourse were each projecting slender plumes of liquid skyward, bright columns of multicolored light piercing the darkness. Reaching their zeniths, each plume of glittering waters divided into cascading showers of glistening droplets, which like small glittering diamonds plummeted back toward their illuminated catch basins.

On both sides of the grand concourse, hundreds of dazzling laser beams were directed skyward, together they formed a peaked broad corridor, their beams of light reminiscent of shining crossed sabers.

Standing with Admiral Secretary Eryan Kyrie, Admirals Mer Shawn, Ron Cloud, and Dylan Cord were wearing full dress uniforms. They were all the best of friends and they stood happily together on the top step before the Glas Dinnein Planetary Assembly building. Its majestic architecture was warmly glowing with a soft illumination.

A clear clarion series of musical notes called out along the concourse. The soft excited murmurings of tens of thousands of conversations quieted; the Guardian Force anthem rose in timbre, intensifying in an escalating melodious fugue.

The throng of people standing together turned and looked East to observe the dark horizon. Then, low on the skyline a brilliant light suddenly appeared. While everyone watched, approaching from a distant vanishing point, the light moved toward the crossing laser beams. As the light came nearer, it divided into five separate lights, their radiance immediately drawing the eyes of the observers. The forms of Cruiser Lan and his four Scouts became discernible. Then, oscillating waves of cheering rolled along the full length of the concourse.

Proceeding slowly, the Guardian ships moved majestically beneath the crossing laser beams, passing along the entire length of the concourse. Holding a tight formation, Lan was in the center, two Scouts were above and slightly offset from the centerline. The remaining two Scout ships were athwart ship, one to the port and the other starboard.

As the five ships moved above the crowds, a deep resonant rumbling shook the ground beneath everyone's feet, every person feeling the vibrations through the soles of their shoes.

Nearly two years had passed since Lan had without fanfare departed Glas Dinnein. They had been two difficult years. During that interval a new star system was explored, and a remote group of humans had been reunited with their larger family.

As Mer stood watching the five ships approach, their hulls brilliantly shimmering white with bands of glistening gold trim, he felt an upwelling pride for their accomplishment. Lan was home again. Being the man who was responsible for having sent them into harm's way, more than most he was glad to see them safely return mostly intact and triumphant.

Lan and his entourage passed in review before the four happy people standing before the Assembly Building. Then, reaching the end of the grand concourse, the formation made a graceful sweep right to the north, crossing out over the ocean, then the formation gracefully came left and about to an eastern track, precisely returning along their initial path.

Lan's glittering mass was positioned one-hundred meters above the concourse, his Scouts being arranged two scouts on each side.

The roar of the cheering crowds was everywhere deafening, and it energetically welcomed Lan home. When the ships again reached the front of the Planetary Assembly building the deep ground-rumbling thunder softened and faded to silence.

Coming to a full stop, the five ships were hovering directly before the four people standing on the steps of the Planetary Assembly building. The ships then altered their formation, pivoting and maneuvering, each pointing their bows toward the

Planetary Assembly Building. Then, Lan dipped his bow in salute, and the Admirals crisply returned it.

Separating from Lan, three small lights descended directly toward the stairs where Mer and his associates stood.

The three transport disks were each shimmering with the same white-and-gold trim radiance as were the five ships. In precise array, the three disks settled to the ground before the three Admirals and the Admiral Secretary.

Amid the applause and cheers of those standing around the group, and still enveloped by music, Captain Kellon stepped off the leading transport disk. He took the few steps necessary to bring himself directly before the four waiting people. Coming to full attention, he crisply saluted.

"Sirs, Captain Kellon reporting, as ordered."

The three waiting Admirals crisply returned his salute.

"Well done Captain Kellon, exceedingly well done indeed," Mer said.

"We each extend our compliments to Lan, his Scouts, to you, to your entire crew, and to our distinguished visitors."

Stepping back, Kellon turned and beckoned Susie and her companion, Gepeto. As Susie stepped forward off the second transport disk, Gepeto remained in perfect heel close to her left side. They then with dignity stood before the senior members of the Glas Dinnein government. Behind her, Roan and Lieutenant Cloud stepped off the third transport disk. They moved up together and stood behind Susie and Gepeto. Everyone, including Gepeto, was smiling.

In a formal tone, Kellon addressed the four people standing on the steps. "I have the distinct honor to introduce you to Earth's first Ambassador, Ms. Susie Wells. The four-footed mammal with her is Gepeto. Susie has informed me that Gepeto is a very special being. As a friend of the Ambassador, Gepeto has also come to visit.

Kellon turned to look at Susie. "Susie, I am pleased to introduce you to the Admiral Secretary of the Glas Dinnein General Assembly, Eryan Kyrie."

Susie looked at the smiling countenance of the beautiful woman who stood calmly before her. The Admiral Secretary's facial features were serene, and as she extended her hands in greeting, Susie gladly took them in her own.

"Susie and Gepeto, you are both most welcome. May your stay on Glas Dinnein be fruitful and a lasting pleasure within the rich bounty of your lives."

"Madam Secretary, I am both humbled and honored to be here and represent the people of my world, and to express our heartfelt gratitude for your valued assistance. We are most grateful to everyone for all that you have already done and are continuing to do for Earth."

As the formality of introductions passed, the gathered people quickly relaxed and began to press in toward the central group. As they did, the five hovering ships, suddenly and without so much as a whisper, moved vertically upward. Rising to an altitude of one-thousand meters, they hovered for a brief moment, then simply vanished from the night sky. They accomplished their maneuver even as the Guardian Force anthem reached its full crescendo and ended. Silence followed.

For a quiet moment the gentle sea breeze whispered softly along the concourse. Then, the hubbub of conversations of tens of thousands of people broke the silence, again filling the spaces.

At that moment, Susie was happy to be the person from Earth standing on Glas Dinnein and among the happy crowd of well-wishers. Gepeto, as always, was the center of attention.

Roan was standing next to Susie, and she heard Shey's voice happily passing him a priority message. "Zorn says you are not to forget that you owe him six cold brews."

"Shey, inform Zorn he is correct in the tally, but it is Zorn that owes me those cold brews."

Susie was happy and felt exhilarated, "William, are you monitoring and recording the entire scene?"

In his cheery manner, William's voice came from her Ambassador insignia badge attached to her lapel, "Ms. Susie, you may be certain I am fulfilling my duty, as instructed. The group does seem quite nice. But please do not invite them all home for dinner, without first providing at least one-week prior notice."

Susie did not feel like a stranger out of place, but felt like she had just returned home. Smiling, Susie looked down at Gepeto.

"Hey buddy, I think they like us."

She stood looking around at all the excited people, many of whom simply wanted to see, and if possible, meet her. She felt a rising sense of confidence. Whatever the Kreel or the Arkillians might be planning to do, Guardian Force was vigilant and on duty. Earth was not alone.

Epilogue

Within the dark immensity of space, at the distant hub of the Kreel Empire, the preparations for war were swirling and forming the vortex of a coming storm. The ruling Kreel Elite and their select Grand Marshals were methodically planning the next logical expansion of the vast Kreel Empire. That expansion was pointed Apocalyptically at Earth....

Author's Postscript

Guardian Force was written for pleasure, and hopefully you have enjoyed the fruits of that effort. You may also enjoy the sequels—*Earth Guardian*, *Guardian Probe*, *Guardian Strike*, and *Guardian Thunder*. Available from online booksellers and your local Barnes & Noble bookstore.

If you really like the story, then please do recommend the series to your friends. Thank you.

D. Arthur Gusner
Cambria, California
2011

www.ingramcontent.com/pod-product-compliance
Lightning Source LLC
Chambersburg PA
CBHW031055260626
47172CB00001B/71